Laura Andersen has one husband, four children, and a degree in English that she puts to non-profitable use by reading everything she can lay her hands on. Books, shoes, and travel are her fiscal downfalls, which she justifies because all three 'take you places'. She loves the ocean (but not sand), forests (but not camping), good food (but not cooking), and shopping (there is no downside.) She lives in Massachusetts with her family.

To find out more visit www.lauraandersenbooks.com or follow Laura on twitter @LauraSAndersen

'Imaginative... an exciting, action-driven plot containing strong doses of both intrigue and romance... an original and entertaining read that's reminiscent of the best of Philippa Gregory' *Library Journal*

'Gripping... Andersen delves into an alternative Tudor England geared to rivet period fans and newcomers alike... Perfect for Philippa Gregory fans' *Booklist*

'A surprising gem and a thoroughly enjoyable read' *Historical Novels Review*

'[*The Boleyn King*] alive with historical flair and drama, satisfies both curious and imaginative Tudor aficionados... Her multidimensional characters are so real that readers will wish it was history and eagerly await the next in the trilogy'

Also by Laura Andersen:

The Boleyn King
The Boleyn Deceit

The Boleyn Reckoning

Laura Andersen

EBURY
PRESS

1 3 5 7 9 10 8 6 4 2

First published in the United States in 2014 by
Ballantine Books, an imprint of The Random
House Publishing Group, a division of Random House, Inc., New York.

Published in the UK in 2014 by Ebury Press, an imprint of Ebury Publishing
A Random House Group Company

The Random House Group Limited Reg. No. 954009

Addresses for companies within the Random House Group can be found at
www.randomhouse.co.uk

A CIP catalogue record for this book is
available from the British Library

The Random House Group Limited supports The Forest Stewardship
Council® (FSC®), the leading international forest-certification organisation.
Our books carrying the FSC label are printed on FSC® -certified paper.
FSC is the only forest-certification scheme supported by the leading
environmental organisations, including Greenpeace.
Our paper procurement policy can be found at:
www.randomhouse.co.uk/environment

Printed and bound by Clays Ltd, St Ives plc

ISBN 9780091956509

To buy books by your favourite authors and register for offers visit:
www.randomhouse.co.uk

For Chris

Always

The Boleyn
Reckoning

PRELUDE

July 1536

"My lady."

Mary refused to acknowledge the greeting, for Archbishop Cranmer's avoidance of her true title was an insult to her birth and position.

"My lady Mary," the impertinent man pressed, "I bring with me a letter from the king, your father."

That she could not refuse to acknowledge. Wordlessly, she extended her hand and the heretic archbishop handed over the letter. They were alone in a small antechamber at Hatfield House, where Mary fulfilled her duty as lady-in-waiting to her tiny half sister. If Elizabeth *were* her half sister; Mary would have liked to believe that the child was not Henry's at all. But in her heart she knew they were sisters. They shared some of the same colouring, and even at not yet three years old, the precocious Elizabeth had a fearsome will that shouted her royal parentage.

Mary's chest constricted at her father's familiar and beloved handwriting. But it was the message itself that closed off her throat and sent wings of panic fluttering through her body. *The queen is safely delivered of a son. England at last has a Prince of Wales as God intended.*

How could God have intended this? Mary wondered. How could He have allowed her own mother—Henry's true and loyal wife—to die barren and alone while the Boleyn whore bewitched the king? How could such a woman be granted a living son when Catherine of Aragon had been denied? Mary felt for the rosary at her waist and then remembered that she was forbidden to wear it at Hatfield.

"What do you want of me?" she demanded of Cranmer. "Congratulations? I am always glad for my father's happiness, but I cannot congratulate him on a mistaken pride in a son who is not legitimate. How can this boy be Prince of Wales, when my father has never truly been married to that woman?"

"My lady," and despite herself, Mary recognized the kindness beneath the archbishop's inflexibility, "your care for your mother's honour does you great credit. But your father wishes nothing more than to be reconciled with you. Why separate yourself from the comfort of the king's love and care when you need not? He asks so little."

"I know what he asks—that I proclaim my mother's marriage a lie, her virtue a hoax, her faith an inconvenience. The king asks me to brand myself a bastard for the sake of that woman's children."

"The king asks you to accept the inevitable. My lady, this is a fight you cannot win. Ask yourself—does God wish you to go on in defiance against your father's wishes? To live out your life in rebellion and servitude? Whatever the state of your parents' marriage, you were conceived in good faith and were born for better things."

Mary thought of how much she hated Hatfield, being in a house of Protestants who despised not only her and her mother but the Church as well. With Cranmer being so reasonable and soft-spoken, she asked cautiously, "What would I receive in return?"

"In return for your signature, your father will grant you the manor of Beaulieu for life. There, you will be permitted to retain a single confessor and attendants of your own choosing."

A confessor . . . Mary closed her eyes and shivered. Henry knew his women. He knew how much she longed for a household of her own again, where she could wear her rosary and pray without the sneers of heretics and be counseled by a true priest. But to sign away her rights . . . the rights her mother had died upholding . . .

"Your father is also prepared to consider the wisdom of a proper marriage, providing your behavior is acceptable."

And that was the final blow to her resistance. Though her intellect knew that "consider" was not the same thing as "arrange" or "allow," it was considerably better than her current state. She was twenty years old and had been often betrothed in her childhood. But she would never be allowed to marry while she continued in defiance of her father's wishes. With each year, she would grow older—and even more than marriage, Mary wanted children.

Mother, she offered up silently, *what should I do?*

The words were so immediate and clear to her mind that Mary knew at once it was her answer. *Do what you must for now—and wait for your moment. God means you to turn England back to Him.*

Mary opened her eyes, her pride protesting but her conscience unwavering. "I will sign."

And then I will wait, she vowed silently. *And when my moment comes—I will act.*

CHAPTER ONE

18 March 1556
Richmond Palace

Today the Duke of Northumberland stands trial at Westminster Hall. Dominic traveled to London yesterday to take part, though I know he is conflicted. Robert Dudley has told him that someone other than his father is behind all the twists of treachery these last two years, but Robert will say no more to Dominic. He has demanded, rather, to see Elizabeth. Dominic asked me to help persuade her, but I did not try very hard. Why should she go? Whether there is one traitor or twenty in this, it was Northumberland himself who held Elizabeth and me prisoner. For that alone he must answer.

Besides, all Elizabeth can think of just now is William. It has been three months since the nightmare of his smallpox and the effects . . . linger.

Perhaps the resolution of Northumberland's fate will release us all from this sense that we are snared in the moment before action. The tension of waiting is almost more than I can bear.

The trial of John Dudley, Duke of Northumberland, was presided over by George Boleyn, Duke of Rochford and Lord Chancellor of England. Traditionally, it was the Earl Marshal of England who conducted such trials, but William had delayed bestowing that hereditary office on the young Duke of Norfolk after his grandfather's death. Certainly Rochford did not appear to mind.

While Dominic settled into place with the other peers who today would sit in judgment of Northumberland, his attention was almost wholly given over to contemplating Rochford himself. Three months ago the imprisoned Robert Dudley had made an enigmatic accusation aimed at the Lord Chancellor but had thus far refused to provide any details. Robert seemed to believe that even if his father were convicted today, William would be merciful as to the sentence and so there would continue to be time to consider the matter.

Dominic knew better.

The doors at the back of the hall opened and Northumberland was escorted in. The hall at Westminster was a rich backdrop to today's trial. A stage had been erected in preparation, hung with tapestries and a canopy beneath which was a bench for Northumberland. Dominic viewed the tableau with a cynicism that he had learned from Rochford—the trappings might argue respect for the accused, but they served primarily to remind those watching how far the man had fallen.

Now in his early fifties, Northumberland had always been the image of a rough, plainspoken outsider, his physical presence a reminder of his military prowess. But today he looked diminished, his high, broad forehead and dark pointed beard emphasizing rather than hiding the new gauntness of his face. He conducted himself with gravity, three times reverencing himself to the ground before the judges. Dominic thought wryly it was the most humility he'd ever seen from John Dudley.

The hall was crowded with spectators, including members of

London City's guilds as well as diplomats and foreign merchants who would no doubt be taking careful notes and sending word of the proceedings far and wide across Europe. England had been the subject of intense Continental scrutiny for quite some time—what with her young and untried king, her inflammatory religious divide, and her highly desirable and unwed royal princess. England might not be a powerhouse like France or Spain, but it was very often the critical piece that determined the balance of power.

And now a peer of the realm was being tried for his life. Not to mention that a mere five months ago—despite a peace treaty—a French army had engaged English troops in battle on the Scots border, and since that time England's king had been mostly absent from public view. Everyone in England and Europe knew that William had been ill, and some correctly guessed at the smallpox that had driven him to seclusion. Now even his own people were beginning to grow restless. They had waited years for William to grow old enough to take his father's place as a reigning monarch. They were not content to leave the government in the hands of men like Rochford and Northumberland, rightly distrusting the motives of such powerful men. The people wanted their king.

This trial was the first step in appeasing the public. Northumberland was hugely unpopular. Although Dominic had not been in London when the duke and four of his sons were paraded through the streets to the Tower, he had heard countless versions of how they were booed and mocked, pelted with rotten fruit and even stones. With William not quite ready to return to public view yet, Northumberland's trial for high treason was a distraction.

It was also a sham. The original plan had been to have Parliament pass an Act of Attainder against Northumberland, avoiding a public trial and allowing the Crown to quickly confiscate the duke's lands. Granting him a trial instead in no way meant that

Northumberland stood a chance of acquittal. There could be no doubt of the verdict; this trial was for the sole purpose of placating the populace.

Rochford opened the proceedings with a reading of the charges, none of which Dominic could dispute: the calculated secret marriage between Northumberland's son, Guildford, and Margaret Clifford, a cousin to the king and thus in line to England's throne. That disastrous marriage had been annulled after Margaret had given birth to a boy, but Northumberland's impudence could not be overlooked in the matter. And then there was the damning charge of *with intent and malice aforethought confining Her Highness, Princess Elizabeth, against her will*: Dominic had seen firsthand the duke's intent to keep hold of Elizabeth in his family castle until William agreed to listen to him. Related to that was also the charge of raising troops against the king—again indisputable. For the last two charges alone, Northumberland's life was forfeit.

But Dominic was less easy about the other charges that had been considered behind the scenes. Charges that Northumberland had conspired to bring down the Howard family two years ago, that the duke had offered alliance with the Low Countries, even claiming in writing that Elizabeth would be a more amenable ruler than her brother . . . Dominic had been the one to find those damning letters in Northumberland's London home. He just wasn't sure how much he believed in them. Papers could be forged. Letters could be planted. Witnesses could be co-opted to a certain testimony. And it hadn't escaped his attention that those particular charges were not being tried in court today.

"We'll keep it simple," Rochford had said. "Leave out the messier aspects of Northumberland's behavior."

And that was why Dominic kept a wary eye on Rochford. Because the messy aspects of this business were also the most open to other interpretations. More than eighteen months ago, the late

Duke of Norfolk had died in the Tower after being arrested for attempting to brand the king a bastard and have his half sister, Mary, crowned queen. Dominic now believed, as most did, that the Duke of Norfolk's fall had been cleverly manipulated.

"What say you, John Dudley?" Rochford asked after the reading of the charges.

"My Lord Chancellor," Northumberland responded, rising. His dark eyes, always alive with intelligence beneath the highly arched brows, looked at each juror in turn, and Dominic felt an unexpected grief at the imminent loss of this bright and capable man. "My lords all," he continued, "I say that my faults have ever only been those of a father. I acknowledge my pride and ambition, and humbly confess that those sins have led me to a state I do greatly regret. But I have not and could never compass a desire to wish or inflict harm upon His Most Gracious Majesty. My acts were those of a desperate father to a willful son. Guildford's death is greatly to be lamented, but I do desire nothing more at this time than to be reconciled to my king and his government."

The presentation of evidence lasted only forty minutes; then Northumberland was led out of the hall and the jury retired to discuss their verdict. It took far less time than Dominic was comfortable with, and the outcome was never in doubt. Rochford and the twenty-year-old Duke of Norfolk (grandson of the man who had died in a false state of treasonable disgrace) were the most vehement of Northumberland's enemies, but every other lord on the jury had cause to resent the duke's arrogance and ambition. And as Dominic studied each man there, he was keenly aware of an undercurrent of fear, deeply hidden perhaps, but real. There was not a single peer present whose family title went further back than Henry VII's reign, and most of them had been ennobled by Henry VIII or William himself. The Tudors had broken the back of the old hereditary nobility, raising instead men whose power resulted from their personal loyalty and royal usefulness. It was true of Dominic himself—the grandson of a king's daughter, perhaps, but in more practical terms only a son of a younger son with no land or title at all until William had granted them to him.

Or consider Rochford, Dominic thought, who might have been only a talented diplomat or secretary if his sister had not been queen.

The problem with being raised up by personal loyalty was that one could as easily be unmade. And thus it was today—the jury would find Northumberland guilty because William wished it as much as because it was right. And after all, Dominic would vote guilty without more than a slight qualm, for he had ridden through the midst of Northumberland's army last autumn and knew that it had been but a hairbreadth of pride and fear from open battle against the king.

They returned to the hall and Northumberland stood to face the jury as, one after another, each member personally delivered his verdict. Dominic saw the glint of tears in Northumberland's eyes as Rochford pronounced the traditional sentence of a traitor—to be hung, drawn, and quartered—and concluded with, "May God have mercy on your soul."

There was open triumph in George Boleyn's voice.

Elizabeth was with her brother when Dominic and Rochford returned to Richmond to report on Northumberland's trial. They met the two dukes in the palace library, a chamber William would once have overlooked. Not that he wasn't well-read and intellectually curious, but before the smallpox that had nearly killed him at Christmas, William would more likely have been found playing cards or dice or tennis or riding through the royal park. Solitude and lassitude were new habits of the king.

Elizabeth studied her younger brother, noting worriedly that he had still not regained all the weight lost during his illness. William had always been tall and lean, but the hollows in his face were new, as was the paleness that could not be ascribed entirely to winter. The pallor of his face was accented by the carefully trimmed dark beard that made him look rather rakish in some lights. The beard was also new since the illness.

The library was not entirely empty of others, but the half-dozen quiet attendants in the chamber were there in case of sudden need, not as entertainment. They kept to themselves at one end of the library, giving the royal siblings plenty of privacy.

And of course, there was Minuette—though these days one hardly needed to specify her presence. Wherever William might be, Minuette was at his side. The only place she didn't follow the king was his bed at night, and Elizabeth wondered how long that restraint would last. Since his illness, William's devotion to the childhood friend he'd secretly betrothed had grown perilously near to obsession.

When Rochford and Dominic entered the library, the Lord Chancellor dismissed the attendants, then offered his official report of Northumberland's conviction. William, seated beneath the colourful canopy of estate, received the news in frozen silence. Another lingering effect: his characteristic restlessness was often submerged beneath lengthy periods of stillness. When Rochford handed the king the execution order to sign, William took it without a word, almost as though he had no interest in the matter.

It was Elizabeth who said, "Thank you, Uncle."

That stirred her brother enough to say flatly, "You may go. Lord Exeter will return the order to you shortly."

Rochford gave them all a long, hard look—lingering with disapproval on Minuette seated so near the king that she was almost beneath the royal canopy of estate. As William intended her to be. There was a time when Minuette would have looked uneasy at

Rochford's fierce attention, but today she merely matched the chancellor's stare with one of her own. It almost made Elizabeth smile. Minuette might look demure and innocent—in her gown of white and amber and with her honey-gold hair artfully arranged with jeweled combs—but her devotion to William was absolute. She would not be cowed from doing what she thought best.

And Rochford, for all his concern, was not ready to bring his discontent to open argument. Elizabeth knew it was coming—this inner circle of just the four of them could not be allowed to last much longer—but for today the Lord Chancellor held his tongue. He left them alone.

They had always been exceptionally close: the "Holy Quartet," Robert Dudley had named them. But since his brush with death, William had kept his sister, his love, and his friend even tighter around him. Was it for comfort? Elizabeth wondered. Or protection?

Alone with those few he trusted absolutely, William stretched out his long legs in a gesture that made the tightness in Elizabeth's shoulders ease. She rejoiced with every moment that spoke of William as he had been before.

"Sentenced to be hanged, disemboweled, and quartered," William said to Dominic, of Northumberland's fate. "I'll commute that to beheading, of course."

"Of course."

"You have nothing else to plead?"

Elizabeth tightened again. They had not told William of Robert Dudley's plea to see her, of his claim that another man had as much to do with Northumberland's fall as his own actions. But despite their silence, William knew Dominic very well. Clearly he sensed there was more than just the usual caution behind his friend's reserve.

But Dominic did not hesitate. "Northumberland held Elizabeth and Minuette against their will in Dudley Castle. He raised an army that could only have been meant to be used against you. I have nothing to plead for him."

William nodded, then stood and crossed to the table where pen and ink waited. The Duke of Northumberland must die. The three of them watched as he signed in swift, bold strokes—*Henry Rex*. His father's name. His ruling name.

He handed the signed order to Dominic, as always entrusting his closest friend to see his will carried out. Of all of them, Dominic appeared the least changed by William's recent near-death. Reserved, loyal, darkly watchful . . . only now and again did Elizabeth see Dominic's green eyes gleam with emotions she could not always name. The gleam today seemed to her one of approval or possibly, like herself, relief that William had taken another step to returning to himself.

As though he read their minds and wished to increase their happiness, William said abruptly, "I've settled on Easter for our return to London. We'll spend it at Whitehall and celebrate lavishly. Masques, tournaments, riding through the streets to Westminster Abbey for service . . ."

Elizabeth added tartly, still trying to gauge when and how to speak to her brother as before, "All elaborately designed to set people's minds at rest and give them reason to rejoice in their brilliant king."

Through everything—Rochford's report, William signing Northumberland's death—Minuette had not moved and her expression had not altered. Another change: that the girl once so bright and merry and easily read now kept her own counsel to a frightening degree. Everything she did seemed calculated for William's sake.

At last she stood and walked to William, facing the king without touching him. There was something poignant, almost painful about the pairing, an indefinable twinge that set Elizabeth's heart wringing, as Minuette smiled gravely and said to William, "The people are waiting to rejoice in their brilliant and handsome king."

William flinched slightly and kept himself angled a little away from Minuette's gaze. Keeping his left side turned always to the shadows.

The smallpox, which had covered his face and chest and arms wholly, had not scarred so thoroughly. Indeed, he had healed almost cleanly, and if one looked at him from the right, one saw only the perfect face with which he'd been born. But on the left, the sores had left a brushstroke of scars behind, like a brush swept carelessly across a canvas.

Minuette was the only one who dared speak of it openly, or to touch. She did so now, resting her hand on William's ruined cheek, which was only partially covered by his newly grown beard. "The people love you, Will, as we do. The rejoicing will be honest. What matters more than that you are still here?"

Only Minuette could make William smile these days. He did so now, and Elizabeth thought if only her brother could be brought to smile more, to be himself more, to quit brooding on the scars, that people would hardly notice them. We see what we expect to see, she thought. Will must make people expect to see only the king and all will be well.

Minuette slipped into Richmond's Newe Park well after dark, shivering in the glooming fog. Only when William retired for the night did he release her from his presence, and then only because he intended to drink heavily before bed. Minuette knew she would have to deal with the drinking at some point, but for now she was only too glad to have the night hours for her husband. The dark was their ally. Their only ally these days.

It was all supposed to have been finished by now. They had wed secretly (and illegally and, according to the Protestants, heretically) last November, with every intention of confessing to the king at Christmas. Then William had been stricken with smallpox. And in the space of days when they feared for his life, plans and confessions had fallen to the wayside.

But not their marriage. And not our love, Minuette thought as Dominic wrapped her in a fierce embrace, his cloak enfolding them both. As she knew every line of his body in the dark, she also responded to his every thought and desire before they were ever expressed, and so their kiss was not so much one of welcome after a long day of secrecy but a kindling of their longed-for marriage bed. Minuette had come to think of herself in these last weeks as one of the marble statues she might come across in the palace or garden. Lovely and impeccable and unfeeling, confined to an ordained form and unable to move at will.

But every time she came into Dominic's arms, the marble shattered and she was a woman again: warmed and passionate and imperfectly real. Before their marriage, Minuette had thought Dominic cold in his behavior, frustrated by the control that left her bewildered and wondering if he wanted her at all. Their weeks at Wynfield Mote as husband and wife had broken that illusion forever and so, even though they could not abandon themselves completely at court, the memory of his hands tracing every inch of her body before following the path with his mouth heated her blood. Tonight she could almost feel that her palms rested on Dominic's bare chest and not the black wool of his doublet.

At last, much too soon, they drew apart just enough to breathe. Minuette let herself rest in Dominic's embrace, his cloak sheltering them both from the petulant wind of too-early spring. Her only peace in an increasingly turbulent world.

"What will happen to his sons?" she asked quietly. She did not need to specify Northumberland's four sons; Dominic read her these days with an ease that went beyond familiarity to the almost uncanny.

"It is the duke himself people hate. His sons will remain in prison for now, but I suspect they will be safe. Not their lands or titles, though—there will not be another Duke of Northumberland for a long time. But I think John Dudley would count the title well lost if it saves his sons."

"Does he still expect to be pardoned?"

She felt Dominic's shrug. "I suppose I will find out when I deliver the order tomorrow."

"I'm sorry it has to be you."

"Better me than Rochford. At least I will not gloat quite so openly."

She drew a little away, so she could see his face—or at least its outlines—as she asked, "What are you going to do about Robert's accusations?"

"When am I going to tell Will about them, do you mean? One step at a time, my love. First let's get him back into the world. Spring is upon us, which means campaigning, which means we'll find out if the French intend to continue their aggressions. I'm watching Rochford, but honestly, after destroying Norfolk and Northumberland, who is left for the man to bring down?"

"You," Minuette answered softly but firmly. "And me. Rochford does not trust your influence with the king, and he despises me heartily." She hesitated over the next part, for she knew her husband's mind, but one of them had to be practical. "Do you never think that, rather than being our enemy, we could turn Rochford to our best ally?"

Against William, she meant, or at least the king's anger. Because William was going to be angry. He was going to be furious when he found out they had married behind his back. While Minuette was secretly betrothed to William himself.

She often wondered what she could have done differently. How had they come to this, the lies and the betrayals? But she and Dominic had made their choices and they could not be unmade. All that could be done now was to mitigate the damage. And for that, they would need allies.

Elizabeth was the obvious choice, but Minuette would not burden her friend with this when she had been so worried about her brother. Besides, the princess had her own touchy royal pride and might not be entirely understanding. But Rochford was, above all, practical. Combined with the fact that he wanted nothing more than to ensure his nephew did not marry a common girl for love alone, and the chancellor seemed the perfect choice to counsel and aid them.

If only Dominic could be persuaded.

She read his resistance in the hard lines of his chest and shoulders and was not surprised when he shook his head. "I do not trust Rochford in the least. And I will not attempt to ally myself with a man who may be a traitor simply because it is convenient for me."

There had been no real chance of a different response. Where Rochford's core principle was practicality, Dominic's was honour. He would never use a man he despised simply because it could benefit him. Minuette had not really expected him to agree. She had only proposed it so he could not accuse her later of acting without consulting him first.

She could never regret having married Dominic, secret and hurried as it had been. But from the moment William's eyes had opened and his slow recovery began, Minuette had felt a great pressure that spoke of unavoidable disaster. She didn't know what form it would take or when it would strike, but every choice she made each day seemed designed only to delay the flood that threatened to overwhelm them all.

Once, she'd been confident in her ability to find a solution that would preserve not only themselves as individuals, but their friendships. Now her confidence was gone and when she wept, which was often, it was for a tangle of troubles far beyond her abilities to solve.

At such times there was a terrible whisper in her head, poisonous and treasonous. *If only William had not survived . . .*

She buried herself in Dominic's arms once more to shut out that thought. William had survived and she was glad of it, and if there were terrible prices to be paid in future she would pay without faltering.

"It will be all right," Dominic whispered, his hands stroking her hair. "It shall all come right in the end."

And there was a measure of how the world had upended itself: that Dominic had all the confidence and she all the doubt.

"After the execution, I will speak to Robert again," Dominic continued. "Perhaps his father's death will loosen his tongue and he'll provide evidence against Rochford."

And whether he does or not, Minuette thought, I shall have to make my own choice about whether to approach Rochford.

CHAPTER TWO

The Duke of Northumberland met his end with more grace and less defiance than Dominic had expected. When Dominic had told him there would be no pardon, only commutation to beheading, Northumberland had gone unnervingly still as if channeling his anger for a rant against the king. But by the time the duke was led out of the Tower on the morning of March 21, he was composed. He asked, and was granted, the customary right to speak to those assembled. He approached the railing of the scaffold and delivered a moving speech.

"Good people, all you that be here present to see me die . . . I am a wretched sinner, and have deserved to die, and most justly am condemned to die by law. And yet this act wherefore I die was not altogether of me, as it is thought, but I was procured and induced thereunto by others. I was, I say, induced thereunto by others, howbeit God forbid that I should name any man unto you. I will name no man unto you, and therefore I beseech you look not for it."

Which was as good as saying, *Hunt down the man who sent me to this bloody end.* Dominic tried to judge the mood of the crowd, to see how many had taken seriously Northumberland's claim of further conspiracies, but failed. At the moment they seemed wholly focused on watching the duke die.

After a brief but seemingly genuine praise of the king and a prayer for God's blessings upon him and England, Northumberland concluded, "I could, good people, rehearse much more but you know I have another thing to do whereunto I must prepare me, for the time draweth away."

It was that sense of irony and humour that Dominic admired and he felt his stomach rise at what the man's pride had brought him to. Northumberland was blindfolded and knelt at the block, speaking softly so that even Dominic, at the front, almost missed it. He thought Northumberland's words were, "I have deserved a thousand deaths."

As he knelt, the blindfold slipped and so did the duke's composure. Northumberland fumbled to move the blindfold back into place, and the executioner, almost at the same moment, swung the ax. Mercifully, it was a clean blow.

Dominic stayed long enough to see the head, respectfully covered, and the body carried into the Tower chapel of St. Peter ad Vincula. Now was the time to speak to Robert Dudley once more, for Beauchamp Tower edged the Tower green and he could have seen his father take his last walk. Robert would be edgy and angry and grieving, and Dominic intended to twist every one of those emotions to his advantage in pressing for information.

"Lord Exeter." A man fell into step beside Dominic as he crossed the green, a man it took him a moment to identify. A wide forehead narrowing to a pointed, goateed chin, the narrowness echoed by a long nose, and watchful, careful eyes . . . Dominic remembered those eyes, observing him on their return journey from France last summer. Francis Walsingham, the intelligencer whom Elizabeth had hired into her household.

"What can I do for you, Walsingham?"

"I wondered if I might attend on Lord Robert with you."

"What makes you think I'm going to see Robert Dudley?"

The slow, intelligent gaze of a man who knows far more than he says . . . "May I accompany you?"

"Why?"

"Her Highness wishes it."

"Does Her Highness know that she wishes it?" Dominic asked suspiciously.

At that, Walsingham smiled. "Those who work for royalty must learn to anticipate what our patrons wish before they themselves know it."

Dominic's first instinct was to send him on his impertinent way, but truth be told, the man was not wrong. Was not his own visit to Robert anticipating what William would wish if—when—he knew about Robert's insinuations? Besides, Walsingham was canny, and Dominic was not so proud as to think he could not benefit from another canny man's advice.

With a sharp nod, Dominic said, "Come on, then."

Robert knew who was coming to see him long before he heard footsteps on the stairs. Dominic was the only one who bothered to see him these days—other than the guards and occasionally the Constable of the Tower—and he would have bet everything he owned that Dominic's sense of duty would bring him here today.

That is, Robert would have bet if he stilled owned anything to gamble with. But he and his brothers had been attainted right along with their father. No land, no titles, no rights in blood to pass anything on to children . . . not that Robert had really had much to begin with. The courtesy title of Lord Robert came only from his father's position; he'd held almost nothing in his own right, and certainly he had no children.

The real problem with attainder was what came after it. Without the status of a gentleman, Robert could be tortured if the king wished it. And William might wish it. Or rather, Elizabeth might and William often granted his sister's wishes. After the debacle at Dudley Castle with Amy, not to mention Elizabeth's imprisonment, her pride was stung. And there was nothing more righteous than the Tudor pride.

Sometimes, in the dark of night, Robert wondered what he might say if it came to torture. The truth? Or whatever lie would be most convenient? He supposed it would depend on who was asking the questions. And on how hard they pressed.

When it came right down to it, torture or not, Robert preferred Dominic asking the questions. The man was infuriatingly good and lacked imagination and his devotion to duty was exhausting . . . but Dominic was honest, a quality Robert was in desperate need of.

The door opened and Robert turned from the window where he had watched his father being led out across the green to the scaffold on Tower Hill. The range of Tower buildings had not allowed him to see his father's death, but he had been able to hear the general tenor of the crowd. He was dressed more for warmth than fashion, and he felt a moment's envy at Dominic's easy grace as he strode across the bare wood floor. Not that he was fashionable, but he had that indefinable air of belonging in the very centers of power—whether in palace or prison cell—all the more noticeable for his being unconscious of it.

Robert caught sight of a second man behind Dominic and frowned. "You've brought a friend. Or is it an interrogator?"

"Francis Walsingham," the man said.

"Yes, I remember you. Came back from France with the princess. Friend of John Dee's."

Walsingham inclined his head in agreement.

Despite himself, Robert could not help the lift of hope in his chest. "Elizabeth sent you?"

"Her Highness," the intelligencer answered repressively, "did not."

"So she still won't speak to me," Robert murmured. Then, louder, to Dominic, "In which case, you might as well go. I'll speak to Elizabeth, or no one."

Dominic held his gaze, with a steadiness that Robert found unnerving. He had always thought it a simple matter to understand Dominic, but there was something new to his expression. That something new continued in the indefinable tone with which he said, "You will speak to me, or you will end as your father. Make no mistake—there are many calling for your head. And as of now, no one asking for clemency."

"Don't try to threaten me, you're not cut out for it."

"I'm not threatening, I'm telling. Your father is dead, Robert. If you try, perhaps you can smell the blood in the air. Your brother, Guildford, met the same end. You, John, Ambrose, Henry . . . all the remaining men of your family are held here, and there are many who hope not one of you leaves these walls alive."

Robert felt his carefully cultivated facade of lighthearted indifference beginning to crack. He had been kept isolated since his imprisonment in November, neither allowed to see his brothers nor receive letters from the outside. Robert was a social creature and the solitude had worn on him more than he'd have thought possible. In his mix of boredom and anxiety, he had taken to carving the stone walls as so many previous prisoners had done. He stared now at his initials, carved confident and deep beneath a pattern of leaves, and admitted to himself that he had never been as sanguine as his father about the chances of mercy. Because Robert knew whose hand was behind all of this—and he knew there was no mercy in that particular hand.

During those endless nights, he had often cursed himself for ever getting involved with George Boleyn. It was true that Lord Rochford was skilled at getting what he wanted, which included manipulating people he wanted to use, but Robert knew he had been eager to be used. His ego had been flattered at working with the foremost power in England. And how could he have refused Rochford's promise to do what he could to ensure Robert's divorce and a chance to seriously court Elizabeth?

In the beginning it had seemed almost like playing. Flirt with a pretty woman, create an illusion of threat to take down an old adversary of his family . . . what could go wrong?

The answer, in hindsight, was plenty. For Alyce de Clare—the pretty woman—was dead, and after the destruction of the Howards, Rochford had turned his sights on Robert's family. And now here he sat in the Tower, cut loose from Rochford and as likely to be executed as forgotten.

Shifting his attention to the other man in the room, the one who came from Elizabeth's household with or without her permission, Robert asked, "Walsingham, will you speak for me to Her Highness? Tell her that I only have her best interests—"

The rest of that sentence was driven back into his lungs by the force of Dominic's shove. Robert's instinct told him to shove back, but Dominic was quick and strong and he had Robert pinned against the wall with one forearm pressed against his windpipe before he could move. Not enough to choke—just enough to let Robert know that he could choke if he wanted to.

How was it he had failed to remember that Dominic was a soldier? He was so quiet and self-effacing that it was easy to forget that he might have any talents at all beyond being William's friend. But then, royalty rarely had use for friends who weren't talented.

"Listen to me," Dominic said. "This is not a game. This is life and death. If it were only your own life you were playing with, then I'd say have at it and I would sit back and watch you play this game straight to the gallows. But there are others at stake. Everyone seems to forget that Elizabeth was not the only prisoner your father took, and it was not the princess who was targeted by an assassin. I want the man behind that."

Robert gave a strangled laugh through the pressure on his throat. "Why is it always about Minuette? You, William—neither of you can think straight when it comes to that woman."

Even as he spoke, the words rang in Robert's head with deeper meaning. Could it be ... Dominic and William so close, sharing everything, but one thing that could never be shared was a woman ...

Robert might have whistled if he hadn't been half choked, but the expression in his eyes must have been sufficient to alert Dominic. "Keep your conjectures to yourself," Dominic said softly, pressing harder on his throat, and this time there was no mistaking the threat.

Abruptly, he released Robert and stepped back. Walsingham had watched it all dispassionately, and Robert wondered what report he would make to Elizabeth. If he reported to her at all in this.

"Easter is in two weeks." Dominic's habitual control was firmly locked in place once more. "The court will be at Whitehall. On Easter Monday, I will come again. And you will tell me everything. Places, orders, plots ... and names."

"If I don't?" Robert couldn't help himself; it was second nature to spar.

"Then I tell William that you have confessed to intending to divorce your wife, marry Elizabeth, and kill the king himself in order to rule England."

There was a sound from Walsingham, something between amusement and approval. Robert looked into Dominic's hard eyes and said slowly, "I understand."

As the two walked out, Robert called after them. "Dominic? Someone has taught you well. But he's still better at ruthless than you are."

William prayed alone, as he did so many things these days. A relative term, to be sure—there was a gentleman standing against the door of his private chapel, with more outside to guard against intrusion—but he had spent more time with fewer people in the last four months than in his entire life.

He prayed silently, the same words he'd offered to Heaven since the moment he'd woken from near-death. *I thank Thee for Thy grace and salvation. I thank Thee for the sign of Thy favour in sparing my life. Make me worthy. Make me Thy weapon, Lord.*

And running beneath, the wordless plea of every waking hour: *May I please Thee, Lord, that Thou wilt make me whole.*

For what could the smallpox have been but a sign of God's displeasure? William had spent many hours contemplating his sins as his body mended, and he had come to two unshakable conclusions. First, that he had sinned greatly with his lies to his people and all of Europe about his marital intentions. Second, that for him to heal completely—and no, he was not necessarily expecting that the scars on his cheek would disappear overnight (though he wasn't necessarily *not* expecting it, either)—and in order for his mind to be settled after the great upheaval of nearly dying, he must tell the truth about the woman he loved.

William let his plea to Heaven settle into his bones, to be carried with him everywhere, and opened his eyes. He did not rise, not yet. Dominic was expected any minute and William would hear the report of Northumberland's end firsthand. But while he remained on his knees, he could think.

There was much to think about. Just because he wanted to tell the truth of his love did not mean it was a straightforward task.

Though William had been physically isolated for much of the last four months, he was not ignorant of the happenings in his kingdom and the wider world. The French troops that had instigated last autumn's battles had seemingly vanished from the Scots landscape. Mary of Guise, regent for her daughter, had made formal protest against the subsequent English incursions but they had lacked heat and the force of righteousness. Which was to be expected, since the French were in the wrong and everyone knew it. Not eighteen months ago William had sat across from King Henri of France as the monarchs signed a treaty of peace. England had kept to the terms. William's betrothal to the young Elisabeth de France still officially held—so what had prompted the French to make that savage thrust across the border and then withdraw?

Obviously they were unhappy with the English gains two summers ago, when they'd picked up Le Havre and Harfleur, and wanted revenge for their losses. But the fact remained that the French had not moved against those cities, but across the English border. A much more intimate threat. Because they had learned that England had approached Spain and (rightly) guessed that William intended to marry his sister to King Philip and then himself abandon the French princess to whom he was betrothed.

William did not mean to marry the young Elisabeth de France, that much was true. But he'd thought he would have more time, that the French betrothal had bought him several years of peace, as Elisabeth was still only ten years old. But someone didn't want him to have those years. Someone was pressing the matter to a head, certain that outside pressure would force him to withdraw from Minuette.

Someone was very much mistaken.

That *someone* might simply be the nameless French observers and politicians who had watched Dominic and Minuette and Elizabeth during their visit to France last summer, but William did not discount the possibility that there might be a very specific some-one, perhaps even in England, who had alerted the French to the peril. There were more than enough Englishmen who did not want him to marry Minuette.

He'd kept his suspicions to himself thus far. The obvious person to discuss it with was Dominic—but their friendship had altered in the previous months. And not as a result of the smallpox.

When William had woken from danger and begun his slow recovery from the illness, everything that had come in the weeks before had been blurry and unfocused. He could remember the outline of events—fighting in Scotland, arresting Northumberland—but details and emotional contexts eluded him.

Except for one very detailed, very emotional memory: the look on Dominic's face when he'd realized how William had used him to trap his friend, Renaud LeClerc.

Not that the trap had come off. The French commander had been meant for death, not a botched assassination attempt that left LeClerc furious and still very much in control of the French armies. But Dominic had seen only his king's betrayal. William knew that, to his dying day, he would remember the contempt in Dominic's voice when his closest friend told him, "You used me . . . and you lied to me about it."

They had not discussed Renaud and Scotland since. William had allowed Dominic to believe the details of their argument had vanished in the mists of his illness and Dominic had not pressed, perhaps remembering his own folly in walking away from the fight in Scotland in a luxury of pride and hurt. It was for the best—let them both forgive the errors they'd made in judgment—but he had not forgotten. And he was certain that neither had Dominic.

William had felt the constraint between them immediately when he'd woken to see Dominic's face. His friend's eyes, though grateful, had been shuttered against him even then, and William knew there were parts of himself Dominic was keeping carefully away from him. William veered between guilt that he'd caused that constraint and fury that the one man he'd always trusted no longer entirely trusted him in return.

There was a discreet knock on the oratory door. William said without turning, "Let Lord Exeter in, and then you are dismissed."

He made a final obeisance to God and stood to face Dominic. "How did it go?"

"As well as could be expected. Northumberland was gracious. And the crowd was less unruly than I'd feared. It was a clean death."

"And now?"

Dominic didn't need to ask what William meant; though there was constraint between them, that didn't change the fact that Dominic knew him better than anyone. "You keep the sons in prison, amply provided for, while you decide what punishment they have earned."

William ticked off the Dudley sons on his fingers. "John's the eldest, but he was not anywhere near Dudley Castle while his father planned his revolt. Rather, he was serving me by guarding Mary. Henry's too foolish to expect much in the way of independence and he doesn't seem to have come anywhere near the girls while they were imprisoned. Nor did Ambrose, but he's a trickier character. Smart enough to keep his hands clean, but that doesn't mean his intentions were pure. Robert . . ."

He paused, staring at the finger that indicated Robert Dudley as though it would help him see into the man's mind.

Dominic continued where the king had left off. "It's always Robert who's the real danger. And the enigma. I would swear that he had nothing to do with his father's seizure of Elizabeth and Minuette—Robert would never risk Elizabeth's regard, not even for blood. And he is the one who freed Minuette and brought his father to surrender without bloodshed."

William flicked his eyes to Dominic. "Robert also distracted Minuette while someone made an attempt to poison her."

"I have not forgotten. But I can almost be persuaded that he was used in that instance, without knowing why. He may be guilty of not asking the right questions, but intent to murder? I don't think that's true."

William asked the pertinent question. "Who used him, then? And don't tell me his father—I know when you are keeping something from me."

It was in the balance whether Dominic would lie to him. And that was something else new, that Dominic would even consider lying to him. Of course he didn't: considering was not doing. "Robert has dropped hints, but no more. I have told him he has until Easter to tell the truth."

"And if he does not? He's been attainted, like his brothers. No longer a gentleman, so no trouble if he's tortured."

Dominic's eyes flickered. "It will be time enough to decide that in two weeks."

William was not surprised that Robert Dudley was ready to offer up another traitor. And Dominic was right: it could wait a few more weeks. At Easter he would spring his own surprise on the court without warning. When he did, any possible traitors would have plenty to act upon, and in their actions they would make mistakes.

But he mustn't let his friend forget who ruled in the end. "Why so wary of torture? You must learn to be harder, Dominic, if you are to sit in the councils of power."

"And you must learn to see the effects of your orders. Have you ever seen someone tortured?"

"Perhaps I'll begin with Robert Dudley."

The constraint reared up between them, almost tangible to the touch. William waited for it to flare into open disagreement, but

Dominic retreated. "Let's get through Easter, and not let politics destroy the celebrations. We all need the joy of your restoration, Will. Time enough for complications afterward."

"There's always time enough for complications."

He wanted Dominic to say something else, some word of approval or satisfaction or even acknowledgment that he was king and, more important even than the title, that Dominic respected his mind and decisions.

What Dominic finally said was, "I wondered if you would be prepared to spar with me in the practice yard later? It's not the same fighting anyone but you."

It was as nearly a gesture of affection as Dominic could make, and William let the satisfaction of it ease the tightness in his shoulders. "Yes, I have missed sparring with you as well. Time to return to more joyful pursuits—and the best fights are always against those who know you perfectly."

CHAPTER THREE

We rode into London with William on Maundy Thursday three days ago. The roads were lined with people, in a manner that reminded me of the celebrations almost two years ago for his eighteenth birthday. But the lavish crowds were more wary than purely celebratory. Northumberland was not popular, but he was powerful. Almost I could hear the thoughts churning in the people's minds: If a man such as the duke can fall, then how secure are any of us?

There was, mercifully, very little notice paid to William's scarred cheek, at least in public. I imagine it is being talked over in public houses and private rooms around the city, but at court discretion prevails. And in the end it is not his face that makes William king. It is his Tudor blood and his mind—and both of those remain ferociously sharp.

Lady Mary is at Whitehall for the festivities. William has commanded her presence at the Easter service at Westminster Abbey this morning. I believe the new Spanish ambassador, Renard, was tasked with persuading her that it will not touch the purity of her faith to support her brother. To all appearances, Renard is here

primarily to see to Mary's interests. That illusion will not last long.
It is Elizabeth he is here for, to arrange matters for her marriage to
Philip of Spain.

Elizabeth will not talk about it. Nor about Robert. Nor, indeed,
about anything more important than William's health. Ever since
Dudley Castle, she has closed off her innermost thoughts to me.

I suppose I cannot blame her, not when my own heart is ringed
round with defenses.

Minuette closed her diary, a worn velvet ribbon her marker, and
replaced it in the jewelry casket that held more pieces now than
ever before. William had gifted her nearly every piece of jewelry
she owned, save the two most meaningful: her mother's rosary,
which Minuette kept concealed beneath the false bottom of the
casket, and the sapphire and pearl necklace that Dominic had given
her for her seventeenth birthday. She let her fingers run over the
coolness of the cabochon-cut sapphires, wishing she could wear it
today, but William would be expecting rather more glamour even
in church. It would have to be one of his more elaborate pieces—
the rubies, perhaps, or the opals. It would depend on the dress.

She looked around the bedchamber for her maid, Carrie, and
was momentarily disoriented. When they'd arrived in London
three days ago, Minuette had attended Elizabeth to her chambers
expecting to be quartered nearby, only to find that, as Elizabeth
had phrased it, "William has assigned you elsewhere." Her tone
made clear it had been without the princess's consent.

Minuette's heart had quailed as she examined her own miniature presence chamber, privy chamber, and bedchamber, the
weight of her secret position pressing in upon her and making it
hard to breathe. These were not the chambers one assigned to a
lady of the privy chamber, nor even to a royal ward who had been
raised with king and princess. The only court women who had

these sorts of suites were Elizabeth herself and Lady Rochford, as wife of the Lord Chancellor.

But there had been another woman in recent memory who'd had chambers like these, from which to exercise her personal influence with the king—William's former mistress and the mother of his young daughter, Eleanor Percy Howard. Minuette might once have feared that these chambers meant William pressing her for greater intimacy, but since the smallpox he was more physically careful with her than ever before. Indeed, at times his restraint resembled Dominic's habitual control.

She found the king's control far more disturbing than his passion. She had once believed William's desire for her was transitory and that when it faded she and Dominic would easily obtain his blessing for their own marriage. But in the wake of the nearly fatal smallpox, William's desire seemed less about her body and more about what she represented: a symbol of peace and possession that could not be tarnished by the winds of politics or religion.

What would William do when that symbol turned to ash?

Carrie entered the bedchamber with an expression that mirrored Minuette's own disquiet at her surroundings, but she said only, "I thought perhaps the silver-edged damask gown for service this morning."

"Good." Minuette smiled at the woman who had once served her mother and had known Minuette since birth. Carrie was more than a maid—she was the keeper of all Minuette's secrets and as loyal a friend as could be hoped. Always neat in appearance and manner, Carrie's round cheeks and glossy brown hair gave her something of the aspect of a cheerful bird.

Minuette continued on the safe subject of her gown. "The blue-gray is a good colour for church, suitably demure. I think the rubies to go with it."

As Carrie finished fitting the headdress and veil on Minuette, two pages appeared in the outer presence chamber bearing a fluid, heavy object wrapped in plain linen. It could only be a gown.

"From the king," one announced, and handed her a note.

She broke William's personal seal, the crowned Tudor rose favoured by his grandfather, and read.

Sweetling,

I would like you to wear this tonight, to the feasting after the service. Come a little late, so that everyone will notice your arrival. The French will be there, and the Spanish ambassador. I want every eye to mark you well when you enter.

Minuette unfolded the covering linen with Carrie's help. She guessed the gown would be costly and fashionable, and would make every woman look at her twice with envy and every man look more than twice with adoration.

The moment the linen fell away enough to see what lay beneath, she felt the colour drain from her face as Carrie gave a small gasp. I should have known, she thought bleakly. William is superb at sending wordless messages.

And tonight, I am to be the message.

"Your Highness." Simon Renard, newly restored Spanish ambassador to England, bowed deeply. "It is a great honour to be with you."

Mary Tudor was not so pure-minded as to not appreciate being treated with the devotion she deserved. Just hearing her rightful title made her blood sing in recognition: *This is who I am, whatever the heretics may say.*

She extended her hand from her appropriately decorated seat and allowed Renard to kiss it. "My heart overflows with joy to know I am not forgotten by His Majesty."

Renard straightened. "Never forgotten, Your Highness. His Majesty is ever watchful of your state and all Spain prays for your health and welfare."

The question was, did they pray for more than just her welfare? It was one thing to uphold Mary's right to the English throne in words—but were those words mere lip service? Or did they conceal hearts and wills ready to fight?

More critically, was Mary's own heart and will prepared to fight? For years she had bided her time, respecting her father's wishes as indeed she was bound to do. If only Henry had not left a son! If she'd had only Elizabeth to contend with, she would have asserted her right to the throne immediately upon her father's death. But was not a king's son a sign of God's will? Even a son conceived before the death of Mary's own mother . . . that was the conundrum. William had always had the support of the people, who rejoiced that Henry's long obsession had finally borne male fruit. But William had been conceived months before Catherine of Aragon's death. If, as Catherine and Mary herself believed—not to mention the Church and most of Europe—Henry's marriage to Catherine had ended only with her death and not through any proclamations issued by wicked men, then William could not possibly be Henry's legitimate son and heir.

Which left only Mary herself.

"Your Highness," Renard said, "in what way may I aid you? Though I am sent here to deal with the king, I gladly offer myself and my household to be at your service."

Mary had given the matter a great deal of thought, from the moment she'd been informed that a Spanish ambassador would be returning to England. She was no fool—no child of Henry Tudor could be—and she had her correspondents at home and abroad. Censored as her letters might be by Rochford and his ilk, Mary knew that Renard's presence betokened only one thing: William wished to negotiate Elizabeth's marriage to King Philip.

Which argued some interesting theories about William's matrimonial intentions and the current French treaty, but Mary's primary concern, as always, was interpreting signs from Heaven. And what else could this be but a most definite sign? A Spanish ambassador offering his services to the only legitimate heir to Henry Tudor's throne ... *Mother, grant me the courage of my convictions.*

"Ambassador," she replied in fluent Spanish, "I thank God for your presence here. And yes, there are ways in which you can serve me and, by serving me, serve the only true and living God. England has much need of us."

Renard's eyes sparked, and Mary knew this was a man whose conscience would align with hers. She smiled, allowing the righteous certainty of her path to settle in her heart. It was time to call England to repentance.

"Not those," Elizabeth snapped, waving away the heavy chains of intricately worked gold offered by one of her ladies-in-waiting. "It's springtime, bring me something ..." She searched for the right description and failed. "Something else."

The woman curtsied and backed away with the offending jewels. Kat Ashley sniffed. "Could you not be more specific?"

Elizabeth gave her former governess a baleful glare. "Minuette would not need me to specify. She would know precisely which jewels I need, without me having to hold her hand."

Kat had lived with her tempers since Elizabeth was a tiny girl. Undeterred, she retorted, "It's no use complaining to me. I'm not the one who swept her away from your household."

"Are you saying I should complain to the king?"

"Are you saying you have not considered it?"

Elizabeth sighed and rubbed her temples. Of course she'd considered protesting. She was territorial about her household and her women, and William had not even consulted her about the change in Minuette's status. He had simply installed her in what had once been their mother's suite at Whitehall Palace and left Elizabeth unsure of what came next. And uncertainty was ever her greatest frustration.

Since her confinement at Dudley Castle last autumn, Elizabeth felt as though she were split in two. One part of her was the impeccable princess who regretted the necessity of Northumberland's execution without being personally moved by it. But the more vulnerable part of her had punishing headaches and spent hours in a darkened bedchamber, trying to forget Amy Dudley and Alyce de Clare and the thought of Robert locked up in the Tower. After Dudley Castle, she had proclaimed that she was finished pleading for Robert Dudley—and she had meant it. But did she still mean it today?

The offending lady-in-waiting returned bearing pearls and diamonds. Elizabeth nodded curtly and said, "Kat will finish. You may go."

Kat added the jewels to Elizabeth's flawless attire of springtime green and delicately embroidered flowers. Then she patted her cheek as though Elizabeth were still a girl of five. "Don't fret about what you cannot change. All you need do is worry about your own choices."

"Simple words," Elizabeth retorted, but kissed Kat affectionately on the cheek. "I will try."

Because of the stir with the jewels, Elizabeth was later into the hall than she had planned. She saw William, speaking to Mary and to the Spanish ambassador while being balefully observed by the ambassador from France. Mary looked pleased with herself, a sight so rare that Elizabeth had to look closely to be certain that it was indeed a small smile she saw on her half sister's face. She had certainly not looked so pleased throughout the Protestant service this morning, although she had behaved with perfect grace. Once, Mary would have retired with dignity after being forced into such a position, but tonight she gave no sign of waiting to assert her righteousness but rather seemed determined to take advantage of being at court.

Dominic stood, as he usually did, on the fringes of the crowd. Always dressed in the sparest fashions and sober colours, he still managed to appear effortlessly attractive, a quality Elizabeth recognized without being at all personally affected. Tonight he wore a jerkin of dark brown wool with the barest decoration of gold cord that had the (no doubt unintended) effect of brightening his green eyes. When she greeted him, he replied with a wordless nod. The surest way to know if Dominic was rattled was that he would speak in more than one word replies.

"Have you seen Minuette?" she asked him, craning to look. On the far side of the hall Rochford and Lord Burghley were in conversation, making an interesting contrast—Rochford dark and lean, Burghley shorter and light-haired—but two great minds and subtle.

"No," Dominic said.

A rustle went through the crowd at the far end of the hall. Elizabeth saw the crowd orienting themselves to look at someone moving toward William. She caught a flash of honey-coloured hair and knew it was Minuette. Why was everyone staring?

Then the crowd eddied as William took three steps to meet her, and Elizabeth could see all of Minuette, from head to toe. She looked remote and untouchable and breathtakingly stunning. There was a fortune of pearls in her hair and around her neck, and her dress was exquisitely cut from velvet and satin, sleeves bound in ermine that touched the floor.

But none of those details were what drew the eyes and caused the ripples of whispers and Rochford's face to darken in fury and the French ambassador to stiffen in outrage.

The dress was purple—the colour reserved for royalty. Even Elizabeth didn't wear purple save for the most solemn occasions in which she needed to be seen as the Princess of Wales rather than simply as William's sister.

William took Minuette's hand and kissed it. He knew how to make a striking tableau: the dark head of England's king bent in near-submission to the golden girl he loved. And not just as a mistress. The colour of that dress meant only one thing—William had thrown caution to the wind. Tonight was his announcement: to his uncle, to his council, to his country and all of Europe.

To hell with treaties and politics: This is the woman I will marry.

Elizabeth blinked and turned to Dominic to pour out a flurry of questions and fears and "what do we do now" panic.

Dominic had vanished.

William had never felt more alive than when he bent to Minuette, resplendent in royal purple, and kissed her hand in sight of everyone in his kingdom who mattered. It was wonderfully freeing to have come to a decision and then acted upon it. The satisfaction buoyed him even as Elizabeth paled and Rochford glowered and the French ambassador stalked out. Dominic's absence was slightly troubling, but no doubt his friend was waiting to scold him privately. Let him—William was past caring about the opinions of others.

Minuette behaved impeccably and William could not have been more proud. Both untouchable and warm; a rare combination, one his mother, Anne, had never mastered, nor even Elizabeth. Their own sense of entitlement kept them always a little aloof from others. But Minuette had not been born to this, nor even aspired to it, and her very humility gave her a common touch of which William approved. Simon Renard, the Spanish ambassador, kissed her hand and murmured to William, "A most charming lady."

"Perhaps the two of us might speak later this week about a royal visit from your masters."

Send King Philip, William was saying without saying it, *and we'll wrap up this Spanish/English marriage as quickly as possible.*

Renard bowed. "It would be my great pleasure, Your Majesty."

He was not surprised to see Renard return to conversation with Mary minutes later. While Minuette made small talk with a rigid and unhappy Lady Suffolk, William watched his half sister and the Spanish ambassador engage in conversation that was clearly more than just polite. He was very curious how Mary would respond to his plans for Elizabeth. Certainly she would approve any alliance with the Spanish, but there must be part of her that would resent watching the much younger Elizabeth make a marriage that Mary might have liked for herself. Still, she was probably the only English person in the room who rejoiced wholly at the blow he'd launched tonight against the French treaty.

Certainly Elizabeth did not appear pleased. He could read his sister's temper in the sharp lines of her shoulders and the angle of her body, and in the way she kept clear of him. Fine. He was in no hurry to fight with Elizabeth. She'd known what was coming—if not quite how soon—and she would simply have to accept it.

"William." Rochford's voice was soft and even, but the fact that the Lord Chancellor used his name and not his title told William how very angry he was.

"Uncle."

"You have your father's gift at keeping a kingdom off balance."

"Is that a criticism, Uncle?"

"It is a fact, nephew. One I should not have overlooked. May we speak privately, William?"

"It's Easter. And I thought the point of this gathering was to show me off to my people and assure them I was in ruling condition."

"Tomorrow, then. Before the council meeting."

William met Rochford's eyes easily. "No."

He was shocked when his uncle gripped his upper arm with a tight hand and whispered angrily, "I am your *chancellor.*"

"And I am your *king,*" William snarled. "Shall I give you cause to remember it? Ask Northumberland how that ends."

Pulling free, William went straight to Minuette and wrapped one proprietary arm around her waist. He knew what he was doing, and the doing of it made him heady with pleasure.

Elizabeth arose on Easter Monday with her conscience clear and her purpose fixed: she would speak with Robert Dudley. Today.

Watching William do precisely as he'd pleased last night and damn the consequences had freed something in her. Her own marriage to Philip of Spain would be fixed and made before anyone had a chance to so much as blink. So be it. But she would not walk that path without deciding first how she felt about Robert. She soothed the tiny pricks of conscience that she was being petty by reminding herself that Robert claimed there was a schemer left in England's government and only she held the power to that revelation.

William was closeted in a privy council meeting that no doubt would be more drawn-out and rancorous than usual. With the court focused on Minuette's sudden elevation and the possibility of French retaliation, it was a relatively simple matter to leave Whitehall in a boat and head downriver to the Tower. Part of the ease of it all was having Walsingham with her. The intelligencer had a knack for slipping in and out of places and situations without notice. And although Elizabeth hardly blended into the background of London, she was at least not in a royal barge flying banners and attracting the eye of everyone on the river and alongside it.

The Water Gate was slimy and black at this tide level; Elizabeth's arrival caused a concerted flurry of activity. The Lieutenant of the Tower was summoned and already apologizing as he approached. "Forgive me, Your Highness, we had no word—"

"I sent none. This is a personal visit, not a state one. I am here to see Robert Dudley."

The inheritance of being royal meant using as few words as possible and not bothering to explain oneself. It certainly came in useful now, for the lieutenant didn't even think of denying her. Why would he? Everyone knew how close she and William were. If she were here, surely it was with the king's permission.

Those useful expectations again.

Whatever Robert's expectations had been, clearly they had not included Elizabeth showing up unannounced in his prison cell. She had never seen him so disconcerted—except for that awful evening last autumn when his wife had walked uninvited into Dudley Castle.

Elizabeth herself had been most unpleasantly surprised that night. She had never met Robert's wife before, and when she'd accepted Northumberland's invitation to Dudley Castle, she had never dreamed Amy Dudley would be so bold. Beyond surprised, Elizabeth had been hurt, and the vulnerability of that feeling worsened a hundredfold when the Duke of Northumberland turned her from honoured guest to royal hostage. Even now Elizabeth was unsure how much of her anger at Robert was legitimately caused by his behavior and how much was simply protection for herself.

When she walked into Robert's cell in Beauchamp Tower, his startled expression instantly gave way to relief.

"Hello, Robert." Best to act as though nothing at all had happened. Certainly she had never been sentimental, though she couldn't help noticing that he'd lost weight since November and there were dark shadows beneath his eyes that made him look older. And grimmer.

But after clearing his throat, his voice was unchanged—light and untroubled and with a promise of warmth to it. "You are looking remarkably well, Your Highness. To what do I owe this honour?"

"You said you would speak to me. I am here. For England's sake, not yours," she warned, though whether the warning was for Robert or herself she didn't know.

"Naturally. Please, though there is nowhere good enough for you, will you sit?"

She allowed Robert to draw out a wooden stool and sank onto it with her bloodred skirts belled out around her. "Join me," she said to Robert, indicating the only other stool in the small chamber. No more than ten feet in any direction, many of the block-stone walls had irregular carvings where prisoners had passed the time in artistry or protest. The wide-planked floor and utilitarian furniture (bed and table only, besides the two stools) were an incongruous backdrop to the luxury-loving, ever-elegant Robert Dudley. Elizabeth imagined being confined here herself and felt a deep, involuntary shudder of revulsion. It wasn't the meanness of the chamber that frightened her, but the thought of being at the mercy of a temperamental and all-powerful king. If men such as Robert, who had known William all his life, could end in the Tower, then who was next?

Robert looked behind her at Walsingham, who had shadowed her steps through the Tower precincts. "What of your man?"

"He'll stand. And listen, and remember." She needed Walsingham to be her ballast, and because she was wise enough to know her own limits where Robert was concerned.

Robert sat facing her, far enough away that touching would be impossible. A nicely judged distance. "How is the king?" he asked.

"In robust health and temper," she snapped. "Tell me what you have to tell me."

"I confess it was not you I expected to see today. Dominic promised me—rather forcefully—that he would be the one to return on this day for my answers. Are you here in his place?"

"I am not a woman to be sent in another's place," she reminded him disdainfully. "Though if you tell me all of what I need to know, then I imagine Lord Exeter will be satisfied and leave you be."

"Has he told you nothing of my claims, then?"

"Only that you claim to have evidence that it was not your father who set up Lord Norfolk and the false Penitent's Confession. Convenient for you, seeing as you would like to escape your father's fate."

"Yes, being locked in the Tower is highly convenient."

"Who is it, Robert?"

"Surely you can guess."

"Surely I can, but I need you to say it."

"George Boleyn, Lord Rochford."

The name hung heavy and menacing in the air, as though the Tower walls themselves did not want to bear witness. For one moment, Elizabeth wished passionately that she had not come so that she might not have to go forward from this claim. But she was not given to long regrets.

It was not as though the name was a surprise—she and Dominic had both guessed that would be Robert's claim—but Rochford had been the bedrock of England's government for almost ten years. Did she seriously consider him capable of treason?

Except it wasn't precisely treason, for Robert's accusations were that Rochford had worked to bring down Norfolk and Northumberland, not the king himself. She didn't think that would make much difference to William. It wasn't Rochford's actions her brother would deplore, but his lies.

Behind Elizabeth, Walsingham's steady voice commented, "That's merely a name, sir. Anyone can accuse—where is your proof?"

Robert looked miserable, and dead serious. "I worked for him, for years. I'm the one who planted the Penitent's Confession at Framlingham after Minuette told me precisely where she would be looking for it. Why do you think Rochford asked you to send someone after her? He knew you would send me. And before that, I wrote coded letters to a woman in your mother's household, using her to stir up old rumours and give Rochford a plausible pretext to move against Norfolk."

"A woman," Elizabeth repeated flatly. "You mean Alyce de Clare."

"Yes."

"The same Alyce de Clare whom you kept in your home for a month, getting her with child before sending her back to court to spy on my mother."

If he lied to her now, it would be over. Like her brother, Elizabeth could abide almost anything but lies.

Robert didn't flinch. "Yes."

"Did you kill her?" For Alyce had broken her neck falling—or being pushed—down a staircase. It was her death that had begun the unraveling of the original Norfolk conspiracy three years ago.

Robert didn't flinch at the question, nor did he hesitate. "No. We argued that night, it's true. Alyce told me she had made arrangements to see William and confess her part in it all—she was unhappy about her last assignment."

Elizabeth remembered that last assignment—a vile broadside depicting Anne Boleyn calling upon Satan for the power to seduce Henry, meant to be planted for salacious viewing at court.

"I had surmised that much," Elizabeth said sharply. "How did she end up at the bottom of the staircase with a broken neck?"

"It was an accident. I swear it, Elizabeth. She'd told me of the child, was angry at my response, and I pushed her away ... God knows I did not mean to hurt her. Certainly not to kill her."

She could never be absolutely certain, but Elizabeth felt how much she wanted to believe him. For now, that was not her primary concern. "All this proves to me is that you were working to blacken my brother's name as a pretext to crush a nonexistent Catholic rebellion. I already knew that. But that might as well have been at your father's direction as my uncle's. More likely, in fact, for why would my uncle entrust any of this to you?"

"Because he knows what I want and promised to help me obtain it. A divorce—clean and final." Robert did not add: *And a chance to marry you.* He did not have to say it.

She would not follow the path of that motivation just now, for she needed to be clear-headed. "As Walsingham said, Robert, where is the evidence that any of this is true?"

"At Kenilworth. My ..." He cleared his throat uneasily. "Amy has in her keeping a chest with a false bottom. Even if she could figure out how to open it, I doubt it would mean much to her— she doesn't read Latin. There are notes and dates and, most important, two messages with Rochford's seal. In themselves they might not be damning, but Dominic knows how to read ciphers, and in conjunction with everything else I think you'll have to at least ask your uncle some very hard questions. Like which operatives told him the Spanish navy was on the move to rescue Mary."

Again Walsingham broke in. "That's a good point, Your Highness. The threat of Spanish naval movements in 1554 was a lie, all my intelligence sources agree."

"Perhaps they wanted Rochford to think they were moving."

Walsingham countered, "Whatever the simplest reason is for a lie, it's usually the true one. Deception is far easier to maintain when simple than when complicated beyond measure."

Elizabeth stood up. "We'll have the chest fetched from Kenilworth. Walsingham and Dominic can go through it and decide from there."

Robert rose more slowly, still graceful despite the hollows in his cheeks. "Do you believe me, Elizabeth?"

"Do I believe that you played shameful games with my mother's reputation and my brother's birth in order to advance your own ambitions? That you took advantage of the woman you were using and ruined her?"

A muscle jumped in his cheek, but he asked steadily enough, "Do you believe that your uncle has maneuvered behind William's back?"

"In more ways than even you can count," she said. "In this particular matter? I will look at your evidence and decide for myself."

"Thank you."

I'm not doing it for you, she nearly said. But that would have been a lie.

CHAPTER FOUR

THE ONLY REASON Dominic didn't drink himself into a stu-
por on Easter night was the knowledge that he would have
to be present at this morning's privy council. Trying to maintain
his tenuous emotional control would be hard enough without a
raging hangover. What he had done instead after fleeing the court
was walk for hours through the London streets surrounding
Whitehall. Not the safest choice, but he'd been armed with both
sword and dagger. Not to mention a driving need to hurt someone.

His anger had kept him sober, but it had not helped him sleep.
Exhaustion pounded behind his eyes as he took his place with the
other men of the privy council, each with varying degrees of
shock and dismay in their expressions. Even Rochford, normally
difficult to read, was openly furious.

If not for his personal stake in the affair, Dominic might have
found it impressive how William controlled the room from the
moment he entered. The king didn't falter or break stride at the
palpable tension in the air, as though this would be nothing more
than a normal council.

William took his gilded chair and faced the circle of advisors
with an air of casual ease that, a day earlier, would have pleased

Dominic. He had not seen his friend behave so effortlessly since before the smallpox.

"France." William cast the word into the silence like a stone skipped into standing water. "Our old enemy, renewed once more."

"Because of your choice." Rochford left little doubt that he would have preferred a stronger word than choice—*folly*, perhaps.

"Because of *their* choices. You were not in the field last autumn, Lord Rochford, to see the effects of their attacks. I was. The French army broke the treaty the moment they crossed our border."

William Cecil, Lord Burghley, cleared his throat. The most level-headed of the privy council, and perhaps the only match for Rochford in strategic planning, the thirty-five-year-old Burghley had a high, broad forehead and wide, cautious eyes. "Are we to understand that the return of a Spanish ambassador to England is pertinent to this discussion?"

"Most pertinent," the king agreed serenely. "Before summer's end, Philip of Spain will visit England to sign a treaty of marriage between himself and the Princess of Wales."

There was only a small rumble of surprise. Burghley kept to the point. "A Spanish treaty to replace the French? That makes it more likely that France will indeed retaliate in force. Will the Spanish move against France itself if, say, they move to retake Le Havre and Harfleur?"

"I have no intention of defending those cities. I only took them two years ago to force Henri to negotiations. We will hold fast to Calais and let the others go."

Sussex, one of the most experienced military commanders now that Northumberland was dead, spoke up. "And if France sends an invasion fleet?" His dour expression was habitual; almost fifty years old, the Earl of Sussex used his age and noble bloodlines as an excuse for bad temper.

With a chilly nod, William replied, "That is the real danger, I concur. Which is why this council's primary business today is to name a new Warden of the Cinque Ports."

One man to take charge of the defenses in southeast England, with all authority to summon men and arms and ships and to command troops against the threat of foreign landings on the coast. George Boleyn himself had once held that post, as had Henry VIII's illegitimate son decades earlier, Henry FitzRoy. Now it should be Sussex, for experience, or Rochford again, for position. But Dominic knew his friend and so it was only a slight surprise—accompanied by a grave sinking in his heart—when William said, without even looking at him, "Lord Exeter will be Lord Warden of the Cinque Ports."

No one seemed any more surprised than Dominic, although some few were displeased. Only Burghley nodded thoughtfully. "The French have good cause to remember Lord Exeter. They will be wary of facing him once again."

Dominic wished he could believe that. The French might have to send ships to reach England, but there would be an army on those ships ready to land and march and only one man would be in command of that army—Renaud LeClerc. Who had been beaten once by having his own tactics turned against him by Dominic. Who had nearly been assassinated by an English arrow last autumn while under promise of safe conduct. Renaud wouldn't be wary. Renaud would be spoiling for a fight.

For the first time since entering the council chamber, William looked directly at Dominic. "What say you, Lord Exeter? Will you lead England's defenses for your king?"

In sardonic silence, Dominic thought, Well done, Will. How can I possibly say no when you put it like that? Aloud, he said, "I serve at your pleasure, Your Majesty."

"That is well done," Rochford cut in, his voice with a ragged edge of temper. "But we must discuss the precipitating event, Your Majesty. We must speak about Mistress Wyatt."

"There is nothing to discuss."

"There is everything to discuss! You cannot throw a common girl into the public eye in that inflammatory colour and then refuse to speak."

"I cannot?"

The temperature dropped instantly. Every man seemed momentarily joined in awareness that they could argue and bluster and rage all they wanted—but the youngest man in the room was the one with all the power. It was almost as though the Duke of Northumberland's headless body lurked in the corner as a reminder of what the king could do.

Bless Lord Burghley for his temperate instincts. Once again he moderated Rochford's words. "Your Majesty, we wish only to serve you and England well. It is difficult to do so if we are kept in the dark about your intentions."

Grudgingly, William said, "My intentions have never been more clear. I need a wife, and I will have none but Mistress Wyatt. There is nothing of substance can be said against her, and it is past time England has a royal marriage untainted by politics. It is not open for discussion."

The hell it isn't, Dominic thought. Because that's *my* wife you're talking about.

When the council meeting adjourned, Dominic was among the first to escape. Once, William would have expected him to remain behind. Now the king didn't even notice when Dominic walked out with Rochford, who seemed glad of the chance to speak with him alone.

"What can we do to persuade William of the folly of dismissing the French so lightly?" Rochford asked urgently.

"I have no idea."

Rochford grunted, the lines around his eyes carved deep. "You're Warden of the Cinque Ports now, I suggest you ensure William knows how vulnerable our coasts are to invasion. Paint him a picture of Portsmouth ablaze, our navy sunk, and foreign troops marching across the southeast of England."

"Why don't you paint him the picture?" Dominic was past trying to please his former master and guardian. These days he could barely keep himself together.

"Because William doesn't listen to me!" Rochford stopped himself. He so rarely lost his temper that Dominic realized anew how deadly serious this all was. William marrying Minuette was such a personal disaster that he had not thought sufficiently about the dangers Rochford had just outlined.

Unfortunately, Rochford was also right about William's refusal to listen. "I'm afraid the king doesn't listen over closely to me these days, either," Dominic admitted. "Not after the battles in Scotland."

Rochford threw him a keen glance. "From which you were so conspicuously absent. Is that where the constraint between you arose? You counseled the king against battle?"

"It doesn't matter. The French withdrew. And now we are all left guessing what their next move might be. Last autumn I had Renaud LeClerc's message that their first attack was meant only as a warning not to provoke them further on the matter of the treaty."

"Throwing that girl in the French ambassador's face dressed in purple is far more than provocation," Rochford spat. "Is there any way you could find out from LeClerc what their intentions are this summer?"

"No." Dominic had been used once, unknowingly, against LeClerc. He would not be used openly.

"Then I suppose I shall have to find another way, as always." Rochford sighed. "Sometimes I think I am the only man in England who is truly concerned with the general welfare of the nation and not just my individual desires."

He stalked away, leaving Dominic staring at his retreating back.

It was not like Rochford to lose his temper and say things he did not mean. But if he had indeed meant that last statement, then he was verging uncomfortably close to what, in another man, could be called treason.

Dominic headed for the stables, for he had promised Robert Dudley he would return to the Tower today and demand an accounting of his evidence. But before he could leave the palace precincts a messenger wearing the crowned falcon badge that Elizabeth had adopted from her mother intercepted him with a request to join the princess as soon as possible. Altering his steps, Dominic thought ruefully that all of this running around at least kept him from the deep—and disastrous—impulse to find both Minuette and the nearest bed and lay claim to the woman everyone else was now looking at only as William's beloved.

When Elizabeth and Walsingham returned from the Tower, the first thing she did was send word to Dominic to join her when he could. Then she closeted herself alone with her intelligencer and sighed deeply. "What do you think?"

The best thing about Walsingham was that, despite having known her such a short time, he understood every twist and turn of her mind. He pondered deeply before answering, another quality she appreciated.

"I think he's telling the truth," he answered at last. "And that makes me uneasy."

Elizabeth closed her eyes. "What do you suggest?"

"Do you need a suggestion from me?"

She smiled, eyes still closed. "I thought it polite to ask."

"The very last thing with which you need to concern yourself is being polite, Your Highness."

A discreet knock sounded on Elizabeth's interior door and she opened her eyes. "Yes?" she asked the lady who appeared.

With a curtsey, the lady said, "Lord Exeter, Your Highness."

Elizabeth made a rapid decision. "Walsingham, speak to Dominic for me. Use my chamber here. Tell him what Robert said and make plans. Knowing Dominic, he will insist on going to Kenilworth himself to retrieve that chest. Let him."

"Yes, Your Highness." Walsingham rose as she did. "We can easily go elsewhere, no need for you to leave."

"I have someone else I would like to consult," she said tersely. She left Walsingham and nodded to Dominic as they passed in the doorway. For once she was grateful for his reticence as he let her pass without question.

Elizabeth made her way to a plainer section of the palace, with tiny chambers opening off whitewashed corridors for lesser guests of the court. The chamber she wanted had its door closed and, unusually for her, she knocked and waited.

The door was opened by Dr. John Dee. When he saw her, the scholar showed a glimmer of surprise, then bowed in welcome. "Your Highness." His eyes, deep-set beneath inquisitive brows, always seemed to Elizabeth to see far more than the physical world.

"May I come in, Dr. Dee?" she asked, with the lightest touch of royal privilege.

"Forgive me, of course you may."

The guest chamber was just large enough for a small pallet bed, a chest at its foot, and a narrow table being used as a desk. The single window showed glimpses of swift-moving clouds and hints of sun. The changeable spring of England, Elizabeth thought. An appropriate mirror to the court's current conditions.

Dr. Dee offered Elizabeth the sole chair; he remained standing. "What may I do for you?"

"You can tell me your impression of the current tenor of the English government."

"Is that all?" he asked drily.

"And then I may have an assignment for you." Though, strictly speaking, Dee did not work for Elizabeth. Strictly speaking, he did not work for anyone just at the moment; he had been in the service of the Duke of Northumberland, but had chosen to warn William of the duke's perfidy in confining Elizabeth to Dudley Castle. Since then Dee had remained at court in a semiofficial state.

Rather like Walsingham, Dee took his time answering her. Elizabeth was patient, knowing that when he did speak, it would be worth listening to. A rare trait at court. "The current tenor is unsettled," he finally offered.

"Is that all?"

"Do you really need me to confirm your own impressions?"

Elizabeth sighed. "I was rather hoping you would tell me I am wrong."

"You are not. The king's illness has unsettled everyone, not least yourself. What is it you fear, Your Highness?"

"My brother is not recovering himself as I had hoped. He is at once both too sensitive and not sensitive enough. William has always been extremely good at judging his moments, at knowing when to act and when to pause. Now he appears deaf even to his own conscience, while being quick to take offense at any criticism of his conduct. He is practically begging the French to land and march across England. What will we do if they send an invasion fleet to the south and send troops across the Scots border at the same time? England is not prepared to fight on two fronts at once."

"Have you told the king so?"

She threw up her hands in frustration. "He doesn't need to be told it! He knows it for himself. He simply doesn't care."

"And that is your true concern."

What was it about John Dee that made her feel as though he anticipated and understood every one of her half-formed fears?

Elizabeth sighed again. "For all my father's stubborn insistence on his own way where his personal life was concerned, he at least managed to preserve England's security. But Will . . . he seems prepared to burn it all himself as long as he can have his Minuette."

"The lady is your friend, I believe. Does it divide your heart to wish her unhappiness?"

"The more time that passes, the more I believe that her happiness is not at stake. Unlike me, Minuette's abiding concern is to please others. She will do what William wishes and not count her own happiness. But she is wise enough to know she is not the right choice for England's queen."

John Dee tapped his fingers along his leg and Elizabeth had a flash of the same déjà vu she'd experienced with him before—that this was neither the first nor the last time she would consult him on matters of some delicacy. Though only a few years older than she, Dee had an ageless quality to his wisdom that Elizabeth respected. At last he asked, "Might I inquire as to the nature of the assignment you spoke of?"

"I wondered if you would care to travel the Continent for a time, finding books to add to my personal library. A man of your talents will know the sort of volumes I'm looking for—humanist, rare, thoughtful. You have contacts in Europe and I thought you might enjoy the opportunity to renew acquaintances."

He regarded her shrewdly. "And perhaps you would be interested in what those acquaintances have to say about conditions in Europe and the political pressures facing England abroad?"

"Very interested."

"Is this your idea, or Walsingham's?" John Dee had known Walsingham longer than Elizabeth had—his was one of the recommendations that had sent the intelligencer to her during her visit to France the year before.

She stood, velvet skirts rustling into place. "Walsingham and I so often see eye to eye. Will you do it?"

John Dee bowed. "It will be an honour, Your Highness."

Ten days after Easter the court moved east to Greenwich and Minuette received a petitioner who she was actually happy to see. Jonathan Percy was a musician and poet who had once courted her—he had gone so far as to propose—and Minuette retained her fondness for the soft-spoken young man. In spite of the fact that his twin sister, Eleanor Percy, had borne William a daughter two years ago and hated Minuette with a ferocity that had landed her in the Tower.

"Jonathan," Minuette said with real pleasure as he kissed her hand in greeting. They were in her privy chamber, small but lovely with its blue and gold décor. Minuette had memories of Anne Boleyn in that chamber, the queen a perfect match for her surroundings. Every now and then she wondered what Anne would make of Minuette's hold on her royal son.

"Mistress Wyatt," Jonathan said in his beautiful musician's voice. "Thank you for being willing to see me."

"I am always willing to see my friends," she said warmly. "Would you care for any refreshment?"

"No, thank you. I wondered if . . . that is, there are two matters I wished to raise with you. If it is convenient."

Minuette signaled to Carrie to leave them. When they were alone, seated at right angles to one another, she said to Jonathan, "What may I do for you?"

His brief smile was a reminder of simpler times. "I suppose everyone wants something from you these days. As to the first matter, I simply wished to inform you that I am going to be married next month."

"I'm so glad! Who is the young woman—do I know her?"

"I doubt it. Her family is from York, Honoria Radclyffe is her name. We will be married at York Minster and the king has agreed to my transfer to the Archbishop of York's service. We prefer to make our home away from court."

"I envy you." She meant it as a wistful wish for a life that was rapidly being shut to her, and only wondered if he took it as personal regret when he eyed her closely. Before he might say something awkward, Minuette asked brightly, "And the second matter?"

"Ah," said Jonathan, looking once more the uncomfortable boy she remembered. "That, I'm afraid, is a request. I wondered if . . . Honoria and I had hoped . . ." He stuttered to a halt, colour rising in his cheeks.

"Jonathan, you need not be afraid of me. I am not yet grown so grand that I cannot be asked a simple favour."

"It is simple, but that doesn't make it easy. Honoria and I would like to be named guardians to my niece, Anne Howard. Eleanor's daughter."

Minuette blinked twice. "Go on."

"Since my sister's arrest, Anne has been passed around various members of the Howard family with little consideration for her welfare, only the convenience of others. The king—" Here he faltered once more.

"The king has formally recognized his daughter, yes," Minuette said for him. "And yet, you are correct, he has not provided her with a household of her own or guardians besides her mother."

"Honoria and I would like to give her a stable home, away from politics. You know me well enough to honestly assure the king that we do not seek this position in order to profit from it. It is the child herself we care for."

His straightforward goodness made Minuette ashamed of herself. I should have married him when I had the chance, she thought blackly, knowing even as the thought formed that it would not have served either of them well.

"I do know," she assured Jonathan. "I will speak to the king. He thinks highly of you. I expect he will gladly grant your request."

His favour asked, Jonathan did not linger. He rose and bowed to her, but when he straightened he added, "It is good of you to do me this kindness. If ever I might be of service, you have only to ask. I would requite the ill my sister has wished you."

"You owe me nothing," Minuette assured him. "And I quite understand that, in Eleanor's eyes, it is I who have done her ill."

"And are you happy?"

How could such a simple question set all her defenses ringing? "Why do you ask?" she parried.

"Because all that time ago, at Hampton Court, when I asked you—" He stopped himself, and his eyes were far too perceptive. Minuette would have looked away if she had not thought it would make her look guilty of something.

Jonathan finished his thought. "When you declined to marry me then, I believed it was for the sake of another man. A man *not* the king."

With a bright, brittle smile, Minuette kissed Jonathan on the cheek. "Go to York and marry your Honoria. And may you both be happy for many years to come."

Within the week, Minuette had spoken to William and secured his agreement to give Anne Howard into her uncle Jonathan's wardship. She thought herself done with Percys then, trying to keep Jonathan's honest appraisal of the past from troubling her waking hours, when a far more troublesome Percy reappeared.

Eleanor wrote to Minuette from the Tower, requesting an interview "with the king's best beloved future queen."

CHAPTER FIVE

I T WAS NEARLY the end of April before Dominic was able to make the trip to Kenilworth and retrieve Robert Dudley's chest. He had insisted on making the trip personally, not trusting anyone else. He'd had to tell William most of the truth to get the king's leave, but he and Elizabeth had not yet told the king that it was Rochford against whom Robert was laying his claims. Dominic didn't know how William would respond to his uncle's ... what to call it? Treason? Treachery? Lies? At the least, Rochford had ruthlessly manipulated events, including blackening his own sister's reputation, in order to eliminate those he saw as rivals. William would not take kindly to being left in the dark. If there was manipulation to be done in England, it was the king's prerogative to have his hand on all the strings.

Dominic made the trip north as quickly as possible with only his man-at-arms, Harrington, as companion. They had worked together since 1553 and Dominic trusted him absolutely. Five inches taller than Dominic and built like an ox, Harrington was one of only three people who knew of Dominic and Minuette's secret marriage: the other two were Carrie, Minuette's maid, and the Catholic priest who had married them. Dominic suspected Harrington's affection for Carrie ran deep, but it was difficult to decipher emotions from such a silent man. Compared to his man-at-arms, even Dominic counted as talkative.

Having been forced into accepting the post as Warden of the Cinque Ports, Dominic would spend much of the spring and summer in the southeast and along the coasts ensuring the defenses were prepared for a possible French fleet invasion. For that reason he didn't remain at Kenilworth above an hour. At least, that was the excuse he gave Amy Dudley, Robert's wife, when she clearly expected him to stay the night.

"But you have come so far!" she protested, widening her eyes in appeal. Amy was pretty in a general sort of way, with blonde hair and fair skin, but it was the prettiness of youth, and already Dominic could see how discontent had marred her appearance. Not that he blamed her for being discontented—she was a woman deeply in love with a husband who seemed to forget her inconvenient existence for months at a time. "And I have been so out of the way here," she continued to plead, "with little news from Robert's family."

What news did she want? Dominic wondered. Details of her father-in-law's trial and execution? The precarious fate of her remaining brothers-in-law? The likelihood of her husband ever coming home?

For pity's sake, Dominic told her, "I have been to see your husband several times. He is being treated well and is in good health. If my errand is successful, I expect he will be released from the Tower before autumn comes. Surely you would wish me speed on such an errand."

She studied the sturdy oak chest Dominic and Harrington had removed from her bedchamber, three feet wide and two feet deep, bound with iron bands and a forbidding lock. Dominic could read the emotions chasing across Amy's face: hope, loneliness, the bitterness of loving a man who had eyes for every woman but her.

At last she shrugged and with feigned indifference said, "I wish you well on your journey, Lord Exeter. Tell Robert I look to hear from him as soon as he is allowed to write."

"I'll tell him," Dominic promised. For the life of him, he could not decide if Amy wanted Robert freed or not. At least while her husband was in the Tower she could be reasonably certain he wasn't visiting other women's beds.

Minuette approached the Tower of London with wary curiosity. She had been unsure of how to go about seeing Eleanor without William's knowledge or permission. (Dominic's knowledge didn't come into it, since he had gone north to fetch Robert Dudley's evidence.) In the end she'd done what she had usually done in the past: gone to Elizabeth for advice.

Though her friend raised both eyebrows when Minuette said she needed aid to see Eleanor Percy, she had not tried very hard to dissuade her. "You might wish to go armed," Elizabeth cautioned wryly. "Barring that, I suppose I can spare Walsingham for a few hours. He'll get you in and out and ensure no blood is shed on either side."

Walsingham did indeed get Minuette in with a minimum of fuss. From the attentiveness of the Lieutenant of the Tower, it appeared her position as William's intended bride had spread beyond court. Minuette let herself play the part of a haughty noblewoman doing her duty to a woman much less fortunate as she followed the lieutenant to the second floor of the circular tower in which Eleanor Percy was confined.

Every time Minuette shared space with Eleanor, she was forcibly reminded of the sheer physical presence of the woman. Not overly tall or classically beautiful, Eleanor Percy inhabited her body as if it were a weapon. Just now her weapon was sheathed, dressed in black and white that Minuette would have considered an attempt at demureness if it weren't such a dramatic backdrop to her blonde hair and ivory complexion. The gown showed less of Eleanor's cleavage than usual, but she still curved in all the right places. Even fully clothed she gave the impression of barely checked passion.

"Mistress Wyatt." Eleanor's curtsey was like a slap, the dislike plain to be seen. But there was something besides dislike in her attitude today, and it confirmed Minuette's suspicions that Eleanor wanted something from her. Her heart beat faster and she knew she was about to embark on something very dangerous indeed. Making an alliance with Eleanor was like trusting a dragon not to eat a kitten.

"You may wait outside, Walsingham." She spoke with all the casual authority she could summon. "I believe Mistress Percy and I have private matters to discuss."

Eleanor's eyes flicked over her. "Do we indeed? This should be . . . intriguing."

Clearly reluctant, but with no orders from Elizabeth to do otherwise, Walsingham stepped outside the door, where no doubt he would wait patiently and try to overhear. When they were alone, Eleanor swept an exaggerated gesture of welcome that took in the curved walls of her prison. They were whitewashed, at least, but the floor was bare wood and there was only a bed, a chest, and a table and chairs in the space. "Won't you make yourself comfortable, Mistress Wyatt? Though I hear you are quite extravagantly provided for at court these days."

Her tone conjured up the very image of Minuette's current chambers: from the tapestries of Artemis and Apollo to the deep-dyed blue hangings of her bed. Eleanor had once known that chamber—and that bed—well. Minuette repressed a shiver ("someone walking on your grave" Carrie would have said) at how small a distance it was from palace suites to Tower cells.

"I'm quite comfortable standing," she answered firmly. "And I don't believe I shall be touching anything you offer me."

If Eleanor had a good quality, it was her directness. She shrugged and said, "The monkshood? You are right to be wary, as I believe I warned you the very day you were struck down. If only you had listened to me."

"If only you had not tried to poison me." Minuette was finding it far too satisfying to speak openly. She must remember to guard her tongue lest she tell Eleanor more than she wanted her to know.

"Are you so certain it was me?"

"Not working alone, but then you did warn me about powerful men as well. I thought you'd meant Northumberland, but now . . ." Minuette eyed her thoughtfully. "What do you want from me?"

"I want what I always want—the ear of the king. It seems you are the only certain means of ensuring William's attention these days. He listened to you in the matter of our daughter's guardianship. I won't thank you for that, because you would not believe me, but I am forced to admit that you are useful."

"I did it for Jonathan's sake, and the child's. I would never want William to turn away from his own daughter."

"No matter how much you despise her mother?" Eleanor murmured. "Did you know that the king had only one condition before allowing my brother to take her? William insisted that her name be changed."

Startled, Minuette asked, "Why?"

With another shrug, Eleanor said, "No doubt, after he gets sons on you, he plans to have at least one legitimate daughter. I imagine he wishes to save the royal names for such an event. He told Jonathan he did not want the girl called Anne any longer. Perhaps he thinks it an insult to his mother, though I wager Anne Boleyn would have understood me well enough."

"So the poor girl is simply going to be called something else? Will that not confuse her?"

"She is only two years old. I have decided on Nora, so that whenever William speaks his daughter's name he will have cause to remember her mother. It is a small price to pay for the king's favour."

It disturbed Minuette deeply, the thought of the little girl being passed around and renamed like a dog or a horse. Had William given any thought to Anne—Nora—beyond providing her an allowance?

Forehead creased, Eleanor asked, "It truly bothers you, doesn't it? I don't understand why. You have got what you wanted . . . for now. But I do not think you will hold it long."

"Why shouldn't I?" Minuette always instinctively argued with Eleanor, whether she believed in her own position or not.

With a patient sigh, as though speaking to a slow child, Eleanor answered, "I know you despise me and think William is all that is good and perfect. But he is not. What he needs, though he may not know it, is a woman as hard as he is. You? He will tear the heart right out of you, if only you were not so eager to do it for him. Your love will not help William, it only weakens him, and one day he will have cause to hate you for it."

Could one's blood actually run cold? Minuette thought numbly. Because hers seemed to be trailing ice beneath her skin. Forcing contempt into her expression and disinterest to her voice, she asked, "What is your point? Besides insulting me."

"Insulting you is not a sufficient point? Oh, very well, I suppose I wished to offer you another warning. Although I knew about the monkshood—and did not especially mind—I was not the instigator of that act. You may think yourself safe while I am locked away, but I am not the one you should fear, Mistress Wyatt. I am a survivor, which means I know when to change the game and how to play it to my advantage. I also know when I am beaten. You do not even know who you are playing against."

"How, precisely, do *you* know so much? There's not a man at court would dare risk being in touch with you just now."

Eleanor gave a lazy smile and shook her head. "I may prefer men in the whole, but if you want to know anything, ask the women. Rochford's intelligence networks have nothing on servants and women."

"I don't suppose you'd care to tell me against whom I am playing?" Minuette could not deny the flicker of fear, but headier than that was the knowledge that here was a woman she could bargain with.

"Not without fair payment."

After appearing to consider, Minuette said, "I can have you released. As you said, I have the ear of the king and I will bring you to his attention. Provided you give me the means to clear you from the attempt on my life," she warned. "William will not let you go as long as he believes you tried to kill me."

"Who would have thought," Eleanor countered musingly, "that the golden girl of the court could play in the mud with the rest of us? I can tell you who instigated the poison attempt, as well as the incident with the adder. And I believe there was something nasty found in your chamber in France?"

It was those last words that convinced Minuette that Eleanor was speaking the truth. She had told not a soul, not even Dominic, of the dead rat and the incendiary drawing that had been slipped into her French chamber in the dead of night last summer. Eleanor had not been in France.

But the woman she served had been.

"Lady Rochford," Minuette said, only partly disbelieving. She had spent all this time looking at which men might be behind Eleanor, and neglected the obvious woman.

A wicked little smile lit Eleanor's face. "I believe there are any number of things I could tell you about Lady Rochford. Her husband, for all his reticence, is inclined to talk in bed."

Minuette blinked once, and swallowed a laugh that verged on hysterical. Eleanor and Lord Rochford? Well, well, well … She could do anything with this information: go straight to William, or share it with Elizabeth and get her measured advice, or tell Dominic and share his distaste.

But she had a much better use for it. Minuette had never felt so kindly to Eleanor, for she had just given her a new piece in the game, and she knew precisely how to play it.

Dominic did not investigate Robert's chest until he'd returned to court. Elizabeth insisted on being present, naturally, and brought Walsingham with her. The three of them alone—Minuette was busy showing herself at William's side while they went riding, and Dominic shoved away a forcible sense of loss that they were not all together as they should be.

The chest was packed with books and papers of all sorts, mostly mathematical in nature. Robert's academic interests, which were genuine and deep, tended to the scientific more than the literary. They scanned each page with a rising sense of impatience, but without wanting to miss anything obvious.

When they had cleared the inoffensive material openly packed in the trunk, they turned to removing the false bottom. It was Walsingham who found the catch first—it was ingeniously well-constructed—and he and Dominic removed the wooden partition that revealed a cavity that ran the length and width of the trunk but only two inches deep. There were papers here as well, mostly in Robert's handwriting and all in Latin. The three of them took turns reading in silence.

After three-quarters of an hour Elizabeth let out a sigh and said pragmatically, "Most of this would not be accepted as evidence. It is only Robert's accounting of what he claims passed between him and Rochford."

"It is very detailed," Dominic pointed out. "Dates, places, times—all things that can be checked. Circumstantially, it is an intriguing account and I can find nothing false in how he fits things together. It is all logical."

"Logic is not the same as evidence."

Walsingham broke in. "These are useful evidence." He held two letters in his hand, creased from delivery and concealment, but the broken seals unmistakably the personal badge of the Duke of Rochford: the maroon background signifying patience and the serpents a token of wisdom.

Dominic rubbed his eyes, not needing to reread the letters. The brief missives were burned into his brain. *I will deliver the document into your hands alone. Keep it on your person at all times until you know where to hide it,* read the first, dated the day before Robert had set off for Framlingham in November 1554. Where the false Penitent's Confession had been hidden in the Lady Chapel specifically for Minuette to find.

The second note read: *If you cannot uncover anything unsavory about the girl, then you can create it. Your talents as a seducer are well known. Perhaps you should turn them to her undoing. Surely you are gifted enough to do so without my niece's knowledge.*

"They are evidence," Elizabeth agreed. "But not conclusive. The girl my uncle speaks of is not necessarily Minuette. He could be challenging Robert to seduce almost any woman. And the document he writes of in the first letter is not named as the Penitent's Confession."

Dominic tried to ignore the thought of Robert eyeing Minuette as amorous prey. With a nod to Walsingham, he said, "It is enough to justify questions. And to question the Lord Chancellor, we must go through the king. It's time William knows it all."

"Agreed." Elizabeth took the offending letters from Walsingham and offered them to Dominic. "You or I?"

"Both of us, I think. But we'll inform Minuette first—she'll be needed to steady William when he finds out."

"How does this end, Dominic?" Elizabeth looked troubled. "Is it wise to bring down one more of the stable voices of England's government?"

"It is always wise to speak the truth," Dominic said, though he felt more than a twinge at his own lies. "William cannot rule without the necessary information. And the knowledge that his Lord Chancellor has maneuvered to bring down his two greatest opponents is very necessary information. What happens after will be up to William."

Dominic was sure that what happened next would be Rochford's arrest. Because if Northumberland hadn't set his son to distract Minuette on that fateful afternoon last year while her necklace was poisoned, then it could only have been Rochford.

There could be no mercy for that.

5 May 1556
Greenwich

Dominic returned last night from Kenilworth and spent hours today closeted with Elizabeth. No doubt they are weighing whatever evidence Robert Dudley has gathered against Rochford. I know what they will do next, because I know them both.

Elizabeth is angry with all the Dudleys still, but her affections are strong. She will be glad of a reason to negotiate Robert into release. And Dominic? He is incapable of ignoring wrongdoing.

I do not think they know me as well as I know them. They think I am too wrapped up in William and personalities. That I am overlooked makes it easier for me to maneuver. When one is underestimated, one can strike all the harder. And so I will move first.

Lord Rochford will never see me coming, but he will have cause before the end to thank me for interfering.

Despite the brave words confided to her diary, Minuette's nerves were pitched to an extreme as she approached Lord Rochford's privy chamber at Greenwich Palace. She had sent him a note asking for a private meeting, and he obliged her relatively quickly. She wished she had Fidelis with her; the enormous Irish wolfhound Dominic had given her for Christmas one year was almost as steadying a presence as Dominic himself. But Fidelis had remained at Wynfield Mote these last six months, the country manor where Minuette had lived as a small child. With the upheaval of William's illness she had not bothered to have the dog returned to court. Surely Fidelis preferred the open sky and fields of the country.

Minuette was received by Rochford's attendants with professional courtesy and soon found herself alone with the Lord Chancellor. "Thank you for seeing me, Your Grace," she said, accepting the seat he indicated across the wide desk from where he regarded her coolly.

"Can I refuse to meet with a woman so dear to the king's heart?" Rochford's tone was all mockery and dislike, and his keen dark eyes—so like his sister, Anne's—pierced through her. Minuette used his contempt to strengthen her resolve.

"I have come to do you a favour," she said.

"I do not think your position is quite so strong that I need worry yet about favours from you."

Perversely, the difficult reception calmed Minuette's nerves, and she let her instincts guide her. She was no stranger to political sparring—she had been trained by Anne Boleyn herself. "Do you know what Lord Exeter was doing in the North?"

"Visiting Amy Dudley at Kenilworth."

"Do you know why?"

"It is no great supposition that my niece would like her favorite released from the Tower. No doubt Lord Exeter is doing her bidding."

"By visiting Robert's wife?" Minuette laughed in genuine surprise. "If you believe that, you are a fool."

The dark eyes narrowed and one hand beat a restless pattern on the desk. "What do you want, Mistress Wyatt?"

"Lord Exeter returned from Kenilworth with a chest of Robert Dudley's papers and letters. Robert claims to have evidence that you were the mastermind behind the Duke of Norfolk's disgrace and the Penitent's Confession."

"Seeing as his father has been executed in part for that affair, of course Robert Dudley would look to save his own name—and neck."

"Dominic believes him, and so does Elizabeth. Who do you think William is going to believe?"

"There is no proof." Was that a flicker of concern in his expression?

Minuette leaned forward confidingly. "There doesn't have to be. William is persuadable. They will bring him to believe it. You are going to fall, Lord Rochford." She let that hang for a few heartbeats, then added gently, "How far you fall? That might be up to me."

"You think you have that kind of power?"

"I know I do. If you preempt the revelations—if you go to William first and tell him the truth—if you have all the Dudley sons released from the Tower . . ." Minuette drew a deep breath, momentarily dizzy with her own daring. "Then I will persuade the king to mercy on your behalf."

She counted it success that he didn't immediately dismiss her. He leaned back in his chair, studying her over his steepled fingers. Minuette had always thought of Rochford as ageless, but now she noted the streaks of silver in his hair and the thinness of the skin beneath his eyes. "Why would you do that?"

"Because you know even less than you think you do. And because a time is coming when I will need all the friends I can get."

"You think I will be your friend for this?"

"I think you will owe me, and you are a man who pays his debts. There is only one requirement—you must convince William that you had nothing to do with my poisoning."

His face grew dark. "The monkshood? I was not behind that."

"You arrested a man who has since been executed for painting my pendant with monkshood. How could you have known the perpetrator if you were not behind the attempt?"

"It was a useful event for my cause, for I could lay it at Northumberland's feet. That is all. I had nothing else to do with the matter."

"It is no secret that you would do anything to remove me from the king's attention."

Rochford put his elbows on the desk and fixed her in his sight. "Trust me in this, Mistress Wyatt—if I wanted you dead, you would *be* dead."

Oh yes, that she could believe. Minuette swallowed. "Eleanor Percy is not prepared to take the entire blame for the monkshood. According to her, you already know who was behind it all. And it was certainly not Northumberland. If you do not confess all to the king, Eleanor will do it for you."

Rochford stilled, watching her like a falcon about to dive on its prey. "What were you doing speaking to Eleanor Percy?"

"Playing the game," she retorted. "As I will continue to do, with or without your aid."

After a long, fraught silence in which Minuette could hear faint footsteps from distant corridors, Rochford nodded once. "You surprise me, Mistress Wyatt. I had thought you incapable of such hardness."

"I learned from your sister, did I not? Do not underestimate what I will dare for those I love."

CHAPTER SIX

SINCE DECEMBER, WILLIAM had fallen into the habit of drinking alone in the last hour before bed, heavily enough to submerge his churning thoughts so that he could sleep. Otherwise he would lie awake for hours dwelling on the things he could not change, and that was certainly not healthy.

No matter which palace he was in, William's bedchamber was always the most favoured and personal of his retreats. At Richmond or Whitehall, Greenwich or Hampton Court or Nonsuch, he always kept a handful of sentimental possessions in the privacy of his bedchamber. His mother's English Bible and his father's love letters to Anne. The silk ribbon Elizabeth had given him to carry on the day of his coronation. Miniatures by Henry VIII's favorite painter, Hans Holbein, of Henry himself and Anne Boleyn.

William was pondering his mother's face while he drank red wine and thinking that it was past time he had a portrait of Minuette when an unexpected knock came on the door.

The gentleman attending him looked askance at William. After a moment he nodded gruffly and the gentleman opened the door a little.

"Might I speak with the king?" Lord Rochford asked.

"I'm not in the mood for lectures, Uncle." William didn't even turn.

"I'm here to confess, not lecture."

The unnatural humility in his uncle's voice startled William almost as much as the words. He pivoted in his chair and squinted in the dim light to make out Rochford's severe figure in the doorway. "Confession? I thought that was a damned heretical practice of which we do not approve."

"Not confession to priests, but some confessions a king must hear."

William waved him in and said to the gentleman, "Wait outside."

When the two of them were alone in the room, William laid aside his mother's miniature and asked, "Is this something you can say sitting down or do you require to kneel at my feet?"

"That will be for you to say."

"But not until I know what you're confessing, so best sit while you can."

Rochford pulled out a chair and sat across from William. He put his hands on the table and laced his fingers together. His expression was, if anything, even more impassive than usual, but there was a tightness to his mouth that told William his uncle was in deadly earnest.

With a heavy sigh, William pushed the wine away. "I suspect I'm going to need to be sober to hear whatever this is."

Rochford did not blink, nor did he mince words. "Northumberland was not the one who planted the Penitent's Confession at Framlingham in 1554 and indicted Norfolk as a traitor. I was."

Of all the confessions William might have imagined his uncle making, this one was so far removed from his immediate thoughts that he didn't take it in at first. "What did you say?"

"The Penitent's Confession and all that went with it two years ago—that was neither a true plot by Norfolk, nor was it manipulated by Northumberland. That particular imaginary Catholic plot was *my* creation."

"Why?"

"Why do you think?" For a second, Rochford's humility slipped into impatience. "To protect you and England. The Catholics might be held at bay, but only just. The end of the regency was a particularly vulnerable time. I am hated, William, I know that. Far better an imaginary plot that I controlled to bring them down than waiting for a real one that might catch us by surprise and do lasting damage."

William shoved his chair away from the table and got to his feet. For the first time since his illness, he was seized with the urge to prowl, and his uncle stood up and watched him as he had so many times before. In the swirl of thoughts rearranging themselves in light of this information, one image blazed glaringly clear before him. "Are you telling me that *you* resurrected that broadside about my mother? You are the one who wanted that vile image seen once more? I thought your crowning virtue was devotion to your sister!"

Rochford's face darkened in anger. "My crowning virtue is devotion to a Protestant England and protecting my sister's children."

"So much for your vaunted sibling love," William went on, as though his uncle had not spoken.

"Don't you ever question my love for Anne!"

"You pinned a knife to my bed! You called my mother an incestuous whore! What can I not question after that?"

Rochford slammed his palms on the table and glared up at William. "It is the Catholics who originated that filth and I used the lies as I saw fit! Norfolk is dead, Mary is on a tight leash, and you are well on your way to consolidating your hold on your people's affections. I did that for *you*."

"And what about Northumberland? He was as devoted a Protestant as could be found in England. Did you send him to his death for my sake as well?"

"He did that himself."

"Entirely?" William's blood cooled a little and his mind began to work more clearly.

"I didn't mind goading him—he made himself such an easy target, what with his touchy pride and open ambitions. I admit that I was happy to cultivate doubts about the evidence against Norfolk and cast suspicion in Northumberland's direction. But I had no idea he would be so stupid as to let his son marry Margaret Clifford—nor that his stupidity would lead him into arming men and holding your sister captive. You can hardly blame me for Northumberland's treachery in that!"

As William's first burst of temper lessened, he realized that his uncle had kept well away from the one crime that Rochford must know he could never forgive: the attempted murder of Minuette. Adopting Dominic's traditional pose of crossed arms and apparently negligent leaning against a wall (it irritated William no end—hopefully Rochford would read in it the same disdain), he contemplated his uncle's clever, lean face. "You tried to kill my future queen. Tell me why I shouldn't drag you straight to the Tower and have your head for that."

"Because it wasn't me."

"Robert Dudley was used to distract Minuette in order to give someone the opportunity to poison her necklace. If it wasn't for his father's sake, then I must assume Robert was under your orders."

"Under my orders to speak with her, yes. To warn her away from you. Neither of us had anything to do with poison."

"It was you who arrested a Northumberland man as the poisoner. Was he truly the poisoner?"

"Yes."

"Was he truly one of Northumberland's men?"

William had his answer in Rochford's hesitation. "No."

"And of course he's been executed for his crime, so I can hardly ask him if he were taking orders from you. Convenient."

"He didn't take orders from me any more than he did from Northumberland. He took his orders from my wife."

William rocked back on his heels, stunned. "Are you trying to tell me that *Lady Rochford* is an assassin? Why wouldn't you tell me that before?"

"Because it was convenient to push Northumberland a little farther away. And because, for all her sins, she is my wife and I did not care to have a woman of my household arrested."

"What possible reason could Jane Boleyn have for killing Minuette? Why does she care whom I love?"

"She might not care, but one of her women cares a very great deal and Jane has always been easy to persuade into malice."

William swore long and inventively. "Eleanor."

His uncle inclined his head in agreement. "A woman of cunning and spite, rather like my wife. The two of them together—"

"And your wife just told you this? In the intimacy of the night—except that you do not spend your nights with her. So where did you hear this?"

"In the intimacy of the night, as you said. But not from Jane."

"You've been sleeping with *Eleanor*?" William let out an explosive laugh that was as much shock as amusement.

"She is quite skilled, Your Majesty."

"You think I don't know that? Or are we trying to dance around the fact that Eleanor was my mistress before she was yours? At least, I'll do you the credit of assuming you waited until I was finished with her. I wouldn't have thought her your type."

"I do not require to respect the women I bed."

William couldn't decide whether to be furious with Rochford's aplomb or to admire it. He shook his head and studied the man: impeccably dressed without ostentation, wearing his authority with ease, arrogantly sure of himself even while confessing to various crimes . . . in short, a man William had often longed to shake during the endless years of the regency. And now Rochford had delivered himself into his hands.

"So your confession, if I may sum it up, is that you conspired against one of the leading members of the nobility—one of your fellow members on my regency council—going so far as to create false evidence that blackened my mother's name as well as others. And don't think I've forgotten Alyce de Clare—a woman who died in the midst of doing your bidding. You further conspired to cast the guilt for those acts onto another member of the nobility, solely to consolidate your own position in the kingdom, in this case using the man's own son against his father's interest. And in the matter of the attempted murder of the only woman I have ever loved, you claim it was your wife's conspiracy—without your knowledge or consent, but with your willingness to shield her afterward. Tell me, *George,* why are you confessing now?"

He had never in his life used his uncle's given name. It made him feel more a man than anything he'd ever done, especially when Rochford flinched. When his uncle answered, his voice was stripped of its usual irony.

"Because Lord Exeter and Princess Elizabeth have an engagement with you tomorrow morning, in which they will accuse me in order to clear Robert Dudley's name and free him from the Tower. Well, that at least is your sister's motive. I don't doubt Courtenay feels it his sole duty to be honest."

"And you thought coming to me first would make me lenient?"

"I haven't actually committed a single crime against the throne or yourself personally. And I have now handed you the women who conspired to kill Mistress Wyatt."

If there was one thing William could do instinctively, it was make quick decisions. There was hardly a pause before he said, "I want you away from court tonight. Don't leave London. You may retire to Charterhouse and wait to hear from me."

That could mean almost anything, but Rochford did not press for details. He bowed in apparently genuine submission. "As you say, Your Majesty."

"One thing more," William added as his uncle straightened warily. "How do you know what Dominic and Elizabeth mean to tell me tomorrow morning? I hardly think it likely they would confide in the man they mean to accuse. Are your spies that embedded in my own court?"

Rochford's expression grew thoughtful. "No, Your Majesty. Though I knew they had each been to see Robert Dudley, I did not know how far things had gone until someone warned me."

"Who?"

The name was the very last one William would ever have predicted. "Mistress Wyatt. She is the one who counseled me to confess before accusations could be laid."

When his uncle had left, William sat up long into the night, drinking and pondering upon Minuette's audacity. What did she think she was doing, meddling with a man like Rochford? Did she not know the dangers of court politics? She was not Anne Boleyn—and William was glad of it. He did not want a queen who made enemies and then broke them.

He would have to make sure Minuette understood her position in his kingdom.

Minuette waited until long after midnight, aware that Rochford had only this one night to preemptively confess and certain that

William would send for her when it was finished. Surely he would be rocked by his uncle's lies. Surely he would want her for comfort or, less likely these days, advice.

But when the palace had grown nearly silent and no summons came, she at last allowed Carrie to undress her.

"Is everything all right?" her maid asked. Carrie's brown eyes were as soft as always, and in the last few months she had gained a little weight, enough so that she no longer looked on the verge of illness, and regained some of the cheer Minuette remembered from her childhood.

"I hope so," Minuette answered. "I will be up early. I am sorry to keep you so late."

Carrie let her hand linger on Minuette's shoulder before she gathered up her gown. "When you worry, I worry. And when you play games, I especially worry."

"It's not a game, Carrie."

"Lord Exeter would not like it."

"Do you make all your choices based on what Harrington would like?"

They had never spoken openly of the growing affection between Carrie and Dominic's right-hand man, Edward Harrington. Carrie had every right to be offended at Minuette's retort, but she merely shook her head. "My choices aren't so likely to get me into trouble as yours are."

Minuette turned those words over in her head for a long time after Carrie left her. The trouble with her choices lately was that whichever way she chose, danger hovered. Was it better to incur Dominic's anger for going behind his back and putting Rochford on his guard, or to allow William to be blindsided by the charges against his uncle? To continue the delicate dance of strengthening William until he could bear the blow of her secret marriage, or to simply run away with Dominic and leave others to pick up the pieces? Where was the safe choice there?

But she knew that, in the end, she had made her choice the moment she married Dominic—and that choice had been entirely about her own desires.

She was up and dressed by eight o'clock the next morning, wearing a gown in a sober shade of blue to emphasize either submissiveness or piety. Perhaps both. Then she sat in her rooms, waiting. She was to meet Dominic and Elizabeth in William's privy chamber at ten. No point trying to write in her diary, she was too fidgety and would blot the ink even if she could calm her thoughts enough to be coherent.

It was half past nine when Carrie came into her presence chamber with a guest: Lady Jane Grey. Minuette blinked with surprise. Jane was the daughter of a duke and the granddaughter of the late king's sister and she had never sought Minuette's company before—why did she do so now?

No matter what she wore, Jane always looked subdued, like a spring garden after a rainstorm. However elaborate her gowns or hair or jewels, something in her very nature made her look wise and almost otherworldly. She wasn't plain, but she behaved as though she were, or as though her appearance was far too trivial to deserve attention. Although Minuette was a year older, Jane always made her feel young and very frivolous.

"Forgive my intrusion," Jane said in her quiet manner. "If it is not convenient, I can come another time."

As it was not inconvenient to pass the time with an unexpected guest, Minuette replied, "You are quite welcome, Lady Jane. Was there a particular conversation you wished to have?"

For all her soberness, Jane showed a flash of ironic humour. "My wishes so rarely enter into anything these days. It is my mother, rather, who wished this conversation to occur. And I thought you might prefer me to her."

Minuette most certainly preferred Jane to the shrewd, formidable Duchess of Suffolk. Frances Brandon had spent her eldest daughter's lifetime positioning her as the only choice for William's queen. The French betrothal had been a great irritation. No doubt Minuette's sudden elevation had sent the duchess into a Tudor rage.

"And what is the subject of this conversation?" she asked Jane.

Beneath her submissive manner, Jane had a streak of stubborn honesty that manifested itself occasionally in bluntness. As now. "Are you and the king quite serious in your intentions?"

Minuette picked over her words cautiously. "Have you ever known William to be less than serious in matters touching his kingdom?"

"He truly intends to marry you?"

"I have not the slightest reason to doubt his intentions."

"You will not persuade him otherwise?" Jane eyed her coolly.

"Lady Suffolk is niece to the late King Henry. Does she really think Henry's son is open to persuasions that oppose his will?"

"My mother is capable of thinking that whatever she wishes must be so, rather like my cousin William." Jane flashed a rueful smile. "I think she will be disappointed in this."

"Does that trouble you?" Minuette's conscience pricked her unexpectedly. Was she injuring Jane's sentiments by stealing away William's love?

The assessing gaze Jane turned on her was, for a moment, a disconcerting echo of Elizabeth's sharpness, and Minuette was reminded that they were all cousins—even Dominic, with his Boleyn mother and royal grandmother. Only Minuette truly stood on the outside.

Finally, Jane said, "The greatest disappointment is my mother's, that I will not be the queen she has always wanted me to be. As for myself, my ambitions have never been so grand. I prefer contemplation and study to the rush and pomp of court. I would be quite content to pass my life in a quiet manner. If I must marry, I would prefer it to be a country gentleman far removed from politics."

"Do you have a particular gentleman in mind?"

"No. But it would not matter if I did. If I am not to be queen, then I must be a duchess. Which leads me to a question on my own account. You are well acquainted with Lord Exeter. He seems a serious-minded man. I wonder only . . ." Jane let her gaze wander around the chamber, flitting from the portrait of Elizabeth of York to the blue and gold curtains at the diamond-paned windows to Minuette's modest jewelry casket. Clearly she was uncomfortable discussing personal matters. Finally, Jane said in a rush, "It is rumoured that Lord Exeter's mother remains devoted to Rome. What are his own religious inclinations, do you know?"

Minuette felt nearly incapable of speech. It was one thing to be quizzed about William—but Dominic? She looked at the fair, slender Jane with her pretty eyes and submissive manner and, in that moment, hated her nearly as much as she was used to hating Eleanor Percy. "So it is Duchess of Exeter your mother aims for, is it?" She could not moderate the sharpness of her words.

"The only other possibility is the Duke of Norfolk, and Lord Exeter is far closer to the king."

"And what is your preference?"

"I want a husband who will respect my convictions and share them, so that our children may be raised in an honourable and honest home. Will Lord Exeter allow me that freedom of conscience?"

Minuette had to subdue the urge to slap that righteous concern from Jane Grey's face. In fact, the force of her violent reaction rather startled her. She managed to keep a level tone through sheer force of will. "I do not know what sort of husband he would make you. I suppose you shall have to decide that for yourself." Minuette stood up in dismissal, though she was by far the lesser-ranked. "I'm sorry to be abrupt, but I have an appointment with the king."

Jane did not appear to take offense, though her expression was thoughtful and Minuette remembered that often the most dangerous people were those on the edges whom everyone tended to overlook. "Whatever my mother's opinion," Jane offered, "I think you are very good for my cousin. You make him happy, and that is never to be taken lightly. I wish you well, whatever difficulties lie ahead."

"Thank you."

Despite feeling ashamed at Jane's generosity, Minuette could not trust herself to say more. Was she going to have to watch Lady Suffolk bear down upon Dominic as she had spent years doing to William, dragging Jane in her wake and thrusting her into his way with single-minded determination? She remembered Aimée at the French court last year, coming out of Dominic's chamber in the middle of the night. Jane was not quite so bad as the voluptuous Frenchwoman. But that didn't mean Minuette wanted to watch while any woman angled for Dominic's attention.

She had to get this business of Rochford straightened out, then put paid to any French invasion plans, so that she and Dominic could cut through their tangled responsibilities and be free.

When Dominic and Elizabeth entered William's privy chamber, Minuette was already, as usual, at her ease with the king. She wore a gown of dark blue that echoed the damask doublet of the king, and Dominic had a sudden vision of her with a crown on her golden hair. How lovely she would look, dressed as a queen.

He blinked and nodded once to his wife, trying to clear his head of that disturbing image. She looked as though she carried unpleasant images of her own, for her hazel eyes were troubled and did not linger over him.

The king's privy chamber at Greenwich retained the furniture and décor of Henry VIII's reign. Although it was May, it was chilly and gray outside and a fire blazed in the wide hearth. Candles added a bit more light to the weak daylight that came through the windows but the whole effect was one of gloomy oppression.

William sat at his ease in a carved and cushioned chair, Minuette in a matching one at his side. The king's expression was more alive than Dominic had seen in months. He instantly realized that was not, at this moment, a good thing. William's mouth was set and squared-off, his keen blue eyes alive with irritation. And when he spoke, the very flatness of his tone announced his fury.

"So, you have come at last to tell me about Robert Dudley's accusations against Lord Rochford."

Dominic caught Elizabeth's sideways glance and supposed she was as little surprised as he was. In some ways, the only surprise was that they hadn't been found out before this.

"My uncle has been before you," William continued. "He made a full confession to me last night."

Dominic stared openly. "Lord Rochford confessed?" The words did not seem to fit together in his mind.

"He seemed to think I would be more lenient if I heard it from him first."

"And will you be?" Elizabeth drawled.

"That," William drew out the word, displeasure heavily colouring his voice, "is not the point. The point is that I was kept in the dark while my sister and my dearest friend went behind my back on a matter touching my throne."

"William," Minuette interposed sweetly, "we were not intending to be deceptive. Only helpful." She let her hand rest on his arm and Dominic twitched at knowing what her touch would feel like to William. Warm and reassuring and ever so enticing . . .

William's eyes lingered on her hand, and then moved slowly, intimately, to her face. Not quite a caress, but near enough to make Dominic twitch again. But then the king spoke, and Dominic grew cold. "And you, sweetling? Would you like to tell the others how you betrayed them to Rochford and counseled him to confess before they could speak? Do Dominic and Elizabeth know that?"

Dominic almost choked holding back the words he instantly wanted to shout: *Minuette? How could you do that? I told you to stay away from him. We don't need a snake like Rochford on our side and I thought we agreed* . . . But Minuette had not agreed. Indeed, he had not asked it of her. He had simply assumed that his word was the last one.

In that split moment of confusion between his head and his mouth, in which Minuette bit her lip and avoided her husband's accusing gaze, Elizabeth spoke first. With characteristic dryness, she said, "Well, Minuette, if your aim were to prove that you belong at William's side, you have achieved that and more. Who would have guessed you could be so calculating?"

Minuette removed her hand from William's arm and straightened in her seat, meeting the watchful eyes of all three with apparent calm. "The lighthearted, merrymaking girl is so easy to overlook."

"So it seems," Elizabeth retorted. "May I take it, William, that Rochford's confession included his manipulation of Robert Dudley?"

"Is that always to be your primary concern—the welfare of Robert Dudley? Just as well you are not England's ruler or your affections might undo us all."

"And yours will not?"

Everyone knew in an instant that Elizabeth's flippant response had crossed the line. Dominic felt that the ceiling had lowered and the air grown dangerous as William's eyes went dark, like a sky about to storm. "Do you have something to say, sister? Come to think of it, I do not believe I have yet received your well wishes on my betrothal. Surely that is an oversight and not an insult to either me or my lady."

William reached for Minuette, taking firm possession of her hand without even looking at her. Dominic couldn't decide where to look: at William's cold fury or Elizabeth's sparking temper or Minuette's shuttered withdrawal. He wanted nothing more than to take his wife by the other hand and get her out of here. Out of this chamber, out of the palace, out of London . . .

Even Elizabeth knew when to submit. "I thought my well wishes were a given. Of course I congratulate you, William, on having had the good sense to fall in love with a woman you do not deserve."

After a heartbeat in which he might have chosen to take offense, William's expression eased. "I suppose I can overlook the insult to me as it is such a truthful compliment to Minuette. I do not deserve her, but I will have her, and whatever your opinion of the politics, I expect your wholehearted and vocal support in the matter."

"Naturally."

Before Dominic could be asked to give that same promise, he said hastily, "What about Lord Rochford?"

William released Minuette, and Dominic had a sudden vision of his wife as a chess piece—one that kept being picked up and put back down at the whim of others. The king leaned back in his seat. "I sent Rochford to Charterhouse last night. I do not mean to have him arrested. But I do think a long absence from court is in order. I will banish him to Blickling Hall and let him ponder the folly of trying to maneuver behind my back."

"He is not to be made to answer for any of his crimes?" Dominic could not help his harshness; as long as Rochford was free, the man could stir up any sort of trouble he liked.

His image of Minuette as a chess piece—silent and played by others—shattered when she said coolly, "What would be the point? The past cannot be changed and it would not profit England to put one more leader in his grave. The king can make known his displeasure with Rochford short of killing him."

The look William turned on Minuette was assessing and not entirely pleased. But he nodded once. "Norfolk and Northumberland are both dead, the first by natural causes and the latter through his own actions. I have already reinstated Norfolk's grandson to the title and estates, and I will release Northumberland's sons from the Tower. His oldest son, John, may retain his earldom of Warwick, but his father's estates remain forfeit to me."

"Those answer the political charges, Your Majesty." Dominic always chose formality when about to disagree with William. "What about the matter of the monkshood?"

"Rochford had some interesting information on that matter. I do have an arrest for you to make, Lord Exeter, one that should please you. The poisoner was Lady Rochford. You may take my aunt from her quarters directly to the Tower."

"Wait . . . what?" Elizabeth held up a hand as though trying to pause the flow of information. "Why would Lady Rochford have taken against Minuette?"

It was Minuette herself who answered, and Dominic could see at once that this was not news to her. "Because she is a trouble-maker for the sake of trouble. And perhaps, in some obscure manner, she thought it would please her husband."

"That's that, then." William stood up. "Arrest my aunt, and then you can go to Charterhouse and make Rochford deliver up the Great Seal. I won't arrest him, but I will not have a man I cannot trust as my chancellor."

"Is that all, Your Majesty?" Dominic felt unbalanced by the rush of revelations. Not least the fact that Minuette appeared to be up to her neck in bargaining behind the scenes.

"Once Rochford is away and his wife in the Tower, you and I will ride the coastlines and see to our defenses. You haven't forgotten you are Warden of the Cinque Ports?"

"I have not."

"And I can presume you have no objections to considering my counsel in the matter of our defenses?"

Cautious of William's leashed temper, and yet irritated himself, Dominic said, "I serve always at your pleasure."

"Yes, you do." William looked carefully at each one of them in turn. "It seems to me that because of our long history and familiarity with one another, the three of you are too quick to forget my position. I am not a child to be coddled, nor a temperamental boy to be persuaded. I am King of England and Ireland, Supreme Head of the Church, the voice of government and power in this realm and that is especially true when you do *not* agree with me. Counsel me all you like, but don't ever go behind my back in the feeble cause of protecting me."

Dominic would have expected this last to be addressed to him, but it was Minuette on whom William had turned, eyes blazing ferociously.

Once, she might have laughed, turning the king's temper to rueful humour. Or gentled her expression and offered her very affection as apology. Today she met William's gaze unblinking. Dominic would have given a great deal to know what was going on behind those serious hazel eyes. With only a slight crease to mar her smooth forehead, Minuette said, "I apologize, Your Majesty. I assure you, I know full well that my position rests entirely on your pleasure."

And don't you forget it . . . Every line of William's body shouted the unspoken threat, and Dominic would have shivered if he hadn't grown numb with misgiving. He hardly sees her anymore, he thought. Not as Minuette, the girl who had been his friend since birth, the one who could always judge his mood and make him happy. William now saw only the queen he meant to make her, and his jealousy was not so much about other men as the fear that he would not be able to control Minuette herself.

Dominic quite understood that fear.

CHAPTER SEVEN

9 May 1556
St. James Palace

It has been three days since Lord Rochford's dismissal as chancellor
and the buzz of gossip remains at a fever pitch. Dominic said he
took it well enough; so well, that he felt perhaps one moment's pity
for him. But only a moment, because Rochford—disgraced or
not—is not a man to receive pity. No doubt he is already planning
for his eventual return. For now, he has been more or less banished
to his birthplace of Blickling Hall.

In his absence, William Cecil, Lord Burghley, has been named
Lord Chancellor. I was pleasantly surprised by this, for William is
usually impatient with the quieter men of the council. But
Burghley is a wise choice: an astute politician who has managed to
serve for years without ruffling many feathers. Elizabeth's sole
comment on the matter was, "Not every effect of the smallpox is
bad. It seems Will has learned prudence in the aftermath—at least
in some things."

But it is Lady Rochford who troubles my thoughts, for there has
been no prudence in her treatment. Unlike her husband, she did
not submit quietly. Dominic led the party that arrested her in her
chambers at Greenwich Palace, and even in his understated way, he

*admitted that she was troublesome and wretched. The less
understated at court have wild stories of her tears and shouts and
imprecations hurled at her absent husband. She scratched at the
guards' faces and I believe Dominic had to subdue her physically.
Now she sits in the Tower, awaiting the king's pleasure in dealing
with her.*

*It may be some time, for Dominic and William leave tomorrow
to tour the southern ports and ensure our navy's readiness to block
the French ships from an invasion. There are times when I cannot
believe it has come to this—the possibility of foreign soldiers on
English soil simply because William fell unwisely in love.*

How much of this is to be laid at my door?

*Before the men leave tomorrow, William has asked (which is a
polite way of saying commanded) that I host a private dinner in
my new chambers here at St. James's. I shall of course do as I am
bidden, though the chambers he has given me are again those most
often used by his mother as queen. I expect it shall be an
uncomfortable night for all concerned.*

Dinner in Minuette's new suite of chambers was every bit as
awful as Dominic had feared. He hated the forced intimacy of
these gatherings, the way the guests watched avidly for every sign
of affection between William and Minuette, just waiting for the
opportunity to increase their own importance by having been in
such close quarters with the king and his unlikely love. Most of
those invited were well under the age of thirty, and though he was
only twenty-five himself, Dominic did not like the careless frivol-
ity of the younger courtiers. All they seemed to care about was
being noticed and they avidly took note of the luxury in which
William had settled Minuette. The plates were silver and the gob-
lets gold, course followed exquisite course from pheasants to sug-
ared novelties, and Minuette wore an ivory gown cut daringly low

that made her skin glow gold in the candlelight and made Dominic ache with the need to touch her.

But the catalyst of disaster turned out to be Margaret Boleyn. She was a lady of very great age—nearly eighty years old—and was great-aunt to not only William and Elizabeth, but Dominic himself through his Boleyn mother. Although her wits might wander, Margaret's tongue was biting.

She kept calling William "Henry" and seemed to think that Minuette, for all her golden hair, was Anne. The family tolerated her lapses, for what could be expected of a woman who had been a child bride in the year that Richard III was defeated and the Tudor dynasty began? One who has lived so long must be expected to forget names and faces. Dominic wondered how many of the guests noted the fact that Minuette flinched every time Margaret called her Anne. Or did she flinch because William was unusually affectionate tonight, twining her hair around his fingers or resting his hand possessively along the back of her neck? Dominic marked every intimate gesture, and felt his control slipping.

As Margaret was helped from her chair at the end of the feast, the old lady motioned for Minuette to stand before her. Pulling her near with gnarled hands, Margaret peered at her closely, examining her up and down.

"Humph," Margaret said in her creaky voice. "So he's talked you round at last. Thought he would. No woman's ever been able to stay out of Henry's bed for long."

The entire chamber seemed to hold its breath as William said sternly, "You speak out of turn, my lady. I am not my father. And Minuette is as chaste as ever she was."

Margaret peered at him, gaze sharpening as her mind cleared briefly. "Henry's son, is it? He'd be ashamed of you. Henry at least knew when a woman had been used. This girl's been in someone's bed. More fool you if it isn't yours."

As Margaret departed, a murmur of voices rose behind her. William was at Minuette's side, whispering reassuring words about age and cruel tongues, and Dominic hardly knew where to look. The one place he could not look was at his wife.

"Well," Elizabeth noted, "I don't suppose Margaret will be asked to the wedding."

William dealt with the awkwardness as he usually did, by ignoring it. "Find me musicians," he ordered, and within five minutes there were violinists standing in the corner of Minuette's presence chamber playing for the small gathering to dance.

There were more men than women present, so Dominic was not the only one to stand along the walls watching the four couples. He felt Minuette's eyes on him several times and knew she was afraid he would take his leave before she could speak to him. But tonight he did not retreat. He watched her dance with William, every step of the pavane between them perfect and painful, and tried not to think too loudly at his king: *I've had her as you never will.*

He was not proud of that possessive instinct.

After several dances William said abruptly, "Do you not care to dance, Lord Exeter?" Dominic could hear the leashed anger and knew that the king had been more troubled by Margaret Boleyn's nastiness than he'd let on.

Dominic was not in the mood to soothe his temper. "It needs the right music and the right partner, Your Majesty."

William spread his hands wide. "Command the musicians as you will."

All eyes were on Dominic as he straightened away from the wall. He kept his eyes on the king, knowing that William expected him to either apologize or back down. Instead, Dominic commanded the silent musicians, "Play a volta."

William gave a short bark of surprise and perhaps even approval. "And the right partner?" the king asked with elaborate courtesy.

"Surely you can spare Mistress Wyatt for one dance."

What could William say? It was you taught me that trick, Dominic thought as William passed Minuette over to him. Ask in public so that one cannot refuse without appearing childish.

His heart misgave him when he realized that William meant only to watch them, which meant that no one else would dance, either. It was reckless to the point of insanity, but as the violin played the opening strains of a volta, Dominic forgot to care. All he knew was that he was going to dance with his wife.

He had never danced a volta with Minuette. It had been years since he'd performed the rather risqué dance at all, but his lack of practice did not show. More than any dance, the volta depended on the connection between partners and that was so strong that he feared the most attentive might actually see the sparks between them.

This girl's been in someone's bed. But not recently enough. The two years he'd waited for Minuette before their marriage was as nothing to the frustrations of the last five months. After those blissful wedding weeks at Wynfield Mote, enforced celibacy had weighed on him more than he would have thought possible. All he could think of was the velvet of Minuette's skin, his fingers tangled in her hair, the length of her body beneath him, her breathless laughter giving way to little gasps of pleasure. It was distracting and infuriating and, when he lifted her every few steps of the volta, his hands curved to her waist and hip, Dominic thought that he would damn them both thoroughly by pushing her against a wall and kissing her.

When the music ended, there was a long silence as everyone waited for the king to speak. When he did, it was to the musicians. "You may go," the king commanded. "The evening is finished."

The guests departed in awkward twos and threes, no doubt eager to spread Margaret Boleyn's slanderous words as well as speculate on the naked tension between the king and his closest friend. On both matters, it didn't matter if anyone believed them. It mattered only that they could repeat them.

All too soon it was just the four of them of old—Dominic and William, Elizabeth and Minuette. What would the king say now that they were alone?

It was not what Dominic had expected. In a conciliatory tone, William asked, "Dom, care to join me in cards tonight?"

He's trying, Dominic realized. If he were wise, he would meet William halfway. But he could not be wise while desire pounded through him like a drumbeat. "I'd promised Minuette a game of chess. If it's all the same to you, Your Majesty."

He saw the flare of quickly controlled temper in William's eyes. "I defer in all things to my lady."

Dominic refused to look away as William gave Minuette a lingering kiss, letting jealousy feed his recklessness. The moment the king and Elizabeth were gone, Dominic opened the door to Minuette's privy chamber. Carrie, supervising the clearing up the table in the presence chamber, closed the door behind them. He assessed the opulently furnished space—the gilded chests and rich tapestries and painted ceiling—and nodded once.

"William has done well by you. I suppose you've earned it." What he meant was, *How have you earned it? What precisely have you done with the king for each dress and each jewel and each piece of furniture?*

"Dominic!" Minuette looked torn between fury and tears.

"I'm sorry. I thought it would be easier after we ... But it's harder."

He stood so near her that surely she must feel the heat pouring off his skin, but he was just gentleman enough not to touch her without consent. For a moment she hesitated, then she opened the second door and led him through to her bedchamber.

They made it to the bed, but just barely. Dominic could not be slow and he could not be gentle. He managed to shed his own clothes along the way, but Minuette was still half dressed when he laid her down. His hands moved from the tangle of her shift to the lines of her bodice and then the bare skin of her arms and shoulders that gleamed beneath him and he was drowning in her scent and taste.

She rested her head on his chest afterward, heavy and warm in his arms.

"I'm sorry," he whispered into her hair.

"I'm not," she said lazily, and Dominic thought that if her voice continued to sound like warm honey he would never be able to leave.

"I put you in an impossible position. Surely William will be suspicious after that dance. How could he not be?"

"William's displeasure was not about suspicion. I know it is painful for you to hear, but he would never dream of suspecting this. He doesn't know that your distance has as much to do with your own guilt as with his actions. William thinks you despise him, because of Renaud and Scotland last year. He looks at you and feels only your contempt. And though he is too proud to say it, or even admit it to himself, he needs you to lean on. Without you, he's . . ." She faltered, searching for the right word.

Dominic supplied his own. "He's dangerous."

"He's lost."

Dominic closed his eyes. Minuette was right, he didn't want to hear this. He didn't want to know that William still looked to him for advice and security, for stability in a world that offered him none. What had William said when he'd made Dominic a duke? *I shall have one duke in England who is loyal only to me.*

He ran his hand down his wife's bare shoulder and calculated how long it would take him to remove what remained of her clothing. "I will try to help him, love. I will try to swallow my own guilt, as well as my desire to rip his arms out every time he touches you."

She relaxed into his embrace. "I wish you didn't have to go."

Dominic tightened his arms. "Even with Carrie standing guard, a chess game can only deceive for so long."

Her next question was so soft he might have imagined it. "What are we going to do?"

Dominic moved his hand to her cheek, drawing his fingers along it before bending to kiss the hollow of her throat. "We will do what we must, together. If anything happens while we are gone from one another . . . We'll think of some kind of code, something that no one else can decipher."

"Like what?" He could hear the smile in her voice.

"Colours, perhaps." He continued to kiss her, moving from throat to collarbone. "If I hear from you that the skies are a lovely blue at Hampton Court, I shall know that all is well and you are safe. What else?"

Minuette's laugh was heavy with desire. "Green. If I send word that I am longing to be at Greenwich again, you shall know that I am longing only for this."

"My bright star." He drew her down then, and set about the pleasurable business of stripping her entirely. But in the activity that followed, she whispered one more colour in his ear. "White is for warning."

When William and Dominic headed southeast to review coastal defenses, Elizabeth remained behind to maintain a royal presence in London. She and Minuette stayed at St. James's Palace, and that was where Robert Dudley made his return to court.

He had been released from the Tower a week earlier, along with his three surviving brothers, but where John, Ambrose, and Henry had retreated to the country as rapidly as possible, Robert wasn't one to run away. Elizabeth knew, from Francis Walsingham, that he had taken up residence at Ely Place—the only London property left to the Dudley family after Northumberland's execution. She had expected Robert sooner, but when he was announced by a disapproving Kat Ashley, Elizabeth still found herself taken by surprise.

He had chosen his moment well, when she was more or less alone in her own chambers. Elizabeth refused to leave the presence chamber for the more intimate privy chamber. Let Robert read into that what he wanted, but she was not going to be afraid of facing him before others or of the talk that would ensue. There were four women with her. Minuette was not among them—she rarely was, these days, and Elizabeth wondered how long before William removed her officially from her service—but those present were biddable and discreet and would release just the right amount of information to the curious.

If she wished for anyone at this meeting, it was Walsingham. She had quickly come to depend on his pragmatic counsel as well as his intelligence gathering. She allowed herself one thrill of nerves and pleasure at Robert's familiar, beloved figure bowing to her with unusual gravity before stiffening her spine beneath her peacock-blue dress edged in brilliant blue and gold feather designs.

"You are looking well, Your Highness," Robert said, striking just the right note of deference.

She studied him before answering, head tilted to the side as she took in his more than usually slender frame and the slightly more sober clothing than normal. She was glad to say truthfully, "You look as though your time in the Tower has not permanently affected you."

"Not physically."

"And what permanent nonphysical effects do you anticipate?"

She had still not invited him to sit, but he gave no sign of impatience. He had the gift of grace whatever his situation. "Confinement is hard on the body, but considerably harder on the spirit. It will be a long time before I stop waking in the night simply to reassure myself that I am free to leave my chamber if I wish it. Before I stop imagining that I hear footsteps approaching to take me somewhere even less desirable."

"Perhaps you will remember that the next time you are tempted to act against the interests of the Crown."

"My intent was never to injure the Crown, but only to advance my own interests. A sin, to be sure, but one motivated by a most sincere and desperate love."

She gestured abruptly for him to take a seat, if only to stop that line of conversation. She did not want to hear about Robert's love today. "What will you do next? Your name has been officially cleared, but I am not certain that my brother will welcome you back with open arms just yet. And for certain Dominic will not."

With a shrug (also familiar—how many of his gestures and mannerisms did she know so intimately?) Robert said, "I am the Crown's to command. Is there some task I can undertake for you while the king is touring defenses?"

When she eyed him narrowly, he hastened to add, "I welcome anything, Elizabeth, no matter how menial."

She did have a service in mind—not menial, but also not pleasant. "Walsingham is liaising with William's household to prepare for the state visit of Philip of Spain. He could use a gentleman to put a better face on some of the interactions. You know how to flatter and inspire, and certainly how to prepare grand ceremonies. I think you would be well suited for this role."

A role designed purely to welcome Elizabeth's future husband to England. She had to give Robert credit—other than the involuntary twitch of a muscle beneath his left eye, he didn't flinch. "It would be an honour, Your Highness."

"Report to Walsingham when you leave here. He will have assignments for you."

With that assured grace Robert rose and Elizabeth extended her hand to allow him to kiss it. It was a less personal kiss than was his wont, but again he was nicely judging his behavior. No liberties, no tantrums, nothing but earnest and humble service.

Elizabeth tightened her hand when he would have released it and said, "I am truly happy to see you, Robert." And then, before his relief could turn to complacency, she added, "Will not Amy regret your continued absence?"

The ironic twist of his mouth was more than familiar—it flooded Elizabeth with all the remembered mischief and laughter and tart wordplay of their years of friendship. "Amy cannot possibly object to any request of yours. She is delighted to share me with the court."

That was as bold-faced a lie as any Robert had ever told . . . and it made Elizabeth's heart sing.

With Northumberland's execution and Rochford's disgrace, the Protestant faction at court was in severe disarray and the Catholics had been handed a rare opportunity to redeem their position and royal favour. And lest vindication leap into something more, there was one woman who had to be managed and placated: Mary Tudor.

Minuette sighed deeply when William asked her to attend his half sister at Beaulieu while he and Dominic were away minding military matters. She had been used as a court messenger before this and, although Mary was suspicious of anyone who came from court—and particularly one partly raised by Anne Boleyn—Minuette had always received a grudging acceptance from the eldest Tudor sibling.

But that was before Framlingham. Almost two years ago Minuette had been the catalyst of the late Duke of Norfolk's arrest. She had discovered the crucial piece of evidence in that case, which led to Norfolk's death and Mary's own house arrest. And now Lord Rochford had admitted to forging that piece of evidence. Minuette did not anticipate a pleasant visit.

She had underestimated the effect on Mary of being allowed to return to her favorite palace of Beaulieu. Released from her hated house arrest, and no doubt buoyed by Rochford's fall, Mary was in a triumphant temper. Minuette, on the other hand, had always found Beaulieu oppressive. The overall effect was of a palace—and a woman—stubbornly clinging to the past. Massive carved chests, bulky velvets and damasks at the windows, and an overabundance of gloomy reds and browns combined with Mary's stifling righteousness left Minuette twitchy and anxious.

Most unusually for Mary, she attempted to tease. "Mistress Wyatt, who could have guessed that you would be the cause of my brother's release from the French betrothal? Almost I could welcome you for that alone."

Minuette curtsied low, startled by the change in Mary's demeanor. Dignified and royal had always been the first words to come to mind when one thought of Mary Tudor, but today she looked contented. Like a sleek cat who has caught its mouse and disdains every being less fortunate than itself.

Despite her teasing words, Minuette knew she was not truly welcomed as William's intended bride. Mary would not even bother to protest that it was not a suitable match, for so much went without saying. Perhaps she believed William would come to his senses and thus, for now, Minuette could be welcomed as a diversion that had disconcerted the French. Another of Mary's old enemies.

Mary had far more old enemies than she had ever bothered to make friends.

"Thank you for allowing me to come to Beaulieu, my lady." Minuette knew how to play the game of pretending Mary was autonomous and not tied to William's every whim.

"I suppose there is a purpose to this visit."

"To enjoy your company is not purpose enough?"

Mary narrowed her eyes, giving her a fleeting but strong resemblance to Elizabeth when displeased. "No one attached to court has fewer than three purposes to every action. Shall I guess yours?"

"If it pleases you, my lady." Minuette could afford to let Mary be haughty; it cost her nothing and gave Mary an easy way to feel superior. Sometimes she thought that was why she was sent to deal with this trickiest Tudor family member—to defuse Mary's pride in attacks on someone of inferior status rather than letting her wounds fester and finally spill into something truly dangerous.

"No doubt one purpose is to do with the proposed visit of King Philip. What does my brother want of me in that regard?"

Straight to the point; Minuette could respect that. "The king knows how greatly it will please you to have Philip in England. It is his wish that you should attend all the royal festivities on the occasion of the Spanish king's state visit."

The state visit that would end in his betrothal to Elizabeth. What, Minuette wondered, would be Mary's reaction to her younger sister of seventeen years wedding a man whom, in another world, Mary might have had for herself? She would know that it was a political marriage, and publicly Mary had to agree that it met every stated wish of her heart—a bond between England and Spain that would put paid to the French connection for years.

But it would be Elizabeth who would reign as Queen of Spain, Elizabeth whose children would carry the same royal blood as Mary's long-suffering mother. Life, Minuette thought with great understatement, is not fair.

Perhaps her pity showed on her face, for Mary's own expression altered and she grew all at once curt. "We shall discuss your other purposes at another time."

Minuette realized that, beneath her elaborate crimson gown and perfectly coiled hair and some private sense of satisfaction, Mary Tudor looked drawn, as though her outward appearance was a thin mask over an expense of nervous energy. Henry's eldest daughter was forty this year, an age when she must begin to admit that patience was never going to be enough to win her the freedom to marry and have children. Her life would always be this: a shadow on her brother's throne, an unpleasant symbol of a broken marriage and a shattered religion that most Englishmen and -women would be happy to forget.

As Minuette curtsied good night, Mary asked suddenly, "Is it true that Lady Rochford has been arrested for an attack upon you?"

"It is true that she has been taken to the Tower," Minuette answered cautiously.

"Because she tried to kill you."

How fast gossip spread, no matter how remote the household. "That is the charge, my lady."

"But Lord Rochford himself is not under arrest, though he plotted behind my brother's back to destroy my own reputation as well as that of the late Duke of Norfolk."

What could possibly be answered to that? It was true enough, in its way.

Mary shook her head slightly, now eyeing Minuette as one would a dangerous animal. "Curious, how the personal has become more important in the realm than the political. You may go."

As Minuette left, she heard Mary mutter a single word behind her. It sounded suspiciously like "Men."

Mary was not a woman prone to sentiment. How could she be? She had spent her adult life in a churning state of suspicion about the motives of everyone around her. But she was forced to admit that there was something rather engaging about Minuette Wyatt. Not that the girl was in the least suitable for a king's wife; charm was all well and good, but to be a queen was a position given by God. Still, if she had to be under the eye of someone from court, she much preferred Minuette to others William could have sent.

She took her time committing to support the state visit from Philip, but that was only for her dignity's sake. Of course she would be there. England must be reminded that Spain had been her friend for long years before her father's bewitchment by that woman. It was God's will that Spain and England be united once more. But perhaps in not quite the way her younger brother intended.

In all the years and insults of her life, there had never been a question that Mary loved William. But even the strongest of earthly loves are but pale imitations of the love of God. Mary had made a vow years before, on the very day she'd heard of William's birth. She had submitted to her father then, signed the document agreeing that her parents' marriage had been wrongly conceived, and allowed herself to be stripped of her title as princess. But she had done so with a vow to God and her mother's memory that she would bide her time and know her moment.

The moment was upon her. The French were furious with William for breaking his betrothal to their princess. Spain was clearly prepared to deal for the hand of an English princess.

How much more might they be eager to match Spain's king with an English queen?

Lord Rochford, as she might once have predicted and most certainly wished, had brought about his own fall from grace. Mary would go to London and court in this newly unsettled atmosphere. Power would be up for grabs now, and the Duke of Norfolk would be anxious to secure some of it for himself. The boy—for he was hardly more than that—was not himself Catholic, but his inclinations and all his strong family loyalty would bring him to see her.

And she would begin the delicate dance that God had saved her for. A dance whose steps she could not predict but of whose outcome she was certain: England with a Catholic monarch firmly on the throne.

The near-giddy satisfaction of embarking at long last on a course of action induced Mary to unusual friendliness with Minuette during her short stay at Beaulieu. She invited the girl to sit with her one morning while Mary worked with her secretary, keeping up a steady flow of chatter designed to put the girl at ease. Only upon later consideration did Mary realize William's young paramour had given away much less information than she'd appeared to.

On the last evening, Mary invited Minuette to dine with her privately, knowing that her brother would take it as a sign of her approval of his betrothed.

"Tell me, Mistress Wyatt, are you much in contact with your stepfather?" she asked. She remembered Stephen Howard's interest in the girl, and it could be useful to have another insight into the tightly enmeshed Howard family.

"Not so often lately," Minuette answered. "Perhaps he does not approve of my new . . . position." She pronounced the word doubtfully, as though she herself was unsure.

Mary gave her credit for recognizing her unsuitability. She'd wondered how William could have been such a fool as to think with his body rather his head in the sacred matter of marriage. But then, even their esteemed father had been bewitched by a woman.

Mary turned to more pressing matters. "As one so close to the king, you must have some idea of what he intends for Lord Rochford's future." Arrest? Permanent exile from court? Neither was answer enough for the upstart George Boleyn's many years of heresy and ill-government, but she needed information to decide how to act in the matter.

"His Majesty does not share political matters with me," Minuette answered.

"He sent you here to negotiate my approval of the Spanish visit," Mary pointed out.

"Because that visit touches on personal affairs, not merely political ones."

Oh, the girl was quite good for being young and of a common background. But then she had been raised largely at court in the company of William and Elizabeth—perhaps it was not surprising that she had learned how to speak without saying anything.

But she herself had been doing the same since before this chit of a girl was even born. "Surely the matter of the king's uncle also touches on personal affairs, not to mention the imprisonment of his own aunt."

"The only matter on the king's mind at present is the security of England's coastline and borders. When the threats of invasion are past, then will the king turn to other matters. Nothing concerns him more than preserving England's security."

Mary allowed herself a genuine smile, almost pitying. "If that were true, then the king would not be in such haste to throw away powerful alliances for a woman who brings him nothing but a pretty face."

She rose from the table, Minuette following suit with an expression devoid of anything but polite attention. "I will not meet with you again, Mistress Wyatt. Tell my brother I shall come to London for Spain's sake, and because I wish it."

And because my time has come, she thought. Mother, guide my steps.

CHAPTER EIGHT

LETTERS FROM DOMINIC COURTENAY
TO MINUETTE WYATT

14 May 1556

Minuette,

William and I are safely arrived at Dover Castle. I will be invested tomorrow with the office of Warden of the Cinque Ports. The gentlemen of the towns as well as the relevant port officials are taking their measure of me, assuming that my primary interest will be in the collection of revenues. If they knew how little I count the riches the king has carelessly granted me. Tiverton and the duchy of Exeter was a far greater gift than I had ever thought to wish for—what need I for even more wealth? All that I need I have in your keeping.

There has been greenery everywhere I looked along this trip. The hard rains of winter have unleashed a riot of growing things and every blade of grass and thrust of flower stem and swish of leaves is bittersweet with memories.

Dominic

22 May 1556

Minuette,

After a tour of the traditional Cinque Ports, we have ridden on to Portsmouth where a French attack is most likely to be made. They'll want to harass as much of the coast as they can, of course—but they'll need a deepwater port for an invasion, and Portsmouth is the most tempting target.

It is an impressive sight, the English ships in port just now. The smaller and faster are at sea, to give warning of French movement, but the two great galleasses—the *Henry and Anne* and the *Elizabeth Rose*—are enough to make one's stomach drop even just standing on solid ground. They each hold more than two hundred men and have an average of thirty guns apiece. As I survey them, I begin to doubt that the French will wish to challenge our command of the seas.

But if they do, rest assured we shall be prepared. You would be proud, Minuette—William and I are working together very well. Almost every afternoon we spend an hour or two in the practice yard and there is great pleasure in remembering how well we know one another's every move. There's nothing like imminent war to sharpen one's mind and put personal grudges aside.

Dominic
From the deep blue seaside at Portsmouth

28 May 1556

Minuette,

William has asked to visit Tiverton with me. I suppose I should be grateful for the king's interest in my home. But I have had to admit to him that, despite what I said upon leaving Yorkshire last autumn, I did not actually travel to Tiverton. It did not seem an important lie in light of the greater dangers of the winter, but I would not wish him to ask around at Tiverton only to discover I had not been there. I told him I went to my mother's home instead. That, at least, is true enough.

Dominic

8 June 1556

Minuette,

So you want to know what Tiverton is like? At the moment, a dreary, cold castle, old-fashioned within and without. There's little I can do about the exterior, short of tearing it down, but the interior could be made quite pleasant with a woman's touch. It has stood empty of family too long. Perhaps, one day, you might advise me on what a woman would find cheerful.

There are many ghost stories associated with the castle. One has haunted me most unpleasantly, though I am not of a superstitious nature. The servants whisper of a spectre known as the Sorrowful Bride, a young woman who hid in a chest during the revels before her wedding. The chest caught tight and would not open from the inside, and the bride was not found until she was dead. In the light of day, I do not believe it anything more than an exaggerated story that could hardly be true. But at night, when I can see neither blue sky nor green grass, my heart misgives me and I find myself praying for all sorrowful brides, whatever their circumstances for pain.

I will be glad to see you again, little star. William and I will meet you and Elizabeth at Hampton Court no later than the twenty-seventh. We would never miss your twentieth birthday.

Dominic

9 June 1556

Minuette,

We leave Tiverton unexpectedly tomorrow, but not to return directly to court. There has been an outbreak of rioting in Norfolk, aimed at Lord Rochford in his exile at Blickling Hall. William wishes to impose his presence on the disorder. This is no ordinary rabble, discontented with the unpopular Rochford. They are disciplined and organized—and there are rumours that they are calling Mary Tudor queen. We still expect to meet you at Hampton Court as planned.

Dominic

By the time William and Dominic rode into Hampton Court, they had gone a long way in restoring equilibrium to their friendship. William had been uneasy seven weeks ago at the thought of so much time alone with Dominic, but Minuette and Elizabeth had both urged him to put aside his resentments. Leave court business behind for a time, they'd counseled him. They had been right.

The first few days had been awkward, with both men avoiding subjects such as Scotland and Renaud. But pressing military affairs had united them in a shared interest, and talk of defenses and tactics and naval prowess provided an easy medium for conversation. Gradually, as Dominic stood at William's shoulder and both men asked for and shared intelligent opinions, they had eased into a more natural companionship. The continual sparring practice, resumed at court somewhat uneasily, had evolved into the more natural rhythm of years spent working together with swords and on horseback. No one ever pushed William like Dominic, and he gave as good as he got. The exercise allowed an outlet for some of the unspoken resentments the two of them had been holding onto, and with each day they grew easier together, more like their friendship of old.

And it didn't hurt that William managed to beat Dominic at least one out of every three matches.

But it was the visit to Tiverton that sealed their renewed bonds. Accustomed as he was to the burdens and privileges of his own authority, William had been impressed by Dominic's easy command and the respect with which he was treated at Tiverton. He was never overbearing, but he didn't have to be. Dominic was plainly a man who lived by the advice he had so often given to William over the years: speak openly, praise honestly, criticize dispassionately, and pay attention to the details of the men who serve you. Dominic's men loved him for it, no matter how little they had known him before he'd been handed the estate.

"A touch of the Plantagenets," William overheard one old crofter say admiringly, and he admitted the truth of it with only a moment's concern. Dominic was indeed descended from that golden king, Edward IV—but so was William. And unlike his royal grandfather, Henry VII, who might have taken that comment as a threat, William's throne was certain and he would never be afraid of diluted bloodlines.

When word came from Norfolk that a Catholic mob had taken possession of Norwich Cathedral and was demanding Rochford's immediate arrest and trial, William found himself listening to Dominic as he had not for too long. They talked late into the night, managing to discuss issues of religion and politics without William feeling that the memory of Renaud LeClerc was hovering over them. Determined to regain Dominic's trust, William was scrupulous in either accepting or rejecting his advice openly. Together, they worked out a course of action and together they set out to implement it.

It took them a week to reach Norwich, William's crimson and

azure royal banner floating alongside Dominic's Exeter arms, the two men leading a mixed force of a hundred soldiers from William's personal guards and those loyal to Tiverton. The Catholics inside the cathedral offered sharp but brief resistance and within twelve hours Norwich was firmly in William's hands and three dozen men were under arrest, including the Bishop of Norwich, who had defiantly made his stand with the rebels.

As William rode into Hampton Court on June 26 with Dominic at his side, he felt for the first time since the French war that he and Dominic were truly working as one. The relief of that mended relationship was nearly as great as when he greeted Minuette, radiant and waiting at their return.

This rediscovered trust came at the right time, for though their flying trip to Norfolk had suppressed the immediate violence, it had raised more questions than it had answered about the mob's supporters. Within two hours of his return, William met with the Duke of Norfolk, who had been openly and blamelessly in London for the last month.

Norfolk's reputation for blunt honesty didn't fail him today. Upon bowing, his first critical comment was, "You are making a mistake, Your Majesty."

William exchanged a long look with Dominic, the only counselor present, and could almost hear his friend's caution. *Don't let him goad you into quick offense.*

With a smile that wiser men than Norfolk knew to fear, William asked softly, "In what way?"

"In seeking to make these riots more than what they were. The men in Norwich were unhappy shopkeepers and merchants. They were not rebels."

"Shopkeepers and merchants with a store of gunpowder and weapons, sufficient for a regiment of soldiers, carefully stowed around the city. They were funded, Norfolk, and dedicated. They began their rebellion with a Roman mass in Norwich Cathedral, offered by my own ungrateful Bishop Thirlby. And to a man, they called me the bastard son of a whore and named my sister, Mary, queen."

Looking suddenly like the twenty-year-old he was, the Duke of Norfolk said, "I . . . I didn't know that, Your Majesty. I can see the danger there."

Dominic, who had sat silently watchful to Norfolk's right, now leaned forward. "Where else do you see danger?"

Norfolk was no fool. He answered Dominic's real question, the one that lay heavily unasked beneath his words. "Examine my correspondence, my household—I swear, you'll find no links to those men."

"No, I don't expect we will," Dominic replied. "This is not an accusation, Norfolk, it's a warning. His Majesty has dealt leniently with the Papists, and they repay him in insults and treason. Leniency is at an end. If more blood is shed, it will not lie on our hands."

William let Dominic's words hang in the silence for a moment before adding, "That is all, my lord Norfolk. For now. Lady Mary will be arriving at Hampton Court tomorrow for the birthday celebrations. I hope no disagreements will mar the festivities."

Wrapping the slightly tattered edges of his position around him, the duke bowed with a touch of arrogance. "Who could possibly wish you harm, Your Majesty?" He stalked out of the chamber in much the way William did when he was displeased.

Dominic's eyes met his after the door shut. "What do you think?" William asked.

"One can never predict what a Howard might do. I'd watch him."

"Norfolk has got the message, and it will spread through the Catholics. Mary is being watched, and her letters read. So what do

I do about Spain? Philip is prepared to come to Dover in a few weeks' time. He seems eager enough to marry Elizabeth, and bringing him here will soothe tempers a bit."

Dominic shrugged. "I'm no good at the politics of matrimony."

William laughed. "You must stop being so particular. All you need do is point your finger and you'd have yourself a wife. And one who is interested in more than your position, if that's what you fear."

With a restless movement, Dominic stood and went to the window that overlooked the privy garden. Maybe he was looking for one of the court women. Maybe not. In the last seven weeks, William had realized that he had no idea what Dominic's personal life entailed. Or if he even had a personal life.

William returned to a conversation they'd had nearly a year ago, and not touched upon since. "Have you considered on Jane Grey as I once asked you to do? The Duchess of Suffolk has made it plain that her daughter is yours for the asking."

"On whose asking—mine or yours?"

"Dominic—"

"Leave it, William. We have more important issues at hand. Like King Philip's visit. And Lady Rochford's trial. And a jilted and restless French army."

"You haven't fallen in love with a married woman, have you? Because that would be a complication. Not necessarily fatal—"

"What of your marriage?" Dominic interrupted. "You've announced no plans for a state wedding."

William paused before answering. "No. We'll make the coronation the grand affair—the wedding will be intimate. Perhaps only you and Elizabeth to witness. I'm thinking Christmas, with the coronation to be held on our twenty-first birthdays next summer. If all goes well, Minuette will be with child by that time."

There was a long silence, long enough for William to feel the tension that had crept into the room. He was trying to understand where it had come from—turning over every word he'd said to see where he'd gone wrong—when Dominic said, "If that's all for now, I'm going to check in with Burghley and see how things are proceeding with Lady Rochford in the Tower."

William let him go with an oddly hollow feeling inside that he tried to dismiss as paranoia. How could weeks of carefully reconstructing their friendship have been undone with one innocent conversation? He'd not even had the chance to tell Dominic of his plans for Minuette's birthday tomorrow. Well enough—if Dominic did not want to share that kind of intimacy, then he could be made to wait until the morning, when he would be notified of his part in the planned ceremonies.

Politics, William thought a bit forlornly, was infinitely easier to cope with than friendships.

Mary arrived by water from Richmond, where she had spent the last month in a greater swirl of activity than she was accustomed to. With King Philip's looming state visit, Mary had been flattered to be consulted by her brother's men even while recognizing that they wanted to disarm her and keep her so busy that she would not think of behind-the-scenes political maneuvering. But she was capable of being both flattered and cautious. No word of disapproval would escape her at Elizabeth being offered to the Spanish king. Not publicly.

In private, she prayed with an intensity that had not been equaled since the early days of Anne Boleyn's rise, when Mary had still believed that wrongs could be righted by pure faith. Twenty years on she knew better. Faith needed righteous force to triumph. And the arrival of Philip, representative of the pure faith in earthly form, might be what she had so long awaited. An opportunity to right wrongs.

Mary knew that many considered her if not unintelligent, then at least unimaginative. But she was her father's daughter and she knew how to manipulate when it was necessary. She also knew the value of symbolism. The Spanish ambassador might have provided the material support for the Norwich protests, but Mary had suggested using Bishop Thirlby, knowing that his acquiescence in Henry VIII's religious reforms had been for form's sake only. And she had been right, for the bishop had seized upon the chance to offer mass to the brave souls now awaiting the punishment of heretics. She trusted Bishop Thirlby's faith would sustain him in the difficult days ahead.

The events in Norwich had been a test. Now Mary was prepared to play in earnest. She began, as Catholics always began in England, with the Duke of Norfolk.

The duke came to see her within two hours of her arrival at Hampton Court. It was easier for Mary to come to court now that the hated false queen was dead, and she took satisfaction in the elegant furnishings and rich fabrics with which her chambers were adorned. She had dressed with special care for this audience, fussing with her still-thick hair so that the increasing strands of gray were not visible, and relying on the structure of her ebony and silver gown to deflect attention from her increasingly stout figure. It was not vanity; she knew that to be treated as royal, one must appear so.

Though this young Duke of Norfolk had been raised Protestant, he still kissed her hand and called her by the title heretics denied her. "It is a great pleasure to see you again, Your Highness."

"You may sit," Mary commanded. Norfolk took a stool that left him half a head shorter than she in her plumply cushioned chair. He seemed unaffected by this, his very young face more handsome than it should be, while his eyes were more cautious than those of most young men of twenty. But then most men of twenty hadn't lost a father to a treason charge at age ten and a grandfather to a Protestant plot just two years ago. A plot masterminded by the man Mary wished to discuss just now.

"Is it true Lord Rochford continues to receive visitors in state at Blickling Hall despite his disgrace?"

"So I have heard, Your Highness." Norfolk cast a covert glance around the chamber, as if looking for spies to this conversation and wondering just how treacherous she intended to make it. "He does not appear to have been overly inconvenienced by the Norwich protests."

Mary knew better than to speak plainly, but who could be surprised at her displeasure with Rochford's continued arrogance? It would be more unusual if she didn't speak of him.

"Is there any chance his status will change when Lady Rochford is brought to trial?" she asked.

"Unlikely. It is well known that Lady Rochford despises her husband. Any claims she makes against him will almost certainly be dismissed as spite. And despite their complicated relationship, Rochford is a great favorite with the king. I do not think William will send his uncle to the Tower, let alone the block."

"So though he is deprived of his position as Lord Chancellor, George Boleyn remains a duke, he retains hold of the greatest private wealth in England, and he continues to work against those of the True Faith," Mary summed up. "What damage might he do while King Philip is here?"

Norfolk shrugged. "What can he do? William has made it very plain he will not go back to the French marriage, so what options are there? One of them must marry a Catholic. William seems only too glad to offer up Elizabeth in exchange for his own liberty."

Discussing marital plans left Mary feeling restless and dissatisfied. She returned to the problem of Rochford sitting at Blickling Hall, unpunished. "He is the most dangerous man in England. He hounded and hunted your own grandfather to his death, smearing the Howard name and honour in the bargain. Not to mention the claims Rochford made against me in the same plot. Why should he remain untouched?"

"Because he is the king's uncle," Norfolk answered bluntly, and despite his youth, he had his grandfather's arrogant surety. "Lady Mary"—no more use of her title now, she noted—"you will never persuade the king to charge his uncle with treason."

She smiled, something she did so rarely that it felt strange on her face. "I do not mean to persuade the king to anything. I mean to act of my own accord. The greatest injury Rochford offered was against me and all Catholics—as their figurehead, I will see that injury punished."

Norfolk looked wary, but not frightened. This young man might not burn with religious fervor, but he hated Rochford with a passion not to be taken lightly. A legacy from his grandfather, despite their ties to the Boleyns. "How?"

"We will speak again soon." No need to tell him that her ideas of vengeance were hazy at best. Mary operated more on theory than practice, counting on the men she inspired to fill in the details. "Can I count on your support?"

A considering pause, but Mary knew her audience. This Duke of Norfolk could be swayed by personal appeal, so she added, "I would be in your debt."

"I could ask for no greater honour, Your Highness."

And that was one piece put in play.

The day before William's twentieth birthday, Elizabeth received Robert Dudley in her favorite chamber at Hampton Court, the one she'd had as her own since she was a child. The palace might be a little old-fashioned now, but she loved the tall, narrow windows and the red-bricked towers and courtyards. She remembered three years ago, looking down through her window to spy Robert's dark head in Clock Court, and knew that however much anger passed between them, part of her would always be looking for Robert wherever she went.

"Tell me," she said playfully as Robert crossed the room to stand next to her at a table spread with jewelry, "which do you think for William's celebrations tomorrow? The Spanish ambassador will be present and I am meant to appear suitably demure."

With raised eyebrows, Robert said, "I do not think even a religious habit would make you appear demure. And if Philip is any sort of man at all, it is yourself he will fall in love with, not some trumped-up image of submissive womanhood."

He surveyed the pieces—pearls and gold and cabochon jewels in brilliant tones—and finally laid a finger on an enameled circlet of Tudor roses. "These, I think. A subtle reminder of position will be more effective than a blatant display of wealth."

Elizabeth had been thinking the same thing, and she shook her head at this unnerving symmetry of thought. "Especially since Spain's wealth is far greater than England's. If Philip has me, it will be for my position and not my riches."

"If Philip does not have you for love alone, than he does not deserve you."

Would there ever be a time when that low, intimate voice failed to stir her blood and make her treacherous heart beat faster? Robert was clever and charming and duplicitous and probably incapable of fidelity . . . but for all that, she had not been so happy in months.

To disguise her pleasure, she retorted, "England has quite enough of royal love matches with William and Minuette. I believe my brother has a grand gesture in mind for their shared birthday tomorrow. I hope he knows what he's doing."

As so many men seemed to ask her lately, Robert inquired, "Do you ever wonder about Minuette's feelings in the matter?"

"Minuette is naturally concerned about the political ramifications, but she has loved William since they were children. Personally, of course she wishes for everyone to be contented. And I must admit, she seems to be learning very quickly. She may not be as far in over her head as I feared."

"You've told me before that, where kings are concerned, love will always be weighted on one side. Does it not seem to you that Minuette's love may not be as highly weighted as William's?"

"Say what you mean, Robert." And why do you care? she wondered. Perhaps because Robert thought his own love weightier than hers, and in a roundabout manner was asking for a reassurance she would never give.

"England has seen this behavior before—a king so in love he defied everyone to have his bride. I know you often wondered about the depth of your mother's love in return. Do you ever worry about Minuette's?"

It was true that Minuette had become far more reticent in the last year or two, much less likely to share her mind with Elizabeth. But surely that was normal when a man became more important than a friend. Surely it only meant Minuette was growing up.

"We are going to Hatfield next week for a respite before King Philip's arrival in August. I will talk to her then. If there is anything for me to worry about, I will know it when we are alone and far away from court."

"Be discreet, Elizabeth. Navigating between two people in love can be a delicate business."

For the first time since Dudley Castle, Robert touched her. His fingertips were light as a summer breeze on her cheek, and Elizabeth crossly noted that her trembling was out of all proportion. Robert's instincts were always pitch-perfect, and gently he curved his hand to her throat and tipped her chin up with his thumb. His kiss was both apology and promise, and Elizabeth let all thoughts of Minuette and William and King Philip slip away.

CHAPTER NINE

It feels strange to be once again at Hampton Court on my birthday,
as though one year's disruption of tradition has made all our
history and memories fragile and insubstantial. Last year I was in
France with Elizabeth and Dominic, while William was in Wales
on royal progress . . . it was the first birthday since we were eight
that William and I have not spent together.

I am not sure that today will restore equilibrium and nostalgia.
I am unnerved by William's hints at my gift. I received another
gown to wear this morning—crimson velvet, so at least the colour is
not as inflammatory as the purple Easter gown. But it is the most
elaborate gown I have seen outside of Elizabeth's ceremonial
wardrobe, and my heart misgives me. I am to be dressed as a queen
today, and I wish I could claim illness and not leave my chambers.
Or that I could close my eyes and open them to the last birthday I
spent at Hampton Court two years ago, the day William and I
both turned eighteen and all he could think of was that he had
reached the age of majority.

And all I could think of was Dominic, leaning over me in the

—

*rain and holding me fast with an expression I had never before seen
on any man's face.*

*But one cannot go back. So I will have Carrie dress me in the
crimson surcoat trimmed with ermine and she will leave my hair
loose and flowing as William asked. I will take part in whatever
William wishes and turn to the court a face of serene indifference.*

With my eyes and my heart only for Dominic.

When William told him of the ceremony planned for Minuette's birthday gift, Dominic was struck well and truly speechless. I
should have seen this coming, he thought frantically. But he hadn't,
and now he had to cope with only an hour's warning.

"With Rochford temporarily banished from court, you and
Norfolk are the only dukes at my disposal," William said. "I need
you both standing by me to lend weight and seriousness. No one
must be in doubt as to my purpose in making Minuette a marquess."

Genevieve Antoinette Wyatt, Marquess of Somerset—how
could anyone be in doubt of William's purpose? Only one woman
in England's history had been granted that title in her own right:
Anne Boleyn, just months before her secret marriage to Henry.
Anne's title of Marquess of Pembroke had been granted her because of the king's upcoming visit with the French king, for which
he had wanted Anne with him. Without a royal divorce, Anne's
position had been a fragile one to take part in such a formidable
state visit, so Henry had granted her a title and lands that made her
the equal of many English nobles.

"I would have liked to give Minuette my mother's same title,"
William went on blithely, unaware of Dominic's clenched-tight
jaw and furious nerves. "But we made William Herbert the Earl of
Pembroke five years ago. And the Somerset title will tie in neatly

with yours, Dom, for the bulk of Minuette's lands will stretch north of the Exeter estates."

Very neat indeed, Dominic wanted to say, *granting a husband and wife adjoining lands.* He ignored the tiny, cynical voice that whispered those combined lands in the traditionally volatile west country would make a good power base from which to resist the Crown.

It would never come to that. He wouldn't let it.

"It's only fitting," William continued. "With King Philip's visit, I want Minuette to have the position she deserves. I will not have Europe say that she is not worthy of riches and power."

"How did she take the news?" Dominic managed to ask. He was finding it harder to speak Minuette's name in William's presence.

The king's grin was a painful reminder of years of uncomplicated friendship. "It's a surprise. I told her what to wear and to be ready for an escort just before noon. I can't wait to see the look on her face."

Neither could Dominic. He was not one of those sent to escort her—that duty fell to several women of the nobility, including the Countess of Pembroke and, with obvious reluctance and distaste, the Duchess of Suffolk—but Dominic stood to the side of William's throne when she entered the Great Hall of Hampton Court and had a perfect view of his wife's pale, composed face. She looked neither surprised nor delighted. Numb, rather.

Obviously Minuette had known what was coming, if only for the few minutes it had taken to walk from her chambers to the Great Hall, for the Countess of Pembroke carried a red robe of estate in her arms and a page in William's own royal livery bore a pillow on which rested a marquess's coronet. There were rustles and the hint of whispers as those in attendance bowed and curtsied as Minuette walked past them to the dais upon which William waited on his throne. The king, Dominic, and the Duke of Norfolk all wore heavy velvet robes of estate capped with creamy ermine fur and their own coronets—William his favorite crown set with diamonds and rubies, the two dukes with the eight stylized strawberry leaves circling the ever-present red velvet.

Minuette looked at no one as she took the last few steps to the dais and then sank into the most graceful of kneeling positions. Dominic's heart wanted to break at the beauty and poignancy of her figure, all alone with the skirt of her vivid gown pooled around her. *Like blood,* his mind whispered—for in memory he could see the red of Alyce de Clare's gown around her broken body three years ago.

Archbishop Cranmer, beginning to look old in the last few months, unrolled the patent he held and read aloud. *"To all and singular, as well nobles and gentles as others to whom these shall come: it is the king's pleasure by this patent to confer on the lady Genevieve Antoinette Wyatt, in her own right and on her offspring, the noble title Marquess of Somerset. And also by this patent to grant her lands worth one thousand five hundred pounds per year for the maintaining of her dignity."*

There was silence, more profound than any gasps, at the amount of property William had granted her. There could be only a handful of men in the kingdom as wealthy as Minuette now was—and of women, only Elizabeth could equal her.

William knew all the practiced moves of royalty and effected them with unusual grace today. He flung back his robe to stand and stepped off the dais to take both Minuette's hands in his. She looked at the king then—how could she not?—and allowed him to raise her up. Dominic could hardly breathe for tension, as William took the coronet of a marquess—similar to the dukes, but decorated with four strawberry leaves and four silver balls—and placed it on Minuette's gloriously golden hair. The king stepped behind her then in order to relieve the Countess of Pembroke of the robe of estate, and with great care placed it around Minuette's shoulders himself. Dominic thought he was not the only one holding his breath as William's hands lingered on her shoulders and then, so everyone could be sure to mark the gesture, he kissed her on the nape of her neck.

Dominic had to close his eyes then. He forced himself to breathe deeply and waited until he heard William's voice. "Your patent of nobility, my lady."

He opened his eyes to see William hand her the patent, and Minuette said tremulously, "Thank you, Your Majesty."

Anyone else would have thought her tremulous because of the great honour and her awareness of what it meant to her future. Perhaps those watching thought her overcome by triumph or awed by what a king's love had set in motion.

But Dominic knew better. Minuette shot one look at him from over William's shoulder and in that instant he saw the tears held deep and the terror that things were so much worse than they had counted on, and how were they ever to extricate themselves from the ties of property and nobility and gratitude?

The Duke of Norfolk laid a cautionary hand on Dominic's arm. "Not happy about this, either?" Norfolk hissed under his breath as the herald announced, "His Majesty, the king, and the Lady Genevieve Wyatt, Marquess of Somerset."

As the king and Minuette processed out of the Great Hall, Dominic set his jaw and looked at Norfolk. "What?"

"He's moving into deep waters," Norfolk continued, obviously guessing he had an ally, although he couldn't possibly guess Dominic's true motive. "I'm not sure marrying his sister to Spain will undo the damage the king has done today."

Dominic stepped abruptly away. He was sick of politics and

everyone at court who saw Minuette solely as a pawn in their games or an obstacle to their plans. Could they not see how troubled she was?

His sudden movement took him into Elizabeth's path, in deep conversation with Lord Burghley, the new Lord Chancellor. The Princess of Wales looked troubled herself, and that impression deepened when she met Dominic's eyes. There was a depth and intensity to the way she searched his face that made Dominic afraid of what he might be showing.

As he escaped the Great Hall, his firm stride and forbidding expression keeping everyone well away, Dominic thought how pathetic it was that once again he was jealous at how William had trumped him in giving Minuette a birthday gift. But William would always trump him, wouldn't he? Dominic had said as much to Minuette once: *You will be queen, Minuette . . . William is everything you could ever want.*

He isn't you, she'd answered. But that had been ages ago, when they had both believed all they need do was want something to make it happen.

If the price for their happiness was the destruction of William himself . . . was that a price Minuette was still willing to pay?

Robert Dudley met with Walsingham in the latter's small chamber at Hampton Court. It was square and plain and devoid of personality, as though the man who rested there took care not to leave any imprint of himself behind. It was the impression Walsingham always seemed to give off—a man of power, but so carefully veiled and manipulated that he could almost be forgotten when not present.

At least he was easier to deal with than Lord Rochford. Robert leaned back in his chair and said, "How much longer do I need to distract the French ambassador with wine and women? It's not as though he isn't aware of our plans with the Spanish. For that matter, what is he still doing in England? Does he want to be taken into custody when the French launch against us at last?"

"You tell me, Lord Robert," Walsingham said without looking up from the papers he was studying. Though Robert's father was dead and the Northumberland title gone, he'd been allowed to retain his courtesy "lord," if only because it was how everyone was accustomed to addressing him. His oldest brother, John, was still nominally Earl of Warwick, but Robert knew how precarious their positions remained. It was why he didn't push Walsingham too far, despite the man's familiar tone.

"All right," Robert responded. "Why is the French ambassador still in England? Perhaps he merely likes our women and wine . . . though that would be more believable in any man not French. In practical terms, he is still here because the possibility of learning something useful continues to outweigh the awkwardness of the situation. King Henri no doubt has his spies in England, but none so near the heart of the court as his own ambassador. Anger with William does not trump the need for information."

"Very good, Lord Robert. And what information have you gleaned in your evenings with the ambassador?"

Robert wondered if Elizabeth knew precisely to what use Walsingham was putting him. Working for her intelligencer was one thing—he didn't think her imagination had stretched to Robert drinking heavily with a man who liked his women pretty and loose. "Nothing practical. He deplores William's new betrothal on political grounds, though he has no objection to Mistress Wyatt's—pardon me, Lady Somerset's—personal charms. Like all the French, he thinks William prudish in not simply making her his permanent mistress, much along the lines of Diane de Poitiers at King Henri's court. And he thinks we are all fools for looking to the Spanish for, as he says, 'an English princess is not an equal balance to their armies and gold.' But that last is mostly bluster. I would say the French are deeply worried about an English-Spanish alliance."

"As to the nature of that alliance . . . has there been any discussion of the Lady Mary?"

Robert's attention sharpened. "No. Should there be?"

Walsingham's gestures could speak volumes. The shrug he gave now encompassed a wealth of possibilities. "Since her visit to court at Easter, Lady Mary has kept up a considerable correspondence with the Duke of Norfolk and the Spanish ambassador. She has naturally taken great pleasure in Lord Rochford's current exile, and perhaps sees England's turn to Spain as an answer to years of prayer."

"Perhaps it is."

"I do not operate on the level of prayers and faith, Lord Robert. What concerns me is the obsessions of the fanatic, and to what interpretation such a person may put current events."

Robert studied Walsingham, brow furrowed until his head ached as he tried to divine the man's mind. "You're talking about Norwich, aren't you?"

"Should I be?"

"Catholic mass, Catholic rebels, protests against Rochford—it's not such a leap to see England's leading Catholic in the shadows. You think Mary would suborn one of her brother's bishops against him and pay men to call her queen?"

"I think Lady Mary will do precisely as she believes God intends her to do, which too often coincides with her own desires."

"Sounds like royalty to me."

"Yes, for not all obsessions are religious in nature. Even love can make fanatics."

Robert shifted in his seat. "So I continue with the French ambassador."

"For now. I may have use for you elsewhere soon enough."

This had better be worth it to Elizabeth, Robert thought as he left. Because it felt all too much like working for Rochford had—secretive, sideways, and with the end always in doubt.

Elizabeth was growing impatient with fretting over her brother and her friend. What was the point? In making Minuette a marquess, William had made it plain to all of Europe that he would do in this matter exactly as he pleased. And whether that pleased or frightened Minuette, she kept her own counsel and seemed in no hurry to share it. When Elizabeth congratulated her on the new title and wealth, with a slight questioning tone to the words that invited confidence, Minuette had replied with courtly formality, "I welcome your good wishes, Your Highness."

Since when am I Your Highness *to you?* Elizabeth nearly asked. But she had a temper of her own and it was being increasingly tried. She would take Minuette and retreat one last time to Hatfield—William had made plain that this visit would entail Minuette as her guest, not as her lady-in-waiting—and give her friend a final chance to discuss her feelings or ask for help or simply rejoice. Elizabeth didn't much care which particular emotion was released as long as Minuette did something other than behave like a perfectly groomed child with no mind of her own.

But before she left court, Elizabeth had final plans to make with Walsingham. She had put him in charge of her household's preparations for King Philip's visit with the express purpose of gathering information from whatever quarter provided it. Liaising with William's household was one thing; dealing with Mary and the other Catholics as protocol demanded was something else.

And it was of Mary that Walsingham had to warn her on the last day of June, if in a rather roundabout manner.

He began by updating her on Dr. John Dee. It had been almost three months since Elizabeth had sent Dee to the Continent on an extended tour of universities and church libraries and already he had sent back some beautiful and rare books of knowledge. Together with Walsingham, they seemed to be forming a backbone of secrets and caution in Elizabeth's household.

"Dee has been in France for three weeks and he writes that matters of military retaliation might not be so straightforward as we suppose. The French king does indeed appear to be preparing for a coastal invasion, but the French ships—although provisioning for an extended time at sea—do not seem to be taking on large numbers of soldiers."

"What of Renaud LeClerc?" Elizabeth knew he was the chief general of France's armies—LeClerc's whereabouts would be a clue to French intentions. He had been Dominic's friend, but when Elizabeth had asked him for insight into Renaud's mind, Dominic had said abruptly, "I don't hear from him any longer and do not expect to. Find your spies elsewhere."

So she had. And now her spymaster looked at her with that expression of knowing far more than he told, and said, "LeClerc has not stirred from the French court except to his own home in the Loire Valley. He has not been seen near any French port. Either Henri intends to invade without his best soldier, or else we are expecting the wrong attack."

"Diplomatic, do you mean? Economic? We are always under attack from the Continent in those ways. I sometimes wonder if we would not be better served making an alliance with the Low Countries once and for all and line up neatly with Protestants against Catholics."

"Easier for England to contemplate that alliance than for the Low Countries themselves, seeing as how we have the sea and a navy between us and the Catholic powers. The Netherlands are not so lucky. Not that they like the thought of England allying with their hated Spanish overlord."

"I can't say I like it much myself," Elizabeth said tartly, "but then I am rather more personally involved than the Low Countries."

She refused to go further in her thoughts on Philip. She just hoped when she finally met him, she would not find him completely abhorrent. She had seen several miniatures of the Spanish king and he appeared to be handsome enough, and certainly he was intelligent. At least he was only six years older than she, though he was a widower of ten years duration and already had a son and heir.

Elizabeth returned to the matter at hand. "So Dr. Dee thinks we should be wary about French intentions. That their naval involvement may be a feint, and not necessarily indicate a planned invasion."

"Possibly they intend to harass the Spanish coasts and try to keep Philip from sailing to England. The king and Lord Burghley have that possibility in mind. The Lord Chancellor tells me that English ships will travel in convoy with the Spanish to make such numbers that the French cannot attack, while still leaving sufficient protection for the ports."

Just how much did the Lord Chancellor share with Walsingham? Elizabeth wondered. They had known one another for some time—Burghley, along with John Dee, had recommended Walsingham to her. Did her brother guess how much Elizabeth's intelligencer knew of his government's affairs?

Walsingham interrupted that train of thought. "Your Highness, have you considered that the French may be more interested in their own territories?"

"What do you mean?" she asked sharply, but even as she questioned, she knew the answer. "Harfleur and Le Havre."

"England has only held those cities since 1554. I imagine the French want them back, considering their loss was one of the points that brought them to the negotiating table in the first place.

If there is no treaty, there is no reason for the French to stay their hands from attempting to reclaim the cities."

"Well, England has certainly won and lost our share of French cities. I will speak to Burghley of the possibility. Unless you would care to do so?" she invited archly.

Walsingham ignored the invitation. "William Cecil, rather than your brother?"

"Burghley is an outstandingly canny man who is not only clever and wise but without the pride to show off about it," Elizabeth retorted, certain she was not telling Walsingham anything he didn't already know. "Although I miss my uncle in many ways, truthfully, Burghley may be the better choice as chancellor. He rules without temperament, which is restful in this court."

"What if the French have more in mind than simply retaking Le Havre and Harfleur?" asked Walsingham.

This time Elizabeth couldn't anticipate him. "What do you mean?"

"Calais." Walsingham pronounced the name delicately and then let it rest, lingering in Elizabeth's shocked mind.

"The French haven't made a serious play for Calais in years. Do you really think they would attempt it now?"

"While English ships patrol the southern ports and keep their soldiers close to home? What better time to attack than when all eyes are elsewhere?"

Elizabeth drew in her breath. "I do not like this possibility at all. Nor will my brother."

"Liking does not enter into it. Only preparation."

"You have made your point, Walsingham, I will speak to William directly about all of Dr. Dee's concerns. Is there anything else?"

"There is. I have some cause for concern in the Lady Mary's correspondence of late."

"You're reading her letters?"

"As your uncle has long done," Walsingham said, unmoved. "And no doubt Burghley has his own methods as well."

Everyone spying on everybody else, Elizabeth thought wryly. How many hands did her own letters pass through on the way to their intended recipients?

"What is my sister saying that concerns you?"

"It's what she's *not* saying, rather. Her letters have become rather pedestrian. One might almost say mundane. Quite unlike her usual style. It leads me to wonder why she is taking such care not to be inflammatory, particularly when she must have opinions on what happened in Norwich."

"Has anyone ever told you that you are too suspicious for your own good?"

"I am not looking to my own good, but to yours. And England's. No suspicion can be too great if it prevents disaster."

"Well, I shall defer to your judgment for now. If Mary does anything to confirm your suspicions, you will let me know."

"I shall write to you at Hatfield, Your Highness."

"Do you expect you will need to cipher your communications?"

He smiled briefly. "Not just yet. But it is a skill with which you may wish to familiarize yourself. One never knows."

One never knows anything, Elizabeth thought, except that where there are kings and princesses and bishops and heretics, there will be trouble. And secrets. And more than enough of both.

Her last afternoon at Hampton Court, Minuette could not settle to anything. While Carrie packed, she flitted from room to room in her near-royal suite, aware at every moment of the scrolled patent of nobility that seemed to watch her from the new gilded and bejeweled chest where it had been stored. She had not been able to think straight since that awful, portentous day when William had placed a coronet on her head and made her a marquess.

She didn't want the coronet or the title or the wealth that went with it. She had never wanted any of this. The only thing William had ever given her that had caused her a thrill of triumph had been the promise, made three years ago on another birthday, that he would allow her to marry where she chose.

Carrie kept looking as though she wanted to say something, but Minuette turned away every time her maid opened her mouth. She was having a private dinner with William in two hours and at some point she had to say goodbye to Dominic as well, but until then all she could do was fret and wander.

And once again, at the height of her nerves and anxiety, Jane Grey appeared unexpectedly. "I hope I'm not interrupting," Jane said hesitantly.

"Not at all," Minuette answered. "Won't you come in?"

"Thank you, my lady." Somehow, hearing "my lady" from the serene, pious Jane made real the weight of her new title.

When they were seated before the empty tile fireplace, Minuette said, as she always seemed to with Jane, "What can I do for you?" Could she be about to ask her again about William's intentions? Jane's mother could hardly be in doubt of them, considering that she had been one of Minuette's escorts during the investiture ceremony. Minuette had felt the duchess glaring at her throughout.

But better that than to ask again about Dominic. Minuette was prepared to be curt and dismissive if Jane mentioned his name at all.

Quiet Jane, however, always seemed to have a surprise in store. "I wondered, my lady, if you would speak to the king on behalf of Lady Rochford."

After a moment, Minuette asked, "Is this your request, or your mother's?" As far as she knew, the Duchess of Suffolk had privately loathed Anne Boleyn's brother and, by extension, his wife. Though the duchess was too politically canny to openly rejoice at George Boleyn's current predicament, surely she was privately glad to see both him and his wife come to grief.

But Jane was not her mother. "Lady Rochford has been all but forgotten in the Tower. I have been to see her and I must tell you that she is not . . . coping all that well. Truth be told, I fear for her mind in continued confinement. Have you not wondered why she has not come to trial yet?"

Minuette was ashamed to admit that she had not wondered, being so busy with her own concerns. "I am sure the king is aware of her condition," she said at last. "But I will speak of it to him." For that was why Jane had sought her out; to use her influence with the king. It was the only reason anyone would ever seek her out again.

"Thank you. It may settle Lady Rochford a little to know she has not been forgotten. Her husband has not made any attempt at contact or comfort."

Well, he wouldn't, would he? the cynical part of Minuette nearly retorted. Rochford was protecting himself from the taint of attempted murder. And to be honest, Minuette herself was not looking forward to Lady Rochford's trial, for then it would all be public knowledge—the adder in her bedchamber, the awful rat and image in France, the monkshood painted on the back of her pendant that had so nearly killed her. She did not relish the thought of her life being picked over by the curious. She wished it would all just go away. Except, of course, that Eleanor Percy had been released from the Tower to a more civilized house arrest in London while she waited her opportunity to openly testify against Lady Rochford. Minuette could not leave Eleanor Percy loose without keeping to her bargain to bring her to William's attention.

"Lord Rochford's concern is ever and always the stability of

England," Minuette said to Jane, hating her own lecturing tone. "He would have little patience for anyone who threatened the king, wife or not."

"But she didn't threaten the king, did she?" Jane countered. "She threatened you."

"Would you care to speak freely?" Minuette asked drily.

Unperturbed, Jane merely studied Minuette with furrowed brow and real concern. "I hope that you are what William needs. A strong king is a strong England, yes, but for his own sake and my affection for my cousin, I want him to be at peace as well."

"You are kind," Minuette said impulsively, and meant it. She herself had once been kind. How long had it been since she had been motivated by anything except her own concerns?

She would remedy that tonight. She would speak to William about Lady Rochford. And, for her sins, Eleanor Percy.

William had been anticipating a quiet, intimate dinner with Minuette in his privy chamber. It was quiet enough, but the intimacy of their last night together for a month was spoiled by Minuette's choice of topic.

"Jane Grey came to see me today," she began, playing with the quail and leek pie on her plate but eating little.

"Yes?" William asked from mere politeness. "You'll have to accustom yourself to many visitors. Everyone will want something from you now."

He did not want to talk about Jane. It seemed to him he had spent half his life fending off his young cousin. Though Jane herself was reserved, even shy, she had a highly ambitious mother whose ambitions had heightened with the overthrow of the French treaty. Despite the title so recently given to Minuette, the Duchess of Suffolk saw what she wanted to see: the French marriage off, the Catholics on increasingly unstable ground, and a daughter with royal blood and impeccable Protestant credentials. His aunt did everything but parade Jane naked in front of him, and if she could have gotten away with that, she would have.

And it was true that he had frequently made use of Jane's company since Easter. He did not fault her for her mother and Jane was convenient and restful company. She was also the only woman at court, other than Elizabeth, who never made sly comments about Minuette. It was useful to be seen riding with Jane or sitting next to her at table or merely giving her his arm while they walked through the galleries. It made the Catholics nervous.

But the last thing he needed was Jane's pious presence evoked in this private space with Minuette.

"She didn't want something for herself. She was asking, rather, after Lady Rochford's welfare. Jane claims that your aunt has been unwell in the Tower."

"Gone mad, you mean?" William said casually. "It seems so. The doctors who've examined her believe she is not feigning merely to avoid trial."

"If she is truly afflicted, where will you send her? Surely you will not continue to keep her at the Tower. She must be moved elsewhere—perhaps one of their homes."

"Do you think my uncle is interested in caring for a lunatic wife?" He did not miss the flinch of Minuette's expression, but she needed to hear the truth. "Her condition does not answer her crimes. She came perilously close to killing you. An attack on you is an attack on me. For that, she will answer."

"How? If she is too ill for a trial—"

"Don't fret about it, Minuette."

"But—"

"I have everything in hand."

"William, surely—"

"Enough!" Why was she pressing him when all he'd wanted was

the joy of her presence? She should be as anxious as he to enjoy their last hour alone. Why did she have to drag politics into it?

She had whitened at his snarl, but met his gaze steadily. "If you do not wish to discuss Lady Rochford, perhaps we should touch upon Eleanor Percy. I know she has been released from the Tower."

Not the change of topic he'd hoped for. "She remains under guard in London. You cannot imagine I would let her anywhere near you—"

"I think you were quite right to release her."

William stopped with his mouth open, dizzy at Minuette's unexpected calm. "You do?" He cleared his throat, and tried to sound more authoritative. "My aunt's guilt does not necessarily equate to Eleanor's innocence. She must answer for herself and her actions."

"I have no doubt that Eleanor will be able to account for herself very well. Though I doubt we shall ever be friendly, I am not afraid of Eleanor Percy, nor am I jealous of her. You must do what you think is best for the mother of your first child."

Once more Minuette had caught him off guard, and it made him unreasonably irritated. "Since when are you concerned with Eleanor's welfare?"

With a cool lift of her curved brows, Minuette said, "I thought my concern for others was one of the things you liked about me."

"Minuette, sweetling, come here." William pushed his chair back from the table and waited until Minuette had hesitantly sat on his lap. He twisted a lock of her hair around his hand and held her face still. "I love everything about you. You are as necessary to me as breath. But I have voices all day and all night telling me what to pay attention to, what is right, what they want and how they want it. I need you to be my sanctuary. No talk of prisons or trials, of governments or armies."

He kissed her lingeringly on the lips. "Be my rest," he murmured, moving his mouth along the curve of her neck. "My heart, my peace, my love." With each endearment he left a kiss in its wake. Only Minuette had the effect of both rousing and relaxing him. His body might strum with the pleasant tension of unmet desire, but his mind was gentled into a quiet only she could offer.

"I hate that you're going to Hatfield," he said softly. "Every time you leave me I fear you will not return."

"I will return, William."

There were unshed tears in her voice and William knew she found it as difficult to part as he did.

CHAPTER TEN

WHEN MINUETTE ANNOUNCED to Elizabeth that she would be paying a visit to Lord Rochford at Blickling Hall before traveling on to Hatfield, the redheaded princess reacted with a temper that had only rarely been turned on Minuette. It flared quickly into a full-scale argument that left Minuette ruffled and unhappy as she approached the home where George Boleyn had been born and where he now spent his days in haughty solitude while waiting to see what further penalties the king might impose.

When Elizabeth attempted to forbid her going, Minuette had summoned all the authority of the position she did not want and replied, "I am no longer part of your household, Your Highness. The king has ordered you to treat me as a guest at Hatfield. And as your guest, I am telling you when I will arrive, not asking."

Only the tiniest part of her would admit the satisfaction of standing her ground and, for once, not worrying about leaving someone else out of temper. Why was it her responsibility to make everyone happy?

Dominic did not argue with her plans to see Rochford, but that was simply because he was not at court and thus had no idea. He had returned to the coastal defenses, although France had made no moves across the Channel as yet. Barring battle, Dominic would be charged with overseeing King Philip's arrival and royal reception at Dover Castle. Minuette told herself that she was willing to stand her ground with her husband as well, but why make her life more difficult than it need be? She knew how deeply unhappy he was about her involvement with Lord Rochford. She didn't think he would forbid her visit, but why risk it?

As she approached Blickling Hall, Minuette briefly wished that she *had* told Dominic so that he might have forbidden her. Or that Elizabeth had gone to William in order to stop her—what on earth was she thinking, taking on Rochford at a game he'd been playing since before she was born? But she steeled herself for the encounter, and by straightening her back and pretending absolute confidence she found enough to go forward.

Rochford met her in his study, an old-fashioned chamber heavily paneled in dark wood that showed its age in the deep-set windows that offered only dim light. The furnishings were also from a previous era, though rather pleasing in their simplicity and lack of ornamentation. The duke offered her the courtesy of rising briefly from his chair. "My lady marquess," he said. Was it possible for him to speak without irony? "I regret not having been at court for the patent of your nobility."

"You regret not being able to prevent the king from bestowing it, you mean."

He waited until Minuette had seated herself to continue. "I may think you all kinds of wrong for my nephew, but I submit when I must. One can only win if one lives to fight another day."

"And so you sit here while your wife marches toward a trial. Have you corresponded with her?"

Rochford's lips tightened. "You may walk in and out of the

king's mind at will, but I do not concede you that right. Although speaking of the king, I do wonder—does William know you are here?"

"Have I come to Blickling because he cannot openly do so without angering others, do you mean? No. I am here on my own account, not at the king's bidding."

"Curiouser and curiouser," Rochford murmured. "If not for William's sake, perhaps for the Duke of Exeter? Dominic Courtenay might have things he'd prefer to say to me behind William's back."

"Lord Exeter does not say anything behind the king's back that he would not say to his face." She managed to make the lie believable. "Lord Rochford, I told you before that a time might come when I would need all the friends I could get. That time is growing nearer."

"If you are so in need of my aid, perhaps you might have ensured that I was not banished from court. What is it you expect me to do from here?"

Minuette drew a steadying breath. She was about to leap into the void, entrust her deepest secret to a man she had never trusted. But time was growing short, especially if her suspicions were correct.

It had been ten weeks since that night in May when Dominic spent two hours in her bed. Ten weeks and no sign of her normal courses. Carrie was watching her closely, perhaps as terrified as Minuette of what it might mean.

But Minuette wasn't just terrified. She was also emboldened. And focused.

"Lord Rochford, I know how deeply you disapprove of William's desire to marry me. What if I told you that I have no intention of becoming the king's wife?"

"I would say that you are either remarkably wise or remarkably foolhardy. Are you saying you would prefer to be his mistress?"

"I would prefer to be his friend, as I have ever been. I love William, but not as he wants. I would do almost anything to ensure his happiness. But I will not marry him."

For the first time ever, Rochford looked at her with something like appreciation. "Dare I hope your decision is for wisdom's sake alone, or do I detect another man in the picture?"

Minuette would never speak openly of her husband, but she had guessed she would not have to. Rochford was perhaps the cleverest man she'd ever known.

"I did think you were looking rather ... what's the politest word?" Rochford queried. "Satisfied? Well used?"

"That is not polite at all," she answered sharply.

He went on as if she had not spoken. "And if there is another man, no prizes for guessing who. I would have said Dominic Courtenay was the least likely man in the world to go behind Will's back. But when there's a woman in it . . ." Rochford shrugged. "I suppose I, of all people, should not be surprised at what a man will do for a woman he has convinced himself he is in love with."

Minuette swallowed her temper and her distaste. "Will you help us?"

"How?"

"We need to leave England." How it grieved her to say so, and how exceedingly difficult it would be to make Dominic agree, but she could see no other course. She had hoped for months that she would be able to mitigate William's anger when he learned of their marriage, but if she were indeed with child . . .

She could not risk being confined to the Tower. They must leave England.

Rochford considered her thoughtfully. "You do not trust to my nephew's mercy? Then you are not the simple girl I took you for. Yes, you will need to be well out of his reach. But your choices for exile are rather thin on the ground just now. Spain will not risk angering William while Philip angles to marry Elizabeth. And even you might have a hard time persuading Courtenay to take refuge in France. That would smack rather strongly of state treason."

"That leaves the Low Countries," Minuette agreed, for she had already thought through the options. "Can you arrange it? It will need to be for four." Because they could not leave Carrie and Harrington behind.

"It's possible. Letters to prepare your way, contacts to get you out of England secretly. But what is in it for me?"

"I've given you your life. How certain are you that, if you had not confessed preemptively to William, he would not have charged you with treason and sent you to the block? You may be banished, but I doubt you'll remain that way. You are too canny at politics."

"While there's life there's hope?" Wonder of wonders, Rochford smiled at her. "I suppose so. But still, if William ever discovered that I helped his beloved flee from him—"

"You can pin it on someone else. The Howard family, perhaps? What with my stepfather being a Howard." It made her stomach knot to say it, but she would warn Stephen Howard as best she could to ensure he would not be caught in Rochford's trap. And if he was—well, she would sacrifice anyone for Dominic and their child.

He laughed. "How I have underestimated you. Almost I want to persuade you that marrying William would be in our best interests after all."

"Almost?"

"No, you are right. If I can get you away from my nephew, then

I win and so does England. No offense, Lady Somerset, but England needs a stronger alliance for all our sakes."

"So you will help?"

He steepled his fingers. "I will put certain things in motion. Do you have an idea of when you would like to vanish?"

She could not afford to leave it too late. "When Philip arrives in August and everyone is busy thinking of the Spanish."

"I will get word to you."

Minuette offered her hand to Rochford, feeling exactly like Judas as she said, "Thank you."

She didn't know which man she had just betrayed more thoroughly: her king or her husband.

Dominic was in conference at the Round Tower, the structure raised during the days of Henry V to guard Portsmouth Harbor, when Harrington brought him news of a visitor. He might have expected a member of the privy council, or one of the town wardens, or an emissary from one of the Cinque Port towns, or even William (Dominic tried to ignore the leap in his heart that always and ever hoped for it to be Minuette), but his expectations were wildly wrong.

"Lord Stephen Howard," Harrington told him. "Seeking to discuss a personal matter with you."

Which could mean something touching upon Minuette, as Stephen Howard had been her mother's second husband. But Howard was also the uncle of the young Duke of Norfolk, and seeing that the Howards breathed politics as easily as air, who could guess what he had come for? Stephen Howard had helped the Crown before, most notably in the matter of the Penitent's Confession in 1554, warning the king through Minuette of his brother's search for that inflammatory document that threatened to bring down William. But his loyalties were so mixed as to be nearly indecipherable: blood ties warring with what had been, by all accounts, a deep and genuine love for Minuette's mother. Dominic would always be wary of a man he couldn't predict.

Dominic returned to Henry VIII's Southsea Castle where he found Stephen Howard on his feet looking out at the view of the harbor. "Thank you for seeing me at such a busy time," Howard said smoothly. He did everything smoothly. He was several inches shorter than Dominic, and both broader and softer than he had likely been as a young man, but there was still something in his bearing that made Dominic think of Robert Dudley. Cleverness? Confidence verging on arrogance? An ironic view of the world that always seemed to find humour?

"What do you want?" Dominic treated him the way he treated Robert, with a brusqueness to conceal his uneasiness. He didn't ask Howard to sit. The man did not seem to take it amiss.

With an amused tilt of his silver-tipped head, Howard said, "Always straight to the point, Lord Exeter. Very well. I have some information about the recent uprisings in Norfolk."

"You are Catholic, Lord Stephen. Why would you give me information about Catholic rebels?"

"As I have pointed out to my stepdaughter before, I am English before I am Catholic. I am also pragmatic and I do not see how ill-considered violence solves anything."

"Why come to me?"

"Because you will see me, where the king likely would not. I need someone who has the ear of the king and no one in this kingdom has it like you do."

"Your stepdaughter does."

Stephen Howard raised an eyebrow. "Would you prefer I involve Genevieve in this matter?"

"No." Dominic bit off the word. "Tell me."

"The rebels were well-funded. You must have seen that. The

weapons in store, the organization—that was not a peasant mob. And where there is funding, there will be a source."

"You are not telling me anything the king has not already considered. Unless you can offer information as to the source of that funding?"

"I have intelligence that says the money came from overseas."

"France?" Never fond of Mary Tudor, but with their current discontent with England and William and the threat of invasion, it was possible. Dominic was already figuring out how to use this information against the French when Howard shattered that thought.

"Spain."

Dominic stared. "King Philip is due to arrive in England within a fortnight."

Howard simply nodded once.

"Damn it," Dominic said under his breath. "How reliable is your intelligence?"

"Reliable enough that I would take it seriously. If Spain is involved, I presume you know in whose household to look for evidence?"

Of course he knew. Mary Tudor—daughter of a Spanish princess. If Spain were truly funding English rebels, the chances that Mary was involved were very high.

Along with the current Duke of Norfolk, Stephen Howard's own nephew.

"Thank you for your information," Dominic said curtly. "I assure you I will take it under consideration, including the implications you so carefully avoided."

"Thomas?" Howard nodded. "My nephew does not confide in me, but I know he's recently seen Lady Mary and I suspect they correspond. No doubt the king—or at least, Burghley—is aware of that."

"No doubt. It does make me wonder why you bothered to come to me at all."

"Because you will not hoard this information, calculating how best to use it to your own advantage. According to Genevieve, you are the most conscientious man in England, ever eager to serve your king to the best of your ability."

Dominic was beginning to choke on that vaunted sense of loyalty. But however deeply he was betraying William personally, he would work that much harder to preserve his public integrity. Within an hour of Howard's departure, Dominic had a courier on the way to William and Burghley detailing the man's allegations.

But if he thought his involvement ended with that duty done, he was mistaken. The very day after Stephen Howard's visit, Robert Dudley appeared at Southsea Castle with a message from Francis Walsingham. Dominic was beginning to grow weary of the constant stream of visitors from court. Couldn't he be left alone to do his job as Warden of the Cinque Ports and leave politics to those better suited to subtlety and deceit?

"Unless you've come with troops to add to our defensive preparations," Dominic told Robert as he strode into the same chamber where he'd met Howard, "then I've neither use nor time for you."

Turning from the view of Portsmouth Harbor—with its impressive collection of English ships and the long horizon where sea met sky in a mingled sweep of blues and grays—Robert offered up his smile of old: ironic, detached, and amused all at once. Dominic had not seen him since the day of Northumberland's execution. Robert looked to have regained his usual sleekness, with his carefully groomed dark hair and impeccably trimmed beard.

But there was an aloofness to his eyes, and a chill edge to his voice that was new. "Do you have time for the Princess of Wales?"

"You're not here at Elizabeth's command."

"I serve with Walsingham at her command, and the princess places a great deal of confidence in the man."

Dominic threw his hands in the air, defeated. "Curse it, Robert, just tell me what you've come to say, plainly and without games."

"Walsingham suspects Lady Mary of intriguing with the Spanish."

That was very plain indeed. "Fine, embroider that a little to enlighten me." But the warning from Stephen Howard was still ringing in Dominic's ears and he knew he didn't want to go down this path. He had enough to worry about without another Tudor royal complicating his life.

"What if Mary has been using her access to the Spanish ambassador in order to plot?"

"Plot what—to end Philip's courtship of Elizabeth before it's signed? Why would Spain want to do that?"

"I'm not saying Mary is rational."

"Spain is very rational," Dominic pointed out curtly. "If they haven't risen in the last twenty years to put Mary on the throne, why would they do it now?"

Robert shrugged. "I'm the messenger, not the intelligencer. No doubt Walsingham has more fears than he shares with me, and probably three-quarters of them are baseless. He wants you to be wary of Spain. That is all I know for certain. But I would guess that Mary Tudor is on very thin ice, and it might break beneath her at any moment."

"Be wary of Spain. Be wary of French invasion. Be wary of Mary's fanaticism. Is there anything in this country about which I do not need to be wary?"

With a wry smile, Robert said, "Now you're beginning to sound like a Tudor courtier. Wariness will keep you alive, Dominic, far longer than loyalty will."

After their argument, Elizabeth had wondered if Minuette would even bother to visit Hatfield. But she came, looking thoughtful but otherwise a good companion. For nearly three weeks now it had been much like earlier years, when the two of them had little more to concern themselves with than flirtatious courtiers and demanding tutors. For once, all talk of future marriage had to do with Elizabeth and Philip rather than William and Minuette, and Elizabeth wondered how she could have gone so long without her friend's caustic and witty comments on everything from property settlements to Philip's lack of interest in learning English. "All the better to manage him," Minuette told Elizabeth. "You'll be able to run your life in eight languages while he can only follow you in two."

One particular evening, as Minuette made her laugh with an impression of the Spanish priests' horrified reactions to their king marrying a heretic princess, Elizabeth had a piercing moment of pure pleasure and thought: *Whatever sort of queen she makes, I shall be so glad to call Minuette my sister in truth.*

The only topic they did not broach was Minuette's visit to Blickling Hall. Whatever business her friend had conducted with Lord Rochford she did not carry into her days at Hatfield, unless the nostalgic streak of mischief and laughter resulted from whatever secrets Minuette harbored. If so, Elizabeth could not entirely regret them.

Robert joined them unexpectedly on July 24, just ten days before King Philip's expected arrival, bringing with him dispatches from both William and Walsingham. William's message was chillingly brief: *Mary has been arrested and confined to the Tower for intriguing with Catholic rebels.*

Minuette was openly shocked at the news; Elizabeth less so. Mary was clever and resourceful and not lacking in courage. Indeed, her only flaw—apart from an understandable animosity toward Anne Boleyn—was her unbending faith. That faith had led her at last to the evidence William's government needed: a letter in Mary's own hand to the Spanish ambassador admitting both sympathy and financial support for Bishop Thirlby of Norwich and his vanquished band of traitors. The missive had been ciphered, but not cleverly enough.

More damaging, it had been written in reply to a letter that never existed—a trap that Walsingham and Lord Burghley between them had sprung when they unlocked the cipher method the Spanish ambassador had been using to communicate with Mary.

According to Robert, who was among the arresting party, Mary had behaved well when the royal guards came for her. She had also been adamant in proclaiming her rights. As the leading Catholic of the realm, she'd insisted, she had a duty to the adherents of the True Faith. God would judge her if she sat idly by and let her people be martyrs. Lord Rochford had much to answer for in spreading heresy through England, and despite the personal abuses of his royally granted power, he remained untouched and uncharged. Where was the king's justice in that matter? Mary protested. And how could any king presume to judge the case of an ordained bishop such as Thirlby?

That unsettling news delivered, Robert accepted Elizabeth's invitation to remain at Hatfield for a day or two. He was no fool, he knew that Mary's arrest might well spoil King Philip's imminent visit. It might even be canceled, for no doubt William's council was now scrambling to discover Spanish duplicity. If Spain had directly financed English rebels, then Elizabeth would have more freedom than she'd had in years as to the matter of her marriage. Not the French, not the Spanish—who was left? Elizabeth saw the calculation in Robert's eyes even as he bent to kiss her hand. Rumours swirled that Amy Dudley was ill.

But their talk that evening, after Minuette had tactfully retired, was not of inconvenient wives or sisters or kings on the matrimonial horizon. They sat before the desultory fire that was more for light than warmth on this summer night and discussed John Dee's latest discoveries in European libraries, the Portuguese colonies recently established in both China and the New World, and the Italian student, Pomponio Algerio, who had been sitting in a Roman prison for nearly a year waiting to be executed for his Lutheran beliefs. And before they separated for the night, Elizabeth allowed Robert to take her in his arms and whisper endearments while he kissed her thoroughly.

The next morning, they rode out together in the watery sunlight as they had hundreds of times before. The best horseman Elizabeth knew, Robert continued his impeccable behavior—witty in his observations and subtle in his flattery. When they returned to the house, laughing together over his description of the French ambassador too drunk to walk a straight line, Carrie was waiting for them near the front door and curtsied to Elizabeth without waiting to be acknowledged. "Your Highness."

Elizabeth looked at the maid negligently, then more carefully as she noted the strain on her face. "What is it?"

"If I might speak with you alone?"

Robert took the cue and vanished gracefully, but even that didn't seem privacy enough to Carrie. She set a rapid pace for the upstairs corridor where Minuette slept. Elizabeth felt the caress of old fear even before Carrie confirmed, "It's her ladyship. She is ill."

Poisoned, like a year ago at court? Certainly not in Elizabeth's home, where she knew every face of every servant and attendant. But her pace increased and Carrie must have read the question in her eyes. The maid hastened to add, "The illness is natural, but I'm beginning to grow worried. I don't know if I can stop it myself."

"Stop what?"

Carrie hesitated at the door to Minuette's chamber, looking wretched. "She's bleeding heavily."

For one moment Elizabeth thought Minuette must have fallen from something, hit her head, perhaps. But the next moment, she knew that there was only one cause of bleeding that would make Carrie cautious in seeking help. In an instant all the pleasure of the last hours with Robert and the previous weeks with Minuette vanished and Elizabeth knew that they stood on the edge of disaster.

Elizabeth didn't need to see the blood-soaked linen beneath Minuette to know she was right. She knew it the moment Minuette fixed her with panic-filled eyes. "Elizabeth, no one can know. Promise me, swear it, not even the servants, it will ruin us . . ."

Elizabeth hushed her and promised secrecy, with one exception. "We need Kat for this, Minuette. You know you can trust her. She's known you almost as long as she's known me—she will not speak."

Perhaps if Minuette had been stronger she would have protested. But then, if she'd been stronger she would not have needed Kat Ashley's help. Carrie was right, she'd lost a lot of blood. Obviously a midwife was out of the question, but Kat was both knowledgeable and discreet. She did not so much as raise an eyebrow when she was summoned, merely set to work.

It was several hours before Elizabeth drew a deep breath. Finally, the bleeding had slowed enough for Kat to pronounce herself satisfied, as long as Minuette heeded instructions and stayed in bed for at least a week. Minuette gave no sign that she'd heard her, just stared blankly at the wall. Between them, Kat and Carrie bundled the soiled linen and removed it. Elizabeth didn't ask how they meant to get rid of it, for she had worries of her own.

The first was simply dealt with. "We must inflict some illness or injury upon you for public notice. If we said that you'd had a fall from a horse, that would serve to keep people away and explain your convalescence at Hatfield for some time. I'll send Robert away first thing in the morning—he can carry the news with him to court."

Minuette continued to stare at the painted stylized lilies above the waist-high paneling of the wall and Elizabeth's throat ached at the untouchable nature of her friend's sorrow. "Minuette, shall I send for William?"

"No!" Minuette gasped with pain as she struggled to sit up, and Elizabeth laid a restraining hand on her shoulder. "No, you mustn't, please, Elizabeth. You can't tell him."

"He'd want to be here. He wouldn't want you grieving alone." Even as she said it, Elizabeth wondered if that was true. William had no stomach for illness; when Minuette had been poisoned, he'd spent the night drinking alone rather than sit with her. Having had smallpox was not likely to have increased his patience for imperfect health. And no matter how inconvenient the timing of the pregnancy, he wouldn't be happy that their first child had been lost so early.

With the air of a trapped bird, frantic in its desperation, Minuette continued to beg. "No, Will can't know! He doesn't know!"

Suspicion dawned in Elizabeth, and the ache in her throat spread to her chest. With gentle hands, she stroked Minuette's hair, damp from pain and effort, away from her forehead. "He didn't know you were pregnant?"

Minuette shook her head, her eyes clouding with tears. "Please, he can't do anything about it. Don't tell him. It doesn't matter now."

"Why didn't you tell him before?" Certainly William would have rejoiced. Her own mother had conceived Elizabeth two months before her marriage.

"I had to be sure. And I wanted it to be ..." Minuette choked back a sob that seemed to come from the depths of her empty womb. "I wanted it to be special." With obvious effort, she got her voice under control and said simply, "You must swear to me not to tell William."

There was nothing else to say. "I swear it."

28 July 1556
Hatfield

Kat and Carrie have finally allowed me to sit up in bed. I asked for my diary, but now find there is nothing I can write.

    There is only sorrow.

CHAPTER ELEVEN

MINUETTE WAS ALLOWED to leave her bed the first week of August. King Philip's arrival had been delayed a week—officially because of inclement weather, less officially because of Mary's arrest—and so Elizabeth remained with her friend for another few days. The bad weather that the Spanish were (perhaps) using as a diplomatic excuse manifested itself at Hatfield in gray, lowering skies that felt more like autumn than early August.

Elizabeth was deeply concerned for Minuette, who had emerged from her chamber a different woman. Still kind and lovely, still capable of behaving as everyone expected, but the spark had been burned out of her. The vivid, joyous girl was gone, bled away with the baby she had so clearly wanted.

William was naturally alarmed when he heard of Minuette's false injury and wanted to send his own physician to see to her. Elizabeth only averted that by a flat-out lie—she wrote her brother that Minuette was recovering nicely but had threatened hysterics at the thought of a male physician. In response, William poured out letters to his beloved, sometimes two a day, which Minuette read privately. She did not, to Elizabeth's knowledge, write back.

On August 7, the day before Elizabeth's departure for Dover

Castle, Dominic rode into Hatfield with a contingent of royal guards. Elizabeth had been expecting the guards—her escort to Dover—but had not expected Dominic to be in their company. "Did William send you?" she asked skeptically, wondering if her brother had asked his friend to spy out Minuette's condition.

Dominic shook his head. "It was my idea. I thought you might like a friendly face along the way, since Minuette will not be traveling with you."

Since when had Dominic ever gone out of his way for her? Elizabeth wondered. But she could hardly turn him away, although she felt a foreboding that she tried to smother in effusive greetings. She sent Carrie to give Minuette warning before dinner, and expected her to keep to her chamber until Dominic had left. But within thirty minutes of Dominic's arrival, Minuette appeared, dressed in a lightweight gown of gray shading to blue on the skirt and sleeves. She would have made a fine model of a Madonna in that gown and Elizabeth hoped Dominic's eyes were not as suspiciously keen as her own.

Minuette was very nearly herself at dinner: colour in her cheeks, laughter threaded through her voice. But Elizabeth was not a casual observer, nor was Dominic. Though he matched her conversation easily, there was a shadow of worry in his eyes. Colour hectic, laughter forced . . . Elizabeth's foreboding increased. Dominic was too clever by half; if anyone could come near to guessing the truth, it would be him.

And why should that be disaster? she asked herself crossly. If they could not trust Dominic, then who could they trust?

Minuette retired straight to her chamber after dinner. It appeared Dominic might request a moment of her time, but he merely stood politely as she left the table, his dark green eyes tracking her until she was out of sight. Elizabeth braced herself for questions she could not answer honestly about Minuette's health, but Dominic seemed lost in his own thoughts. At last he asked her leave to walk in the gardens.

Elizabeth spent an hour reading before the dark was too complete for candlelight to overcome. Even then she was too restless for sleep, so she wrapped herself against the unseasonable summer chill and went outdoors. Her steps took her to the white garden, which was always seen to best advantage in moonlight. She felt her nerves ease as she walked among the beds of fragrant pinks and carnations, snowdrop bellflowers and wide-eyed daisies, pale roses shedding both warmth and light.

She heard a low murmur of voices from the center of the garden, then saw them: Dominic and Minuette seated together on a curved bench beneath an arbor draped in honeysuckle vines. Elizabeth should have retreated at once. Instead, she stepped off the path into deep shadow.

It was Minuette she heard, her voice low and broken. "Dominic, why? I had thought it was a sign, a gift from God to assure us we are doing right. But now . . . I am lost."

"Why did you not tell me?" Dominic's gentleness was the tone one would have used with a skittish horse or a frightened child.

Or a woman whose heart had broken.

"I wanted to be sure," Minuette choked. "And I wanted it—" She broke off.

To be special. Elizabeth completed the answer silently, remembering Minuette's words when Elizabeth had asked her the same question.

No, not precisely the same question. Elizabeth had wanted to know why she had not told William.

Minuette shook with racking sobs. The tears she had choked back in front of Elizabeth, the tears unshed for days, were released in a storm of weeping. Elizabeth could see her leaning into Dominic, clutching his doublet as if he were the only thing keeping her anchored to this world. She watched Dominic's arms curve around Minuette's shaking shoulders and his lips press against her hair with infinite tenderness.

It was as though the earth shifted beneath Elizabeth's feet and the foreboding of disaster she'd felt all day rearranged itself into an unexpected and yet inevitable certainty.

Minuette had spoken only the truth. William had not known about the baby—for the simplest of reasons.

He was not the father.

It was a long time before Minuette stopped weeping. Dominic held her tight, his own chest hurting in sympathy and muscles wound tight with his utter inability to help. Only when her breath at last settled into a slight hitch did he say, "You were right, little star. We need aid. I should have listened to you and gone to Rochford before this happened."

"I already have," she said. She offered the revelation listlessly, as though nothing mattered any longer.

"That is why you warned him to confess," Dominic said slowly, as understanding dawned. "You protected Rochford as best you could in exchange for his future help."

"I went to Blickling Hall just before I came to Hatfield. Lord Rochford is preparing a way for us to take refuge in the Low Countries." She shrugged. "I thought we were in something of a hurry."

Dominic didn't know how to feel at this unexpected disclosure of his wife's plans. To leave England, to flee as a traitor and leave William utterly bereft of friends and love ... but no. Will would have his sister. And his government and his armies and his Parliament. William had everything. Dominic had only Minuette.

And a lost child ...

"Very well," Dominic said. "How soon? I will take you from Hatfield this night if you wish it." Even as he offered, he knew it wasn't possible. He had little knowledge of the damage done to Minuette's body, but it could not be light. It might be weeks before she could ride.

She shook her head. "No. You are needed for the Spanish."

"To hell with the Spanish! To hell with everything—I will do whatever you need me to."

"There is no hurry now." The matter-of-fact words were belied by her shaky voice. "Let us finish our immediate duties. Bring King Philip and Elizabeth together, see them safely betrothed—if that is indeed the outcome—and then we will put ourselves in Rochford's hands."

"Do you think that entirely wise?" Dominic couldn't help asking, long years of wariness not easily dismissed where Lord Rochford was concerned.

"He is eager to rid William of me. And if you leave England as well, then who will be left to guide the king? Rochford will use our flight to restore himself to power."

Dominic took her chin in his hand and raised her head until he could search her face. "Are you certain this is what you wish?"

It had been ages since he'd been able to read her thoughts in her eyes, but tonight they shone clear and nearly broke his own heart. "I am so tired, Dominic. I want a life with you, with children—" She choked and took a ragged breath. "We cannot go back. We can only go on. William will never let me go. What else can we do but run? Unless you no longer find me worth it."

He cupped her face in his hands, not entirely gentle. "How can you say that?"

If she'd had any tears left, she might have wept, but instead her words caught on dry sobs. "How can I not? I have cost you your king, your wealth, your honour ... and now your child. What could you want with a broken wife?"

Blindly trying to feel his way to what she needed to hear, Dominic said, "You are not broken, Minuette, and even if you were, I would not care except for your sake. It is you yourself I cannot do without."

She did, after all, have a few tears left, for they spilled soundlessly onto his fingers. Roughly, desperate to make her believe him, Dominic whispered, "I count the world itself well lost to have you as my wife."

More than anything he wanted to kiss her, to use her body to blot out his own sorrow, and he hated himself for it. Was that not what had brought them to this pass? If he had not pressed himself upon her in a mix of desire and jealousy that night at court, she would not be ill and grieving.

It was Minuette herself who kissed him, pulling him to her with a ferocity that instantly overwhelmed his scruples. Her mouth was hungry for him, and if she still wept, Dominic told himself they were cleansing tears. It could not go on, they were in the middle of Elizabeth's own garden and might be interrupted at any moment and surely Minuette was not in any condition to finish things, but for a few wild, thoughtless minutes the past and the future retreated and all was entirely well.

8 August 1556
Hatfield

Dominic and Elizabeth left this morning for Dover Castle. When I told Elizabeth I was sorry not to be going with her, that I wished I could be with her in the uncertain days ahead, she kissed me on the forehead as she might a young girl.

"I shall do well enough on my own," she said. "It is you I am worried about. You must rest as Kat and Carrie tell you so that you can meet us all at court when Philip's visit is ended."

And then she hugged me fiercely and whispered in my ear, "You can trust me, Minuette, for anything. If you were in trouble . . ."

She cannot imagine the depth of my trouble.

10 August 1556
Hatfield

I forced myself to write to William today, although the couriers will have to follow him to Dover. But his letters have been like coals heaped on my heart—so solicitous and worried, so careful not to hint of any hurt at my silence. I don't know how I will face him again. I don't know how to do this anymore! But I don't know what else to do.

11 August 1556
Hatfield

That is a lie. I know precisely what to do. It is a measure of my cowardice that I am still afraid to do it.

Elizabeth rode into Dover beneath a bright coastal sun on August 11, to cheering crowds and rippling banners. William met her to ride the last mile to the castle together and the siblings no doubt made an impressive spectacle—both upright and slender, William's dark curls encircled with a golden crown, Elizabeth's bright hair a shining memory of the last king. *Mother would have liked this,* Elizabeth thought as they passed through the outer curtain wall by way of Fitzwilliam's Gate. *Her royal children in triumph.*

But the moment, like all moments, passed swiftly away, and inside Dover Castle even the walls themselves seemed tense and anxious. The Spanish ships had been sighted and were even now heading into Dover with an English escort. They would arrive by nightfall, and tomorrow morning King Philip would set foot on English soil.

Whether he came with a proposal or a condemnation was uncertain. An informal council convened in William's privy chamber: William and Dominic, Elizabeth and Lord Burghley, and Walsingham and Robert Dudley.

Philip would be polite, was the consensus. He would hardly have bothered to make the journey if he did not intend to at least meet the king and princess. But whether that meeting would end in a betrothal was anyone's guess.

Burghley, as always, was pragmatic. "We cannot know anything until we have met with King Philip. By tomorrow evening we will have a much clearer idea of what he intends."

"And so we simply parade the Princess of Wales as a lure before him?" Robert asked. "That's rather cold-blooded."

William's face darkened. "The princess is not your concern."

"The princess," Elizabeth intervened, before either man could lose his temper, "is quite capable of doing what is best for England. I do not object to being a pretext for a personal meeting if the results are greater security for all."

She went to bed in a temper of her own, for the first time since Hatfield thinking of something other than Minuette and Dominic's love affair. Although she still did not know how she was going to extricate the two of them from their folly, for now she could only gird herself for Philip of Spain. Husband—or enemy?

Or possibly both.

Dressed in his most elaborate ceremonial wardrobe, draped with velvet and silk and heavy chains of gold, a crown set with rubies and opals circling his head, William waited for Philip of Spain. Elizabeth sat in a throne next to his, looking effortlessly royal and icily beautiful in cloth-of-gold and a pearl-encrusted headdress. Around her neck she wore a simple circlet of enameled Tudor roses. Before them, the King's Hall of the Great Tower—built by that energetic and farseeing king, Henry II—was filled with most of the nobles of England, as well as William's privy council.

As Lord Burghley ceremoniously opened the doors, all eyes turned to the small Spanish party and the man at their heart. William noted Dominic walking behind the group, but he had eyes only for Philip. He'd had reports of the monarch's appearance, even seen portraits, but so much of a king's presence depended on how he carried himself. King Philip of Spain was clearly a master of royal presence: he was shorter than William by several inches and somewhat slight of figure, but one forgot that quickly when faced with Philip's elegant carriage and grave expression. His eyes were wide and pale blue, his hair and beard a dark shade between brown and red, and he was dressed impeccably in black and gold.

William rose and stepped off the low dais to greet his fellow king on equal ground. In serviceable Spanish, William said, "You are most welcome to England, our dear friend of Spain."

They clasped hands and Philip replied in less serviceable and strongly accented English, "To meet our dear England is ever an honour." Then, in rapid Latin, "Shall we converse in a more mutual language?"

William didn't answer that his Spanish was perfectly good enough for conversation, for it would have highlighted the fact that Philip's language facility was more limited. In Latin, William turned to the dais and summoned Elizabeth forward. "The greater honour is to meet my sister, Elizabeth."

"And so it is," Philip agreed, his expression giving nothing away of his ultimate intentions toward William's sister. Nor did Elizabeth's face betray any emotion other than polite welcome.

"Your Majesty." Elizabeth had a store of curtsies; this particular one offered genuine respect mingled with a sense of her own worth.

Philip replied in kind, a deep bow followed by a kiss of her hand. "Portraits do not do you justice, Your Highness."

Bestowing a smile upon the flattery, Elizabeth answered, "Yours did you justice very well, for you are quite as handsome as in your pictures."

Did she mean it? William wondered. Impossible to tell with his sister. She had been assigned a part, and she would play it well—so well that none would ever know what she really felt unless she chose to share it. William found himself looking for Robert Dudley, curious about his reaction. Robert's expression was not as unreadable as the royals': he was unhappy.

I hope I make you much more unhappy before the Spanish depart, William thought fervently. They needed Spain. Pray Heaven Philip had come to offer for Elizabeth. If he hadn't, then England could be in serious trouble.

Within an hour, Elizabeth knew that Philip did not intend to barter for her hand in marriage. Not yet. He might be considering her, or he might equally be playing with them all, but either way the Spanish would depart England without a royal betrothal.

Perversely, that certainty made it easier to appreciate Philip and enjoy his company. Elizabeth was accustomed to learned and wealthy men, had spent weeks at the French court last summer in company with well-born, self-assured men who had flattered and flirted with her. Philip was a different matter. He did not bother to flirt, and scarcely to flatter, for each word gave the impression of having been carefully weighed out beforehand. Rather than give his conversation the appearance of calculation, it instead bestowed an impression of a man who spoke only what he truly believed.

He was nothing at all like Robert Dudley.

As they dined in private company—the two kings, Elizabeth, the Spanish ambassador Simon Renard, Lord Burghley, and Dominic—Elizabeth assessed her own impressions of the Spanish king and was a little surprised to discover that she found him personally attractive. She liked his rare smile and the cool gravity of the way he looked at her. Here is a man I could match, she thought, and fancied she saw mild regret in Philip's eyes that a betrothal was not on offer today.

After the meal, Elizabeth was politely dismissed so that the men might have a private word about kingdoms and politics—and a half-Spanish princess locked up in the Tower. Philip escorted her, their steps matching perfectly across the chamber. He took the opportunity to speak a few soft words for her ears alone. In Spanish, a generous acknowledgment of Elizabeth's fluency.

"Your Highness, I confess I shall leave England with greater regret than I had anticipated. It is a pity our two kingdoms cannot be friends as I've long wished."

A less than honest wish, as Philip knew it was in his power to make them friends. Rather more than friends. For the first time in a lifetime of arranged possibilities for her future, Elizabeth thought that this was a man who would be a worthy partner—and perhaps opponent. The one did not preclude the other.

"Your Majesty," she replied. "Whatever political tensions arise, I personally shall be most interested in further . . . friendship."

If it had been Robert, he would have kissed her at that flirtatiously offered challenge. Philip, however, simply regarded her, his smile the only sign that he appreciated her words. "Your Highness," he murmured, and lifted her hand to his lips. "I find myself hoping you and I shall have many years of friendship before us."

Elizabeth retired that night looking forward to the next day: riding out with her brother and Philip and, after an afternoon of the two monarchs consulting privately, dancing at the farewell banquet. Surely Philip was an excellent dancer; he moved with such controlled grace.

But when she woke, it was to news that the Spanish had set sail at dawn. They had taken their ambassador, Simon Renard, with them and left behind a message that scarcely bothered to be polite about unexpected weather and the need not to be delayed in an English port if a storm blew up.

It was Robert who brought her the news. He at least had the grace not to openly gloat. But when Elizabeth snapped, "Well, I imagine you are the only one in Dover who is wholeheartedly relieved to see the back of Philip," Robert answered readily, "For my own sake, yes. If his ungracious flight displeases you, then I am sorry for your pain."

She sighed and shook her head. It was not fair that Robert moved her heart so easily. She knew she treated him casually, sometimes cruelly, but only because she hated being vulnerable to any man.

Extending her hand in invitation, she waited until Robert held it firmly before speaking. "Robert, if I had to do with only one man for the rest of my life, it would be you. Kings are all well and good, but none can be my eyes as you are."

Even as he kissed her and Elizabeth let herself be pulled into him by her own desire as much as Robert's, she knew she had not spoken the whole truth.

CHAPTER TWELVE

FROM THE MOMENT he'd left Hatfield, Dominic had felt it was a mistake to leave Minuette behind. What did he care about France or Philip or Elizabeth's betrothal when his wife needed him? He should simply have scooped her up and left. He should have taken her when he could, snatched her free of the court and its trappings and—if they could not get across the sea—headed west, to the combined strongholds of Tiverton and Minuette's Somerset lands.

But Dominic was long accustomed to subduing his desires to the demands of duty, and so he'd gone to Dover and played his part at William's side and hardly listened to a word that passed between the Spanish and the English. When the visit was cut so unceremoniously short, Dominic knew without caring that Elizabeth would not be marrying Philip of Spain. At least not this year. He sent a note to Minuette at Hatfield, telling her that they would be going to London from here and hoping she would meet them. When they reached London, he would go to Rochford himself and bully the man into finishing his arrangements to spirit them to the Netherlands.

He was up at dawn to deal with reports from along the coastlines. Fears of a French invasion had, if not entirely vanished, largely receded. But Dominic would not leave any command of his half done. If he had not been up and about the castle, the news might have been delivered to Burghley first, but Dominic intercepted the message from the captain of one of the small English ships that regularly patrolled the Channel. They had seen Spanish ships in force, the message ran, and not those of the royal party just departed. More was not committed to paper, so Dominic followed the messenger to the ship itself and questioned her captain.

"Moving fast." The man spat on the deck of his ship. "And out of their own waters. Toward France."

"Take me out," Dominic decided. If William decided to leave Dover today, he could catch up with them later. "I want to see these ships for myself."

He took Harrington with him, leaving word for the king that there was an anomaly at sea he wished to see for himself.

They set sail from Dover in the brigantine that had brought word, the low, swift ship easy to maneuver and much used in piracy and espionage. Dominic's nerves were unsettled and his body tensed up the longer they were at sea. He was accustomed to the bigger, more comfortable ships that carried ladies of the court between England and France and he was not a natural sailor. But it was his imagination that fueled his unease, for he could think of multiple reasons for Spain to be sailing toward France, and not one of them was good.

They headed south where the brigantine had last sighted the Spanish, sailing well into the night and picking up again at dawn. Before the sun had been up for long, there was a smudge of ships on the horizon. The captain passed the sea glass to Dominic and assured him that the vessels were Spanish. They were not the elegant royal ships that had brought King Philip and his party to England, but warships. Sitting well off the French coast and motionless. A warning. Or a blockade.

"You know what's behind them," the captain said.

"Le Havre."

The captain nodded. "They're not deployed to fight, more to keep away any English ships that might care to fight."

"To keep us from reaching our newest French cities?" Dominic didn't need to ask, and the captain didn't bother to answer.

Dominic took a last look through the sea glass, foreboding strung tightly through his body. If Spain was attempting to keep the English out of Le Havre, it argued either an attack of its own against English interests or an agreement with the French.

And if Spain and France were working together . . .

"Get me back to Dover," he ordered.

Dominic's messenger brought word of the Spanish fleet's appearance off the French coast just half a day before the French ambassador himself, Antoine de Noailles, delivered a formal announcement to William and the privy council. The day after reaching Whitehall, William sat in the circular council chamber surrounded by men as grim faced as he was. Dominic was still on the road from Dover, no doubt riding hard for London, but everyone else was there: canny Lord Burghley, bitter and seasoned veterans like Sussex and Oxford, and the young men. Of the latter, William kept a careful watch on the Duke of Norfolk.

De Noailles bore himself gravely, as befit a man nearing the end of his career. He'd served his first diplomatic mission years before Anne Boleyn's marriage to Henry VIII and gave the impression of having seen it all and not being impressed by much of anything. He did not openly flaunt France's success (for no doubt he did not wish to see the inside of an English prison) but managed to assert it as a natural consequence of William's actions without overtly blaming the English king.

"We regret the loss of friendship between us, Your Majesty. But as England seems determined to break with us, we have had no choice but to look to our own security," the ambassador said.

William did not trust himself to speak, though he felt the ripples of discontent and dismay among the councilors attending him. Lord Burghley, ever calm in the face of disaster, spoke for the English. "Unlike France, we have offered no violence beyond our own borders."

"We would like to ensure it remains that way."

"A strange way to seek peace, by provoking retaliation."

De Noailles spoke straight to William, his direct gaze an arrogant contrast to his measured language. "Your options for retaliation are somewhat sparse just now, for we have not only retaken Le Havre and Harfleur."

William hated being forced to speak, but de Noailles knew how to wait. Rather like Dominic—or Rochford. William would have given much to have either of them at his side just now. Since he did not, he asked the question he'd been diplomatically maneuvered into asking. "What else have you taken from us?"

The two syllables pierced William like a dagger, though he'd known it was the only answer. "Calais."

Calais: the last remnant of England's empire. Seized two hundred years ago by Edward III, possessed and retained through the plague and the Wars of the Roses and even Joan of Arc.

"Elaborate," William said, jaw so tight he thought he might have cracked a tooth, "on the presence of Spanish ships off the French coast."

"King Henri has proposed a treaty of peace with King Philip. They will meet in four weeks' time to discuss terms, including the betrothal of Princess Elisabeth de France to the Spanish king. As a gesture of goodwill, we assure you that neither party has an interest in pursuing further aggression. For now."

Well, William had wanted out of the French marriage. This

wasn't quite how he'd envisioned it, however. Philip was meant to marry the English Elizabeth and provide the Continental security that England needed.

With a flick of his finger, William directed the Earl of Pembroke. "Take Monsieur de Noailles into custody. Not the Tower"—not yet—"but he is not to leave Whitehall without our express permission. No visitors. No correspondence."

The ambassador seemed unaffected; no doubt he'd been expecting as much. He knew he was more or less untouchable unless William was prepared to turn the combined might of France and Spain against him at once.

When de Noailles had been escorted out, the council burst into a buzz of outrage and concern and plans. The immediate impression was of the younger men itching to fight and the older men urging caution. But William knew how to look beneath surfaces and it did not escape him that the Duke of Norfolk—youngest man in the room save himself—said nothing at all. "Enough!" William finally thundered. "What is the point in twittering about what is lost? All that matters now is what we do next."

"Can we trust that France and Spain are not even now planning a joint invasion?" asked the Duke of Norfolk in measured tones.

"I think so," William said bitterly. "If only because they consider us beneath them. They expect to overawe us with their combined might, like little children made to wait in the corner until the adults are finished with business. So we will go about our own business. What we need is a distraction."

"Such as?" Lord Burghley demanded.

"It's past time Lady Rochford answered formally for her crimes. Her trial will begin in three days. Send word to my uncle that his presence in London is required." William stood and stared down his furious and, yes, frightened councilors. "For today, I will pay a visit to my sister Mary. I would like to break the news of Spain's betrayal myself."

And see if she is surprised, he thought grimly. Or if this might not be exactly what Mary, in her twisted sense of duty and righteousness, wanted to happen. And before he left Whitehall, he had a word with Burghley and ensured the Duke of Norfolk would be well watched for now.

William rode to the Tower through the city of London, paying no attention to the cheers and shouts of his citizens. He'd been cheered since he was born; it was nothing new. He would notice only when they stopped cheering.

As he and his guards rode in through the Middle Gate and were met by a visibly astonished constable, William tried to remember the last time he'd been to the Tower of London. Could it really be that he had not been here since the night before his coronation? He remembered that night vividly, lodging with his mother and uncle in the temporarily lavish suite of rooms in Wakefield Tower. At the age of ten, he had not appreciated the fact that Henry VI had been murdered in that very suite while at prayer. That last night before William was officially crowned and anointed, he had mostly been interested in Dominic's sword, for his friend at fifteen had been a knight already and infinitely more impressive to a boy than the robed clergy and councilors who'd surrounded him in those days.

He brought himself forcibly back to the present moment. "I'm here to see the Lady Mary," he snapped to the constable, cutting off the man's nervous flow of words. It was almost a pleasure how quickly silence fell, and he stalked along the uneven cobbles at a rapid pace, forcing the others to keep up.

Why make them pay the price of your anger at the French? The disapproving voice was, as always, Dominic's.

Because I can. It wasn't as satisfying as saying it to Dom's face, but it would have to suffice for now.

The path to Mary led them down the cobbles of Water Lane, with the Thames lapping grimly against the steps of the waterside gate. Above that stone river entry was St. Thomas's Tower, the gothic chambers constructed by Edward I for his personal use. An arching, crenullated passageway stretched across Water Lane, connecting St. Thomas's Tower to Wakefield with its circular stone walls and rectangular paired windows. Then beneath the heavy square of Bloody Tower that controlled access to the Inner Ward of the complex, William turned right, crossing before the serene bulk of the Conqueror's White Tower to the royal apartments.

As a show of deference to her position, Mary was housed in the queen's chambers where Anne Boleyn had stayed before her own coronation, and on the surface she had all the elegance and luxury she could demand. But Henry's children were skilled at looking beneath the surfaces, acutely touchy about their position and due deference, and no doubt she thought it an insult to share space with a dead woman's hated memory.

William read his sister's discontent as clearly as if she had shouted it rather than curtseying deeply. "Your Majesty," she said, in that perfectly English voice that still managed to have a hint of foreignness to it. As though she had imbibed her mother's accent along with her defiant spirit.

"You may sit," William said abruptly. Mary narrowed her eyes at his tone but complied placidly. William remained standing, too much anger pent up to confine himself to a chair.

Instead, he took a slow turn around the square room, the walls softened and warmed with tapestries. He studied the mementos Mary had brought with her and recognized many of the religious items; crucifixes abounded, along with devotional reliquaries and books by Cardinal Fisher and Thomas More.

"Do you know why you are here?" he asked, back turned discourteously on his sister.

"Because you do not trust me."

It was a surprisingly blunt and perceptive answer. William turned to her with appreciation. "Usually this is where you blame my evil councilors."

She met his gaze without flinching. "You are king. If you trusted me, then no amount of wicked counsel could turn your heart from me. It grieves me to admit that, for I have never been anything but a loving sister and a loyal subject."

"Clearly our definitions of loyalty differ greatly. If I do not trust you, it is because you have given me cause."

"Honouring God and the Holy Church does not lessen my loyalty to you personally."

"It does when that honour compels you to support armed rebellion. Those men in the North were not rabble, Mary. They were organized and armed . . . and they called you queen."

"I cannot help what people say."

"But you can help what they do, especially when it comes to Spain. Someone funded those men, someone outside England."

"How could it be Spain when Philip is preparing even now to marry Elizabeth?"

William could not mistake the edge of jealousy in Mary's voice. Any marriage of Elizabeth's must pain her, being so forcibly kept single until now she could no longer hope for marriage or children. But the thought of Elizabeth marrying the King of Spain, the beloved homeland of Mary's mother, must be particularly bitter. Not that she would have to worry about that now.

"Spain has decided they would rather have France. Spanish ships have aided French armies in taking Calais."

His sister's face blanched. "What can you mean?"

"Calais is lost."

It was like gall and wormwood to admit it aloud. The last reminder of England's brilliant victories in generations past, stolen away. He saw his own bitterness mirrored in Mary's eyes as she whispered, "How father would weep."

William's melancholy cleared. "Not weep," he said sternly. "Father would rage. And he would have vengeance. I am not foolish enough to rush to an unequal war, but I will not forget. And I will not forgive—either France or Spain."

He approached the chair, looming over her so she was forced to look up at him awkwardly. This close, he could see the lines around her eyes and the sag of her once sharp jawline. "I offer you fair warning, sister. You are already implicated in encouraging Spain to arm the Norwich rebels. I know well that, even from the Tower, plots can be laid. If you ever want to return to Beaulieu and freedom, you will keep clear of even the appearance of evil. Do not mistake my sibling care for political carelessness. I will be watching you. Don't make me do something we will both regret."

CHAPTER THIRTEEN

THE TRIAL OF Jane Parker Boleyn, Duchess of Rochford, for treason and attempted murder, was held on the last day of August, amidst a sweltering heat that seemed to capture all the uneasiness and tension of a populace bitterly unhappy at having lost Calais. Dominic felt the heavy air as a tangible thing, pressing down on him so that he could hardly breathe. As a duchess and aunt of the king, Jane's trial took place at Westminster Hall. Dominic took his place on the bench, thinking wearily that he had seen too much of this chamber this year. He could almost see the figure of Northumberland before them, penitent and surprised at his sentence just months ago.

Jane Boleyn was not penitent. She was also not entirely coherent. Dominic twitched through her mercifully brief appearance before the judges, skin crawling at her unmistakable imbalance. How much of it was inherent in her nature and how much forced into being by her time in the Tower and relentless interrogations was hard to say, but he could not believe they were being asked to judge her. She should be locked up, perhaps for her own good, but to execute her seemed hardly necessary.

The star witness against the Duchess of Rochford was Eleanor Percy. Surprisingly, Eleanor testified in person rather than through a written statement. Dominic almost didn't recognize her, dressed as soberly as a nun in black and gray, her straw-blonde hair coiled sedately around her head and covered by a gauzy veil. Her personality was as subdued as her attire. Despite his dislike and distrust of the woman, he couldn't help but be impressed by her apparently straightforward account.

She wove in words an image of Jane Boleyn as a cunning and manipulative woman who had used Eleanor's love for her daughter to ensure her aid in persecuting Minuette. Tricks, at first, like the adder in the bedchamber. And the spreading of rumours, of course. But Eleanor claimed she had been shocked when she realized Jane had used her as a distraction in order to attempt murder.

"I did not know of Lady Rochford's intent," Eleanor stated plainly, and she was such a practiced liar that Dominic almost didn't know himself whether to believe her. "I was horrified to realize what she had done."

"Then why," Lord Burghley asked, "did you not inform someone in authority?"

"Lady Rochford threatened me. She knew that I had been ... that her husband and I had ..." Eleanor paused delicately. "I did say something to Lord Rochford, and who could be a higher authority than the chancellor? But he wished to protect his wife's name and assured me the young lady would be kept safe. What else could I do, with my daughter to protect on my own?"

Nicely played, Dominic realized. Eleanor had managed to not only provide a strong witness against Lady Rochford, but to balance perfectly her words about Lord Rochford himself. If William decided to let his uncle remain free, then Eleanor had not condemned him. But if the king chose to disbelieve that his aunt had acted of her own accord, then Eleanor could be pressed to say more about Lord Rochford's guilt.

And somehow Eleanor had kept herself above the tawdriness of it all, for who could not be moved by a young widow trying to protect her child? The king's child, in point of fact, a detail made all the clearer to the men in the hall by Eleanor's refusal to highlight it.

"I was in the power of a woman who meant murder," confessed Eleanor, "and a man who could ruin my entire family with a word. And I did offer what warning I could, to Mistress Wyatt herself. Ask her if I did not caution her against trusting anyone, on the very day she so blessedly survived the attempt on her life."

Jane Boleyn, Duchess of Rochford, was found guilty of attempted murder and treason for acting against the interests of the king and sentenced to death. She spit words of fury and venom as the guards took her out, to return to the Tower and await William's pleasure.

With his aunt's fate set, William could no longer avoid dealing directly with Eleanor Percy. At least he didn't have to return to the Tower; William had sent her weeks ago to Ely Place, the London home still belonging to the Dudley family. It had been something of a conundrum where to send her: nowhere the Howard family could get to her, obviously, and Charterhouse, which he might once have considered, belonged to Rochford. And although William had forgiven his uncle the affair with Eleanor, he did not mean to facilitate its continuation.

Not that he was jealous. So he'd convinced himself, right up until the moment a guard escorted Eleanor into the solarium where William waited. She sank into an immediate and graceful curtsey when she entered, and he stared mutely at the top of her blonde head, remembering the silk of her hair brushing against his face and chest. For a blinding moment he wanted nothing more than to strip the prim silk gown from her and bury himself in her curves and generosity and forget forever that she had been in his uncle's bed.

He was no saint; since his months of devotional celibacy to Minuette had ended in Eleanor's bed a year ago, William had enjoyed many nights in a woman's arms. Though "enjoyed" might be a bit strong; no woman had ever given him the pure abandon that Eleanor had. And as much as he worshipped Minuette, William could not deny that his body very much wanted Eleanor every single time he encountered her.

"You may go," he told the guard, and let Eleanor remain in her submissive position for several long moments—schooling his expression to indifference—before sharply gesturing her to stand.

They faced each other head on, as he realized now they had always done. At seventeen, William had thought her the perfect companion for him. So she may have been, but perhaps not solely for the youthful lust he'd assumed. Eleanor was as practical as he was. She had never looked at him with disappointment or wanted him to be different than he was and, though he knew that did not make for a wise paramour, it was restful in its way.

Besides, he had used Eleanor for his own pleasure (and still would, if he let himself), and though she had used him in the same manner, it did not change what he owed her. Especially for the little girl, now named Nora and living with her uncle, two years old and his acknowledged daughter. William had only seen the child once, but it had been enough to seal her care upon his heart.

"You are free to go," he told her abruptly, because if he was not abrupt he might stop thinking altogether and do something stupid. "I've allowed you to retain control of the estate in Cumbria I gifted your late husband. If you continue to prove that you can be trusted, then I will consider allowing Nora to join you there in time."

"I can always be trusted to look to your interests, Your Majesty." Eleanor said it without irony or inflection, her wide blue eyes and fair skin lending her an illusion of innocence.

"Then you must allow me to decide what is in my own interest, and that means accepting Lady Somerset as my wife. We are planning a Christmas wedding. I expect your gracious acquiescence and support in the matter."

Why did he care? he wondered. Eleanor herself was not powerful, and though her late husband had been an uncle to the current Duke of Norfolk, the Howard family had not embraced Eleanor as one of their own. What matter if this cunning, beautiful, seductive woman acquiesced in his choice of bride?

Eleanor was silent, an unusual state, and seemed to be considering what to say, or perhaps how to say it. "William," she at last ventured, and he did not protest at the familiarity of his name for she made no attempt to touch him. "I have been and always will be your devoted servant. Your position is a difficult one, surrounded by so many who will take what they can get without thought to whether it's in your interest. I have only ever wanted to ensure that you are not taken advantage of, for even those closest to you—such as Lady Rochford—have too often betrayed your generosity."

"And you have not? Since when is sleeping with my uncle and chancellor not a betrayal?"

She bit her lip, a gesture so evocative of past intimacies that William felt an instant, unbidden arousal. He very nearly groaned aloud and would have admitted at that moment that he did not blame Rochford for taking Eleanor to bed. Any man who could resist her when she looked like that—all promised passion and skill—was beyond a saint.

"I cannot apologize sufficiently for my part in that, though I assure you it was not I who instigated the affair. But I was angry with you at the time, and so I behaved foolishly." Eleanor sighed, her expression softening to affection. "I regret the secrets I kept from you, and I promise that I shall never do so again. Those who lie to you do not deserve your trust, and I swear that I shall give you cause to trust me once more."

It took her three steps to reach William, her oval face tipped up in appeal. "Perhaps one day we can again be friends."

As she leaned in and kissed him lightly on his unscarred cheek, William thought, But we were never friends. And what he wanted from her just now was what he had always wanted: passion unburdened by love, release without responsibility, refuge from thought.

When he seized her by the arms and pulled her into a more reckless kiss, he could almost feel the smile as her mouth opened beneath his. Guilt stood no chance against Eleanor's hands and his own hungry body.

3 September 1556
Whitehall Palace

I had hoped to remain at Hatfield until the end of August, but with the failure of King Philip's visit and the devastating loss of Calais, William begged me to return "as soon as your health will permit." My physical health presented no obstacles, for I have healed quickly and both Kat and Carrie assured me that I should have no trouble in future. So I came when William called. For the last time.

He has been distracted and irritable and worried over the possible French-Spanish alliance and Lady Rochford's conviction, but in the midst of all that he has been heartbreakingly solicitous of my welfare after my false fall from a horse. I have been lying to him for months, nearly two years now, so why do these last lies weigh so heavily?

Lord Rochford has sent me a note from Charterhouse, where he has been staying since his wife's trial. He asked me to call upon him soon: "For," he wrote, "mid-September should bring our joint concern to fruition."

So long we have waited, and now so little time remaining.

10 September 1556
Whitehall Palace

In the midst of all the rumours and opinions of Lady Rochford's state of mind and health and what that might mean to her sentence, the privy council has issued an edict allowing for the execution of the insane. If I were not so tired and downhearted, I might try to speak to William about the wisdom of this, but I have nothing left to give.

If Jane Grey wishes to intervene, she can speak to William herself.

13 September 1556
Whitehall Palace

Jane Boleyn, Lady Rochford, was beheaded on a private scaffold on Tower Green this morning.

Tomorrow, Dominic will go to Charterhouse and receive whatever instructions Lord Rochford has for us.

My life at court is down to days, if not hours.

"Minuette?" Elizabeth spoke softly, but even so Minuette startled badly. Elizabeth waited while her friend closed her diary and turned in her seat. Dressed for bed, with her dark honey curls bound in a single plait, she looked about fifteen years old.

Elizabeth had rehearsed what she might say to Minuette, how

to delicately broach the subject of Dominic and their evident affair, and had not yet found the nerve. Minuette always seemed so fragile, should she not wait until her friend was well?

Smoothing a tiny crease on her gold damask overskirt, the only outward sign of her uncertainty, Elizabeth said, "You were missed at dinner. William and Dominic are both highly worried. I told them you needed only rest, and time. Prove me right, Minuette, and heal quickly."

She hesitated, knowing that time was slipping away, that a world of hurt was waiting for her brother, that something had to be said sooner rather than later . . . and in that hesitation, Minuette spoke.

"Elizabeth." Her voice, so soft it hardly touched the air of the chamber, made Elizabeth blink.

She crossed to the bed and sat down, taking Minuette's hands in her own, and waited in silence.

"Elizabeth . . . I'm in trouble."

Those first words were like the breaking of a dam. She poured out everything to Elizabeth, in a jumble of words and chronology that threatened to be unintelligible. But having had weeks to consider Dominic as Minuette's lover, Elizabeth was quick to grasp the fact of their marriage. If anything, it was the detail of the Catholic priest that surprised her most. Who would have thought Dominic would do something so heretical?

But if the use of a priest surprised Elizabeth, the revelation of Minuette negotiating with Rochford positively astonished her. "How very devious of you," she said with admiration. "And wise. You say that my uncle's preparations are complete?"

"Dominic is to meet with him tomorrow. For instructions and papers, I suppose."

"Carrie and Dominic's man—Harrington, is it?—have been informed?"

Colour had returned to Minuette's face the more she'd unburdened herself. "Yes. They will travel with us."

"You were really going to leave me without saying goodbye?" Elizabeth tried not to sound critical, but the hurt was real.

Minuette's breath caught, a prelude to tears. "Not for lack of love, Elizabeth. It seemed safer."

"Because you did not trust me to help?"

"Safer for you as well. William—" Minuette broke off, perhaps swallowing the urge to cry. "William will need you. I would not take that last relationship away from him."

For all her belief that she was not sentimental, Elizabeth had to force her voice to evenness. "Will there ever be a day when you are not looking out for us, Minuette?" She hugged her friend, hoping that Minuette would feel the same comfort that she had so often given to Elizabeth. "You are right, leaving England is the safest course for now. Let my uncle aid you, go to the Netherlands, and I shall do all in my power to soften William's anger and bring him to forgiveness. However long the breach takes to mend, I trust you and Dominic will be part of England's court for many years to come."

When Dominic arrived at Charterhouse on September 14, he noted new lines on George Boleyn's previously ageless face, sharply engraved around his mouth and eyes. These months of royal displeasure—as well, perhaps, as his wife's violent end—had marred the elegance of the king's uncle. But the power was still in full evidence, checked though it might be. Indeed, Rochford behaved precisely as though he were still sitting at the center of power in Whitehall rather than at his own private residence at Charterhouse.

Rochford raised a smooth and ironic eyebrow. "Am I to take it that, rather chivalrously, you are here in place of the Marquess of Somerset?"

The contemptuous reference to his wife made Dominic's temper rise. He'd spent half an hour with Minuette this morning, in which she'd told him of her confession to Elizabeth and, for what it was worth, the princess's blessing on their planned flight. Because they needed Rochford to ensure their safety, Dominic checked his tongue. A little. "You have the necessary papers?"

"So anxious to leave England?" Rochford shook his head. "I confess, I cannot grasp the hold the lady has over both you and William. All this trouble and torment for love of a mere woman."

"You sit where you do because of a man's love for a woman," Dominic retorted.

"Oh, I understand when such a love brings reward. But you are throwing away titles and lands and future."

Dominic did not expect George Boleyn to understand. Here was a man happy to spend his passion with his nephew's former mistress, so how could he grasp what Dominic felt? "Where are the promised papers?" he demanded.

"They will be in my possession tonight. Tomorrow afternoon, the king will join me here to dine privately. While we are thus engaged, I'll send a man of mine to meet you at the Greenwich docks with the necessary documents and information on your passage. Attempt to blend in by dressing plainly and travel with all you need. I take it you do not expect to return to England anytime soon?"

"You know your nephew as well as I do."

"Yes, I would not expect quick forgiveness." Rochford shrugged. "But I will do what I can to mitigate his anger. Your young lady did me a favor and, as she once noted, I am a man who pays his debts."

Rochford rose from behind the desk and offered his hand. Somewhat surprised, Dominic shook it.

"Farewell, Courtenay," Rochford said. "You are a man of honour, which is not always an easy thing in this world. I respect that. I should like to think we will meet again."

Dominic returned to Whitehall, painfully conscious of every sight and sound and person he passed. Tomorrow night he would set sail and might never again see England, and that knowledge was like a dagger placed, not to kill, but to wound. His entire adult life had been spent trying to reclaim his father's honour, wrapped in the very heart of English royal life. He had dreamed what it would be to walk away from all the bad things—the vicious politics and the personal jealousies, the lies and the betrayals, but now he counted the good things that would be lost as well. Men like Lord Burghley, who sought honestly to bring balance and peace to England; the joy of riding out under the banner of his family and king; being at the center of a world that attracted the talented and learned. Not to mention Elizabeth, who had been like a sister to him through all these years. He could not help but wonder what Elizabeth thought of him now that she knew the whole of his actions.

And, always and ever, William.

When Dominic reached Whitehall, he turned by instinct to William's presence chamber, where this afternoon the king was enthusing over some exotic gifts brought by an explorer, including a lively monkey that was wreaking havoc in the polished chamber.

The light and joy in William's eyes was an extra twist of the dagger. Keenly aware that he had less than a day remaining, Dominic looked past the man whom he had lately seen only as a rival and found anew the boy who had made of him a brother.

It was that boy Dominic was loath to leave, for William's enthusiasm today would not last. It would fade away, as it so often did these days, into brooding. Ever since the smallpox, William had been unstable in his moods and liable to overreact. Not that he hadn't been before, but the illness had stripped away the protections he'd once had. Now William was likely to take everything personally. And when Dominic very personally took the woman he loved out of his grasp, what would William have left?

When the other attendants and courtiers were dismissed, Dominic and William remained alone as they had so many times. The king paced the length of the chamber and Dominic leaned against the wall with a throat that was almost too tight to swallow as, for the last time, William asked his opinion.

"How long can I continue to keep Mary in the Tower before the Catholics mount more than a vocal protest?" William asked.

"The answer to that depends on whether you would prefer the Catholics to protest physically."

William shot him a keen glance. "If I can draw them into a confrontation I expect, all the better for us."

"True." Dominic shrugged. "How little do you trust Mary?"

"Little enough to suspect her of almost anything, but not so much that I will manufacture evidence. Mary will have to damn herself. I will not do it for her."

"Wise enough."

William grinned. "Why, Dom, was that a compliment? I don't believe you've ever paid me a compliment before."

"And that is a flaw, Your Majesty. I know I have been hard on you. I hardly know why myself. Except that I see your talents and gifts and know what you may accomplish for England. My lack of praise has only ever been about my own reticence and not a comment on your worth."

With creased brows that conveyed equal puzzlement and pleasure, William asked, "Why so generous now?"

Because soon enough I will never be able to say these things to you, and I am sorry for it, Dominic thought. He cleared his throat and said, "You have ever been a clever and learned prince and have shown Europe that you are a monarch to be reckoned with. I am proud that you are my king, and my friend."

William's unscarred cheek twitched once and Dominic knew he was moved. "If I am a good king," he replied, "it is due to my father and my mother and my uncle . . . and to you. There are very few living whose good opinion I care for. To know that you think well of me is an honour."

"I do think well of you."

"Even when I fall short of your ideals?" Behind William's light words was the memory of Yorkshire and Dominic's anger over the attempt on Renaud's life.

"We all fall short, Will. I have long forgiven you for any injury I may have—fairly or unfairly—laid to your charge. You owe me nothing."

"I'm glad of it," William said curtly. "For with France and Spain allied against us, I have need of men who trust me."

Dominic could not have continued speaking if his life depended on it. He nodded once in acknowledgment, then excused himself. "I know you have private plans tonight."

"Yes. But I'll see you tomorrow in the tiltyard. You haven't forgotten that we are set to spar?"

"I have not forgotten."

He would not sleep between now and then. One last night at court, one more sparring bout with Will . . . then he and Minuette would take to flight.

By the time Minuette appeared in his privy chamber for dinner, William's restless mood had swung from his earlier enjoyment to a more usual melancholy. Dominic had been so very solemn earlier—not that he was ever a beacon of cheer—and though William had been moved by Dominic's words of confidence and trust, he was also perversely struck by self-doubt. A condition only Dominic had ever been able to induce.

Every time he'd closed his eyes this last week, he had seen his aunt's face in the darkness. Jane Boleyn had never been a favorite of his—the duchess was not a woman to endear herself to children—but nevertheless she had been part of that inner circle of family that was now so perilously small. When Minuette entered the softly lit chamber, romantic with candles and flowers, William asked abruptly, "Do you remember the incident in the gardens at Blickling Hall?"

For one moment she seemed startled. Then remembered laughter lit her eyes. "Oh dear, we were far too mischievous for our own good. I remember distinctly how very angry Lady Rochford was at the beheading of her tulips."

"And I remember you saying most solemnly to my aunt, 'But when one is fighting a dragon, there are likely to be innocent casualties.' Right before my aunt repossessed our wooden swords."

"This has been a most difficult week for you. I wish I could make it easier." Beneath the laughter, understanding lurked in Minuette's voice. She sat next to him at the circular table filled with delicacies that held no appeal for William. All he wanted was the wine, and he'd had more than one cup already.

He took Minuette's hand, caressing her fingers as he studied her face. She'd looked so drawn since Hatfield, her brightness dimmed and uncertain. But her beauty was all the greater for it, especially the gold-green eyes that shone luminous in the candlelight.

"You make everything better, sweetling." But better didn't necessarily mean easy, just easier to live with. There was no avoiding the fact that Jane Boleyn had died at the hands of William's executioner. Though he did not regret the punishment, he did regret its necessity. If only his aunt had stayed out of his marital plans, then he would not be plagued by memories of her sculptured face and sharp tongue while imagining how she'd changed as prison broke her in body and spirit.

"I am told she made a good end," William said. "Left her blessing on me and England. Apologized for her offenses."

Minuette sat silent for long minutes while William brooded and caressed her hand with his fingertips. When she spoke, it was soft and far away, almost as though she were talking to herself. "I know what it is to be haunted by one's actions. I never told you . . ."

And now she faced him fully, her eyes alive but wary. "I've never told anyone this. Only Dominic knows, and that is because he was there. When Giles Howard died at Framlingham, it was not Dominic who killed him. It was me."

The words seemed to echo from every corner of the room, whispering from the swish of the curtains stirred by drafts and the pops and crackles of the fire. Finally, William asked, "Why didn't you tell me before?"

"I did not want to talk about it, and I did not want you to think less of me. A woman who could kill a man, even for her own protection?" Minuette shrugged. "It is not likely to make anyone think better of her."

"Sweetling—"

"Don't tell me it's all right," she said firmly. "I'm not asking for your comfort. I simply wanted you to know that I understand what it is to have taken what seems the only possible course of action and yet to regret it. For months after Framlingham, I would wake certain that my hands were still covered in blood. The dreams come infrequently now, but I do not think they will ever entirely pass. I have his death on my conscience, justified or not."

William did not know what to say, or even to feel. It was true, the thought of Minuette's hands covered in blood disturbed him.

Mostly because he wished he could have been the one to kill Giles Howard himself. At least he no longer need feel jealous that Dominic had avenged her rather than him. It seemed Minuette was capable of avenging herself.

But it was the phrase about her conscience that struck him most forcibly. Was that what troubled him so much? He had far more blood on his hands than Minuette ever could: from the tutor turned traitor of his childhood, Edward Aylmer, through Northumberland and now his own aunt. And what of the men who'd died in France or Scotland fighting his battles? William didn't believe he'd done wrong—but there was something in what Minuette said about waking from dreams.

He had a flash of memory, back to the day Aylmer had been executed. He and Minuette had retreated to the gardens at Hampton Court. Looking at her now, for the first time in months, he saw beneath the beautiful face of the woman he loved to the familiar face of his friend. Minuette alone had been able to speak to him about Aylmer, the only one who knew how to address the pain without letting it consume him. He had forgotten what it was like to let her be his friend, thinking of her only as a woman to bed at night and a queen by his side in the day.

But Minuette had ever been so much more than that.

A little hoarsely, he said, "I believe I did right, signing my aunt's execution order. She committed treason, after all. But sometimes, in the night—" He broke off, not sure how to say what he wanted.

"In the night, our fears loom large," Minuette finished softly.

"It wasn't always like this," William said. "Before last winter, before the . . ." He touched his scarred cheek, still superstitiously afraid of naming the illness that had almost killed him. "When I was so ill, I seemed to wander in a fever of black omens. England burning, my people destroying one another, my crown trampled into the mud. At times I could see a hand plucking it away from me, like my grandfather pulling Richard's crown out of the bushes at Bosworth. I have always had enemies. But those terrible nights when I did not know if I would emerge from my nightmares, I seemed to feel it more than ever before. Men hate me, Minuette. Men I know—have known my whole life—would kill me if they could. How am I to live each day feeling that hatred?"

"Not by drinking it away," Minuette answered, moving the wine away from him. "Drinking too much might buy you a few hours of forgetfulness, but it will not teach you how to rule."

"Then what will?"

"Your own conscience. The guidance of men who both love and respect you. Do not focus all your attention on your enemies, Will. For there are many, like Lord Burghley, who serve not for the sake of expediency but because they believe in you."

"And you." William touched her cheek with his fingertips. "You have always been my best and truest champion." As he traced the line of her cheek, the sensation went beyond pleasure to something both more familiar and more intimate.

She must have seen the many shades of emotions in his face, for her eyes filled with tears. "Were it in my power, Will, I would give you all the confidence and courage and wisdom you could ever need."

"You give me all of that." He hesitated. "I do hope that I give you something in return."

A tear slid down her cheek and William brushed it away with his thumb. She reached up and clasped her hand over his, twining them together as she moved it to her lap. "The King of England thinks he has nothing to offer?" she said, aiming for lightness and only just falling short.

But he would not be swept aside. "Another woman might love me for my position, and from another woman I might be satisfied with so much. But not from you."

She closed her eyes and he contented himself watching the sweep of her lashes, so much darker than her hair, against her skin. When she opened her eyes and spoke, her voice, which he knew as well as anyone's, seemed to thrum beneath his skin.

"I love you as I love my own soul, Will, for we are so nearly the same. We act before we think, we risk all for our hearts, and we drive everyone around us mad with our impulses. Don't ever think that it is your position I covet, for I would love you if you had nothing to your name but your own self."

She put her hands on his cheeks and looked deep into his eyes. "Tell me you believe me."

William let his head drop forward, until their foreheads were touching. He was suddenly shy but there was something he wanted, so badly that he could taste it. Something he'd never wanted from anyone before.

"Will you stay with me tonight?" he whispered, head still against hers so he couldn't see her reaction. "Not like that. I don't mean . . . well, what you might think I mean. But you're right that the only way I've slept at all these last months is drinking more than is wise. And then my sleep is restless and broken by dreams. I am so tired, Minuette. Will you stay long enough to see me to sleep?"

He sounded like a child, scared of the dark and the shadows. She must think him laughable. And it would open her to the worst of rumours. Gossips would assume that she had finally given in, that they had anticipated their wedding night as his father had with Anne Boleyn. But William was suddenly, absolutely certain that if she would just stay by him for a few hours, he would sleep better than he had since the smallpox.

He only realized she was crying when she withdrew her hands and moved back. Her cheeks shone wet and she looked unbearably sad, but her voice was steady. "I will stay."

They spoke very little after that. Minuette ate an apple and, to please her, William ignored the wine and had some bread and stewed pheasant. When the food had been cleared, his attendants knew to withdraw and leave him be unless summoned.

Looking doubtfully at Minuette's highly decorated gown, William said, "I'm not trying to ... that is ... I don't suppose you're meant to lie down in such a dress."

Her laughter seemed nearly tears, but she said practically, "I'll take off the gown, for I have quite enough layers on beneath for modesty's sake."

But there was nothing in the least modest about watching Minuette as she unlaced the tight sides of the heavy blue velvet and drew it off. William didn't dare move, for fear that if he helped her, then he wouldn't be able to stop until he had stripped her completely. She was so unbearably lovely in a kirtle the colour of the summer sky, its simplicity a more stunning setting for her golden beauty than any court gown had ever been. The linen sleeves of her smock showed the length and delicate bones of her arms, and the squared-off line of the kirtle highlighted her collarbone and the perfect sweep of her neck. And, yes, her breasts.

Her hair was braided and coiled in an intricate pattern, too formal for this night. "May I?" he asked, his hands moving to the first of the pins, and when she nodded, William gave himself over to the sensory pleasure of unloosing that glorious hair, the colour and weight of darkened honey. When it finally hung loose halfway down her back, he buried his hands in the waves and closed his eyes against dizziness.

It was Minuette who moved into a kiss, soft and warm beneath his mouth, and William knew—he *knew*—that if he pressed for more, she would offer it willingly. She would offer all of herself tonight, as she always had.

He could wait.

Not that he deprived himself the luxury of kissing her for a while, more intoxicated by her scent and taste than he'd ever been by wine. But at last he stepped back and whispered, "I made you a promise. I intend to keep it."

He stripped off his doublet and jerkin, but made himself stop at the shirt. If he felt too much of her against his bare skin, this night would have a different ending than he'd promised. There was something melancholy and yet peaceful in the way Minuette curled up against him on the bed, the skirts of her kirtle and petticoat crushed aside so she could lie nestled in the crook of his arm.

William had fallen asleep next to women before, but never had he felt so vulnerable, his arm curved around Minuette, aware of each rise and fall of his chest and her golden head moving with it. At the last minute he'd been afraid that, this close to her, desire would eat away at him and steal any chance of sleep. But his first instinct had been right. He fell asleep much faster than he'd dared hope.

Hours later he was dimly aware of her moving carefully away, but he let himself drift back into the first pleasant dreams he'd had in a year: dreams of the sons he and Minuette would have together. And a daughter, too, as merry and golden as her mother.

Somewhere in that dream he heard Minuette whisper: *I have ever loved you, William. Remember that.*

CHAPTER FOURTEEN

15 September 1556
Whitehall Palace

After returning to my own chamber in the early hours of the morning, head held high against the sidelong glances of William's attendants, I spent a long time upon my knees in prayer. Occasionally I even slipped into heretical Latin in my head, for I have always found peace in ritual.

God alone knows how near I came to betraying my marriage vows last night. If William had pressed . . . but he did not.

Something broke in me last night. Something that will never be mended.

When Minuette finished writing, she returned the diary to her jewelry casket—empty now of all except her mother's rosary and Dominic's sapphire necklace—and gave it into Carrie's keeping to pack. She had told Carrie at Hatfield of what was ahead of them and she knew her maid had all in order ready to leave England.

As Carrie dressed her for this last morning at court, Minuette wondered how her friend felt about abandoning her home and the graves of her husband and children back at Wynfield Mote. Minuette herself could hardly bear the thought of leaving her steward and housekeeper and tenants without word and she had wept over Fidelis, knowing there was no simple way to bring the wolfhound overseas with them. How long before the faithful dog forgot her entirely?

But if Carrie felt any natural resentment, she would never betray it. "Thank you," Minuette said impulsively, as the maid finished adjusting the leaf-green sleeves and damask bodice of her gown. "For everything."

Only for a second did Carrie let affection and concern show in her brown eyes. Then she said briskly, "Off with you. The princess will be waiting."

Minuette met Elizabeth in her chambers and they walked together through the maze that was Whitehall Palace toward the tiltyard. They said little. When the sparring was finished, William would go to Charterhouse to see Lord Rochford and then planned to spend the afternoon with his treasurer before dining with various guild leaders from the City. By the time dinner was completed, Minuette and Dominic would be aboard a ship bound for Europe.

The weather should do nicely, Minuette thought, desperate to keep to banal topics even in her head. The heat of August had broken in a series of violent storms in early September, and the last four days had bestowed blue skies and brisk winds that would see a sailing ship quickly on its way.

The women reached one of the interior courtyards and Minuette's attention caught at the sight of two stone-faced yeomen flanking the entrance. She just had time to wonder what they were meant to be guarding against when she heard raised voices from the courtyard beyond.

"You were released on condition that you stay away from court. Go to Cumbria where I sent you, Eleanor, or I shall see you back in the Tower." It was William, warning but not yet angry.

"Are you certain you want me so far away? I had thought perhaps we might renegotiate our ... understanding." In the pause, Minuette could imagine Eleanor drawing near to William, perhaps trailing her hand along his arm.

Elizabeth tugged once on Minuette's sleeve to move her along, but she stayed rooted to the spot. The guards ignored them, possibly because their orders were unclear as to the king's sister and future wife.

With a crispness that betokened increasing impatience, William said, "I am sorry to disappoint you, but there is no understanding. And you are not in a position to negotiate with me."

"Am I not? I know about Hatfield."

Minuette felt her heart stutter and she knew clearly in that moment what was about to happen. How could she have been such a fool as to believe Eleanor had bargained fairly with her? Eleanor would say or do anything in order to get back into the king's graces. What was it she'd said all those months ago in the Tower?

If you want to know anything, ask the women. Rochford's intelligence networks have nothing on servants and women.

Eleanor's voice dropped to a purr. "I will give you a son next time. I know how you long for that."

"My son will be royal and his mother pure." The whipcrack of temper in the king's voice hung heavy with threat.

"Oh, William," Eleanor said sadly. "Do you imagine you're deceiving anyone? How long has she shared your bed—six months, a year? You want her pregnant so you can force the marriage through your council. Your precious Minuette is no purer than I am. I at least had a husband's name when I bore your child. And you should not forget that—I *bore* your child, alive and healthy. Minuette could not even keep the child you got her with!"

Minuette's ears roared like waves breaking on a beach, and she might have fallen if not for Elizabeth's quick grasp of her arm. She heard her friend's intake of breath and knew they were thinking the same thing: *How had Eleanor found out?*

William spoke in the cold, clear voice of royal rage. "If you were not a woman, I would strike you for that."

"Can it be . . ." Eleanor paused, and in her next words Minuette heard comprehension dawn. "Did you not know? Did she really not tell you? Oh, William, you are too trusting! Go to Hatfield and ask. There's a woman in the village whose sister washed a great deal of bloody linen on the night your precious betrothed fell ill. She was never injured in a fall. Your perfect Minuette lost your child that night."

Even in this ultimate moment of disaster, Minuette was bitterly amused at how thoroughly Eleanor had missed the point. She had meant only to use the miscarriage to bargain with William, to ensure that she might at least share the king with Minuette, but instead Eleanor had just razed her enemy into the dust. And she didn't even know it.

Shaking off Elizabeth, Minuette stepped past the guards and into the courtyard that was half sunlight, half shadow. William had his back to her, his hands on Eleanor's shoulders as though he'd been shaking her. Eleanor's eyes widened when she saw Minuette, and she gave a spiteful smile that must have alerted William. He turned, still holding tight to Eleanor.

Minuette heard Elizabeth whispering low words, urging her to come away and leave them be, and knew her friend was really begging her to keep silent or else to face down this accusation with a scorn that William would believe. Escape was so close—all she needed was a few hours and she and Dominic would be safely out of reach. William looked at Eleanor with loathing, no doubt prepared to believe that his mistress was once again tormenting Minuette for her own purposes. Minuette knew she could get away with a denial. And what, in the end, was one more lie?

She stared at William's furious, familiar face, and knew it was one lie she could not tell.

Ignoring Elizabeth, Minuette stepped forward, near enough to William to see the dark of his eyes, wide and black with anger. She spoke clearly, so that there might be no misunderstanding.

"It is true."

William's vision dimmed, until all he could see was Minuette's steady face. As her words rang in his head, Eleanor twisted in his grasp and he dropped his hands.

"Get out, Eleanor," he rasped.

His mistress went without comment. William could not tear his eyes away from Minuette. He knew every line and shade of her face and he could not fathom how she could look so unchanged, as though the world had not just tilted off balance with three simple words. *It is true.*

He'd never had such a hard time finding his voice. "I don't . . . Minuette?"

"It is true, William. I was not injured."

"You . . . were with child?" He didn't even know his own voice, he sounded to himself like a stranger. *How?* he nearly demanded, but that was stupid, he knew how. What he meant was *who,* and *why.* She had been in his arms just last night, half dressed and pliant, and he had restrained himself and left her untouched. Who had touched her if not him?

But Minuette had more than one secret. "I am married. I have been married these ten months."

"Married?" With part of his mind, William noted Elizabeth's lack of reaction as she hovered near Minuette and realized his sister had already known. He stored that knowledge away for future handling.

Not a lover, but a husband. So much worse, to know that Minuette hadn't given herself lightly to some ambitious lord who'd wanted only her body; no, she had bound herself both body and soul. He struggled to grasp the meaning of it, but he kept seeing her with that glorious hair loose, eyes closed and shoulders bare, breathing ever quicker beneath a man who . . .

Wasn't him. "Who?" he ground out between clenched teeth.

But there could only ever be one *who*. William knew it even as he asked the question.

He read the answer in Minuette's pitying eyes and turned his back before she could say it aloud and complete his destruction. This was . . . how could . . . what was he supposed to do now? Everything he was, everything he trusted, wrenched away in a dozen words.

He didn't know she'd moved until he felt her hand on his arm. "I am so sorry, Will."

In one swift movement he turned and struck her with the back of his hand. The ruby ring he wore caught her across the cheekbone and raised an ugly welt. She made no sound despite the tears in her eyes, just dropped her hand and waited for him to hit her again.

"Don't call me that," he spat out, hating the unsteadiness of his voice.

They stared at each other for a long moment, her hazel eyes steady as ever, as William let the swirls of hurt and confusion settle into clarity. At last he lowered his arm, which had indeed been raised for a second blow. "Guards!"

The two yeomen stepped into the courtyard and William gave crisp orders. "Escort Lady Somerset to her chamber. She is unwell. Ensure that she is not disturbed."

She went without protest. When they had gone, Elizabeth said desperately, "William, don't let your anger get the better of you. Think before you act."

"I am thinking. I am thinking that I'm scheduled to meet Dominic in the tiltyard in ten minutes. I am thinking that today we will not fight with wooden swords. I am thinking that you had best go straight to the gallery to watch. Don't say a word to anyone."

He turned on her ferociously. "I am also thinking that you were keeping secrets from me, sister. I shall deal with you in due course. Do I make myself clear?"

"Perfectly clear, Your Majesty."

Dominic stood at the south end of the famous Whitehall tiltyard, searching the gallery for Minuette. He saw Elizabeth seated in the front row, looking remote and solitary despite the many surrounding her. Perhaps Minuette was resting. Or perhaps she simply could not face anyone in these last hours.

Harrington came from behind and pulled him into the shadows cast by the viewing stands. "Carrie passed me a message from Mistress Wyatt." Dropping his voice to a whisper, the big man added, "She bids you remember that, next time you play chess, you have promised her the white queen."

The message was so nonsensical that Dominic could only stare. Chess? They hadn't played chess in months. And when had Minuette ever cared what colour she played?

Colour.

White.

White is for warning.

Before Dominic could think what to say or do, William approached from beneath the stands. He wore a linen shirt and dark blue doublet of unusual plainness suitable for sparring. The padded leather jerkin which would protect his chest was still only partly laced. Dominic's attire was a near-perfect match to the king's, differing only in the green of his doublet, and he realized that the tiltyard was the one place he had ever felt himself William's equal.

The king did not look at Dominic as he spoke, turning a short dagger restlessly over and over in his hands. "We've quite an assembly to watch us today. What do you say to giving them a show? Forget wood—let's use steel."

"Rebated?" Dominic asked without really paying attention, for he was trying to decipher Minuette's vague warning.

There was a heartbeat's pause before William laughed. "Naturally. I wouldn't want to harm you." The king's eyes turned to him then like a hawk's, fixed and unblinking. "And I can only presume you would not wish to run me through. At least not in front of witnesses."

He knows.

Dominic couldn't move, couldn't breathe. What had William done with Minuette?

William strode away, calling back as he went. "I'll send the arms master with a sword."

Dominic turned on Harrington. "Where is she?"

"In her chambers, with a guard posted outside. Carrie brought me the message."

"What happened?"

"I don't know."

"Find out."

Harrington vanished as Dominic watched William swinging a heavy, broad-bladed sword in the middle of the yard. Even blunt-edged for training, it looked deadly. It kept catching the sun, deflecting the light into Dominic's eyes.

Within a minute Dominic held a similar sword and he tested it, weighing the balance and fitting his hand to the best position. He slowed his breathing and tried to focus on the coming bout. William looked in no mood to be gentle.

The thought of Minuette under guard didn't make Dominic feel especially gentle himself.

Both securely laced into training gear, the two men met in the middle of the tiltyard and saluted each other. Dominic was taken aback by the ferocity of William's initial lunge and for a moment he thought the king had overreached in his anger. The shock of that first blow rang through Dominic's sword and up his arms, but he knew what he was about. He instantly gauged the strength of William's thrust and met the force with corresponding weakness. He allowed William's sword to trap his and push it down, but Dominic was already moving by then, charging through so that he could bring his sword up and at William's side from an unexpected direction. Only a quick sidestep on the king's part saved him from a hit, and the crowd roared in appreciation.

After that first emotional attack, William got control of himself and set about moving with skill and precision. He used his anger well, as Dominic had taught him, letting it fuel him without the loss of control that would lead to mistakes. Dominic found himself evaluating William as he had in the training exercises of their youth. Economical in his grace, nothing showy or flowery, just sharp, neat movements and disciplined footwork. And always those blue eyes, gauging and judging and storing up offenses to avenge. But Dominic was confident in his own skills and greater experience, hampered only by the fact that he didn't particularly want to injure his opponent.

William had no such scruples. He landed several hits on Dominic's chest and side, including a long slashing cut below his rib cage that would have finished him if the sword had been sharp. As it was, Dominic knew he'd have a wicked bruise in the morning.

Think, he commanded himself. He'd taught William everything he knew—what would the king try to win this? Even as he thought, Dominic saw William plant his feet, preparatory to kicking upward in a move borrowed from Dominic's service in Wales. Dominic dropped his sword hand behind him in an instant, out of reach. But William hadn't been aiming for his sword. The kick landed hard in the center of Dominic's stomach and he ended on his knees, doubled over and gasping for breath.

Where he realized his immediate problem was not lack of air.

The silver blade at his throat was perfectly steady, the edge of the dagger close enough that Dominic could feel it as he breathed out. He raised his eyes to William's, no longer opaque but blazing in fury, and thought, *He might do it.*

Several women in the crowd cried out, but all settled swiftly into a smothering silence. And still Dominic stared at William. At last, very softly, so only the two of them could hear, Dominic said, "That's cheating."

"That's winning." William moved the dagger until it rested flat and cold against Dominic's cheek. "Do the unexpected. Your advice, was it not? Was that before or after you made her a *whore*?"

Like flint to tinder, fury surged through Dominic. He forgot the crowds, forgot his own doubt and guilt, forgot that William had some right to feel betrayed. To hell with fairness.

Dominic allowed his eyes to drop, until he was staring at William's boots. The dagger against his cheek moved slightly, not to draw blood, but in a slight relaxation of tension. When the dagger moved, so did Dominic, propelling himself off his heels, his head meeting William's stomach with satisfying force.

William was still wheezing for breath by the time Dominic was on his feet. The dagger was on the ground, but William held tight to his sword. The look blazing from the king's eyes was murderous. Dominic could have moved then and dealt him serious harm before he'd recovered, but he wanted the satisfaction of beating his rival fairly.

This time William unloosed his ferocity entirely—and this time Dominic met it in kind. The force of each blow vibrated clear to his shoulders, but Dominic kept moving, matching cut for cut and thrust for thrust. Without the distractions of conscience, Dominic's experience and strength came to the fore. William could not match his battlefield instincts. Dominic simply moved, reading a dozen different signals at once so that he always knew from the balance of William's feet or the shift of a shoulder from where the next blow was coming. Dominic was a master of countercutting: his defensive moves were also offensive, turning every thrust to his own advantage. William could not hope to match him.

The swell and roar of the watching crowd could have been the clamour of a battlefield. Dominic knew there must be shock and doubt among some of those watching, but more of them simply reveled in this sudden eruption of violence between the king and his closest friend.

There came a moment when William stepped out of reach and Dominic had a brief hope that it was over. But before he could even finish the thought, he saw that the king had given himself just enough room to lunge. Dominic moved at the same instant. This time it wasn't swords that met but flesh, Dominic's left hand holding off William's sword while his own right hand was caught in the king's vicious grasp. Dominic felt the pulse of hate and anger and pain flowing through William and knew that this was what his friend wanted, that nothing else would do but that he tear at Dominic with his bare hands.

Locked hand-to-hand and eye-to-eye, time slowed and Dominic saw a friendship's memories between one painful breath and the next: his early days of training with William, and his first flash of respect for an eight-year-old prince who refused to be coddled;

a ten-year-old's solemn face as he gripped the orb and scepter and took upon himself the weight of a realm; a changeable sixteen-year-old, quick to take offense and quicker to apologize.

A friend who had, above all else, valued Dominic for his uncomfortable honesty.

Dominic dropped his arms so abruptly that William stumbled forward. They released their desperate hold on each other, William's breath rasping harshly and Dominic beginning to be aware of numerous aches and pains that the heat of the fight had masked.

He wasn't certain what he expected. The possibilities flew through his mind: arrested or killed where he stood. He had time for one wild moment of regret when a sudden force and sound rocked the air. Dominic stumbled, ears ringing, at the unmistakable release of black powder.

In seconds William was surrounded by guards. There was another explosion and another and a breathless guard came running into the tiltyard.

"What's happening?" the king shouted at the newcomer.

The stricken guard seemed unsure of delivering his message so publicly.

"What?" William demanded, in a voice that brooked no delay.

"Explosions between here and the Tower. Perhaps an attempt to free the Lady Mary—"

"Get my horse and half-armor," William shouted, and several of his guards broke into protest. "Now!"

"Your Majesty, this could be an attempt on your life—"

"Then get me a damned *unrebated* sword and arm yourselves. We're riding to the Tower!"

This was fear as much as fury, Dominic knew. Always William preferred to spring into action when uncertainty arose. That didn't make it the wrong move.

Even now, with all in ashes around him, Dominic's first instinct was to stand with William. He'd be needed for this. He took one step before he remembered that, needed or not, he wouldn't be at William's side. Not today. Perhaps not ever again.

Across the length of the tiltyard William shot him an unreadable glance. Dominic waited for the king to summon guards, to place him under arrest as surely he'd already placed Minuette.

William opened his mouth, then shut it and strode away.

The spectators broke into a swirl of noise, women's panicked voices rising and men rushing to arm themselves and join the king while Dominic stood frozen in the middle of the yard. He didn't even blink until Harrington's urgent voice sounded once more in his ear. "I'd get out of here if I were you."

"Where is she?" Dominic demanded, following Harrington into a secluded spot beneath the stands, unlacing the bulky leather training jerkin as they went.

"Still in her chambers. No one's saying much. All Carrie knows is that she was escorted back under guard. I don't think she's been arrested, but I'd say it's a safe bet your secret is known."

"Did Carrie say . . . Is Minuette all right?"

"She's fine. Except . . ."

"What?"

"According to Carrie, she had the mark of a man's hand across her face."

Everything around him went red. "He hit her."

The voice that replied was cool, composed—and feminine. "He slapped her," Elizabeth corrected, stepping forward from the gallery.

Dominic clenched his hands and tried to match her tone. "What happened?"

"Eleanor Percy happened. We should have guessed that if anyone could unearth your darkest secrets, it would be her, though clearly she did not know the whole of what she'd uncovered. And rather than lie her way out of the matter, Minuette told William the truth—all of it. The marriage, the child . . . how could she have been so stupid?"

"Stay out of this, Elizabeth."

She went on as if he hadn't spoken at all. "William just rode out with a dozen lords and a regiment of guards. Almost, I might think you responsible for staging this attack on the Tower. It's certainly convenient, for it seems William has neglected to leave any orders as to your person. I should take care to be gone before he returns."

"I won't run."

"You were set to run in just a few hours. Go to my uncle and get the papers you need now." Elizabeth's composure was not as complete as he'd thought. Her voice thinned around the edges as she snapped, "This isn't a game or test of honour. You have devastated him. I do not wish to see my brother injure you. Better to remove yourself and leave him to calm down in his own time."

"I'm not leaving Minuette."

"He will not harm her." She raised her hand as he opened his mouth to protest. "Yes, he struck her this morning, but that was in the heat of anger. It won't happen again."

Dominic gave each word equal weight. "I'm not going anywhere without my wife."

Even in the midst of his desperation, Dominic felt a moment's thrill at that. *My wife.* It was the first time he'd ever called her that aloud.

Elizabeth's lips tightened. "Let me be plain, Dominic. You are in the wrong. As far as I'm concerned, this catastrophe rests on your head. It's only because I know you so well—both of you—that I can believe it was not ill-intended. It was folly, but not malice." She sighed, and her face crumpled slightly. "What do you need?"

He didn't dare answer for a moment, afraid that he'd misunderstood. But she continued to regard him gravely. Dominic drew a deep breath. "Can you get Minuette away from the guards and out of the palace?"

It was an eternity before she answered. "Yes."

"Do it." He calculated quickly. "An hour and a half, bring her to the outer walls near Westminster Abbey. It would be best that she dress for riding, just in case. I'll go to Rochford and hope we can move things up a little."

Dominic didn't even risk going back to his room, sending Harrington to retrieve the few personal items already packed and then to fetch horses, including Dominic's own favored gray stallion, Daybreak, and the white jennet William had given Minuette on her seventeenth birthday. Then he headed northeast on foot to George Boleyn's elaborate home at Charterhouse. Only when he'd cleared the last of Whitehall's warren of entrances and gates did he begin to breathe easy. He'd kept expecting a guard to come from behind and detain him.

He presented himself at Charterhouse's outer entrance to the first of Rochford's men, all with the distinctive serpent badges and something of the same air of detached intelligence as their master. For the first time in his life Dominic was grateful for his position, for it enabled him to pass quickly through the several layers of protection around the former Lord Chancellor. Only when he came face-to-face with Rochford's secretary did he stutter to a halt.

"I'm sorry, Lord Exeter, but Lord Rochford is closeted with representatives of the Spanish guilds. They are trying to salvage economic ties in the wake of Spain's upcoming talks with France."

"As he's speaking to the Spanish, then he'll definitely want to know that the Tower is currently under attack and the king has ridden out to engage. Did you not hear the explosions?"

"I was instructed not to disturb the gentlemen. You know how little His Grace likes being disregarded."

"I am sure he would be even less pleased to discover that his nephew may be under personal threat and you made no move to inform him." Dominic pushed his way past the man, using his size and leashed panic to intimidate. "Let his wrath be on my head." For tomorrow I'll be out of reach, he thought. And anyway, Rochford would have to line up behind Will at this point if he wants my head.

The secretary let him pass, but stayed prudently out of sight of the door to Rochford's study. Dominic flung it open, prepared to apologize brusquely and get the Spanish representatives out of the room as quickly and rudely as possible.

But the study was empty. Dominic stopped short, instinct taking over as his eyes roamed about the chamber. There were two chairs in front of Rochford's desk, shoved casually aside as though they had just been vacated. Rochford's high-backed, heavily carved seat was pushed roughly parallel to the desk. Where had everyone gone?

Even as the question went through his head, Dominic had his answer—or, more precisely, two answers. The first was provided by the French windows that gave onto a balcony fronting a garden with a low wall. It would be a simple matter to depart this chamber without alerting the secretary or guards and climb over the wall into the city streets. There would usually be men in that garden, but clearly Rochford had required absolute privacy for this meeting.

The second answer was more blunt, and awful—not everyone in this chamber had gone. Perhaps he could smell the blood or perhaps the last moment of violence lingered in the air, pressing against his skin, but Dominic knew what he would find even before he crossed the room in long strides and shoved Rochford's chair out of the way.

George Boleyn lay on his side, the dagger handle protruding

from beneath his ribs where a very careful and skilled assassin had plunged it into his heart. Dominic squatted on his haunches and touched his finger to the blood. Still warm. He shut his eyes and swore long and vividly, though well under his breath so as not to alert the secretary hovering out of sight beyond the door. He could not afford to get caught up in this. There wasn't time.

Swiftly, he checked each document case stacked on Rochford's desk, hoping against hope to find the papers prepared for him and Minuette. He found nothing in his first sweep and knew he couldn't risk searching any longer. Probably the papers were already gone: given into the hands of some nameless, faceless man who was meant to meet them in Greenwich later. They would never make it—Greenwich was east of the Tower of London where the king and his soldiers were now swarming against whatever threat had presented. The east was closed to them now.

Even as Dominic's thoughts focused on their immediately precarious situation, considering and discarding options, another part of his mind assessed the larger issue. An explosion—just the first one—had been set off close to Whitehall. More had been set nearer the Tower along with, apparently, enough armed men to make it seem a rescue attempt was under way. But what if the true target had been Rochford? Could the explosions have been merely a feint, to distract attention away from George Boleyn's murder while his killers escaped?

If it were a week earlier, or even just a day, Dominic would have called Rochford's secretary in and grilled him about the men. He would have sent guards to scour the streets at once, tracking down the assassins.

But it was now, this hour, and if he didn't move fast he and Minuette both would join Mary Tudor in the Tower. They needed to take flight—without Rochford's preparations to aid them.

Although much thought had passed since he'd entered Rochford's study, no more than four minutes had elapsed. Dominic took to the French windows as the last visitors had and spared one glance back for his former guardian.

"What's William going to do without you?" he asked softly into the air, then scaled the wall as the assassins had done before him and lost himself in the London streets.

Harrington met him outside Whitehall's precincts with the horses that would now be their salvation. It couldn't be a good idea for Minuette to ride so soon and for so long after losing the baby, but there was no choice. The women appeared within minutes. His eyes went straight to Minuette, who looked ashen, but she smiled briefly. He took in the welt on her cheek where William had struck her and the guilt that kept threatening to swamp him vanished in icy rage.

Dominic stood ready to help her mount, but she hesitated and looked instead at Elizabeth, solemn and silent. "I—"

"Don't say anything," Elizabeth commanded. "Just go."

After helping Minuette onto Winterfall, Dominic mounted Daybreak and broke the news to Elizabeth. "Find Lord Burghley and your man, Walsingham. Lord Rochford has been assassinated. You need to take control at Charterhouse before the news spreads."

Elizabeth paled, then flushed. "My uncle is dead?"

He'd forced himself to wait until they were mounted to tell her, so that Minuette could not be moved to compassion and delay their parting. He jerked his head at Harrington to lead the way out and said, "I'm sorry."

Did Elizabeth watch them ride away? Dominic did not turn back to see. But he guessed that, being herself, she had not waited but gone straight to her duty.

God help England now.

CHAPTER FIFTEEN

19 September 1556
Wynfield Mote

We rode in at dusk last night. I nearly fell off my horse, so weakened was I by the pace we were forced to keep. Fortunately there has been no return of the bleeding, but my body remembers too well that it is only eight weeks since I lost the child. Carrie has put me to bed and ordered everyone—including Dominic—to leave us be.

I did not want to come here. I thought we would head for Tiverton, where Dominic has men at his command. But I could not ride that far and Dominic is not prepared to take up arms. I do not fault him for that, but I am burdened at the thought of the danger we have brought with us to my quiet home.

The only moment of pure pleasure was when Fidelis launched himself at me before I'd even dismounted. Fortunately, Winterfall is well acquainted with the hound or my horse might have shied at the enormous shaggy bulk running full speed toward her. Dominic tried to keep Fidelis off me, but if my husband cannot wrap me safe in his arms through the night, then the faithful dog he gifted me will do. For now.

30 September 1556
Wynfield Mote

I have been up and about for five days. I cannot remember ever being so unhappy at Wynfield. Perhaps it is only our own rebellion poisoning the walls.

For that is what we are, is it not? Rebels and traitors. Every waking moment, part of me is attuned to each sound and vibration, waiting to hear the drumming of hooves as armed men are sent to retrieve us. It is unnerving, the waiting. Never have I been so cut off from the court, for no one dares write to us. It is as though Dominic and I are utterly adrift, not knowing what is coming and hardly knowing how we got here in the first place.

Dominic courteously leaves me to deal with my own household, and I have assured Asherton that I have no intention of arming my tenants and setting the king's armies at defiance. If it comes to that . . .

It will come to that. But I will not let my people pay for my own sins.

20 October 1556
Wynfield Mote

We have had our first communiqué from the outside world. Not surprisingly, it came from the Duke of Norfolk. It appears he has retreated to the North after his failed attempt to free Lady Mary from the Tower. Of course we knew of Rochford's assassination, but Norfolk did not know that and so he referred to it cautiously, no doubt wary of his words being intercepted. There can be little doubt that he and/or the Spanish were behind the murder. Though Norfolk writes warily, he also writes as though he takes for granted that Dominic is on his side. Why would he not? We have fled the king as Norfolk has. Surely all sides are expecting Dominic to join the Catholics in armed rebellion.

I do not know what Dominic will do. I dare not ask him.

4 November 1556
Wynfield Mote

Today I received a letter from Elizabeth. I could hardly believe my good fortune—she had her intelligencer, Walsingham, find some way to deliver it without betrayal. It had been written twelve days ago, which shows the lengths Walsingham went to for misdirection. Naturally, she did not waste time in regrets or sentiment, but gave us what she knew we would most crave: information.

The inquiry into Rochford's assassination has been relentless. Thirteen men, eleven of them Spanish, have been arrested and interrogated. The two remaining men were English Catholics and have also been tortured for not only their confessions, but the names of other conspirators. As Elizabeth wrote: "It surprises no one that Norfolk has been named, seeing as he so precipitously fled London in the aftermath. But another name is desperately unsettling. Under torture, half of the men have named Mary as the head of the conspiracy to kill my uncle. What William will do with this knowledge is anyone's guess."

When Dominic read it, he reminded me that men under duress of torture will say whatever their interrogators want to hear. I'm not sure which I would rather believe—that Lady Mary, a woman I know personally, openly ordered the assassination of Lord Rochford, or that the government (meaning William) is determined to believe it of her.

Either way, it cannot lead to a good end.

12 November 1556
Wynfield Mote

I stare at my diary and feel myself the most awful coward. Anyone reading these pages would think me indifferent to the consequences of my actions. But the truth is too near to write.

What do I say? That I live torn between what I have lost and what may never be gained? I don't know what I thought would happen when Dominic and I fled. But this is not it.

Dominic brought me a gift of fabric today in honour of our wedding anniversary. Having left almost all my clothing behind when we fled, it is rather more a necessity than a pleasure. His expression was distant when he wished me a happy day and I cannot help feeling that he wishes he had never behaved so recklessly a year ago. Between the wife and the king, I believe he would rather have the king.

I do not mean to sound bitter. Mostly, I feel sorry for these two men I have injured in a manner that can never be repaired. I have spent this month looking back and wondering where I went wrong. At what point could pain have been avoided? That night at Hever, perhaps, if I had not gone to William to offer comfort. If he had not reached for me in his grief for his mother, he might never have thought himself in love with me. Or perhaps when Jonathan Percy proposed—what if I had said yes and married him before he left for France? Dominic would have mourned the loss of me, or his idea of me, for a time and then swiftly forgotten.

But now William is facing a rebellion without the one counselor he most needs and Dominic has become the thing he most fears: traitor. We pretend that all is well, we behave impeccably before the servants, but when night falls the pretense dies. I want him and I am glad of him, but all the while I feel William poised between us, like a sword laid between two bodies to ensure chastity.

4 December 1556
Wynfield Mote

Winter has begun in earnest and still we are left unmolested.
What is William waiting for?

Happy Christmas, Will.

She was murmuring in his ear, he could feel her breath, teasing and arousing, igniting a storm in his blood. In a moment he would turn and pull her close, but for this moment he let the liquid flame of her nearness flow through him. A Christmas wedding, a long-anticipated wedding night ...

William's eyes snapped open and Minuette vanished into the ether from which she'd come. He breathed in the frigid air and looked unmoved on the thirteen heads protruding from spikes above him on Tower Bridge. The thirteen men arrested, hung from gauntlets and put to the rack, and at last executed for the treasonable murder of George Boleyn, Duke of Rochford.

Theirs were not the only heads: older ones, mostly dating to late September, relentlessly rotted above as well. Those were the men from the summer's Norwich rebellion, including William's own recalcitrant Bishop Thirlby. The bishop had defied the king in his trial and thrown himself on the mercy of salvation found in the Roman Catholic Church. "For God knows I strove for peace in this realm, but not at the expense of my own soul," Thirlby had declaimed from the scaffold.

After a long, steady survey, William turned his horse and headed east to Greenwich where, as traditional, he kept his Christmas court. He went slowly, daring his subjects to take his measure— firm, resolved, and implacable. Let them see that there was no profit in treason. He was very aware of the Tower looming over all and of Mary, locked behind its walls awaiting her own punishment. She was no longer in the comfort of the queen's apartments but in a more spartan cell in Bloody Tower.

He spent the remainder of Christmas day in subdued celebration. Elizabeth was present, with Robert Dudley and several dozen others whom William did not so much as speak to. The hall felt at once too crowded and too empty.

Every chamber was too empty without Minuette.

The guests veered between hilarity and anxious watchfulness. He caught the darting glances, sliding away before anyone risked meeting his eyes, and felt a dark pleasure that he had them so unsettled. No doubt they were wondering what he would do next, and on whom his vengeance would fall. All of England and even Europe had been wondering that for months.

Dominic and Minuette were at Wynfield Mote, and there had been much speculation at court about Dominic's choice. If he meant to defy the king, Wynfield offered no protection. Tiverton Castle was another matter. In his own castle, on his family lands, surrounded by men who would die for him merely because of his name . . . Tiverton was where Dominic should be. Instead, he had spent the last three months in an indefensible medieval manor, with none but farmers surrounding him.

There were those who thought Dominic had made a mistake. William was not among them. Dominic didn't make mistakes like that. He was waiting for William, and whether it was some sort of trap or merely an unshakable assurance that the king would never harm him, the effect was the same. William waited for the perfect moment, and trusted that he would know what to do when the time arose.

After the quickly suppressed attempt to storm the Tower and free Mary, the Duke of Norfolk had fled to his own estates, no doubt spending the winter months gathering an army. There were reports of French troops crossing to Scotland, ready to sweep across the border the moment the tinder of rebellion caught hold. It couldn't be far off.

Jane Grey slipped noiselessly into the seat next to him. That was bolder than she usually was, but she was getting older and with Minuette's defection her mother could practically taste the crown.

"Happy Christmas, Your Majesty."

Happy Christmas, Will.

He answered roughly. "Enjoying yourself?"

One could never tell with Jane. She appeared as perfectly composed as ever, her fair hair modestly restrained beneath a pearl-bordered hood and veil, thin hands folded across her court gown, a deep chestnut colour shot through with gold thread. She wore no jewels save an enameled cameo flower tied with a ribbon around her neck.

Jane hesitated before answering. "I would enjoy myself more if I could bring you repose." She blushed when he looked at her in surprise, but her voice remained steady. "You have been ill-used, and I dislike seeing you suffer."

With a harsh smile, he reminded her, "It could be to your benefit."

In her quick blinking back of tears, William saw that he had hurt her. "As for myself, Your Majesty, I would be nowhere more content than in a peaceful retreat, devoting myself to my studies. I have no ambitions except, as your kinswoman, to wish you peace. And as your subject, I naturally wish you a long and successful reign in tearing down heresies and false doctrines."

As she retreated with a dignity fit for a queen, William thought dismally that he would have to apologize. Perhaps he had misjudged. She seemed earnest enough in her kindness—it was not her fault that he saw deception behind every female face. Jane was not Minuette.

She would never be Minuette.

He rose abruptly, causing the musicians to halt and the chatter of his guests to die away. He ignored everyone equally as he left, from his sister to Lord Burghley keeping quiet watch in one corner of the hall. William didn't care what they thought. Let Elizabeth thank them and soothe any ruffled tempers.

His scowl was apparently sufficient to warn off anyone from speaking to him. The gentlemen attending gave him a wide berth when he stalked into his public chambers. Through the presence and privy chambers, right on to the most secluded room in the palace. He shut the door in the face of the only attendant dim enough to try and follow, then flung himself onto the bed and stared blankly at the embroidered canopy high above.

And he asked himself the question he'd been asking since the moment Minuette had confessed.

Not *How could she?*

Not *How could they?*

How could *he?*

More than any man he'd ever known—more even than Lord Rochford or his own father—William had trusted Dominic. Trusted his advice, his loyalty, his maddening habit of speaking truths William didn't want to hear. Even now he still found himself instinctively looking for Dominic's opinion. It was Dom he thought of first when anything delicate needed doing, and there had been nothing but delicate matters in the last three months.

And then would come anew the burning moment of realization: that it was Dominic who had betrayed him. Dominic who had married his Minuette and bedded her and got her with child, all the while listening to William pour out his own frustrated desire and anxious love. How often had Dominic gone from the king's councils to Minuette's bed? How many times had they come together while William slept alone? And what of tonight, this almost-wedding night when she should have been coming to him, virgin-pure and trembling? Was she trembling in a traitor's arms right now, her breath coming ever quicker, her eyes closed and back arched and lips parted . . .

With a sudden savage energy, William pushed himself off the bed and strode across the room. Throwing the door open, he commanded the nearest guard, "Find me a woman. Any woman. Just . . ." He considered for a moment. "I want her dark-haired. And eager."

He slammed the door, wondering, not for the first time, if it was possible for the blackness of misery to kill.

Christmas week at Greenwich was charged with the underlying, unspoken tensions of Rochford's assassination, the executions of the plotters, and the still-unresolved issue of Mary's involvement. Not to mention the Duke of Norfolk's conspicuous flight to his own strongholds and, as always, the continuing whispers about Dominic and Minuette. More about Dominic, really. Men might have a few moments to spare for lascivious discussion of how Minuette had managed to ensnare the king and Lord Exeter both, but it was Dominic's abandonment they could not understand and turned over ceaselessly, metaphorically throwing up their hands at his folly.

Elizabeth wondered how many besides herself realized just how great a hole Dominic's absence had created. He had always been so quiet that perhaps only the most perceptive recognized how that quietness had been a ballast to both her brother and his government. Lord Burghley felt it, at least. That was the topic under discussion three days after Christmas in Elizabeth's chambers at Greenwich.

Present were herself, Lord Burghley, and Walsingham. Elizabeth felt slightly uneasy having a private discussion with her brother's

Lord Chancellor, but she could not sit back and wait for William to jump in some unspecified direction without warning. If he would not discuss his plans with her, then she must take some matters into her own hands in order to protect England from his simmering need for vengeance.

"Has the privy council made any concessions to preparing for war?" she asked Burghley.

The chancellor's usual equanimity had been strained these last months. He continued to be modest in his dress and manner, but grooves had been etched into the corners of his mouth—of concern or disapproval, it was hard to tell—and the occasional strand of gray could be seen in his light hair. "We cannot raise taxes now, not with Norfolk offering an outlet for any resentment. The best that can be hoped is that France and Spain will truly leave us be and not force us to face both an inner and an outer conflict at the same time."

"What say your sources, Walsingham?" Elizabeth asked.

"The Spanish have not committed themselves to France as yet, but they continue to play and no doubt it's a stronger alliance by far than any we offered. Word is France will wait for the sport of watching England tear herself apart. The real peril begins if Norfolk gains ground. If there is a decent chance of Catholics regaining power here, both France and Spain will want to commit money if not men to that cause. And Spain continues to hammer at us about the Lady Mary's imprisonment in the Tower."

"So," Elizabeth mused aloud. "We must keep Norfolk hemmed in, while giving the discontented Catholics no reason to join him in revolt. And we must present a strong front from our government so that the Continent sees no chance of widening the gaps in our populace."

"What does the king mean to do with Lady Mary?" Burghley pressed.

"Surely you've asked him as his Lord Chancellor."

"The king is not inclined to discuss family matters with me."

"As if Mary has ever been solely a family matter!" Elizabeth took to her feet to pace, both men rising courteously when she did. "I have asked William, as you have, what he means to do. He has said he will know what to do when the time is right. Which is the same answer he gives when I ask him what he means to do about the Duke of Exeter." Elizabeth had only asked that latter question once. Her brother's countenance had warned her off broaching the subject a second time.

"He would be wise to leave Exeter alone," Walsingham counseled. Her intelligencer was always quick to offer reliable advice. Unlike Burghley, the dark-countenanced Walsingham appeared the same as he ever had. Perhaps because he always lived on the razor's edge of paranoia. "My reading of Dominic Courtenay is that he will stay out of political and military maneuverings unless he is pushed into it. And the last thing we could endure is the West rising in concert with the North. If Norfolk persuades Exeter to command rebels from the West, the king's armies will have an exceptionally difficult fight."

Elizabeth stared him down coldly. "If you have a suggestion for how to speak to the king about a man nearly his brother who betrayed him in the most personal manner, please . . . offer it."

Walsingham dipped his head, quick to recognize when he'd overstepped. "I apologize."

"You are, however, right. William must separate England's needs from his own wishes just now. Dominic is an unknown factor. My sister is most decidedly known. We must press on the matter of Mary so that we are not caught unprepared when William decides to act." Elizabeth indicated the letter that lay on the table where she had left it after reading. The perfectness of Mary's script only heightened the poison of its contents: a missive directed to the

Duke of Norfolk, congratulating him on the success of George Boleyn's assassination and assurances that the Spanish had gold to spare for his troops.

"What is it you fear, Your Highness?" Walsingham asked, for she had not decided yet what to do with that letter. The intelligencer had brought it to her and Burghley, leaving the decision in their hands. But Burghley would do what she directed. The choice was Elizabeth's.

She would not name her most foolish fears, the ones that slipped into her mind in darkest night, whispering that Minuette and Dominic's abandonment had taken with them William's reason. Her brother hardly seemed to see her these days, at least not as anything more than another hectoring voice that bothered him beyond reason. He was angry with her, naturally, for helping Minuette slip away with Dominic. But it wasn't William's anger that she feared. It was his detachment, as though Elizabeth and Mary and Norfolk and the Catholics and even Europe itself were nothing more than obstacles in his way. To what lengths would he go to overrun those obstacles? And how deeply would England pay?

"We must be prepared for anything," she answered finally. "England cannot be allowed to be riven by the flaws of any one man, no matter who that man may be. I will see Mary myself, and then decide."

It said a great deal about the current state of William's government that his own chancellor nodded gravely at her near-treasonous words.

Mary Tudor faced the long winter of her imprisonment in the Tower with more than equanimity, sustained by righteousness. She spent hours each day on her knees in prayer and her greatest regret was not the loss of her freedom of movement, not the loss of luxurious surroundings or sufficient retainers or lavish meals: it was the denial of a confessor. But even that was made bearable by the thought of the Boleyn siblings gone from the earth, her mother's tormentors now in Hell, as well as the knowledge that the Duke of Norfolk was rallying true Catholics to her cause.

I waited, Mother. I endured. I have been patient and faithful. Now is the moment for God to strike. I am ready.

So it was that when Elizabeth deigned to visit the Tower as the year drew to a bitter close, Mary greeted her with composure and the surety of her position. "Sister," she offered fairly.

Elizabeth was not so gracious. "You've been playing dangerous games, Mary," she said softly, the two of them alone in the chill stone-walled chamber. "I cannot decide if you do not see the danger, or if you see it and do not care."

"How can you imagine me ignorant?" Mary retorted ironically. "I have been put in Bloody Tower, have I not? Meant as a threat, no doubt. Or perhaps they imagine me susceptible to ghosts, and hope the spectres of Edward IV's poor murdered boys will drive me mad. But I live by God's light, and do not fear the darkness. Not when I have done nothing against God's law or my own conscience."

"The murder of an unarmed man is not a mortal sin?"

Mary narrowed her eyes at Elizabeth's impudence. She had tried to love her sister all these years, and retained a certain stubborn affection against all logic. Perhaps only because Elizabeth had their father stamped firmly in her features and bearing. Henry VIII's hair had dulled over time, but Mary could remember when it had shone with the same red-gold fire as Elizabeth's. The way her younger sister spoke and argued and even teased . . . those were all legacies from their shared father.

Her affection ran side by side with envy—which *was* a sin. But how could she not envy the young princess who had stolen her title and her youth and all the opportunities for marriage and children that belonged, by right, to her? And Elizabeth treated them so lightly, with her arrogant cloth-of-silver gown and fur-lined cloak of finest wool and an astonishing vanity of jewelry about her person.

Elizabeth did not deserve her gifts.

With an impatient shake of her head, clearly ignoring whatever Mary might be thinking, Elizabeth continued, "What would you say if I told you that I have in my possession certain letters of yours meant for Lord Norfolk? Letters that near enough prove the two of you were in collusion over Lord Rochford's murder, and which encourage the duke to approach Spain for further funds in arming his rebels? Letters that prove you are actively working to destroy the king?"

Mary blinked. Elizabeth was guessing; she must be. Those letters had been entrusted to the most devout Catholics. "I would say you are bluffing."

"Then you would be utterly, disastrously wrong. You are too trusting, Mary. Because your faith is stubborn enough to overcome all earthly temptations, you expect the same of others. But most men are more venal. They can be bought—and I mean that literally. Your courier has been in my agent's employ for months. Every letter that has passed between you and Lord Norfolk has been intercepted and read first by my men. And now I must decide what to do about it."

"If you've come to beg me to recant—"

"I don't beg, sister. You know that. I was willing to let you be, even after your triumph at my uncle's death. But I will not allow you to move against William. It is over, Mary. Your plotting is finished. When the spring comes, the king's armies will sweep north and destroy the rebels. And you will never be free again."

"As if I have ever been free!" Mary fought to control her tongue, but years of resentment finally burst forth against this young, beautiful, bastard sister. "I have been imprisoned in a land of heretics and liars since the moment your mother bewitched my father. My life has been a prison of mockery and pretense, ever having to guard my tongue against those who bowed to the king's will over God's will. I have been submissive and humble as long as my soul can stand. No more. Your mother was nothing but a king's mistress, and neither you nor your brother have any right before Heaven to his throne. I have given William every chance to rule. I would gladly go to my grave honouring him as an earthly king if only he would honour God. But I cannot let the faithful fall and do nothing. If William will not guard the truth, then I must."

Elizabeth rose, not a trace of womanly pity in her expression. "Your letters will be handed over to the privy council. What happens next will be up to them."

"As if I care for the councils of men," Mary retorted dismissively. "I would rather die a martyr than live a hypocrite."

"I will do everything in my power to ensure you don't die."

"Don't do me any favours," Mary spat.

Raising one smooth, cool eyebrow, Elizabeth said, "I'm not doing it for you."

CHAPTER SIXTEEN

FROM THE MOMENT Dominic reached Wynfield Mote, he was beset with doubts about their choice of refuge. All his strength lay at Tiverton, and he knew the concerns of Minuette's health had been little more than a quickly grasped excuse to not have to decide immediately whether he would fight. But all he had done was delay the matter. As far as the Catholics were concerned, he was the king's enemy now, and that meant he was in their camp. Norfolk kept up a constant stream of letters and messengers through the autumn. The pressure eased with the winter weather, but Dominic knew Norfolk had not abandoned hope of securing Dominic and Tiverton for his spring rebellion.

Cut off from his former friends, Dominic took what news he could from wherever it came. So it was through Norfolk that he learned the details of the rescue attempt for the Lady Mary on the day he and Minuette had fled London. William's forces had cut off the rebels from their reinforcements and arrested thirteen men. Trials and executions had followed, with a swift brutality that sickened Dominic. He found himself offering silent counsel to William. *Cruelty ensures that open rebellion comes sooner—and harder. Norfolk is a formidable enemy, Will, and you're pushing men into his camp with every public vivisection.*

That was the worst of it—to feel every loyalty pulling him to William and yet know himself a traitor. Not even sleep brought forgetfulness, for he found himself dreaming of his father's shadowy end in the Tower. He would wake to his father's plea, written to Henry VIII, echoing in his head: *Whither have I fallen? What have I done?*

Minuette appeared as locked in her own mind as Dominic was in his, and it seemed their marital intimacy would pay the price. He needed her too badly at first to keep away entirely, but each encounter left him increasingly restless as it was only his body that was sated. After one encounter in early November, Dominic left her bed to sleep in the room he had used before their marriage. He did not come near her again, for he could not bear the thought of using his wife as he might have any convenient woman who could provide temporary oblivion.

It wasn't as though they argued. He spoke to her much as he always had, and she replied with equal civility. But they lied fluently to each other, if only by avoiding any topic of importance. William was never mentioned, nor even Elizabeth. They did not speak of court or the Catholics or the trials or the continued imprisonment of Lady Mary. Anyone listening would have thought them a quiet young country couple, content to live among farmers and concerned with nothing more than winter weather.

As a dreary Christmas passed and 1557 dawned, letters from Norfolk came more frequently despite the weather, pressing Dominic to declare for the rebels, using everything from flattery to blunt warning. And still Dominic delayed, watching the shifts of political winds as a farmer watches the sky, waiting for the storm to break.

In the middle of February he and Minuette spent an hour one night with her tenants and their families in the medieval hall at Wynfield. The company was a change from their usual solitude, and Minuette was in her element, moving among her people with a kind word for each of them and a thorough knowledge of their troubles and small illnesses. She played blindman's buff with the children, and Dominic overheard Asherton, her steward, say to Harrington, "That is a lady, and no mistake."

And so she was, a lady not dependent on position or wardrobe or jewels. She had dressed plainly since their flight from London; her gown tonight was a lightweight charcoal wool with unlined sleeves. Her hair was twisted neatly beneath a linen veil, as became a married woman not at court, and her only adornment was the pearl and sapphire necklace that Dominic had given her a lifetime ago.

It made his heart ache to see how others called forth her joy when it seemed all he had brought her this last year was misery. She swayed to the music of a single violin, laughing with the children as their parents danced. One little girl, just old enough to walk, clung to her skirts until Minuette swung her up and twirled with her a few times. And then the child laid her head against Minuette's shoulder and Minuette rested her own head against the child's and the flickering light cast by the fire was enough for Dominic to see the jewel-like tears that hovered on his wife's eyelashes. And only then did he remember.

February—when their own child should have been born.

The shock of it went through him like a blow shattering glass and Dominic had to swallow against tears of his own. They had never spoken of all they had lost and he knew right then that their silence had been a mistake. How were they meant to be husband and wife when they shared nothing more than house space?

When Minuette returned the sleeping girl to her mother, Dominic came up behind her and caught her hand, twining his fingers tightly with hers. She gave him one brief, startled look, then softened into place beside him. Together they bid farewell to her families, and when they were alone, they did not speak, but their silence this time was not fraught with tension or choked-back words.

It was Minuette who finally broke the silence, in the hushed darkness of the hall after Carrie had tactfully swept the housekeeper and maids away. "There are many things I regret, Dominic—but being your wife will never be one of them. Just because we made mistakes, it doesn't follow that everything is tainted."

He pulled her to him and kissed her, just once. Then he let go, afraid of breaking the fragile bridge they had built this night.

But Minuette had ever been the braver one. She pulled him back, her hands tight on his black doublet, and kissed him with a thoroughness of intent that made him shudder in response. Thank heaven for Carrie's discretion, because they never made it out of the hall. The table was hard, but both of them were too fierce and frantic to care about niceties like mattresses. He might have worried about hurting her as he plucked her veil loose and tugged at the far too many laces that kept him from her—but Minuette tore impatiently at his own clothing until she could run her hands across his chest and then his back, her fingernails urging him on.

They laughed afterward, and then cried a little, and both were cleansing. Leaving their clothes for Carrie to deal with, Dominic picked up his wife and carried her upstairs to bed.

She smiled the next morning to find him still in bed with her, and through the other emotions evoked, Dominic felt a lift of hope that all their lives could yet be well if only they would be left alone.

That hope lasted until early afternoon, when Mistress Holly appeared in the hall with Francis Walsingham close on her heels.

Dominic heard Minuette's slight gasp of surprise and fear and he voiced quickly what his wife was thinking. "Elizabeth?"

"The princess is well," Walsingham assured them. "In body, if not in spirit."

"Then why are you here?" Minuette asked. "Elizabeth would not have sent you for something trivial. She is taking care to keep away from us."

Did Elizabeth's self-protective distance bother Minuette? Dominic wondered. He had not dared ask. But she sounded without resentment and, in the end, Minuette was more practical than sentimental.

"Her Royal Highness had news she did not dare commit to paper and it could not wait for a more roundabout messenger. Lady Mary has been tried for high treason for the assassination of Lord Rochford and the arming of the Catholic rebels in the North. She has been convicted and sentenced to death."

If he had guessed for a hundred years, Dominic would never have guessed this. He saw his own shock mirrored in his wife's face, but her eyes were also deeply sad. "Why?" she asked, and whether she was speaking to Walsingham or Dominic or herself was unclear.

"Her Highness wished you to know, so that you might be prepared for any . . . repercussions that might follow."

"He won't really do it, will he?" Dominic asked, and he was definitely asking his wife. "William would not execute a woman." But even as he said it, he remembered Jane Boleyn and the council's cynical law that had allowed the execution of an insane woman.

It was the first time the king's name had been spoken aloud at Wynfield and a slight shiver passed through the air as though a barrier had been crossed once and for all. The storm is breaking, Dominic realized.

"The William we knew would not do such a thing," Minuette said slowly. "But the William our betrayal has created . . ." She faltered.

Walsingham cleared his throat. "I'll be on my way immediately, but I have one more message from the princess. She urges that, if possible, you find a way to leave England before spring. She cannot predict which direction the king's armies will march when campaigning season begins."

"He will march where the rebels are," Dominic said. "Tell Elizabeth we understand."

Which was not the same thing as agreeing. For himself, the time of flight had passed. He would live or die in England, come what may.

The specifics of how he would live or die, he had yet to decide. Dominic had told himself he must discuss it with Minuette, but this was not something she could decide for him. And he did not want her to. His wife had made the only possible choice for her in telling William the truth. He must make his own choice about taking arms against his king.

Robert Dudley rode to the Tower of London on the icy morning of February 18. Never again would he willingly enter the Tower from the river; the Water Gate was tainted forever by the sick memory of being deposited there in the dead of night with his brothers, uncertain if any of them would ever leave the precincts alive. He would be delighted never to lay eyes on the Tower again, and would have been tempted to say no to William's orders, but Elizabeth had asked this of him as well.

She had asked him to watch her sister die at her brother's hand and to tell her about it afterward.

What is happening to England? Robert wondered as he left his horse in the outer precincts and walked into the inner courtyard. The green was covered in a thin rime of frost and a heavier layer of mud churned up through the winter grass. At the north end of the White Tower, with the Chapel of St. Peter ad Vincula and

Tower Green to one side, a low scaffold had been built so the spectators might clearly see Mary's end. As the daughter of a king, she would not be exposed to the boisterous crowds outside the Tower walls. Today's witnesses would number no more than two hundred; enough to see the king's justice and spread word of it far and wide.

Robert watched Lord Burghley exit the Queen's Lodging, where Mary had been returned after her conviction to live out her last days in relative comfort. Robert did not envy the man his position. As Lord Chancellor, Burghley'd had the task of informing Mary just an hour ago that she would die today. Robert wondered how she'd taken the news. Did she fight? Did she beg? He hoped not. He'd known Mary Tudor since he was a little boy, and though he did not like her in the slightest and thought her very dangerous, he did not relish the thought of standing by while a woman he knew had to be dragged to her death.

He should have known better. Mary's hallmark had always been her dignity—that, and her faith. Both stood her in good stead on her last day. When she emerged from the Queen's Lodging with two weeping attendants behind her, her own face was pale but perfectly composed. She was dressed as richly as Robert had ever seen her: cloth-of-gold gown, elaborately belled sleeves, all impeccably embroidered and finished until she looked rather like a stiff doll. She carried a rosary in her hands and Robert could see her fingers moving ceaselessly along the jet beads. It was the only sign of tension she betrayed.

The witnesses were nearly silent as Mary processed to the foot of the scaffold. There she stood waiting for someone to offer their hand. Lord Burghley complied and she thanked him when she stood on the scaffold beside the single priest William had allowed his sister. The executioner waited quietly to the side. Her ladies hovered at the foot of the steps while Lord Burghley courteously asked Mary if she would like to speak to the crowd.

She considered, seeming to rake each individual member with her sharp and unforgiving eyes. Robert nearly shuddered when she looked him over, but her expression never wavered: somewhere between righteousness and contempt.

"Those come for to see me die," she spoke at last, in an even voice, "I wish you joy of it. If my death serves to restore but one lost soul to God's true fold, I myself rejoice greatly. And for the king, my brother, I do thank God for granting England a king and with my last breath I pray for his salvation and that of all his people."

Trust Mary to turn her final words into a tractate on religion, Robert thought. Mary's ladies joined her on the scaffold now and helped their mistress remove the heavy, elaborate overgown (why ruin good fabric with blood? he thought cynically) so that she suddenly looked older and harmless, an aging woman in a kirtle that was less than flattering. Then they removed Mary's stiff French hood, revealing that her abundant red hair had been severely coiled beneath a simple coif of white linen. Robert felt his stomach knot and wished it had occurred to him to drink heavily before this. For certain he would drink after.

Mary kissed her rosary and gave it to the priest who stood by and now offered his final murmured blessing. She allowed one of her ladies to blindfold her and then kissed them both and sent them off the scaffold. Robert felt each beat of his heart pressing hard against his chest, as though a drum were keeping count of the rising tension as Mary made the sign of the cross and then, only slightly less than graceful, knelt to the block, using her hands to position herself.

The executioner was quick and clean—before Robert could

blink the ax had swung and Mary's head dropped and rolled to the edge of the scaffold. There was a murmur from the crowd, but no outcry. Committed Protestants, all of them, and thus not too shattered to see the end of England's royal Catholic figurehead. Robert squeezed his eyes shut and imagined he could taste the tang of the blood. Against the backdrop of his eyelids he saw the ax fall once more, only this time it was his father's head that rolled . . .

He opened his eyes and watched while attendants gently carried Mary and her cloth-draped head into the Chapel of St. Peter ad Vincula for hasty interment. Time to report to Elizabeth. And ask her how in the name of Heaven and its angels she meant to stop her brother from destroying his own country.

Because there was another reason those watching today had been subdued, besides simple respect. Everyone in England knew that the young Duke of Norfolk was gathering an army in the North and East. All it needed for civil war to flare was a spark— like that caused by the execution of the woman who loyal Catholics were convinced had been England's rightful ruler.

Not for the first time, Robert cursed Dominic Courtenay soundly and thoroughly. Without him, he didn't think there was any man left in England able to talk sense into William. It was up to Elizabeth now to keep the country from tearing itself to pieces.

For a precious three weeks there was peace at Wynfield. Fragile and dearly bought, but Minuette soaked up every moment with her husband, knowing each day that brought them nearer to spring also brought them nearer to the edge of no return. They still did not discuss William freely, but the ice had been broken by Walsingham's news and so they were able to talk about Elizabeth and Lord Burghley and Norfolk and the possibility of Continental involvement in any Catholic uprising.

She did not know what Dominic would do. She knew he received missives from Norfolk's camp, nearly every day as time went on, and she knew he was deeply conflicted. She kept her own counsel, as her husband had always allowed her to do, and gave him her tacit approval to do whatever he felt he must. She would not make his choices for him.

But then two things happened on top of each other, within twenty-four hours in the first week of March. First, Harrington brought word from a visit to Stratford-upon-Avon that Mary Tudor had been executed inside the Tower of London. Minuette wept when she heard it, and not only for the lonely, bitter, royal woman whom Minuette had known and, if not liked, at least respected. Her tears were also for William, and for the nightmares he must be living through now without anyone to comfort him.

The very next morning, just two hours after dawn, Renaud LeClerc appeared at Wynfield Mote.

Carrie woke her to the news that Dominic and Renaud were speaking together in the hall. "Renaud LeClerc?" Minuette asked, disbelieving. "Are you sure?"

But of course Carrie was sure; she had met him during their stay in France. Minuette hastily dressed in a guest-appropriate gown of richly dyed green, like the starkness of evergreens in the frigid winter, and descended into the hall where Dominic and Renaud sat in two chairs before the enormous medieval fireplace, locked in intense conversation.

Renaud rose when he saw her, Dominic half a beat behind. "It is a great pleasure to meet you again," the Frenchman said, kissing the hand she offered. "And especially to meet you as Madame Courtenay. I had not dared hope Dominic would be so fortunate."

"Is he fortunate?" she asked tartly. "The price has been high."

"No price is too high for love."

"Thus speaks the Frenchman who is *not* estranged from his king." No need to be coy; they all knew where they stood. And Minuette didn't need to be told why Renaud was there.

He told her anyway. "I come, *madame,* with an offer of passage to France and a promise of safety in my country."

"Did you not take a great risk in coming here? I thought the last time you were on this island you got an arrow in the back."

"Last time I did not take care to disguise my coming. A single man with a good weapon arm can pass anywhere with relative ease."

But to cross the Channel in winter was not a matter of relative ease. It argued Renaud's deep seriousness of purpose. "Your king wants Dominic in his army," she said bluntly.

Renaud shook his head. "This is my offer, not my king's, and it is one of friendship, not calculation. There is no expectation on my part or that of my masters. Only safe haven and a place to be free."

Minuette looked between Renaud and her husband. Dominic's face was unreadable; an expression she was long familiar with. His eyes flicked to her for a moment and she froze, for he registered her with only the greatest detachment. She bit down on the inside of her cheek so as not to react, but before it could become unbearable there was a flare from Dominic and she knew that he had not retreated wholly.

"I need to speak to my wife," Dominic said. "Do you mind waiting here?"

Renaud smiled and indicated the wine, bread, and cheese that Mistress Holly had provided. "I am comfortable. Take your time— but not too much."

Minuette led Dominic into a ground-floor chamber at the back of the house that had been her father's study. It still held his collection of books and Minuette had a few memories of playing on the floor while her father studied. *What do we do?* she offered up silently.

It was the question Dominic put to her with a single word. "Well?"

Minuette circled the room restlessly until she came to the window, where she paused and stared at her mother's rose garden. The bare stems were black outlines against the soil, with no sign of the buds that would spring forth in a few months' time. "My answer is simple: I go where you go."

"That is not an answer."

"I made my choice when I married you, Dominic. I do not promise that I will allow you to make all my choices for me," she smiled at him briefly, "but on this matter, the choice is yours." Because it is you who will be giving up the most, she thought. I am half French, but you are wholly English and wholly loyal.

"What if my choice is for you to go, and myself to stay?"

She whirled away from the window, shocked. "You would not ask that of me!"

"And if I did? Would you go?"

"Absolutely not, under any circumstances."

"What if you were with child again?"

"I am not."

"You could be, at any time now. And if you were—"

"Stop it! We could do this forever. What if William marches on Wynfield next month, what if Norfolk sweeps in and cuts down the king's army, what if the Spanish land in retaliation for Mary, what if the sweating sickness sweeps through here and kills us both? I will not make decisions based on fears that may never come to pass or things that we cannot control."

Dominic took her hands in his, studying her face with an expression that was not at all detached. "I cannot leave England, Minuette. Whatever happens, must happen here."

"I agree."

He wrapped her in his arms and she allowed herself to relax into him, marveling that she could feel happy at such a disastrous time. Dominic kissed her cheek, then allowed his mouth to trail down her jaw to the hollow of her throat. With reluctance, he pulled back and said, "We'll see Renaud safely off."

Like a good Frenchman, Renaud gave a shrug of apparent indifference when they declined his offer. But his words were more direct. "I hope you will not come to regret it, Dominic," he warned. "You know what will be asked of you if you stay."

"He's already been asked," Minuette retorted. "And we all must make the best choices for ourselves."

With a sad little smile, Renaud lifted her hand and pressed it to his lips. "So we must, *madame.* To be honest, I did not have much hope of persuading him. But you both should know, the offer will never be rescinded. You will always have a friend across the sea ready to come to your aid."

"Thank you."

"Dominic," Renaud turned to him, "would you tell your man to ready my horse? I will not stay."

When Dominic had left, Renaud turned back to Minuette. Urgently, he said, "Take care of him, *madame.* Men of rigid honour can be so easily broken."

"Like yourself?" she countered, though an icicle of fear poised at the base of her neck.

"I am by nature more . . . pliable. But Dominic—I fear for him in what is coming."

"So do I fear, for all of us. I cannot undo the bonds of friendship and history that tie us to others, nor would I wish to. But as I also do not wish my marriage undone, I ask you, *monsieur* . . . what would you do in my place?"

"I cannot tell. But remember that my offer of sanctuary is not solely for your husband. If ever you require aid and must act alone, you have only to ask."

The fear stabbed chilly through her at the word "alone" and Minuette wished Renaud had never said it. Not that the thoughts didn't lurk in the shadows, but she did not want them acknowledged. She had Dominic; she must think of today and not, as she had said to him, worry about a future that they could not control.

"Are you ready?" Dominic asked from the door; Minuette wondered how long he'd been standing there and what he had heard.

"Farewell, *madame,*" Renaud told her, with a kiss for each cheek. "I hope we may meet again on a happier day."

"So do I."

She watched the two men walk away and felt that another bridge had been crossed and set ablaze behind them. Was there another bridge ahead, she wondered, or only a chasm?

CHAPTER SEVENTEEN

WITH MARY'S EXECUTION the murky path ahead that William had spent so long trying to divine miraculously cleared. He knew precisely what to do. No more waiting for Norfolk and the Catholics to decide when and where they would strike—it was time to take the battle to them. William made clear his orders in the first privy council meeting that followed Mary's death.

"I expect an army ready to move by mid-March," he announced to the grim-faced table. "Lord Sussex, you are in command. You have three weeks to muster troops to London to guard the city and a larger force to march."

"In which direction will the troops march?" Lord Burghley asked delicately.

"In whichever direction I send them," William bit off. "I will not wait for our enemies to encircle us. We will sweep up the traitors wherever we find them."

If his uncle had been here, he would have pressed the issue. William did not expect that from anyone else, but Burghley was surprisingly persistent. "Does that include Lord Exeter?"

The time had passed for private fury, but William would not

allow impudence, even if it was disguised as concern. "Do you see Dominic Courtenay at this table? Every man here knows his crimes. And every man here also knows his strengths. Would you have me leave the West Country vulnerable to his leadership?"

He wasn't sure what expression crossed Burghley's face—relief, perhaps, or sorrow. Or perhaps something of both. "No, Your Majesty. The threats to the Crown must be confronted."

It didn't answer the unasked questions about how and when and where William meant to confront Dominic. Some of those unasked questions were the king's own. He could not ponder too long upon the subject without losing himself in a mire of rage and doubt. And he could not allow himself to doubt. Rochford was gone and Dominic was gone and Minuette was gone . . . William could rely on no one but himself.

Which is why he decided, "I will lead the army personally when we take to the field. I will not sit in safety while my kingdom is threatened." Also, he could then make the decisions the moment they came to him.

If there was any doubt about his choice, no one on the council said a word. Perhaps they trusted him more than Dominic ever had, or perhaps they feared him more, so they dared not voice their honest opinions. Whatever the reason, William was savagely glad of his unopposed command.

"I will appoint a regent while I am in the field," he continued. "To ensure the government in London does not languish for lack of immediate care."

He knew what they expected to hear: surely it would be Elizabeth. Who else was left to him?

But he no longer trusted his sister as he once had. Elizabeth had been the one to talk Minuette away from the guards he'd set on her that disastrous day of confession; she had allowed Minuette to slip through his grasp. They had never spoken of it, but William would wager Elizabeth had simply been waiting to be punished. Here was her punishment, although she did not know it yet.

"Lord Burghley," William announced. "You will act as regent in my name while I am in the field. Any actions that must be taken so quickly that I cannot be consulted will be in your hands."

Burghley looked more unhappy than shocked. "The Princess of Wales—" he began.

"The Princess Elizabeth will be retiring to Hatfield for a season. The strain of this year has been too much for her."

He wondered if anyone there believed him, for no matter how much strain she might be under, Elizabeth would never be less than poised and prepared and in control. Better if they didn't believe him, for then they would all the better read in this action what he wanted them to: that no one, not even his full sister, was immune from the consequences of her actions.

No one protested, although Burghley looked both thoughtful and concerned as the council dispersed. William ignored him. The man would do as he was asked; Burghley was almost as constitutionally dependable as Dominic had once been.

William would break the news to Elizabeth later that night. First, he had a woman or two to see.

His aunt, the Duchess of Suffolk, was simple to locate. She had taken to hovering at court like a large, persistent dog, unwilling to miss the slightest chance at William. Truthfully, he had delayed the inevitable this long only to annoy her. That same desire led him to wave her off when he entered the chamber where she held a small court of her own and say abruptly, "I would speak privately with Jane."

He didn't miss the flash of jubilation from his aunt, nor the devouring eyes of those around her. When Jane hesitated, he beckoned her sharply. With a blush, she rose from her seat and made her way to his side. With several dozen pairs of eyes on them, William led Jane into a corridor. He ordered his guards to keep out anyone foolish enough to eavesdrop.

He might once have been kind. He might once have taken the trouble to speak softly, to offer compliments, to woo even a woman he did not love. For most of his life he had not expected to marry a woman he loved—but he had expected to be courteous.

That time had passed. "When the matter of the rebels is settled, the privy council will approve our marriage. We will marry this autumn."

Jane did not flinch, did not smile, did not betray in any way that she had even heard him except for a unique quality to her stillness. With exquisite irony, William asked, "I assume you have no objections?"

Give her credit; Jane's response held a hint of her own irony. "What possible objection could I make?"

"None at all that I can see. You will be Queen of England. Have you not longed for the opportunity to ensure our country is kept free from Catholicism?"

"I am grateful for the opportunity to serve God and England."

William's irritation grew with each cool, composed reply. Heaven knew he no longer wanted a wife who would endanger his happiness and peace of mind, but it would be nice if she didn't look quite so much like he was the worst part of the bargain.

Abruptly, he seized her by the shoulders and kissed her. Jane, as he might have predicted, was stiff and surprised and unresponsive, even when William backed her against the wall and trailed kisses from her mouth along her slender jaw and throat. And in a flash of unbidden memory he was not in a corridor with Jane Grey, but at Hever with Minuette.

Suddenly he was aware of everything, every inch of him alight with her touch. He kissed her again, his hands moving up her back to twine into her heavy, loosely plaited hair. She returned his kisses with a hunger that may have started in grief but changed rapidly to desire—he knew the signs well enough. Her hands swept through the tangle of his wet curls, keeping his head pulled firmly down to hers.

With a gasp, William pushed himself off Jane and stumbled backward. From being unresponsive a moment ago, Jane looked suddenly concerned. "Your Majesty?" she asked, taking a tentative step forward.

"You may go," he snarled. "Tell your mother she's won."

She hesitated, then said in a rush, "William, I am sensible of the great honour you do me. I promise, I will never give you cause for grief."

Nor for joy, William thought bleakly, but he managed a nod to the slight, upright figure of his future bride. For a woman so committed to the Protestant faith, she dressed remarkably like a nun, all dark colours and severe lines, as though beauty were an offense to God. She curtsied deeply and left, back straight and shoulders set.

William closed his eyes and tried not to be swept away by dizziness and desire. Not for Jane, not for a stranger, not for any of the women he had ever enjoyed in his bed ... the only woman he desired these days was the one woman utterly out of his reach.

He wished he could believe that everything about Minuette had been a lie. It would be easier to despise her if he believed that she had never loved him, that every time he'd touched her she'd simply endured it. But William knew better. He had made her shiver in response, he had roused her desire to match his, she had never recoiled from him. Not even when the smallpox left him scarred. That last night before her flight, in what William could now recognize as Minuette's unspoken farewell, she had undressed and lain in his arms and made herself vulnerable to whatever he wanted of her.

And despite all of that, she had still chosen Dominic.

Was there no one in this world who loved only him?

A tangle of bedsheets, a throaty laugh, eager hands and voluptuous curves and a proud mother of his child . . . William opened his eyes and breathed deeply.

He would send for Eleanor. The only woman who had never pretended to be anything other than what she was: amoral and greedy and sensuous. And absolutely devoted to him.

27 February 1557
Wynfield Mote

It has been ten days since we heard of Mary's execution and Wynfield has suddenly become a beehive of activity. There are riders twice, sometimes three times a day from the North. I know that Dominic has sent messages to his holdings at Tiverton. To all appearances, he is preparing to lead from the West.

5 March 1557
Wynfield Mote

Walsingham managed to send us another letter from Elizabeth in unofficial exile at Hatfield. She is furious, of course, at being summarily banished from court, however William may have prettied it up by claiming she needed rest. But unlike her brother, I have never known fury to overwhelm Elizabeth—nor indeed any emotion. Not that she does not feel deeply, for she does. But she was born with the ability to see always the wider picture no matter the details that threaten to overwhelm her. And for her, always, the wider picture will be England's safety. I know that her fury at being

banished is less about her pride and more about her fear that,
without her, William will heed no counsel.

And is that not the true source of my regrets, and Dominic's?
That the consequences of our actions reverberate far beyond our own
two lives.

On the day of the vernal equinox a handful of riders appeared at Wynfield Mote—two of whom commanded a much greater flurry of attention than any others over the previous weeks. The two men at the center of the small party dismounted, wearing no identifying badges, only travel-stained riding leathers. The first man Minuette had been waiting for and so knew him at once: the young Duke of Norfolk.

But it was Norfolk's companion that made her nerves flare to a high pitch: older, more familiar, and much more injurious to her peace of mind.

Stephen Howard. Uncle to the Duke of Norfolk, and Minuette's stepfather.

Dominic and Minuette greeted the men in the hall. She uttered the words she would have used with any guest, though she was certain they would not stay. "Shall I prepare a chamber?"

Norfolk hardly looked at her, so anxious was he to get to Dominic. "No, my lady. I have a matter to discuss with your husband, and then I shall relieve you of my presence. Perhaps we might walk?" This last was addressed to Dominic.

Minuette perched on one of the embroidered stools flanking the fireplace and looked up at the duke with wide, innocent eyes. "No need for that. I assume, Lord Norfolk, that you are unashamed of what you are about to propose. Let us hear it openly."

She wasn't sure whether it was Dominic or her stepfather who smothered a short laugh. Probably Stephen Howard; he was always irreverent.

Despite his clear annoyance, the duke spoke politely. "Such a beautiful woman has no need to trouble herself with affairs of state."

Dominic met her eyes and his lips twitched in a smile. "Her house, her husband. She stays. And you're a fool, Norfolk, if you think she doesn't know precisely what you're about to propose."

"I told him so," Stephen Howard announced to the chamber at large. "I warned him that Wyatt women were stubborn to the core."

It seemed the Duke of Norfolk was not a man to waste time on peripheral issues. He turned his back on Minuette and Stephen Howard and spoke to Dominic as if they were alone. "The army has left London, split into two forces. One marches straight north—the other is marching northwest, less than a half-day's ride from here. You can't sit on the fence any longer, Exeter. And you're the fool if you think this army is not coming to scorch and burn all you hold."

Minuette held her tongue and watched her husband intently as he asked Norfolk, "Are your forces in the North ready?"

"We're ready. The French are ready. The question is . . . whose side are you on?"

Dominic's face did not change at all. "My own."

"You have mixed feelings about the king, I respect that. You've known him all his life. But what has that got you? Exile, a permanent state of uncertainty? Do you really think he'll let this marriage stand? He's waited, God knows why, but he won't wait forever. Once you're in his hands, your marriage will be dissolved. You will never see her again. And like as not she'll end up his mistress one way or another."

Dominic took a step forward in obvious fury and Norfolk thrust up a hand in conciliation. "Forgive me, but we haven't time to be anything but blunt. William is his father all over again—

what he wants, he gets. And he'll burn and scorch whatever is in his way. That you were his friend makes vengeance more certain, not less."

Minuette thought it time she intervened to bring the matter to the point. "What is it you want, Lord Norfolk?"

He answered promptly. "An assurance that your husband has a sufficient force to deride the royal army, and the will to use it."

"You want me to raise the West Country." Dominic's voice had lost all inflection.

"As your uncle did before you." Norfolk smiled coldly. "I hit them in the north, with the French coming in across the Scots border. You sweep up behind them from the west, barring retreat and keeping reinforcements from arriving."

"And once you've dealt with the royal army," Minuette prodded, "what is your goal?"

"To bring the king to reason and remove the heavy burdens beneath which his Catholic subjects labor. He has murdered a princess royal, a born daughter of a king, and that cannot be forgotten. The king must show his willingness to mend his errors."

"And if he does not?" she pressed.

But Norfolk would be drawn no further. "May I speak to you privately, Lord Exeter?" the duke urged.

Dominic nodded. Minuette tracked her husband as they left the hall, heart wrung for him and hating everything about this moment.

Her mood was not improved by Stephen Howard's customary drawl. "So, daughter—forgive me, stepdaughter—what a fine mess you have gotten yourself into."

"I might say the same of you, coming into armed rebellion at last."

He smiled lazily. "Have you seen me take up arms yet? But my nephew is right. Our young king is digging himself deeper every day. He will tear this country to pieces if he is not sharply checked."

"And if he will not be checked?" she countered, knowing the answer but wanting someone other than her to say it aloud.

"With Mary Tudor dead, the Catholics consider Mary Stuart the legitimate ruler of England. There is a reason France has given support to our forces."

"And you know how much all English people, Protestant or Catholic, despise the thought of a Queen of France ruling us. What is the Duke of Norfolk's true goal?"

"Can you not guess?"

Minuette looked away. She could guess. The young Duke of Norfolk might be catering to the Catholics, but he was too proud and too English to turn the throne over to Mary Stuart as long as she was betrothed to the French heir. If he beat William's armies and brought down the king, then the duke might try to convince the French king to allow him to wed Mary Stuart himself, or else he would spurn France altogether and mollify the Protestants by marrying Elizabeth. Norfolk was maneuvering for a crown of his own. He would not care which woman helped him achieve it.

Stephen Howard gentled his voice. "I told you once you were playing in deep waters. Friendship with royalty—particularly Tudor royalty—is a losing proposition."

"You cannot imagine that Elizabeth would marry a man who had brought her own brother to ruin and death."

"Nor can I imagine Her Highness allowing France to rule this island. I think Elizabeth is even more practical than you are. Rumour has it she is running her own shadow government out of Hatfield House."

"To keep herself apprised of events, not to work against William!"

"Are you so sure?" he taunted. "How long has it been since you've spoken with her directly?"

Of course she was not sure. She was not sure of anything—except Dominic's goodness and her own love.

To her surprise, Stephen Howard knelt down before her. Softly, he pleaded, "Minuette, is there any hope of persuading you to leave England? I can arrange it. I cannot think you want to be here when all goes to Hell."

"What I want does not enter into it. We are all walking the only path we know how."

He sighed. "Then I wish you well, daughter, and hope that your good heart will guide you truly in whatever comes."

He kissed her cheek, then rose and looked down on her a little sadly. "Farewell, Minuette. Try not to blame yourself for this war—it's been a long time coming. You were just a convenient spark."

Was that supposed to make her feel better? she wondered. Surely those destroyed in the fire didn't care whether the spark had meant to destroy or not.

Dominic walked Norfolk out of the house, leaving a watchful Minuette behind. He had a question he did not want her to hear.

"What happens to William if his armies are defeated?"

The duke was no fool, he gave the answer he must know Dominic wanted. "He will be asked to voluntarily relinquish his throne, to admit his illegitimacy and retire from public life."

"We both know the king will never agree. You'll have to kill him."

With a shrug, Norfolk said, "One step at a time. First, we defeat his armies. Then we repair the breaches in England."

"And Elizabeth?"

"I have no interest in harming a woman. As long as Elizabeth accepts the status quo, she will remain at liberty. Perhaps rather more than liberty."

Meaning her only chance of survival would be to marry Norfolk himself and set a seal upon his victory. Rather as her grandfather had married the niece of the Yorkist king he'd killed in battle.

Stephen Howard joined them, looking troubled as he mounted. As Norfolk followed, one more question slipped out, one Dominic hadn't been aware of thinking. "Does William remain in London?"

"You know him better than that. To answer your real question—the king is marching with the northern force. You need not fear, I would not put you head-to-head against him. Too risky. I couldn't predict what either of you might do." Norfolk looked down at him and said, not unkindly, "You've given up everything for her. Don't let it come to naught over some misplaced sense of loyalty. You were a traitor the moment you took her from him. Turn it to the only victory you can."

When Norfolk and Howard were gone, Dominic headed for the creek that burbled along one edge of the kitchen garden, where he sat on the bank and threw pebbles into the icy water, counting each one as if they were the beats of his heart.

One. *That you were his friend makes vengeance more certain, not less.*

Two. *I am not my father. I keep my fealty.*

Three. *There is no man on this earth I trust more than you.*

Four. *You were a traitor the moment you took her from him.*

Five. *Whither have I fallen? What have I done?*

With a force that splashed him, Dominic flung in a handful of stones and stood up. Norfolk was right. Their only chance for a future lay with the rebels. Dominic had held off as long as he could, fearing that final step that cut him off from every previous loyalty. He couldn't afford the niceties of conscience any longer, not with a royal army on the move. He must get Minuette safely sequestered in the western strongholds at Tiverton and commit himself to the only possible course of action.

But first he would ride out and see this force for himself. Less than a half-day's ride, Norfolk had said. The information he gathered would be useful, when it came to fighting them. He ignored the voice that told him he was still stalling, and went to the stables. The moon would be full tonight, he and Minuette could ride through the night for Tiverton.

He found Harrington in the stables. "Tell Minuette I'll be gone for several hours."

Harrington eyed him carefully. "I'll tell her, if you'll wait for me. You shouldn't ride out alone."

Dominic opened his mouth, then decided he didn't have the time to spare on argument. "I'll wait."

He was afraid that Minuette might follow Harrington back, to ask him where he was going and why. She didn't. And Harrington was as blessedly taciturn as ever, though Dominic suspected he asked no questions because he already had a shrewd idea of the answers.

By the time they saw the dust kicked up by countless horses and men, twilight was not far off. Neither was the army. It was less than eight miles east, and Dominic's heart stopped beating as he calculated how little time they had. He and Minuette should be riding for Tiverton at this hour. Instead, his sentimentality had tied his hands in indecision until it was nearly too late.

It was Harrington who pointed out the obvious, slowing Dominic's heart a little. "They're camped. And I see no tracks along this road. They've not sent anyone ahead."

Dominic stood beside him at the edge of a long stretch of forest, the horses tethered safely out of sight farther back. They were near enough to see the tents laid out before them, the bright colours of the banners flattened somewhat by the slowly dimming sun. It appeared Sussex was leading this force, and Dominic saw the banners for Westmoreland and Essex as well.

Harrington was already drawing back into the trees, though there was little chance they would be seen in their dark clothes against the deep shadows. Dominic huddled into his warm cloak and cast one more glance over the encampment, calculating numbers in his head and storing away details that would help him fight this army. The rebels might be outnumbered, but the leadership advantage lay with Norfolk and the French.

Not to mention that Dominic himself would be hitting them with a force they were only half expecting. He would tip the balance in Norfolk's battle.

And that, he thought bleakly, is how one turns from traitor to savior. Simply by shifting one's point of view. He turned to slip into the forest. As he did, the wind kicked up and he caught something out of the corner of his eye—a banner that had been hidden behind Westmoreland's at the center of the camp. Dominic stopped and stared, hoping he was wrong, knowing he was not.

Crimson and azure—lions and lilies.

Norfolk's intelligence had been wrong. William was not with the northern force.

William was here.

Dominic might have stayed frozen there all night if Harrington hadn't pulled him away. He didn't remember the ride back. He saw nothing but the royal banner, planted like a stake in his heart. Only when they reached the stables did Dominic come to himself.

He dismounted as Harrington asked, "Shall I get fresh horses readied?"

He spoke with absolute neutrality. Dominic didn't believe in that indifference. Harrington surely had an opinion on whether they should throw in their lot with Norfolk or wait for the royal army to take them.

As Minuette surely had an opinion . . .

"I'll be back," he said over his shoulder. "Do nothing until I tell you."

Minuette was in the solarium. She must have seen him ride in, for she was on her feet when he entered. With the same neutrality as Harrington, she said, "I can be ready in half an hour."

In that moment Dominic really thought his heart might break. She was prepared to follow wherever he led, whatever the consequences, with no reference to her own wishes or regrets.

There was no way to do this gently. "William is with the army. I saw his banner myself."

Her eyes flickered but she continued to regard him gravely, waiting.

"I had persuaded myself to believe Norfolk. I told myself that this could not all be for nothing, that we deserved a future and that I would do what I must to secure it." He broke off and swallowed hard, wondering how to make himself understood.

In the end, it was simple. It had always been simple. "I swore an oath, Minuette, not to the throne or the crown or some other abstraction. I swore it to *Will*. And though I have twisted it and trampled upon it, I cannot break it utterly. I will not take arms against him. Not even for you."

"I would not love you if you could."

"It means—"

"I know what it means."

He broke off, wishing he could take her in his arms. But if he did that, his resolve might weaken. "I must tell Harrington not to bother with horses tonight. Tomorrow, I will ride out and give myself up."

He hesitated, knowing she would not want to hear his next plea, but he had to try. "Is there no chance you will consider leaving? You and Carrie and Harrington could ride out well before dawn, and I could wait and give you time to get—"

"Where?" she broke in. "Where can I go, Dominic? To the Somerset lands William gave me, to raise the armies you will not? To Scotland or Wales or across the sea, leaving those I have loved to tear each other to pieces? I will not leave."

"Then promise me that you will let me go in the morning without you. Most likely William will send some troops here to guard you, but he will not offer you harm. Please, Minuette, stay here. For my sake."

"I promise that I will let you ride out alone."

If he touched her now, he would never be able to finish his work. With only a curt nod of acknowledgment, he strode out to speak to the household.

Harrington received his orders without comment, though he clapped Dominic on the shoulder as if in approval. He spoke to Asherton as well, letting him know that a detachment of soldiers might well be quartered at Wynfield as of tomorrow. Dominic would do what he could to persuade William to leave Minuette alone, but best to be prepared for every eventuality. The steward received the news without comment, save to say, "It's our mistress we serve, and her we will always stand by."

By the time Dominic finished, it was full dark. He stood in the bleak garden for a while, remembering his wedding day, how Minuette had looked and sounded here amidst the roses. A little over a year they'd had . . .

Dominic was under no illusions. He knew that William would

never forgive them, not to the extent of allowing their marriage to stand. The most that could be hoped for was Minuette's liberty. As for himself, he was prepared for whatever punishment William inflicted.

He rather hoped for death. At least then he would not have to live knowing that Minuette belonged to someone else.

Minuette sat on the deep stone sill of her bedroom window, hugging her knees to her chest. She knew that Dominic was in the gardens and she had briefly considered going after him. Instead, she'd had Carrie help her into a loose white gown, wrapped herself in a fringed silk shawl, and curled up here. She looked away east, as if she could pierce the darkness and the distance and see William and his army and whatever fate awaited them all at the end of the road.

She heard Dominic's soft footsteps and closed her eyes for a moment, savoring the sense of his presence, before turning her head. For one dreadful moment his face held that detached expression, so common this winter, that made her feel as though he were looking right through her. And then the mask crumpled into despair and love and regret and Minuette felt a wild joy that he had come to her.

They came together fiercely, grief and rage and guilt transformed into a cleansing, abandoned passion that drove away all thought and left them breathlessly tangled amidst the bed linen. She dozed briefly and woke to her husband's touch, his fingertips exploring the arch of her back and the curve of her shoulders and the line of her jaw, as if he were memorizing the contours of her body. She did the same, noting every tactile subtlety, from the smooth hardness of his chest to the scratchy stubble of his beard. They made love again, slow and sweet—every moment a benediction, an act of both blessing and farewell.

When the first gray of not-quite-spring dawn crept into the sky, Dominic slipped away from the bed. With heavy heart, Minuette rose and summoned Carrie. She would face this day as a lady, armored in her dress and her manners. She would not bid him goodbye looking drawn and ill.

It seemed forever that she waited, and she had just about decided to go to the stables herself when she heard the ring of his boots in the hall. Dominic strode in, dressed for riding and wearing his old colours—plain gold battle tunic, with none of the markings of the Duke of Exeter. Her throat tightened at the sight and she hoped that William would take it as the sign of humility that it was and not as an arrogant rejection of his gift.

There was little to say, though even that could barely be managed. *I love you.* What more need be acknowledged? They had been in the wrong, they knew it, and now it must be paid for. They would face it as they must, and never concede that it had not been worth it.

She knew without needing to be told that he could not bear to ride off if she were watching him. So she made it easy for him and stayed behind when he left the hall.

He did not look back.

CHAPTER EIGHTEEN

A FTER A RESTLESS night, William was up with the dawn. The camp stirred around him, eager to be on their way to wiping out the rebels. He walked silently through his men, for orders were already given and awaited only daylight to be put into action. While Sussex led the army northeast to join up with the rest of the royal forces, William would ride to Wynfield.

He could have gone last night, of course. Some of his men plainly believed him mad that he had not. Only Sussex had the nerve to say aloud what they were all thinking. *It's as good as handing him freedom. They'll be halfway to Tiverton by dawn.*

They thought William sentimental. They thought him hesitant for affection's sake, allowing Dominic a chance to evade arrest once more. They were wrong. He wasn't offering Dominic freedom—he was offering him the rope with which to hang himself. When Dominic threw in his lot with the rebels, his future would be sealed. Then William could have no compunction in meting out justice.

He reached the western edge of the camp and studied the stretch of road that wound through the trees. He remembered his sole visit to Wynfield almost two years ago, the serenity of the moated house with its old-fashioned feel and sleepy sense of rightness. How had Minuette felt at abandoning Wynfield? Would she have wanted to remain here, or had she gone gladly with Dominic to Tiverton?

He drew a ragged breath and prepared himself for what lay ahead. A small detachment of guards left at Wynfield, merely to remind the retainers and farmers who was in charge and to keep any loyal servants from aiding their fled mistress. Then a rapid march north and the earliest possible encounter with Norfolk's forces. English springs were precarious and he wanted this done with once and for all.

William saw the approaching rider at almost the same moment the forward watch did. Halting them with a word, he stared at the single, solitary figure that meant the overturning of all his expectations.

He would have known that rider anywhere.

"Your Majesty?"

It was Robert Dudley, alert and attentive, if somewhat detached, in his service. He had regained his customary sleekness, looking elegant even in the plain attire of a military campaign, and he did not seem to resent being folded into royal service rather than marching under his family's banner. "You should withdraw until we know who comes and for what purpose."

"I know who it is," William said, but his mind churned on the question of purpose. What the hell was Dom doing?

It didn't matter. William would turn this to his own advantage. "Dudley, take four men and escort him in. Bring him to my tent."

Robert motioned to several of the watch, then swung up on his own horse. William called sharply after him, "I want him untouched."

"And if he's armed, Your Majesty?"

"He isn't." Disconcerted by his own certainty, William turned on his heel and stalked to his tent. He dismissed everyone and waited alone for the one man in the world who could still unsettle him.

By the time Robert Dudley drew back the entrance to his tent, William was braced and ready. Dominic entered as though nothing at all had happened, as though he had come here for one of any number of reasons, none of which included treason. William waved off Robert from following. He wanted to be alone for this.

Dominic watched him unblinkingly. If betrayal and flight had left their mark on him, it was inward. Outwardly, he was as casually sure of himself as ever, right down to the plain gold tunic he wore. As though the last four years had never happened. As though he hadn't been granted titles and wealth and position by William. As though Dominic expected simply to walk in here and resume his customary place as an impatient, disapproving elder brother.

William regarded him coldly, and with an equal chill to his voice said, "If you're hoping for clemency, you're too late. You were too late the moment you touched her."

"I'm not looking for clemency. I'm not looking for anything, except my own peace of conscience. I have injured you, and I will carry the grief of that to my death."

"Where is she?" He could not keep himself from asking.

"At Wynfield. I understand if you feel it necessary to leave a detachment of guards behind, but I assure you, they won't be needed. Minuette is not about to lead an insurrection."

Even now, Dominic was so effortlessly in control. William found himself having to struggle to keep his voice and expression even. Although he wanted nothing more than to scream, *Stop telling me what to do,* he wouldn't give Dominic the satisfaction of knowing he'd rattled him.

"Matters of state are no longer your affair, except as they concern you. The fact that you are under arrest, for instance. I see you've already anticipated the attainder of your title," he said dismissively, indicating Dominic's plain gold tunic.

Dominic's neutral expression flickered briefly. "I truly am sorry. No punishment you can devise will match the penance of my own soul."

"You underestimate my imagination." William raised his voice. "Dudley!"

Robert came in and stood next to Dominic, his neutrality firmly back in place, as William said formally, "Dominic Courtenay, Duke of Exeter, you are under arrest for crimes against the state and the person of the king. You will be returned to London and held in the Tower until such time as you are called to answer for your crimes."

At a jerk of William's chin, Robert took Dominic's arm and pulled him round. Dominic kept his eyes on William, no doubt waiting to be asked for his parole as any gentleman would be.

As William stared at that aloof, self-contained face, he felt an overpowering urge to shatter that confidence. "Dudley," he said, staring all the while at Dominic, "put him in chains."

He felt a moment's satisfaction at the shock in Dominic's eyes. And then they were gone, and he stood alone once more.

As he always would from now.

When Dominic had passed out of sight, Minuette went to her jewelry casket. Since they had fled court, it contained only three items: her diary, the sapphire and pearl choker with a single filigree star that Dominic had given her years ago, and the jet black beads and heavy silver cross of her mother's rosary. She touched each of them in turn, unsure what she meant to do. Any other day of her life she would have worn the star pendant for courage, but she knew that would be a grave mistake today. The rosary was always a mistake, no more so than when a royal army was marching to subdue a Catholic rebellion. And her diary? If she were wise, she would burn it.

If she were wise, she wouldn't be in this position in the first place.

Once she made her decision, she moved swiftly. She gathered up the contents of her casket and placed them into a plain linen bag with the simple embroidery of a child's possessions. She would give it into Carrie's keeping and hope for the best.

She had always been more cynical than Dominic. He might think his surrender would mean William marching away from Wynfield—or at most sending troops to guard her home—but Minuette knew William too well to believe that. The king would come for her. All she had left was the choice to move first.

She looked around her chamber, wondering if she'd thought of everything, and was suddenly swamped by the memories of her wedding night, overlaid with last night's final hours with her husband. She drew in a sharp breath of regret and swallowed it away. She could not afford to be lost in the past; now was the time for clear-eyed action.

Carrie waited in the hall below, coming to her feet the moment she heard Minuette's footsteps. Minuette felt as though she were noticing everything with the razor-sharp clarity afforded last moments. Carrie's plump cheeks and glossy brown hair, the crease of concern between her eyes, were as dear and familiar as childhood, and Minuette's heart ached to cause her pain. But she knew better than to protest at her maid's devotion.

Harrington was in the hall as well, a solidly comforting presence in both size and silence. Minuette knew the only reason he had not accompanied Dominic was because he'd been ordered to stay with her. She hoped he would understand her intentions.

"Prepare horses," she said to Harrington. "For the three of us. We are riding to the king's camp."

"You promised Courtenay you would stay here," he rumbled. The use of Dominic's last name rather than his title wrung hard at her heart, and she had to swallow against tears.

But she would not be deterred. "I promised him that I would let him ride out alone. I was careful in my choice of words."

"He wants you to be careful with your person."

"I will not sit here and wait. Do you not think me as honourable as my husband?"

Carrie stepped between the two of them, so small and so fierce. "We knew what you would do. The horses are ready. I have packed the necessities. Is there anything else?"

Suddenly choked, Minuette handed Carrie the linen bag with her most precious possessions. "I am ready."

She could not keep back the tears when Fidelis rose from his customary spot outside the front door. The wolfhound clearly expected to go with her, as he always had this winter, and Minuette's sobs escaped despite herself. "Not this time," she whispered to the hound. "You must stay here."

He must have sensed her distress, for he did not go easily. In the end, Harrington had to use his full strength to draw Fidelis into the stables and shut him in one of the stalls. His howls echoed in Minuette's ears as she mounted Winterfall and rode out of her home.

With Harrington leading the way, Carrie riding pillion behind him, Minuette schooled her thoughts with each passing mile to calmness. She would need to be perfect when she came to the royal camp. Not just for William's sake, or Dominic's, but her own. The only way to do this was without looking back and without letting herself think twice. It shouldn't be so hard: she had spent months, if not years, playing a part at court. Now she would call upon all her skill to give her courage as she submitted herself to the will of a scorned king.

The royal camp was in motion; she could hear the clatter of men and horses as they drew near. But they had not set off just yet, so it was hard to tell which men would be headed to Wynfield. It didn't matter—there were only two men in the world she had ever cared for, and every inch of her was alert knowing how near they both were.

They were met by forward guards, who received her with cold hostility. She was wary, knowing the sorts of things that had once been shouted at Anne Boleyn. It would not have shocked her to have names thrown at her, but these men were disciplined enough. They asked the three of them to dismount and searched Harrington for weapons before proceeding on foot.

She spotted the royal tent, not yet taken down, and her heart skipped several beats when the flaps were thrown back and a familiar, long-legged figure appeared. The ground was soggy and the air heavy with the threat of rain, but weak sunlight filtered through the clouds here and there, one beam casting a sheen on William's dark hair. He'd let it grow since she'd seen him last; it curled down to his collar and she had a startlingly clear memory of her hands tangled in those curls at Hever so long ago.

William did not falter, but she saw the tension in the set of his shoulders as he came forward and then halted, waiting for her to take the last steps. She stopped a few paces from him and tried to remember how to breathe normally. His gaze swept her from head to toe, taking in the subdued cut of her riding gown, the lack of adornment, her hair plaited and pinned at the nape of her neck.

A greedy silence spread through the camp as word passed of what was happening. She moved to curtsey, and William stopped her. "Hold," he commanded. "Your audience is not complete."

So she held her ground and waited for Dominic to be led out. The look on her husband's face was not betrayal, at least, but a deep despair that rocked her nonetheless. His hands were chained together in front and Robert Dudley stood at his side. She stared at her husband, hoping he could read her devotion and love whatever came next.

"So." William's voice carried in the heavy air. "Have you come to beg my forgiveness?"

She tore her gaze away from Dominic. "Yes, Your Majesty."

Their eyes locked. "Then beg," he commanded, vicious.

She knelt as gracefully as she could, feeling the uneven ground through the layers of her skirts. With her head bowed low, she said, "I beg pardon for all my offenses, Your Majesty. It was done thoughtlessly, but not with malice. I could never wish you other than well, and I will never forgive myself for the injuries I have caused."

"The only lasting injuries have been to yourself. Now you must pay."

"Yes, Your Majesty."

William circled her, and she could feel his eyes burning into her bowed head. He stopped in front of her—his boots near enough that she could have kissed them if she'd bent farther—and suddenly she was being jerked to her feet, William's hands like a vise around her upper arms. *Don't react,* she silently begged Dominic. *Don't make it worse.*

She felt the combined intake of breath from the men watching as William bored his eyes into hers, the normal clear blue grown opaque with contempt. "I've had a lot of time to consider how to make you pay," he said, pitching his voice so that Dominic could not miss a word. "Perhaps I'll begin with Wynfield. Your home may be relatively inconsequential, but I well remember how devoted your people are to you. It would not do to leave a pocket of resistance behind me."

"Wynfield is no threat at all," she said, struggling to keep her voice even. She was walking such a narrow path; she could not afford the slightest stumble or William would pounce and others would pay the price for her mistakes. "They have had nothing to do with any of this."

"They harbored fugitives," William said. "That is a crime. And fugitives from the king, at that, which might make it treason."

She dared say nothing else, simply met his eyes and hoped something in her gaze would calm him.

Releasing her, William turned abruptly on his heel. "Sussex," he called, "get the men ready to march north. Leave fifty with me. Dudley, return the prisoner to your tent and stay with him." He gestured to two men-at-arms. "Take the maid and manservant into custody as well."

"And the woman?"

William shot her a smile over his shoulder, an expression that made her blood run cold. "Put her in my tent. We have negotiations to conclude."

The tone of his voice left no doubt what he intended to extract in those negotiations. Minuette had hoped for the best, but now braced herself for the worst. As long as Dominic kept control, so could she.

She did not dare look at her husband as Robert Dudley led him away and she gave a heartfelt prayer of thanks for Dominic's silence. Because he behaved, so did Harrington and Carrie. A guard took Minuette's arm and escorted her to William's tent. It was plain by court standards, though lavish by camp ones. The walls and roof might be cloth, but the interior was high-ceilinged and the ground thickly covered in rugs. There was a long oak table and chairs for councils of war, two chests no doubt filled with clothing and armor, and a bed. A large bed, with a real mattress and fine linens. Minuette looked away, shivering from her imagination as much as from the cold.

She waited a quarter hour before William entered. He had a linen bag in his hand, which he tossed on the table. It was hers, the one containing her diary and jewels. "Should make interesting reading," he mused. "And a rosary as well ... you have been dabbling with rebellion all along, haven't you?"

He moved behind her, and she tried not to stiffen as he rested a possessive hand on the curve of her neck. It was a familiar gesture, and so she was prepared for the kiss that followed.

"So," he said, and his voice was soft and all the more dangerous for it, "you wish to keep Wynfield and your people safe. What will you give me in return?"

"I do not believe you would offer the innocent harm."

"Do you not? Perhaps you do not know me as well as you should."

"I know you perfectly."

He turned her to face him and tipped her chin up with the hand that was not still resting on her neck. Something in the pose was suggestive of how easily a neck could be snapped and she repressed a shudder. "Then you know that your people, as well as Dominic, are in my hands. He has admitted his treason. There is no need for him to ever reach London or face trial. I am within my rights to execute him this very hour. Will you negotiate for that?"

It was why she had come. "Will you give me your word that my people at Wynfield will not be harmed? Your word that Dominic will face an open trial by jury in London?" Not that it would matter in the end—the jury would give the verdict William wanted. But Minuette knew it was beyond her power to stand in this camp and watch her husband die today.

"My word . . ." William's hand shifted along her throat until it rested at the neckline of her gown, "for your willingness?"

She met his eyes without wavering. "For my willingness."

William kissed her.

Even with her eyes closed, there was no hope of pretense. As William slid experienced hands across laces and fabric, removing her gown with caresses and kisses, Minuette felt her soul being stripped just as bare. She had bargained for the use of her body— she had not expected that her heart, so long twined with William in friendship, would demand its share of this hour.

William spoke only once. "Sweetling," he whispered when he laid her down, as though he had forgotten all the betrayal and fury of this year.

Minuette began to cry.

Is this punishment or is this penance? Am I whore, or am I savior? I feel him trembling against me and I do not know if I am his tormentor or his comforter . . . Forgive me, Lord . . . Forgive me, Dominic . . . Forgive me, Will . . .

Forgive me.

Robert Dudley was impressed with the extent of Dominic's control. They sat in a tent for two hours, waiting, and Dominic did not move from where he perched on the edge of the camp bed. He mostly kept his elbows braced on his knees, resting his forehead above the chains around his wrists. It was Robert who could not keep still. What the devil was taking the king so long?

Wrong question. He knew—everyone knew—what the king was doing.

Only once did Dominic speak. "Why just you? Isn't the king afraid I'll overwhelm a single guard?"

"There are armed men outside, you wouldn't get far. And if you did kill me, you might be doing the king a favour."

"Well," Dominic said distantly, "we wouldn't want that."

At long last a guard entered the tent. "We're moving. The king wants the prisoner mounted, but he remains chained."

"Where are we going?" Robert asked. Surely William didn't mean to drag Dominic along for the battles like a pet. Though on second thought . . .

But the guard answered, "We're going to Wynfield Mote."

Dominic's head came up at that, but he managed not to say anything. He submitted with perfect courtesy to Robert's necessary ministrations in getting him out of the tent and to his horse. Only when both men were mounted, along with twenty guards, did William escort Minuette from his tent.

Something in the way she moved reminded Robert of Elizabeth at her most imperious, as though she had locked away the core of herself and all that remained was the outward image. Robert wanted to curse at the uselessness of all this. He had warned Minuette more than once that she should walk away from William; how little he had realized that the real danger began the moment she did just that.

She accepted William's aid in mounting her white jennet, and William took a moment to lay a possessive hand on the mare. "You've ridden her well," he said, double meaning plain to be heard. Robert felt, rather than saw, a shudder run through Dominic, but when the king led them out, Dominic seemed indifferent.

It was the worst ride of Robert's life. He hadn't wanted to be with the army in the first place, serving a king who still half hated him and would never trust him. But Elizabeth had asked him to go. Robert hoped she wasn't counting on him to keep William in line. His only plan was to keep his head down and do as he was told.

William led the way, with Minuette's aristocratic jennet nearly even with his. They made a beautiful pairing, Robert thought: one dark and one gold and both able to look on the world with indifference. They did not speak to each other, nor even look at each other. After them rode six guards, followed by Robert and Dominic, and the remainder of the men behind with Harrington and Carrie in their midst.

Wynfield Mote was a square, old-fashioned stone manor house surrounded by low-bordered gardens and timber outbuildings, with cultivated fields and a handful of cottages in the distance. The company pulled up in good view, and after a few minutes in which the household might have been discussing what to do, the front door opened. A broad-shouldered man with silver hair and a countryman's unflappable gaze stepped outside.

"Asherton, isn't it?" William asked. He swung off his horse and helped Minuette down, then gestured to the others to follow.

The steward, for that he must be, waited patiently until all movement had settled, then tipped his head in Minuette's direction. "Are you well, mistress?"

"You don't call her 'lady'?" William asked in a deceptively mild voice. "But then, you must have known she only got that title through her deceit."

"I'm perfectly well," Minuette assured Asherton, and made a motion with her hand for him to be calm.

"How may we be of service, Your Majesty?" Asherton asked.

"How many are resident on this estate?"

"Eight household servants. Sixty or so on the farms."

William paced back and forth in a line between Asherton and Minuette, hands clasped behind his back in an attitude of deep thought. "Crops ready to go into the ground, I suppose?"

"Yes, Your Majesty."

William paused in front of Minuette and faced her. "You still believe me incapable of harming the innocent?"

She didn't answer, perhaps sensing that there was no safe answer to be found. There was a flush to the king's face Robert didn't like, and he thought: *This is all wrong.*

Abruptly, William stepped away from Minuette and faced Asherton. "You have one hour to clear the house and the cottages. One hour's grace for the people, thanks to your mistress's negotiating skills."

It was Minuette who asked, "And then?"

William met her eyes coldly, then away. "Guards! When the hour is passed . . ."

He returned his gaze to Minuette. "Burn it. Burn it all."

CHAPTER NINETEEN

23 March 1557

The most gracious Royal Highness Elizabeth,

After a two-night delay near Stratford-upon-Avon, His Majesty once again moved north today. We should catch the main body of the royal army tomorrow and continue on to our destined fight with Norfolk's rebels.

No doubt you have heard of Dominic and Minuette's surrender. Courtenay is being returned to London in chains, to await His Majesty's justice in the Tower. The lady, under separate guard, is headed for Beaulieu. A more gracious confinement, but a confinement nonetheless.

The king has ensured her people's submission by burning her estate to the ground. The main house, being outwardly stone, retains at least walls and substance. But the cottages of her small holdings are gone and her people scattered to seek what mercy they can find. I thought Your Highness would wish to know.

Take care in all things, from your most devoted servant and eyes in the North,

Robert Dudley

31 March 1557

Your Highness,

We have reached Nottingham, encountering only wisps of Norfolk's army, mostly in the form of scouts who vanish as quick as they come. It appears Norfolk has kept his army on the move as well, perhaps trying to slip past the king to London. I trust Lord Burghley knows his business, but it will ease my mind to know you are also aware of the possibilities. No one knows the twists of a devious mind better than you do, Your Highness, and you will be aware of the threat of a rebel army moving close enough to the coast to be reachable by a foreign fleet.

The king's army will begin moving south and east tomorrow, to intercept.

All care,

Robert Dudley

7 April 1557

Your Highness,

I scribble this by candlelight a few miles outside Bishop's Lynn (the locals still reference its ancient name, rather than King's Lynn as your father decreed it when he gained the bishop's holdings). The port here is the true danger, but there have been no sightings of French or Spanish ships that we can tell. Norfolk's army holds the city, but as long as he does not receive foreign reinforcements, our forces are sufficient for the clash. It will come within the next day or two, for the king is anxious to finish the matter and not draw it out in sieges and feints.

With all care for your gracious and royal self, I remain forever your servant,

Robert Dudley

"Well," Elizabeth said drily, "I'll wager that the name of King's Lynn will adhere to the town after the rebels' defeat."

It was April 15, and the fickle spring manifested itself today in gusts of cold rain followed by brief periods of watery sunlight. She was closeted in her study at Hatfield with Francis Walsingham and Lord Burghley. As chancellor, Burghley had himself brought Elizabeth the news of William's victory at King's Lynn. It had been as much rout as simple victory, for Norfolk had learned the painful lesson that French promises were not to be trusted. France had not set a single foot across the Scots border, and without Dominic's western forces, Norfolk had never stood a chance.

She appreciated Burghley's consideration in coming to Hatfield, especially as she knew his position was as delicate as her own. William had not forbidden Elizabeth to correspond with those at court, but no doubt he did not anticipate his own chancellor being quite so friendly with the sister he had sent away.

Elizabeth didn't especially care. Someone had to keep an eye on William, and Burghley was wise enough to know that and clever enough to manage things out of the king's sight. And of course there was Walsingham, who had proven his usefulness and discretion a hundred times over this last year. Elizabeth never asked for specifics of how he gained information, although she knew it often involved large sums of money. She had given him a relatively free hand since Minuette's flight from court and was not disappointed in the quality of his intelligence.

"Now what?" she asked Burghley. He was a different creature entirely from Rochford—more self-made man and less figure of elegance and languid grace—but he had a similar subtlety to his mind and much of the practicality that had marked her uncle. Without the arrogance or the ambition, and without the blood ties that had always given Rochford a wedge to use against his niece and nephew. "The rebel army is defeated and disbanded, but Norfolk has managed to slip through our fingers." She had no trouble using a royal "we" in this case—she considered herself as much England as William was.

Burghley said, "Norfolk fled by ship, almost certainly headed for France or Spain. It's a guess which country will want to deal with him: Spain is the most righteously angry because of Mary's execution. But France holds Mary Stuart and proclaims her England's rightful Catholic queen now. Either way, Norfolk can continue to stir up trouble abroad."

"Your men are watching?" Elizabeth asked Walsingham.

"Yes, Your Highness. Including John Dee, who is not a man of mine, per se, but a loyal servant to your cause."

"To England's cause," Elizabeth corrected sharply. No matter how angry she grew with William, she would allow no one to forget her brother's position in her presence.

"Of course, Your Highness."

"Lord Burghley, upon my brother's return to London, I trust you will endeavor to persuade him to recall me to court. I am uneasy at being long separated from one I love so dearly." *And one I trust so little when he is angry and injured.*

"Your Highness, it is my great aim to restore you to the heart and soul of England's court, for none graces it so well as you do."

Another difference between Burghley and Rochford—her uncle had never troubled much with praise, and when he did it had always been tinged with irony. But though he might speak flattering words, Burghley's eyes on her were thoughtful and appraising. She trusted his judgment and thus extended her hand and allowed him to kiss it. "I am indebted to you, Lord Burghley," she said. "You serve England well and I will not forget it."

"Thank you, Your Highness."

When Burghley had bowed himself out, Elizabeth said to Walsingham, "Your men will keep an eye on William's movements? I should like to have advance notice if he does not return straight to London."

If he went on to Beaulieu instead, she meant. She came close to shivering at the memory of her sister, Mary, who had spent much of her adult life in that manor. A restricted, circumscribed life, with little but the illusion of freedom. What did William intend sending Minuette there? Did he mean to keep her under lock and key like a slave, a mistress always at his disposal? Or had he locked her away from himself, a protection against memories of the past that were too painful to be looked on?

But unpleasant though Beaulieu might be, at least it was not the Tower. Elizabeth spared a moment's thought for Dominic and his no doubt certain end, then shoved it away. She could not help anyone unless she was in a position to help herself first. All her energies must bend to returning to court.

After the humiliation of being brought to the Tower in chains by men who would once have accepted his authority without question, Dominic had prepared himself for an onerous imprisonment, or even a speedy trial and execution. He was housed in Bell Tower in the corner of the inner ward and he passed the first weeks in an excess of mind-numbing boredom—no books, no paper, no visitors.

At least boredom was better than the waves of rage and jealousy that had swept through him at regular intervals during the long escorted ride back to London. Being jealous of William was not new; Dominic had hated every minute the king spent alone with Minuette over the last few years, had flinched with every royal caress bestowed on his wife.

But this was different. He knew, as well as if he'd been in the royal tent with them, what had passed between Minuette and William. And although he did not blame his wife, a wounded part of his soul kept screaming: *I would rather be dead than live with this.*

But as he'd had no doubts that the guards would be quizzed by William on his behavior, there was no way in hell he would give the king the satisfaction of knowing how he'd been hurt. So he schooled his face and body into indifference. And in that effort his spirit became, if not indifferent, at least calm. Whatever had happened in the camp outside Wynfield had happened and could not be changed. What mattered now was the future. For Minuette's sake, if not his own.

He was under no illusions as to his future: interrogation, trial, execution. Except that no one seemed in a particular hurry to begin. He was admitted to the Tower precincts on a cold, damp night at the end of March, and entering by the dreaded Water Gate had sent a single shudder through him that he harshly channeled into arrogance. Worse than that had been his solitude. Harrington was brought to London with him, but they were kept separate along the road, and in the Tower, Harrington was imprisoned separately.

Dominic spent twenty-two days seeing no one except the Lieutenant of the Tower (who had received him the first night with grim neutrality and no sign that they had ever met before) and the rotation of guards who stood outside the door to his double chamber and handed him food twice a day. The guards wouldn't speak to him, and Dominic didn't know which was worse: that he had no news of Minuette or that he didn't know what was happening to the royal army.

At last in mid-April, the Lieutenant of the Tower appeared once again, with Harrington at his heels. "The king, having successfully routed the rebel army, has decided to be gracious and allow your man to stay with you."

"Is the king returned to London?" Dominic asked.

The lieutenant hesitated, and Dominic brought to bear all the old authority he had once worn so easily. It was mostly a matter of straightening his posture and focusing his gaze, allowing anger to become arrogance until he looked at the lieutenant with all the contempt he could not direct at William.

At last the lieutenant said grudgingly, "His Majesty is at Hampton Court."

He would not be drawn further, but thankfully Harrington had more news at his disposal. "No one minds the servant as much as the master," he told Dominic. "I've picked up pieces of what happened."

Dominic could not believe how good it was to see Harrington. For the first time in weeks he sat at the table in the outer chamber and felt his shoulders relax. He hadn't realized just how tense he'd been every moment until he felt the pull of aching muscles as they readjusted themselves. "Have you been treated well?" he asked. It had been one of his fears in the night; that, barring specific instructions for Dominic, the guards or interrogators would do their worst to Harrington instead. He looked the same: six and a half feet of solidly built frame, no evidence of injury or insult. But a man that size and temperament could absorb a lot of punishment without sign.

Harrington skipped right over the matter of his treatment with a shrug. "Not interested in me. They kept me with two other prisoners, London merchants, both of them, who received regular letters from outside. The king won his battle, but has lost Norfolk. It's said the duke took ship for refuge in France."

"And the remains of the rebel army?" Dominic asked, thinking despite himself of tactics and maneuvers.

"The king has let it disband with only a handful of arrests. Stephen Howard was one of them. According to a friendly guard, he was brought to the Tower last night in lieu of his nephew."

Dominic spared a moment's regret for Minuette's stepfather, but that was all he could muster. The man had known what he was doing.

Finally, he asked the only thing that mattered. "And the women?"

Harrington's jaw tightened briefly and Dominic knew the man was as concerned for Carrie as he himself was for Minuette. "No news. Except that they're not here, and every day they are not in the Tower is good news."

Dominic nodded in agreement, but his heart sank. If he'd thought his guards were in the least bribable, he'd have given everything he owned in the world for word of Minuette. Just as well they weren't, because everything he owned in the world just now amounted to the clothes he wore.

"And you?" Harrington asked. "Have there been questions?"

"Not a single one."

"What do you suppose he's waiting for?"

He'd had time to ponder that question, but even more, he had many years of friendship and familiarity to teach him William's mind. "He wants to do one thing at a time. Now that the rebel army is dealt with, he'll turn his attention to me." With clear-eyed understatement, Dominic added, "It won't be a pleasant summer."

As spring gently turned to early summer, William did not find the season as pleasant as in years past. As long as he could remember, April and May and early June had brought with them not only longer days and bolder sunlight and cheerful flowers, but also the childlike anticipation of his birthday. This year, the spring seemed colder, grayer, wetter. His approaching twenty-first birthday only reminded him that Minuette would be twenty-one as well.

He had not seen her since Wynfield. She had stood, white-faced but unmoving, while his guards had methodically set fire to her home and estate. The only emotion he'd seen was the brief anguish in her eyes as she'd ridden away from her people, now homeless and beyond her aid. But she had bit back any public reproach and remained cloaked in unapproachability. He had sent her to a tent of her own in the camp that night—well guarded, naturally—and had not turned out to see her ride away the next morning with an escort of armed men. Not because he was ashamed. Not exactly.

How long had he waited for Minuette? How many nights had he dreamed of finally having her in his arms, lost to everything but desire? Maybe it was just that he'd never imagined he would have her only with her husband very nearly watching them. Maybe it was simply that nothing so long anticipated could live up to the dreams.

Minuette kept her word—she had been willing. But willing was not the same as eager, and he'd never had a partner who'd been less than eager. William had found pleasure with her, but it was brief and weighted with unlooked-for guilt. What had he to feel guilty about? he raged silently. He had not lied to his friends, he had not broken the trust of a king ... but even so, he did not want to be alone with Minuette immediately after. A matter of prudence.

His council did not seem to appreciate his prudence in other matters. Summoned to Hampton Court, where William had chosen to retreat after the victory at King's Lynn, his once-more reduced privy council spent an hour hectoring him about letting almost all the rebels retreat to their homes rather than forcing punishment on a large scale.

"I thought my restraint would be appreciated, as I have been accused in the past of too-hasty action." William stared down Lord Burghley. "Their royal champion is dead and their commander routed. More than that, the French did not march at all. What more do you want?"

Burghley spoke delicately. "Lord Norfolk is capable of creating trouble for us still. Your Majesty, would it not be wise to approach the French and attempt to mend matters between us sufficiently that they will be disinclined to support Norfolk?"

"It is for the French to mend matters with us," William said sharply.

"Then at the least increase the number of men in readiness along the southeast coast. If the French decide to invade, or even lend Norfolk ships—"

"How much money and time did we waste last summer waiting for an invasion that never came close to occurring? You're the one who keeps pointing out the burden of taxes on my people. Leave it. Our defenses are sufficient to give us warning and the people will rise if there is the slightest danger."

Burghley subsided on that matter, but pressed another. "There is much talk at court about the Princess Elizabeth's continuing absence. Surely Your Majesty does not wish to give rise to rumours of your estrangement."

Were they estranged? William wondered. He hadn't meant to be. But Elizabeth was so damned uncomfortable with her questions and her penetrating eyes and her almost thorough knowledge of his heart.

But damned if he would allow this last relationship fall prey to gossip and the vicious-minded. "Of course I wish my sister's company. I intended to send for her this week, that she will be well in time for the birthday celebrations."

He would summon her; and not just for his birthday. There would be another event on June 28, one intended to pacify his council and country. Surely Elizabeth would want to be present when he married Jane Grey.

By the time William's summons arrived at Hatfield, Elizabeth had been contemplating open rebellion for weeks. It was infuriating having to wait, but she filled her days as best she could with her voluminous correspondence. Robert had not dared come see her, precarious as his position was at court, but he wrote and so did Lord Burghley. And John Dee wrote faithfully from France, where Norfolk had indeed appeared after his retreat. The duke had not, as yet, been publicly received at the French court, but nor had he been sent away. It seemed he was in a sort of limbo, awaiting the decisions of kings on both sides of the Channel.

John Dee seemed to know as much about Minuette from his far distance as anyone. *Word in France is that she is being kept secluded at Beaulieu,* he wrote to Elizabeth. *With only a single maid allowed to attend her. No one else sees her; everything, including meals, goes through her woman.* And then, unnervingly prescient, Dee added: *Do not fret for her state of mind, Your Highness. Your friend is bright and charming, but mostly she is resilient. Her stars will guard her right.*

Stars, thought Elizabeth bitterly. What use are stars that are nothing but vague reassurances of personality, rather than markers of how to proceed? But she knew her displeasure was coloured by her own worry and enforced idleness.

She shrank from confronting her brother directly, even by letter. From Robert and Burghley, Elizabeth drew a picture of a court that was similarly wary. It was a perilous balance they were all ne-gotiating, with a king who had become dangerously unpredictable. He'd had Eleanor returned to court in the aftermath of victory, and set her up in chambers that shouted her regained status as king's concubine.

Elizabeth attempted twice to write to Minuette, but had no way of knowing if her letters were getting through. She did not receive any in return. She made no attempt to contact Dominic in the Tower, for two reasons. First, because she was looking to herself. Selfish that might be, but Elizabeth had no wish to bring down William's wrath upon her own head.

And second, because she thought there might come a time in future when she would want all the influence she could command. Best not to spend it too early.

So when the royal summons came, Elizabeth ignored her brother's peremptory tone and set off gladly for Hampton Court, hopeful that now she could discover for herself precisely what her brother's mood was and how best to work with it. William sent a royal barge for her comfort, and as she sailed past the Tower, its walls and turrets looming sternly on the Thames, she wondered how Dominic was enduring his imprisonment. William had made no move to bring the friend once known as the King's Shadow to trial as yet. Indeed, as far as she could ascertain, William had not so much as mentioned Dominic's name since the arrest. She distrusted that silence, for it was all the more likely to erupt in sudden violence. Perhaps William meant to leave him there for years. Perhaps William himself didn't know what he was doing.

To only her slight surprise, William avoided her upon her arrival at Hampton Court. She was in her usual apartments, but Hampton Court more than any other palace was haunted by memories of Minuette. Elizabeth counted herself neither sentimental nor nostalgic, but she kept thinking she caught glimpses out of the corner of her eye—skirts swirling, golden-honey hair flashing—and occasionally a drift of laughter seemed to contain the music of Minuette's voice.

Robert was a link to that past but he was also, reassuringly, firmly focused on the present. The travails of the last two years had sharpened his mind and made him wary, but they had also deepened his character. Odd, she thought, that actions begun in secrecy and mischief could end in making him firmer. Like a steel blade tempered by fire.

Not that she had forgotten his sins. But her options for friendship had never been more limited and she trusted Robert—if not quite wholly, then more than she trusted anyone else at the moment.

"How is he?" she asked Robert without preamble as he took the offered seat next to her in the window. It was informal and the slightest bit improper, but who cared about flirtations and gossip when England's king might any day erupt into violence?

"Erratic. Some days he throws himself into court life with all the energy and enthusiasm one could wish. Other days he is present, but irritable and quick to snap. But the real concern is days like this one, when he withdraws completely from public life and no one sees him for two or three days at a time save his personal attendants. He will not even admit Lord Burghley when such moods come upon him."

"Is he ill?" she asked. "A lingering effect of the smallpox?"

Robert shrugged. "I'd say a lingering effect of indecision. I do not understand him, Elizabeth. But I do believe that nothing will get better so long as he leaves the matter of Dominic and Minuette open. For better or worse, matters must be brought to a head."

"Are you telling me I should encourage my brother to execute his closest friend?"

"If anyone can persuade him to mercy, it is you. But if you cannot . . . then yes, even an execution would be an end."

Robert's words haunted her in the days leading up to William's birthday. Though the king emerged from his chambers two days after Elizabeth's arrival, he did not go out of his way to speak to her privately. Her unease grew with each hour until she herself was ill with worry. Robert had not been wrong, nor Burghley, nor

Walsingham. Each had warned her of some facet of the change in her brother's personality. It wasn't a complete surprise, for he had not been wholly the same since the smallpox. But the differences now were more pronounced, and in her most cynical moments Elizabeth wondered how deeply England would pay for her king's discontent.

Finally, William sent for her alone. She dressed with greater than normal care, irritated that she was nervous about meeting her own brother, but still taking efforts to appear unruffled and in control. Kat Ashley supervised, sniffing approval only when the deep green damask gown with its cream-coloured silk sleeves and stiffly pointed bodice were impeccable. Then she patted Elizabeth on the cheek and said softly, "Remind him how you love him."

That resolve lasted for all of two minutes when she was shown into William's privy chamber. He was dressed richly, but there was something off-putting about it, something in the puffs and slashes and velvet and jewels that combined to create an image of a king rather than expressing the king's nature itself.

But it was the glitter to his eyes and the dark hollows beneath them that concerned her most. "I've missed you, Will," she said impulsively and moved to embrace him. He did no more than submit to a brief touch before he stepped away.

"I welcome your presence, sister," he said. Something of the formality reminded Elizabeth of the way he had always spoken to Mary—sibling duty rather than affection.

She instinctively matched her attitude to his. "How could I ever be content away from Your Majesty?"

A smile, small and cool, ghosted his face before vanishing. "I would ask your presence tomorrow at noon in the Chapel Royal. Will you come?"

"Are you willing to tell me why?"

His blue eyes, so strikingly like their father's, held deep wells of pain and bitterness, but his voice remained remote. "To witness my marriage to Jane Grey."

A million thoughts rushed through her head in the space of a single breath, but Elizabeth always knew how to choose the right one to speak aloud. "My congratulations. A most worthy bride. You must be happy."

You do not look happy, she thought. You look as though you do not remember who you are.

CHAPTER TWENTY

T HE MOST DIFFICULT part of Minuette's confinement at Beaulieu was the utter solitude. She had never been so lonely in her life. She did not even have interaction with her guards, for William had instructed the men to deal only with Carrie. It was infuriating and humiliating being shut into just two rooms of this palace, and having to retreat into the inner room whenever a guard appeared with food or to deal with other necessities. She would have thrown a tantrum every hour for as many days as it took to get noticed were it not for one simple fact: Dominic was in William's hands. She had sacrificed much to ensure her husband's safety. She could endure loneliness for his sake.

If only solitude didn't allow quite so much scope for memory. With no one but Carrie to talk to, no books or letters or diary— not even dice or a chess set—Minuette had little to do but remember. The acrid smoke of Wynfield burning; the stunned faces of her tenants; Fidelis's warm coat beneath her hands as she'd commanded the dog to stay with Asherton in the shell that had been her home ... She wallowed in those memories until she could smell the fire and hear the flames and feel the hollow tightness that had overtaken her that afternoon.

If she dwelt in that particular hell, she did not have to remember the one that had preceded it in William's tent.

Her fear and regret made her short-tempered and she found herself apologizing to Carrie at least four times a day. It was a measure of Carrie's own strain that she did not insist such apologies were unnecessary. She had uttered no word of reproach to her mistress, though Minuette knew how Carrie worried about Harrington, and the maid had every right to blame her for the predicament they were all in.

The guards grudgingly gave Carrie news of the royal army's victory and Lord Norfolk's flight, and Minuette braced herself for William's return. Surely he meant to see her. Why else would he send her to Beaulieu rather than the Tower? But as the days, and then weeks, passed, she realized he might not intend to make her his mistress after all. Which was just as well, because her negotiation of willingness had been a onetime only offer, even if William had not violated the spirit of their agreement by burning her home.

To her dying day—which was surely not far off—she would never forget the weight of Dominic's careful indifference as they had all ridden to Wynfield after . . . well, afterward. Her husband had neither looked at nor spoken to her, and every hour she was awake Minuette carried a prayer in her heart: *Lord, let him understand and forgive me.*

Let me forgive myself.

When she became ill after her arrival at Beaulieu, Minuette thought it nothing more than nerves and solitude. But the nausea did not pass and first one month and then a second slipped by without any sign of her female courses. Carrie did not comment on her lack of bleeding. She did not have to. Only once in her life had Minuette missed her monthly bleeding—during the too-short-lived pregnancy last summer.

By the time her twenty-first birthday arrived, fourteen weeks after her last night at Wynfield with Dominic—and her hours with William in his tent—Minuette knew that God had devised the cruelest punishment of all for her sins.

She was once more with child.

On the first day of July, the guards came for Dominic in Bell Tower and the interrogations began. He knew his inquisitors, naturally, the chief among them being the increasingly aged Archbishop Cranmer. The cleric coughed a great deal and looked as though he hadn't eaten or slept in months. Though there was awkwardness on both sides, there seemed little of malice and the questions were so random as to be meaningless. It was only after the third or fourth of these sessions that Dominic realized William hadn't told his inquisitors what exactly he wished them to prove. Catholic collaborator? Personal treason? Attempted murder? Until William decided which course to pursue, the interrogations were mild. They served more to tell Dominic what was happening in the outside world than to fill him with foreboding.

Just at dusk on the sixth of July, Dominic sat playing dice with Harrington and two squires who had come from Tiverton and requested to stay with him, determined to prove their loyalty to a Courtenay. He knew something unusual was happening when the door opened to admit the Constable of the Tower, a man who left most duties to his lieutenant.

"Come with me." His voice was blank with authority.

Another interrogation, then. Perhaps they were ready to get serious in their questions. When the constable didn't lead him to the usual chamber, however, Dominic felt a flicker of worry. Would it be torture this time?

But their path did not lead to the chamber Dominic had been in twice before and still recalled with a rolling stomach. Rather, they ended up outside a wooden door in Wakefield Tower and Dominic's confusion increased. What the hell was he doing outside the records room? Did they expect the sight of hundreds of account books to induce him to confession?

The constable opened the door and there stood William, looking lean and hungry and with a banked fire in his eyes that set off all Dominic's alarms.

Probably not torture. But perhaps swords at twenty paces, or daggers, or sheer, bloody hatred in hand-to-hand combat.

Dominic forced himself back to rationality. William hadn't come here to kill him. If—when—William killed him, it would be at a safe remove, and with the widest possible audience. A nice, safe, judicial murder.

"Leave us."

When the door was shut and they were alone, William came forward one slow step at a time, until only a dozen inches separated them. "You do not offer congratulations?"

"On what?"

"My wife."

Dominic's throat closed off. Wife? He couldn't mean . . .

William smiled, a nasty, insinuating smile. "You don't really think I'd take your cast-offs, do you? I have uses for Minuette, now that she's broken in, but I could hardly make her queen. No, I've rewarded the Protestants for their support in recent uprisings."

Dominic's throat loosened enough for him to speak. "Jane Grey."

"We're closing ranks, Dom, isolating our enemies, striking wherever we find discontent. It's astonishing the number of priests in this country, when one troubles to look. In even the quietest households. Such as your mother's."

He froze for only a moment, then with a bitter laugh, Dominic shook his head. "What did you do with him, William? Send him out of the country? Throw him in prison?"

"Burnt him," William answered bluntly. "Made quite a spectacle in the middle of the village. I understand your mother was somewhat distressed."

Dominic turned away. Killing the priest who had married them . . . he should have seen that coming. And now his mother was bereft of the only comfort she'd known in years. Courtenay men: between them, he and his father had done a decent job of destroying his mother's life.

"What do you want? To gloat? Why don't we just take it as read? You won, I lost."

William sauntered to the quartet of narrow rectangular windows set in the rounded wall. "Nice view of Water Gate. I'm sorry I couldn't be here to watch you brought in, but the fighting, you know. Still, there are other prisoner arrivals to observe."

In spite of himself, Dominic crossed to the window and looked down, wondering who it was William wanted him to see. His mother, raving mad? Some other of his mother's household, brought here for no reason than because they mattered to him? Asherton dragged back from the ruins of Wynfield Mote?

From this vantage, Dominic could see clearly the Water Gate used for transportation of the most important prisoners. He'd come in this way himself, three months ago. Tonight a regiment of guards lined Water Lane, with bracketed torches casting long shadows. The constable himself stood at the top of the wooden steps leading down to the river.

A barge appeared, skillfully brought alongside the stairs by a wizened boatman. There were two cloaked women in the barge and Dominic tried to discern which might be his mother. A guard stood up, extending his hand to one of the women.

The woman stood and Dominic's body recognized her before his mind could work it out in words. He thought he might be sick, for as the woman balanced in the small boat, the hood of her cloak fell back and a spill of golden hair gleamed in the torchlight.

For one long moment Minuette stood in the slightly swaying barge and stared at the offered hand. Then she picked up her skirts with both hands and stepped quickly, if a little clumsily, onto the first step.

William's voice was low and vicious in his triumph. "Proud girl. What was that phrase? All eyes and legs and spirit."

Dominic did not allow the contemptuous words to distract him from Minuette. In spite of her icy demeanor, she was frightened. He could see it in the little things: the stiffness of her movements, the way her hands clenched on the fabric of her skirt, how her eyes darted away from the constable as if looking for a way to escape. One of the guards stepped forward to take her by the arm and Dominic saw her freeze like a hunted hart. For a blinding moment, he was afraid she was going to panic. God help him, if he had to watch her dragged away screaming, he would break William's neck.

Minuette's hands relaxed. She stared scornfully at the guard— Dominic couldn't see her face, but he knew from the set of her head and shoulders that her eyes blazed with scorn—until the man stepped back. The constable led the way and she followed on her own, back straight and head held high.

She was almost out of sight, ready to pass beneath the arch that led to the green around which ranged most of the Tower buildings. And then, with a suddenness that caused a guard to bump into her, she stopped walking. Absently, she shook the guard off where he had touched her shoulder and raised her head. With unerring instinct, she looked straight at Dominic.

He knew she couldn't see him in the unlit room, or at least no more of him than his outline. But she didn't need more than that, maybe not even that much. She knew he was there.

With a dazzling smile, she lowered her head and walked away.

"I hope you looked well." Venom laced William's voice. "You'll never see her again."

"I didn't expect to see her today. And I don't need to look to remember her." He saw her every time he closed his eyes, he felt her beneath his hands, the length of her body pressed against him that last night, even hear the beat of her heart, swifter and lighter than his own.

William's control was beginning to slip. "It's not as if you had her pure on your wedding night. Virgin she may have been then, but only just."

"It was her body alone that you touched. You'll never have more of her than that."

"Do you not remember Wynfield and our negotiations?" William's smile was cold with fury. "I had her in ways you are too rigidly honourable to dream. And she didn't protest. She came to my bed willingly. With you not fifty feet away."

Stamping hard on the images William's words called up, Dominic said, "I've never doubted she came to you without force. But it wasn't for love, either, you've ensured that. She came to you for pity's sake."

He didn't try to avoid William's fist. Dominic's head snapped to the side with the impact and he rocked back on his heels. *Come on,* he urged silently. *Hit me again. Hit me until you've burned out all your anger and jealousy and fear.*

But William had learned his lessons well, the lessons of control and restraint that Dominic had always been so eager to teach him. That might have been a mistake, he reflected, watching William's eyes cool and his body relax. *He's learned too well to twist and calculate, he cannot just let go.*

That will be his undoing—and mine.

William eaten alive with bitterness, Minuette held in the Tower . . . the situation could not possibly be worse.

And then, with a casual twist that was reminiscent of Lord Rochford at his most cruel, William announced, "And as for your pure wife, you should know one thing: she is with child. Pity she's not quite so pure as to be certain of the father."

6 July 1557
Beauchamp Tower

He is here. I saw him, as they brought me in.
    No, not saw him, not really. Felt him.

10 July 1557
Beauchamp Tower

This is hardly a formal diary, being only a sheaf of paper without binding, and it is no doubt folly to continue to set down my thoughts. I hate the thought of William reading my diary—or worse, passing it to his council to condemn me. But as I have already established that I am not wise when it comes to words, it can hardly do me more damage now. And at least it is something to do!

I suppose I should not complain of boredom, as the alternatives could certainly be worse, but I find it difficult being once again confined to two rooms with only Carrie for company. I was assured that I might bring three or four women with me—it seems I am not to be treated without some consideration—but the only ones I could have borne to have near me now I also care about too much to drag into this. Carrie is only here because I knew it would require violence to keep her away. Besides, Harrington is in the

Tower as well. I suppose she might see him, or at least hear of him. More chance, anyway, than of my seeing Dominic.

After three days, I have yet to be asked a single question. This is not aimed at me—it is aimed at Dominic. William intends to break him, and he thinks he can do it through me.

8 August 1557
Beauchamp Tower

I have finally been interrogated. It was something of a relief after four weeks of tedious waiting, though the interrogators were not especially polite. If ever a man had spoken to me in the nasty, insinuating manner these men did, I would once have haughtily ignored him.

Today, I could not afford haughtiness. I had to keep my head, and answer honestly what I was asked without volunteering anything that might damage us further. It was not as easy as it sounds, particularly when they probed for intimate information— was I a virgin when I wed? What about Jonathan Percy—had I not lain with him before he left for France? Had I not spent hours alone with the king, enticing him to the point that he agreed to marry me? There were significant glances at my shape, just starting to show beneath looser gowns, and it was all very sordid and depressing. By the end I nearly wanted to say, "Just kill me and be done with it."

But Dominic would not approve of my giving in.

29 August 1557
Beauchamp Tower

I have been questioned at erratic intervals over the last three weeks, always more of the same. More unpleasant leering as they ask

*things that anyone who knows me couldn't possibly believe to be
true. Truth, it seems, is not the guiding principle of this
investigation.*

*That was hammered home today. I faced a roomful of men, all
of whom I have known for years, and most of whom have long
disapproved of me. Or at least, of William's attachment to me.*

*Today, the questions were different. Today, I was accused of
trying to murder William.*

*I was so astonished by the accusation that even now I'm not
entirely clear on the details. To be frank, I'm not sure my
interrogators were clear on the details, either. It seemed to me that
they were fishing, prepared to fashion the particulars in whatever
convenient manner they could devise. Something about poison—
monkshood, no less—and a garment of mine that I had sent to
Will. One of my enticements, I can only presume. The timing of
this attempt was also unclear; I heard dates ranging from last
summer, just before we fled court, to as long ago as the winter of
1554. Perhaps they're trying to prove a pattern of murder attempts.*

*The details don't much matter—it is the accusation itself that is
revealing. If William is prepared to charge me with this, then he is
prepared to kill me.*

*31 August 1557
Beauchamp Tower*

*When I was summoned today, I went as usual, expecting to face all
and sundry and defend myself against sheer imagination.*

It was only Will.

*He looks different—harder, more remote. He did not say much.
I congratulated him on his queen, which was perhaps not the wisest
choice. But when face-to-face with him, my temper flared. I know*

he holds my life in his hands. More important, he holds Dominic's. But my tongue was quicker than my brain, and I wanted to provoke him. If I did, he hid it well. His face has become blank— only those blue eyes are alive. Those devouring eyes that studied the unmistakable swell of my body with an intensity that scorched me to my bones. As though he were already laying claim to the child I carry.

He made me an offer, of course. I've been expecting it for months, but still I was speechless when he actually said it aloud. It's quite simple—I come to his bed, willingly and for as long as he wishes it, and Dominic lives. He threw in some additional inducements, such as my title and promises of titles and land for any children we might have ("including this one," he said, with a pointed look at my growing figure), but he knows the only thing that matters is Dominic's life.

I said no. That was all—just the one word. He retreated after that.

He will be back.

1 October 1557
Beauchamp Tower

He has been back, twice a week for the last month. Nine times he has asked me now, and nine times I have said no.

Today, my willful tongue being what it is, I finally asked him why bother with the pretense of consent? I am in his custody and at his mercy. He had me securely confined at Beaulieu—why not leave me there and force the issue after the child is born?

His face darkened and he raised his hand as if to strike me as he did once before. But he merely closed his hand into a fist and slammed it into the door on his way out of the room.

*And then I knew. He wants what Dominic had, and that does
not include taking me by force. Almost I wish I did not know that,
for I am still capable of hurting for Will. And this is a hurt that
can never be mended.*

5 October 1557
Beauchamp Tower

*I have not seen the king since he stormed away from me. But it
seems I have provoked him in a manner I did not intend.*
Dominic stands trial tomorrow.

THE TRIAL OF DOMINIC COURTENAY, DUKE OF EXETER
WESTMINSTER HALL
6 OCTOBER 1557

*In the eleventh year of the reign of King Henry IX: for rebelliously
conspiring against and endeavoring the subversion of the government
by confederacy with various Popish traitors and accomplices.*

*Then the Lord High Constable of the Tower, the Lieutenant of
the Tower, and the Gentleman Porter, who carried the ax before the
prisoner came first in, and the prisoner followed and made his appearance at the bar.*

*Then were summoned the peers of Dominic, Duke of Exeter, to
sit in judgment, having due regard to their own conscience.*

The trial lasted less than two hours. Dominic supposed he
should be grateful that it lasted even that long. The worst of it was
not the sketchy evidence or the twisting of events or the flat-out
lies. It was not even anxious anticipation of the verdict, for he was
never in doubt of that.

The worst of it was watching men he had commanded in battle

and counseled with in peace pretending that this was anything but a sham. At least they seemed more or less ashamed of themselves, enough that most of them would not look at him directly. Only Lord Burghley met his eyes boldly, and Dominic was certain of the sympathy he read there. But sympathy could not help him now.

Dominic barely concerned himself with the details of the day. It was enough to be lumped in with Norfolk's rebels, to have his relationship with Renaud examined in light of a French-Catholic conspiracy aimed at deposing William and putting either Mary Tudor or Mary Stuart on the throne. They even managed to claim that, as a great-grandson of Edward IV, Dominic had intended to wed one of the Marys himself and rule with her. How he was supposed to manage that when he was already married—legitimately, as far as the Catholics were concerned—was glossed over. The suspicion was enough.

> *The Attorney General to the Lord Judges: Let me note unto you that he hath long lived in friendship with this prince, and so highly advanced by His Majesty's favor that he should have trembled to think of such rebellion as he now has enterprised. Doth not my lord of Exeter now enjoy his title by the gift of this prince? Was he not made Lieutenant of the March at the mere age of twenty? One of His Majesty's council? To be Warden of the Cinque Ports, set above men who were his superior in both sense and experience? Yet all these were as cleverly forgotten as if they had never been.*

When the examinations had been made, Dominic was removed from the hall for a short time. Too short, he thought wryly, following the lieutenant back in after less than twenty minutes. Though he hadn't expected salvation, it was disconcerting to be proven right so quickly.

The lords were polled individually. He listened without moving as, one by one, each lord stood with bared head, placed his left hand on his right side, and proclaimed Dominic guilty. When they had finished, all eyes turned to the bar.

> Lord High Steward: Dominic, Duke of Exeter, you must go to the place from whence you came and there remain during His Majesty's pleasure, from thence to be drawn on a hurdle through London streets, and so to the place of execution, where you shall be hanged, boweled, and quartered. Your head and quarters to be disposed of at His Majesty's pleasure, and so God have mercy on your soul.

Dominic was asked if he had anything he wished to say.

This was the moment he'd been waiting for, and he invested his final words with as much humility as he could muster. "My lords, do but send to me at the time of my death and you shall see how penitent and humble I will be in acknowledging His Majesty's exceeding favours to myself. And I do most humbly desire His Majesty that my death may put a period to my offenses committed, and be no more remembered by His Grace."

It was the nearest he could come to petitioning William directly for Minuette's life.

CHAPTER TWENTY-ONE

"Tell me, Dr. Dee, did you see Dominic Courtenay's fate in the stars when you spoke to us at Greenwich? Did you know then how all this would end in blood and tears?"

Elizabeth prowled her presence chamber at Hampton Court, the glittering space empty apart from herself, Francis Walsingham, and John Dee, who had arrived in England from his Continental travels just the day before. Though Dee's face bore the marks of fatigue and long hours of hard journeying, his eyes and voice were steady as ever.

"Your Highness, I have told you many times that I see only what the stars lay out according to men's natures and positions. I do not tell the future, nor do I ordain it. We are all as God made us in our various spheres."

"That's not good enough!" Elizabeth slammed one palm on a tabletop, not sure if her temper was fury or grief.

Or terror.

Because Minuette would stand trial for high treason the day after tomorrow. If William could indeed condemn Dominic to the executioner's block, what else might he be capable of?

With effort, Elizabeth pulled the edges of her unraveling self together. "How has God made me, Doctor? Do I act according to my impulses, or restrain myself to prudence?"

There was a long silence, and Elizabeth turned to face the men. Walsingham caught her eye and she was more grateful than she could say that she had met him. A man committed wholly to her service was such a luxury of relief. Dominic had once been that man for William . . .

When John Dee spoke, Elizabeth felt that odd sense of present and future combining. She had felt it the first time she met him, a certainty that this was a man important to her, a man she would seek out again and again in the years to come. A man who would give her not easy answers but a path to find the hard ones.

"God made you to see widely, Your Highness. Rarely will you be blinded by immediate troubles, looking always to what will follow from how you deal with them."

"So I am cold and prudent?"

"You are wise. That does not mean you do not feel. Only those who feel deeply can judge rightly the effects of their own and others' choices."

There were times when Elizabeth would like someone to tell her that she was lighthearted or merry or restful . . . but she was too clearheaded and ambitious for those moments to last long. Now she sighed, and finally sat down. Waving the two men to seats of their own, she said, "What is the latest word from France?"

None of it was good. The Duke of Norfolk had at last been received at the French court and King Henri appeared to be giving serious consideration to providing the duke with troops and ships in the spring to launch a new offensive in England. The seriousness of the offer was underscored by the news that Norfolk was negotiating a marriage to the daughter of one of the French king's courtiers. Elizabeth wondered how much Henri's maneuvering of Norfolk was simply a gamble to see if England could be plucked away from the troublesome Tudors with someone else bearing the physical brunt of the work. Money and mercenaries were relatively simple to come by, compared with a leader in whom burned a righteous fervor. Also, Mary Stuart, Queen of Scotland and the lead Catholic contender for England's throne, would soon be fifteen. Rumour was she would finally marry the French dauphin in the next year. What better wedding gift for her new father-in-law than an island ruled jointly by Mary and her French husband?

"Your Highness," Walsingham finally said. "Have you given thought to Mistress Wyatt's condition?"

The entirety of Europe knew that Minuette was now seven months pregnant. If her trial ended in a conviction and sentence of death, she would at the very least be spared long enough to give birth. That gave Elizabeth precious time in which to maneuver. If she decided to maneuver. That was the thrust of Walsingham's question, for he knew the princess very well indeed. If she decided to aid Minuette, then Walsingham would be her hands.

"I am constantly giving thought to her condition," Elizabeth answered. "I have asked Robert Dudley to attend her trial. When he brings word to me of the verdict, it will be time enough for you and I to speak."

Because she still had hope, slender though it was, that the jury would not convict a pregnant woman. That if they did, they would soften her sentence. That even if Minuette were condemned, William would be moved to one of those careless acts of mercy which he favored. She would not undermine her brother while she still had hope.

LETTER FROM ROBERT DUDLEY TO ELIZABETH TUDOR

10 October 1557

Elizabeth,

It is done. I am truly sorry. She has been convicted and sentenced to death.

Early on it seemed the case might founder, for the witnesses were either so vague as to be meaningless or so openly hostile as to discredit themselves more than her. The greatest sensation of the morning was poor Jonathan Percy, summoned from his quiet life of musical composition to provide evidence of Minuette's early moral laxness. He would not play their game. As he poetically put it, "She is as pure as the snow and as good as a springtime morning." And then he denounced all as a scourge of hypocrites, and stalked out. They didn't even try to bring him back. They knew their most damaging witness was still to come.

Unlike her twin brother, Eleanor Percy is such a skillful liar she could make the Pope believe that Martin Luther was a reasonable man. She spoke of her brother's admirable if ill-conceived defense of a woman he had once loved, twisting that defense into a matter of honour rather than truth.

But Eleanor had more. She did not so much as bat an eyelash when she claimed that Minuette had sought out "unnatural practices" to keep the king enslaved to her body and soul. I have a shrewd idea of what practices Eleanor meant—and how she comes to know about them. But none of that matters. All that matters is that she painted a convincing picture of a scheming, manipulative whore who was sleeping with half the court and either wanted to kill William to prevent him finding out or wished to get herself pregnant so William would have to marry her.

Minuette is back in the Tower tonight, she and Dominic both, waiting for William.

Don't do anything rash.

Robert

Elizabeth exercised all her control to stand still. Pacing would have been both unfeminine and far too revealing of her state of mind. She must appear calm, appealing to reason rather than emotion, or she wouldn't have a chance.

She sank into a graceful curtsey the moment the door opened and kept her eyes carefully lowered until she was spoken to.

"Elizabeth," her brother said flatly, then to whoever was with him, "Leave us."

Elizabeth drew a shaky breath as footsteps receded and the door was closed.

Straightening, she fixed her brother with what she hoped was a look of modest submissiveness. Not that she could overplay it, for William knew her far too well.

"I don't recall inviting your presence today, sister." His words were like a slap, but she knew that he wasn't furious so much as afraid. He didn't want her here because at least part of him was ashamed of himself.

She knew him even better than he knew her.

"I have come to petition for a commutation of sentence."

His eyes flickered. "Which prisoner?"

She had toyed briefly with the idea of pleading for both, but had reluctantly concluded that Dominic was beyond anyone's aid, especially as his execution order had already been signed for tomorrow. "Minuette."

His face might as well have been carved from granite for all the expression in it. He has finally learned to control his countenance, she realized wryly, as he said, "She was tried and convicted fairly. I cannot overturn the court's verdict."

Repressing her opinion of the trial's fairness, Elizabeth said quickly, "But you can commute it. A death sentence is not valid until you have signed the execution order. Leave her in prison, or send her to house arrest far from here. Surely she need not die merely to assuage your wounded heart."

She tried to bite back the last words, but too late. William's eyes hardened. "She will die because she is a liar and a whore and a traitor. Her life is mine."

"And the life of the child?"

She thought for a heartbeat she might have overreached, but William answered, if rather glacially. "Of course she will live long enough to safely deliver the child."

"And then?"

"If it is a girl . . . I have no need of another daughter. But if it is a boy, I will acknowledge it. Neither son nor daughter will save the mother."

It was the first confirmation that he had reason to at least consider the child might be his. Elizabeth wanted to weep at the thought of what that experience had cost Minuette and William both, and it was that emotion that wrung out in her next words. "William, please, you are not yourself, you must not do this."

"Go back to Hatfield, Elizabeth. I will send for you when you are wanted."

As she tried desperately to think of any words that might suffice, William added abruptly, "Jane is pregnant."

Startled, she met his eyes—and she knew. Why death, and why now. He thought he could bury his pain and regret in blood. He wanted to be free of his ghosts before his legitimate son was born.

So much for hope. Now was the time for action.

By sunset of his last night on earth, Dominic was ready. He had written his will, disposing of those few items that had been wholly his—horse, saddles, books, sword—and, more terribly, a last letter to his wife. He had pressed that upon Harrington, who had reluctantly been released earlier that day.

"I'll stay," Harrington had said stubbornly, when told by the lieutenant that he was free to go with no charges laid against him.

"You'll go," Dominic ordered.

The lieutenant had withdrawn and allowed the two men to fight it out among themselves. Dominic had won. Harrington's continued presence would accomplish nothing but a show of support in his last hours, and though Dominic valued that, it was more important that Harrington be free. "There is nothing you can do for me," he'd told the big man who'd become his friend, "but you might be able to help Minuette. And if not, then Carrie will need you. Keep your head low, but stay in London. I'll bet you that within a day, Walsingham will have found you for Princess Elizabeth's sake. They will tell you if there's anything you can do."

So Harrington had gone, bearing Dominic's farewell to his wife and leaving him, grateful for the twists of fate—and Lord Rochford's scheming—that had brought the two of them together.

If it were not for his memory of the night Minuette had been poisoned, Dominic would have thought this the longest night there had ever been. But even counting down the hours to his own certain death was not as difficult as the hours he'd waited in desperate uncertainty of hers.

He stood at the window of the inner chamber, from where he could see little but the bulk of Middle Tower to the west. He could smell the river and tried to let his mind ease into the tidal rhythm of the Thames. When the door opened behind him, Dominic ignored it. If it was William, come to gloat at the end, he would not engage.

He recognized the lieutenant's voice. "One hour." Then foot-steps retreating, and the door closing. Then absolute silence.

No, not absolute. Someone was with him—someone whose breath came soft and fast. He closed his eyes, afraid to turn around for fear that he was dreaming. If it were a dream, he didn't want it to end.

But even in dreams, self-control extends only so far. He turned.

If he were dreaming her, surely he'd dream her in her wedding dress—or nothing at all. Minuette wore a gown he'd never seen before, dark brown and clumsily cut. There were shadows beneath her eyes and lines around her mouth. She looked older, and weary. Only her hair was unchanged, hanging loose to her waist and seeming to warm the air around her. And beneath the gown, cut high just under her breasts, the perfect shape of a woman heavily pregnant.

One moment they were staring at each other, the next moment she was in his arms and he was crushing his wife against him and breathing out a prayer of thanks to whatever god or mortal had given them this hour.

Beneath his almost terrifying joy—and the round swell of the child—Dominic was aware of how thin Minuette was, her neck and shoulders as fragile as a bird's. He was afraid he might break something if he held her too tight. Slowly, he eased the embrace until he could see her face. She looked as dazed as he felt.

"Come here." He led her to the hard, neatly made bed in the corner of the room. "You look as though you haven't slept in a week."

Her voice was stronger than he'd expected. "You don't think I'll sleep now."

"No."

She raised an eyebrow in inquiry and he laughed, a half-choked laugh at the gift of her expression. "Nor do I expect anything else.

THE BOLEYN RECKONING · 319

It's the most comfortable spot in the room. We'll sit, love, and talk."

He braced his back against the wall and Minuette nestled beneath his arm. He was dizzy from the feel of her and the scent of her, as though all his senses were heightened, imprinting this moment upon him so that he would remember it . . .

The rest of his life.

They talked, much in the manner they had in the first weeks of their marriage. At night, after other activities, they would lie drowsily tangled and play "Do you remember?" And so they did tonight. They rambled in memory through every moment of their brief times together—the day she'd jumped to him at sixteen and tipped the balance of his heart forever, the night she'd confronted him in anger in Hampton Court's kitchen lanes, the perfect moment when he'd kissed her for the first time, setting a seal upon their future.

Beneath the surface words and pleasant memories, Dominic was achingly aware of the opportunity he'd been given. He had said nothing of this in the letter he'd written her, but now that she was here, now that he could see her face-to-face, there was something he must say. A favour he must plead.

She wasn't going to like it.

"Minuette," he said softly, his hand twined in the silk of her hair as she leaned against him, "has William been to see you?"

He felt the answer in the slight stiffening of her body, and hoped she would not bother to lie. They didn't have time for that.

She didn't lie. "Yes."

"More than once?"

"Yes."

She drew breath to say more, and he stopped her. "I can guess. He has offered to spare your life if you will be his mistress."

Her answer was quick and tart. "Since he cannot have me when

I am dead, my life is a necessity, not a bargain." When she continued, her voice wavered. "He offered your life. Was I wrong to refuse?"

He kissed her hair. "You need not ask me that. I would not want
a life in which you were kept from me, and I doubt he would have
kept his word in any case. But there's something more I must say
and I want you to listen until I am finished."

She nodded warily.

"Tomorrow, when I am ... William will come to you once
more. He will give you one last opportunity to choose—him or
the scaffold." He could not look at her as he finished. "Minuette,
choose him."

He heard the shock, even a twist of betrayal in her voice. "You
would have me sell myself?"

You haven't already? he nearly answered. But that was jealousy,
not reason. "I would have you *live*. Bear children ..." He touched
her stomach and felt the lazy kick of the child within. "Find a
measure of happiness."

She was silent for a long time. At last she faced him, her hazel
eyes steady and unequivocal. "I would not do it for your life—
I won't do it for mine."

She kissed him once, then slipped back into the comfort of his
embrace. "Besides, you are wrong. William is finished with me. He
will not offer again."

By some inner sense, they knew when the hour was nearly
done. Without a word, he helped her to stand and wrapped his
arms around her, made clumsy and unfamiliar by her shape.

She flinched when the knock sounded. "Oh, God."

Dominic looked to the half-open door and met the lieutenant's
eyes. "One minute. Please."

The man drew the door to without shutting it completely.

Minuette was shaking and Dominic felt his own panic building.

She couldn't fall apart now, he couldn't take it, he knew it was self-ish but he needed her to be calm.

He whispered in her ear, a plea for himself. "I can do anything if you are strong, my star. Just a little longer."

She drew a deep, shuddering breath, and asked a most unexpected question. "Will it hurt?"

His arms tightened in reflex, but he managed to answer without hesitation. "No, love, it will be too quick to hurt." He didn't even know if she were afraid for him or for herself, but he plunged ahead recklessly, offering the only comfort that came to mind. "It's a jump, Minuette, that's all it is. A jump out of this world, straight into my arms."

Incredibly, she managed to smile. "You will catch me?"

He pressed his lips against hers. "Always."

When the lieutenant entered, they were ready. One kiss—one last, hard kiss—and Minuette was walking away.

He could not have been more proud of her. She did not cry or linger or force the lieutenant to assert his authority to remove her. She did what he needed her to do—she went without looking back.

But if he thought that was the end of things, he was very much mistaken. Against all odds and expectations, Dominic managed to sleep until sometime deep in the utter blackness of the hours after midnight he was woken by a stinging slap to his face. He sat bolt upright, seeing only the outline of two men, and in spite of the months of imprisonment he still reached instinctively for a dagger that was no longer there. He kicked out and caught one man in the stomach, hearing the man's garbled cry, but then there were two more men in the doorway and he was outnumbered and couldn't for the life of him figure out what was going on. Was William not to be satisfied with hanging, disemboweling, and beheading?

It seemed not. For the fifth man that came through the door, though cloaked in heavy dark wool, was unmistakably the king.

Dominic swore as the other four men held him fast (he was proud of how hard they had to work, for he was past the point of honour or instinctive loyalty and would gladly have done what damage he could to William before the end). William removed his cloak and though there was not moonlight enough through the tiny, deep-set window to read expressions, Dominic knew he was taking his time to savor the moment before he struck.

The beating was vicious, and all the more so for being perfectly controlled. William knew just where and how hard to hit and kick to do maximum damage without sinking Dominic into unconsciousness. He seemed particularly interested in Dominic's face, landing blow after blow until his jaw throbbed and he was sure he'd lose several teeth (not that it much mattered—he wasn't going to go hungry between now and the scaffold) and his eyes began to swell shut. Blood trickled from several gashes on his forehead, deliberately inflicted by the heavy rings on William's hands.

The only pride Dominic could summon was to keep his mouth shut and not ask why. When William stepped back for several long moments, he thought dizzily that it was over. But then the king drew the sword he wore and held it out for Dominic to consider. Even with the faintest of light, Dominic knew that sword, knew that if he could see clearly he would recognize the four star-shaped gems laid into the hilt. A gift for his friend and king, offered a lifetime ago. Dominic kept his eyes as open as he could manage through the blood and stinging and waited for William to kill him.

When the blow came, it was not the blade that struck, but that sentimentally decorative hilt. William slammed the butt of the sword into Dominic's temple and he crumpled into blackness.

———

Minuette walked blindly away from Dominic's farewell, her eyes so blurred with unshed tears that she could see only one step ahead of her. She would not think of that farewell, she would not think of anything, better to blink away her tears and look around her. Force herself to look at the White Tower, stark in its medieval outlines, and beyond that the outline of the chapel, and Minuette forced herself to notice and to care that it was lit from within. Who was praying at this hour?

As they reached the entrance to Beauchamp Tower, she continued to stare at the chapel entrance. Someone stood near the doorway, a cloaked figure lit from the side. The lieutenant took her arm to escort her within, and at that moment the figure moved, throwing back the enveloping hood of the cloak. Though Minuette was too far away to see clearly the face, she knew the hair, that bright red-gold hair. There was no more distinctive marker of the Tudors.

Elizabeth raised one of her long-fingered, slender hands and held it in a gesture of goodbye. Minuette gave a slight nod that she knew her friend would never see, but it was the most she could manage without collapse.

Beauchamp Tower rose above her and she was glad to mount the stairs and finally be shut behind her own door. After Carrie had helped her change, her round face creased with sympathy and shared grief, she hovered, hesitating. Minuette looked at her inquiringly.

From the bodice of her gown Carrie withdrew a square of paper, folded small and tight. "Harrington found a guard willing to bring this to you. It's from him."

The uncertain pronoun wasn't in the least confusing, and Minuette grasped the precious letter tightly. She would not read it yet, but just to hold it was enough for this moment.

"Anything else, my lady?"

"No."

As Carrie rested a kind hand on her shoulder, Minuette added, "Yes, Carrie. Don't disturb me in the morning. I shan't want breakfast. I shan't want anything. I will come out when I am ready."

Sunrise found Minuette sitting on her bed in the tiny inner chamber of her prison, leaning against the wall to balance the heaviness of the child. It all went swiftly after that. She heard the roar of the crowds outside the Tower as Dominic was taken by cart to Tower Hill. She followed him in her imagination, dry-eyed and unblinking. From the cart to the scaffold, built high so that thousands could witness a traitor's end.

She didn't break when her imagination conjured the ax descending swiftly to his neck. She didn't break when the crowds cheered and the bells of the Tower began to ring. When it was over, she rose dry-eyed and retrieved Dominic's sealed letter. She unfolded and read it where she stood.

My bright and merry star,
    Things I would tell our child if I could—

1. Love matters.
2. So does friendship.
3. Everyone makes mistakes, including you. Be generous with others' errors, and honest about your own.
4. Your mother is the truest, kindest, sweetest soul I've ever known. I love her. And I love you—for your own sake, not solely for your mother's.

Dominic

Only then did she break. Sinking to the floor, covering her head with her arms, Minuette huddled and wept.

William came by boat from Greenwich, with only one guard and the boatman for company. Through the journey, he kept his mind blank of everything but the image that had kept him taut and uncertain and desperate for the last seven months. Minuette beneath him, her hair spread loose and gold, eyes closed . . .

He'd thought that having her just once would clear his blood of the feverish need for her, that afterward he would be himself again. But the burning in his brain had continued after the camp outside Wynfield, the spells of retreat when he could not bear anything but solitude and darkness.

Take me and be done with it, she'd said to him so scornfully. Why not? He'd tell her tonight, now that Dominic could no longer live between them, that she would be his mistress whether she liked it or not.

But standing outside the door behind which she waited, William wondered if that could really undo the spell she'd woven. What if it were some kind of witchcraft? Would forcing her break it, or only seal it upon him forever? He shook his head and told himself to be reasonable. Minuette was only a woman. And he knew what to do with a woman.

He opened the door without knocking. Minuette stood in the middle of the room, braced to meet him, hands clasped beneath the great swell of the child. She was alone, as William had commanded she be. Brought up against that familiar face, studying him gravely and without a flicker of expression in her eyes, William felt a moment's doubt. He had never taken a woman by force. Could he really begin with Minuette?

Stop thinking of her as Minuette, he told himself. *She is a liar and a whore. She deserves what she gets.*

She did not retreat when he moved forward. She did not struggle as he ran his hands across her breasts, larger and heavier with pregnancy. Sealing his possession of her, William bent to kiss them where they swelled and, as he had once before, pushed her up against a stone wall. He'd wondered if her late pregnancy would be an impediment to his desire, but his body was aroused and responsive. His mind, though, was unpleasantly active as well, noticing her stillness, her submissiveness, almost her lack of awareness, as though she wasn't really there and it was only her body that he touched, not her, not the essence of who she was . . .

He pushed himself off her and turned away in a mix of fury and despair. He felt like throwing something or hitting something but he didn't, he just stood with his back to her and breathed in and out until he could face her with some semblance of control.

She stood against the wall of her prison, hair tumbled and cheeks red and one lip a little swollen where possibly he'd bitten her. She didn't look at him. In a moment, as suddenly as it had struck years before, William's desire vanished. He felt sick.

"I'm sorry, William."

He had to choke back a bitter laugh at that. "You're not sorry for me, you hate me. If you're sorry, it's for yourself."

"I don't hate you, and I am sorry for you. You were my friend."

"Kings don't have friends." He dropped the words like coals between them, wishing he'd learned that lesson earlier.

"We were your friends," she whispered. "We loved you. Not because you are king, but because you are Will."

The only way to beat back the misery that threatened was to take offense. "*We*—always *we*. Always you and Dominic. Why could you not love *me*?" He threw the words at her, wanting to hurt her, wanting to break her, wanting her to acknowledge that all of this was her fault. If only she had loved him . . .

Laying her hands on either side of his face, she drew it down and kissed him on the forehead. He caught at her wrists and leaned his head against hers.

He closed his eyes and, for one moment, he was back in his mother's room at Hever. He could smell the rain, he could feel his own clothes soaking wet and Minuette's hands clutching him as she cried. For one moment he remembered what it felt like to love her simply and completely as his friend, before desire intervened, twisting his regard for her into something tantalizing and forbidden and out of his reach.

She came to you for pity's sake.

He stepped back hastily. Almost he looked round, for Dominic's voice had rung so clearly that he seemed to be in the room with them.

He threw the door wide and half stumbled down the stairs and into the chilly October night. The boat was drawn up near the western entrance, past Traitor's Gate, past Bell Tower where Dominic had lived out his last months.

The boat slipped away from the Tower, away from ghosts and pity and everything William could not control. He sank his head into his hands and realized he was shaking.

By the time the boat reached Greenwich, William was burning with fever.

CHAPTER TWENTY-TWO

LETTER FROM ROBERT DUDLEY TO ELIZABETH TUDOR

14 October 1557

Elizabeth,

I thought the burning of Bishop Bonner was the worst sight I should ever see. Yesterday was worse. The intensity of the crowd was frightening, all the more so for being impersonal. I doubt one person in a hundred knew more of Dominic than his name and association with the king, but they were all in a frenzy to watch him die.

So many were crammed into the streets outside the Tower that I could not get closer than a hundred yards. I was glad enough for the distance when it began. He had been beaten, Elizabeth, thoroughly and with more than professional detachment. He could barely walk unassisted even before they strung him up, and the blindfold could not conceal the damage done to his face. I expect the blindfold was to increase his sense of unease, not knowing what was coming.

He was not even given a chance to speak, though it would not have mattered. They had cut out his tongue, Elizabeth, before he was brought out of the Tower. That touch seems particularly cruel, though no worse than the tearing into his bowels while he still lived. He managed to scream despite the loss of his tongue, and bless the executioner for being less of a sadist than whoever beat Dominic beforehand, for he struck his head off neatly and competently.

You did say you wanted details. I will always take you at your word, though it grieves me that you should know such things.

I am, as always, yours to command,

Robert

Elizabeth looked at Walsingham, the two of them quite alone at Hatfield but still speaking sotto voce just in case. "Can you do it?" she asked.

"The doing of it is not the issue—it's the not getting caught afterward, and gaining enough time for her to reach the ship."

"Then can you do *that*?"

Walsingham's shrewd gaze was more unreadable than normal. "I can, with help. There is a prisoner in the Tower whom I believe could be induced to aid us in creating a distraction."

"Minuette going into early labor and importing a flurry of necessary women is not distraction enough?"

"I meant a distraction that will take eyes *off* Mistress Courtenay rather than focusing all attention on her. Stephen Howard is in the Tower, rather forlornly forgotten by the government in the aftermath of Norfolk's rebellion. I have been to see him, and I believe him truly interested in the welfare of his stepdaughter."

"And in his own, no doubt. What have you promised him for his aid?"

"Nothing. It is likely that he will not live to receive any gifts."

Elizabeth stared. "Just what sort of distraction are you contemplating?"

Walsingham didn't bother to say aloud, *Do you really want to know?* They knew each other well enough not to ask pointless questions.

With a shrug that was only half careless, Elizabeth ruthlessly put away concern for everyone but Minuette. This was all she could do, and she meant to succeed. "So, Minuette goes into early labor, two women enter the Tower to aid her, then two women leave, presumably in the midst of whatever distraction you have in mind for Stephen Howard. The women who are brought in will be safe?"

"If we're lucky, those women will also be able to slip away during Howard's distraction. But if they are caught, then we need you in a position to speak with authority. Ideally, we need the king to leave London and its closer environs. You must be the one Lord Burghley seeks out for advice in the matter."

"Then Minuette and her maid are put on a ship for France, where Renaud LeClerc will be waiting for them."

Walsingham gave a single nod.

Elizabeth closed her eyes, imagining all the things that could go wrong. Imagining William's reaction when he discovered Minuette had flown. She had no illusions—her brother would know it was her. But she would not be cowed by William.

Walsingham had just one question. "Shall I travel with them, Your Highness?"

"No. I have someone else in mind for that."

Robert would do it, without a second thought. And she would tell him not to return to England until she could assure him he would not be touched by William's wrath.

"We cannot leave it too long, Your Highness. Mistress Courtenay's condition . . ."

Elizabeth knew very well how swiftly they needed to move. Minuette was only six weeks away from giving birth. "If William shows no sign of leaving London within a week, I will manufacture a reason for him to do so," she said, with more confidence than she felt. Being a conspirator sat uneasily on her, even when she was confident of her rightness.

But events seemed determined to draw her into conspiracy, for the very day after Dominic's execution, Walsingham brought Elizabeth a letter from a Low Countries merchant resident in London.

The letter was from Philip of Spain.

To Her Most Royal Highness, Elizabeth, Princess of Wales,

It was with interest and concern I write you. I regret the necessity of subterfuge, but circumstances have not been wholly in our favour.

You know that France has offered me their own royal Elisabeth, and we have met to discuss terms. I will consider her carefully as I must, for my first concern must ever and always be my kingdom's welfare. But I do you the credit of speaking frankly— What use have I for a child bride? It will be some years before she could make me a wife.

Unlike you.

I had not thought to like you so well as I did. I expected to meet only a heretic, and instead found a woman as learned as the most clever of princes. I fear that my thoughts turn to you more than wisdom dictates they should. And not only in admiration of your mind, for Your Highness surely knows that you are beautiful.

England is on the brink of disaster. Your brother is not wise, and I admit I do not much mind the spectacle he is making of himself and his nation. I think you will be called on to exercise much wisdom and much power in the coming months.

Though I fear I would make no good husband to the Princess of Wales, I regret the loss of Elizabeth Tudor. For that regret, I offer assurance that, for yet a little while, Spain will not entangle itself with France in a treaty. I am a ruler who likes to consider every option before I commit.

Yours in respect and the goodness of Christ,
Philip

Elizabeth watched the dangerous letter burn, as surely Philip had meant her to do, and as the Spanish king's words turned to ash, other words echoed in her ears. *What did you see?* she'd asked John Dee years ago.

You will command men and guide nations . . . This is the hand of a woman, Your Highness. But it is also the hand of a ruler.

She sat alone long into the night, wondering precisely what God meant her to do.

William burned with fever for two days after his final visit to Minuette. When he arose on the third day, he didn't delay more than an hour before leaving Whitehall and London far behind. Jane was at Richmond Palace, being well-coddled for the duration of her royal pregnancy, but it was not west that he headed. It was north. He took six guards with him and no personal attendants. Only Lord Burghley had been told his destination: the manor house in Cumbria he had bestowed as a wedding gift upon the late Giles Howard.

Burghley assumed he was following Eleanor, who had returned north as soon as delivering her devastating testimony at Minuette's trial. And so he was going to see her—for who better to wipe the taint of his failure with Minuette from his mind and body?

But even his Lord Chancellor did not know all his secrets.

It took seven solid days of riding to reach Lakehill House just south of the market town of Kendal. The manor was medieval in its lines and history, and thus well fortified. William had never been there before. For a moment he found himself comparing it to Wynfield Mote. Where Minuette's home had radiated warmth and good cheer, Lakehill House lowered against the sullen grey of the skies. Its moat was not mainly decorative, the greasy black water itself seeming to shout "keep away" to any unwary travelers.

Perfect.

William sent an outrider ahead of him, so Eleanor had half a day's warning of his arrival. As always, his mistress's preparations were impeccable. The guards were directed into the care of her steward, an iron-faced northerner who scarcely could be bothered to bow to William. Fair enough—this job required taciturn and uninterested tongues.

"Would you care to take refreshment first?" Eleanor purred, slipping her hand through his arm as they walked alone into the hall. She looked like a rich and contented wife in her jewel-toned blue gown, hair neatly confined beneath a hood. But her eyes couldn't be wifely if they tried; William felt her calculation as she led him inside. The interior of the manor, at least, was elegantly furnished and decorated, even ostentatious. "Or you could visit Nora. She chatters like a little bird, you'd be enchanted."

"She is here?" William pulled up sharply, shaken at the news. "Why has she left your brother?"

"You said I might have her with me if you could trust me."

"Send her away," William ordered. "Back to Jonathan, at once. I don't want her here this winter." Not with the darkness he himself had imported. Far better his daughter be with the infuriatingly loyal Jonathan Percy.

Eleanor bit her bottom lip, a gesture William remembered well, and changed the subject. "Your bedchamber is ready for you." *And so am I* she did not need to add. Everything about her shouted it.

He stopped abruptly and kissed her hard in the middle of the reception hall. Her response was immediate and reassuring. But

Eleanor, though a pleasant distraction, was not his primary purpose in coming here.

When her caresses had sated the edges of his temper, William stepped away. "You know what I want. Business before pleasure."

Although this business would also be pleasurable. Very much so.

Eleanor led him to the oldest part of the house, to a round tower that looked uninhabitable above the ground floor. But there was an oak door, six inches thick and with a sturdy iron lock and bolt, that led to a flight of steps descending into blackness. They each carried a lantern, Eleanor going first, her voice floating up to him as they went down.

"Fortunately, the servants here are not much interested in anything beyond themselves and what they're paid. And I have a reputation as being somewhat . . . what's the word? *Erratic* in my tastes and habits. I imagine they think I have a lover chained down here, what with my being the only one in attendance."

William ignored her, for he had the fanciful notion that he could feel the man waiting below, could track the mind and emotions—tightly reined, no doubt, but perhaps the fiercer for it.

It would be a long time before William broke down that fierceness.

Eleanor reached the last step and William followed her down a short length of corridor with four iron-gated doors opening off it, two on each side. Only the last one on the right-hand side was barred shut. A dim light radiated from a single torch set in the wall outside the dungeon door.

William stepped up to the door and raised the lantern so his face could be clearly seen. "Hello, Dominic."

Dominic blinked against the strong light, not surprised by the familiar voice. "Hello, William. Come for another round?"

He had been very surprised indeed when he had come back

to consciousness all those days ago in a tightly closed, jolting carriage that had made him retch with the constant motion and after-effects of his beating. Why wasn't he dead? William had gotten his satisfaction—why not then hand him off for the public pain and humiliation of his execution?

He'd been in so much pain, slipping in and out of consciousness for days of rough travel, that he couldn't concentrate on why. He'd begun to put fragments together, suspicions, but only when the coach stopped for the final time and he'd been hooded before being marched along and down stone floors and he was chained to the wall of his new prison did he finally grasp it.

William wasn't finished with him yet. For the space of an hour Dominic wondered where he was, who William had enlisted in this secret. For secret he had surely kept it—he would not want Minuette having hope. William wanted her desperate and alone and sunk in grief.

When Eleanor Percy appeared, looking angelic with her light hair and exquisite cream-coloured gown, Dominic had been startled enough to exclaim, "Son of a bitch."

"Close, but it's a daughter I have. Though a son will surely follow, a son with a royal father. Pity your bitch wasn't so smart."

The chains brought him up well short of the iron door. It was the only time he lost control. After that he didn't speak to Eleanor at all when she appeared twice a day to bring him food.

He'd wondered how long William would be able to keep away. By his count it was nine days now since his supposed death. And here was the king, looking at him as though he were a specimen in a menagerie.

"Can't you deal with the waste?" William said sharply to Eleanor.

"By myself? Do I look like a maidservant?"

"Fine. There must be someone in your household without the

wits to put together two words. Have them do it. And get him some water to wash himself. Now."

Eleanor had learned submission, or at least how to approximate it. She took her lantern and walked away. Only when her light could not be seen did Dominic speak.

"Suddenly concerned about my condition?"

"There's no need to make an animal out of you."

"Because it's more fun if I remain the gentleman?"

Was that a jolt of hurt in William's eyes? Probably just disgust, Dominic decided. To keep William from broaching the subject first, he asked abruptly, "How was my execution? Sufficiently brutal, I suppose. How long did it take you to find a man who looked enough like me to pass at a distance?"

"Not long. You're tall and black-haired—who ever looked at you enough to see beyond that?" William studied him. "Aren't you going to ask me about Minuette?"

Not for anything in this world would Dominic speak of her to William. Because he couldn't trust his mouth to keep his mind's intention, he kept it firmly shut.

William shook his head at Dominic's stubborn silence but didn't try to break it. Was he going to beat him again? Dominic didn't much care, although his previous injuries were finally beginning to heal, slowed by darkness and cold and solitude.

Slow, shuffling footsteps followed Eleanor's quicker ones. A young man came behind her, carrying a bucket of water and with the undoubted look of a child in an adult's body. Eleanor unlocked the iron door herself, and gestured sharply for the man to put the water inside and shove it with his foot. Then he picked up the foul bucket of waste and retreated with it.

"Anything else, my lord?" Eleanor asked mockingly, and Dominic felt a great longing to wrap his hands around her neck and squeeze hard.

He kept his eyes on the king, wishing he could read the face he had once known better than his own. What was he thinking?

Curtly, William said, "I'll be back. When Minuette's child is born, I'll return and report. Surely you'll be interested in the outcome. Almost as interested as I am."

Then he walked away, leaving Eleanor to scramble after him.

Dominic let out his breath and sank down with his back to the wall. He put his aching head in his hands and wondered how long a man could last in such a place without either dying or going mad.

CHAPTER TWENTY-THREE

WHEN CARRIE WHISPERED in Minuette's ear that there was a plan devised for escape, a way out of the Tower— that she needed to be ready to fake an early labor the moment she was told to—she was almost too numb with grief to care. Something essential in her nature had been broken, and if there was still a tiny flame of reason and hope left, it was buried so far that she'd lost sight of it. All she could manage was to keep breathing and that was labor enough.

"What does it matter?" she heard herself say, surprised she could manage even that much. Dominic had been dead for three days. All she wanted was to join him.

Carrie was not cowed. "This matters," she'd hissed fiercely, laying her hand on Minuette's heavily rounded stomach. As if in agreement, the child gave a series of urgent kicks just then, so that Carrie's hand moved with it.

Minuette had worked very hard to distance herself from the fact of her pregnancy. What was the point of attachment, she'd thought, when she would never know her baby, when the moment she was delivered they would take the child from her, give it into someone else's care, and then cut off her own head? When she said to Carrie,

"What does it matter?" what she meant was: *This child will never be mine. Why care about something I can't have?*

But something about these particular kicks penetrated Minuette's numbness and she fancied there was a touch of familiar frustration to it, like Dominic when he was irritated with her stubbornness. It was enough to start the tears, though Minuette clamped down hard. She could not afford to get lost just now, because the sharp kicks had tumbled loose her grief and only now was she beginning to understand what Carrie was telling her. That there might be a way out, for both their child and herself.

She blinked and drew a hard, cleansing breath that was far shallower than usual. This child was determined to make itself felt in every way possible, apparently. "I understand," she said, and found to her surprise that hope was not dead yet. "I'll be ready."

Six days after Dominic's death Carrie received a message with their evening meal. "Tonight," she barely breathed out to Minuette, as though the walls themselves were straining to overhear. "You should begin now."

It was an amateur performance at best, for Minuette had never given birth, had never even attended a birth. But she could manage to moan and cry and whimper and Carrie was good at giving slight direction with only a nod or a shake of her head. It was also useful to have such a well of unshed emotion to call upon; Minuette directed her grief and fury into giving herself and her child a chance, and there came a time when she half believed in her own performance and wondered superstitiously if she were going to curse herself and bring the child too early.

Carrie flitted in and out with water and blankets and soft words, and kept badgering the guards to send for a midwife. Hours after Minuette began her performance, when the time was creeping near midnight, the door opened. Two women were admitted, wearing heavy woolen dresses and cloaks against the late autumn cold, one of them as large and broad as an obscenely well-fed man.

Swiftly, Minuette traded clothing with the larger woman, the garments padded out at the shoulders with extra linen so that she looked enormous all over and not just her belly. Her golden hair was plaited tightly to her head and bundled beneath a linen coif and cap. She had a moment's memory of her escape from Dudley Castle two years ago, but tension made her jittery and unfocused.

"Now what?" she whispered to Carrie, who had remained in her own green gown, round face fiercely determined.

"We wait until we hear the sounds of a disturbance."

"What disturbance?"

Carrie shrugged. "I wasn't given the details."

"How long do we wait?"

"No more than an hour. If there's nothing, then Walsingham's instructions were for us to leave as though I am going with one of the midwives to gather further supplies."

Minuette looked doubtfully at the two women who would be left behind in such an event and wondered if they were prepared for the consequences. They met her gaze steadily and the larger one nodded in understanding. Minuette could only suppose Walsingham had explained the risks and made it worth their while. How much did it cost, she wondered, to get two strangers to risk their lives for hers?

It wasn't nearly as long as an hour before there were shouts from elsewhere in the Tower. Carrie counted to five, then threw open the door and said imperiously to the guards, "She's in a bad way. We need to get her somewhere safer to deliver than this cold Tower room!"

"She doesn't leave."

"That may be the king's son she's carrying—do you want to tell him his babe is dead because you hadn't the wit to act responsibly?"

The guard blinked, but was stubborn. "No leaving."

Carrie drew breath to begin the argument that she and one of the midwives be allowed out to gather more of what they needed, Minuette sweating beneath the heavy layers of clothing on top of her already bulky body, and the two midwives shut behind the inner chamber door. But suddenly there was the sound of running feet and the next moment a man burst up the stairs and, without hesitation, drove a sword through the nearest guard. The second guard pulled his sword but wasn't nearly fast enough. He, too, was run through.

"Well, stepdaughter," Stephen Howard said breathlessly, pulling his bloodied sword free of the second dead guard. "You do get yourself into the most interesting of troubles."

"What are you doing?" She couldn't decide if she was relieved or appalled.

"Offering one last service to your mother. Don't make it in vain—get to the Water Gate. There's a boat, but it won't wait long."

Minuette couldn't decide whether to cry or laugh and knew that she was on the verge of hysteria. Carrie was quicker, and called to the midwives to escape with them as well. Then she had Minuette by the arm and was moving her along the corridor.

Shaking her off, Minuette turned back. "Aren't you coming?" she asked her stepfather.

"You need time and distraction, and I can give you that."

"They'll kill you."

"Don't fret for me, Minuette. I've lived my life and made my choices. And this way I get to take a few men down with me. It's all to the good."

She surprised herself—and him—by throwing herself on him in a fierce hug. He patted her back awkwardly, then kissed her forehead. "I don't want another Wyatt woman dying in childbirth. Get yourself out of here. Take care of Marie's grandchild."

They made it unmolested through the precincts of the Tower, past guards who gave them only a cursory glance as they rushed toward Stephen Howard and his sword, down the icy steps of the Water Gate and into the small fishing boat where Harrington himself waited for them. Only when they were far enough up the Thames that the Tower could no longer be seen did Minuette absorb the fact that she had one more man's death on her conscience.

She laid her hand on her stomach and prayed silently for the soul of Stephen Howard.

As soon as Elizabeth heard that Minuette and Robert Dudley were safely on a ship to France—and Heaven bless they would have fair weather long enough to cross—she left Hatfield for Whitehall. Since William would summon her the moment he heard what had happened, she might as well anticipate him. Oddly enough, in those days of waiting she found herself thinking most often of Stephen Howard, who had killed three Tower guards and led them on a merry chase before himself being trapped and mercilessly hacked down by a number of swords. She didn't suppose William would take Howard's death as putting an end to the matter.

It was a jittery four days before William returned with the rush and clatter of an extraordinarily angry man. Burghley must have alerted him that Elizabeth was already in residence, for he did not even bother to change out of his travel-stained riding clothes but stormed straight to her privy chamber.

"Out," he commanded her women, and they did not even wait for Elizabeth's permission to scurry away.

Elizabeth rose and met him on her feet, braced for a fight. She couldn't decide if he looked more angry or more ill. How long and fast had he been riding? Burghley had told her only that he'd been in the North. Word must have caught him on the road, because he looked as though he hadn't slept for at least two days.

His blue eyes were opaque above smudged shadows of fatigue. But his voice was as sharp as ever. "I won't ask why. I won't ask what you were thinking. I won't even ask who helped you, for I have already discovered Robert Dudley's absence. You sent her to France, I imagine? I hope saving her was worth it."

"I was rather hoping to save you as well," Elizabeth replied steadily. "You are not yourself, William. Executing Dominic was one thing—friend or not, he was sworn to your service and he betrayed you and that is treason. But Minuette—"

"Do not speak of her!"

"If you killed her, you would never be able to live with yourself. Let her go, Will. Be the king you are meant to be."

For one startled, horrifying moment, she feared he would strike her. But he tightened his hand and locked it at his side. "What do you know of ruling? This is my kingdom, you will not tell me who I am or am not!"

She softened her voice. "I didn't mean that. William, I apologize—"

"It's too late. There are guards outside waiting to escort you out of Whitehall."

"I don't need to be guarded back to Hatfield."

"You're not returning to Hatfield. You have proven you cannot be trusted. And since you were so eager to release Minuette from the Tower . . . then you can take her place."

Elizabeth was struck by a gust of dizziness. Only by sheer force of will did she keep steady on her feet. "That is not necessary."

"I say it is."

She would not beg. Instead, with considerable effort, she curtsied to her brother. "As it pleases Your Majesty."

"There is nothing left can please me."

17 November 1557
Chateau de Blanclair

*On my first crossing of the Channel, I was excited and cheerful
and very young and every moment was delightful. The second
crossing I was in a temper and shut myself up belowdecks.*

*This third crossing was like Purgatory, if we were allowed to
believe in Purgatory. Although I suppose now I can, seeing as I am
in a Catholic household in a Catholic country.*

*Granted, crossing in late October is a considerably chancier
business than in midsummer. Robert, Carrie, and I waited tensely
in a small inn outside Dover for two days, praying all the while
that the weather would turn. It did, but the seas were rough and
the wind cold and I was so damned uncomfortable.*

*But the truly hellish part of the Channel crossing was that I
kept thinking I could hear Dominic, lecturing one of the young
girls from our first crossing, or see his face taut with anger and
disappointment at my folly during our second crossing. Perhaps it is
as well that I am exiled to France, for though I know Dominic was
once a guest at Renaud's home, I have no memories of him here.*

*Here, it is only Carrie and I and Harrington. And soon my
child.*

19 November 1557
Chateau de Blanclair

*Carrie and Harrington were married today. They only waited this
long because Harrington flatly refused to be married by a Catholic*

*priest. "No offense to you, mistress," he told me gravely, and I
assured him with equal gravity that no offense was taken.*

*Robert Dudley, who has been reluctantly confined here with us
since our arrival, gladly took the challenge to locate a Protestant
cleric for the ceremony. He was gone for three days and returned in
a sort of manic cheer with a suitably reformist priest in tow.
Renaud and Nicole, impeccably gracious hosts, welcomed the man
and provided a beautiful wedding in a small salon of their home,
papered in blue damask and looking like an underwater grotto.*

*Carrie was neat and lovely in one of Nicole's older gowns, and
Renaud had suitably outfitted Harrington in a no doubt
made-to-order jerkin and doublet. For a moment I was amused at
the great difference in their sizes: Harrington looms over everyone
like a granite outcropping and Carrie is like a little wren tucked
beneath his arm. But when they look at each other, there is
something innately right about the match. And when they look at
me, I see their fierce loyalty and am glad to have them in this new
world of mine.*

*22 November 1557
Chateau de Blanclair*

*Robert left the morning after the wedding. He claims he wished to
be nearer the French court to determine how things stand with
Norfolk's negotiations. But I think he cannot bear to be still and,
though I know Elizabeth told him to remain in France until she
sent for him, I wager he will make his way back across the
Channel as soon as he can arrange it.*

*I am finding it hard to keep awake these days. Partly because
the baby is nearing its time (so say both Carrie and Nicole) and
partly, I think, because it is a form of retreat. If I am sleeping, I do
not have to remember.*

29 *November* 1557
Chateau de Blanclair

*The sun has made its early departure from the winter sky and my
pains grow in earnest. They have been erratic all day, but now they
are regular and of a quality that announces the time is now.*

I will not cry.

Minuette did not cry, not precisely. Carrie encouraged her to
cry, or scream, or curse, but that all seemed far too much work.
Though Minuette had always been told how transparent she was
in her emotions, how everything she felt was there for others to
see immediately, perhaps the last years of secrets and lies had taught
her concealment. Or perhaps she was only comfortable being
transparent on her own terms. In any case, in the extremity of the
pain Minuette closed in on herself. She knew she moaned, when
it seemed as though the pain wanted to pull her under, with barely
a breath or two between surges, and she seemed to be whispering
things under her breath, but even she wasn't entirely sure what she
said. *Please* was in there a lot, and so was *Help,* and several times
Mother.

It went on and on until Carrie told her the sun was just beginning to rise. "How much longer?" Minuette croaked to the French
midwife who had been chattering volubly all night. She didn't
even know if she managed to speak in French, or if it was English,
but the midwife patted her hand and smiled. "Good girl," she said.
"Almost."

There seemed a longer pause than she'd had for hours, and then
Minuette felt a gush of something warm. She'd heard of a woman's
waters, but this was nothing like what she'd thought. One moment
she spared an almost amused thought for the mess of all this, and

then she was swept by something more terrifying even than the pain: an urge to push that was primitive in its demands.

"Carrie," she gasped, reaching blindly for her friend's hand, "what . . ."

But she couldn't talk, she couldn't think, she couldn't do anything except what her body wanted. Carrie spoke low and warm and reassuring in her ear. "Don't fret, let it come, this is good, trust yourself . . ."

There was no time after that, just the demands of her body and the awful thought that she would do anything for this to be over, even die, and why would any woman do this more than once?

Finally, after much too long (though even five minutes of that was much too long), a sharper pain, like burning, and the midwife crooning to her in French and Carrie cautioning her to breathe deep and go slowly, but how was one supposed to control any of this?

And then a rush and the horrible pushing sensation vanished and Minuette realized she could breathe deeply for the first time in months and she had completely forgotten what all this was in aid of, so desperately relieved was she that it was over.

Until a sharp, aggrieved wail reached through the morass of her spent body and plucked once—hard and deep and eternal—on the very chords of Minuette's soul.

Her child.

"Carrie?"

"Ten fingers, ten toes, and a cry to wake the dead. A healthy, imperious girl, just like her mother."

"A girl?" And just like that, she burst into tears.

She cried for herself and her daughter, cried for England and all those she would never see again, but mostly she cried for Dominic because he would never have a chance to be either glad or sorry that he'd had a daughter rather than a son ... or to wonder if the child was even his.

She cried for so long and so untouchably that she must have alarmed all the women present. It was a man's voice that finally brought her back to her body and her bed and all the present pain that was, in a way, an anchor against the overwhelming pains and regrets of the past.

Renaud LeClerc laid the tightly bundled baby girl in her arms and said simply, "Dominic would want his daughter to have a name, *madame.*"

It was precisely the right thing to say, and the right way to say it. Compassionate but matter-of-fact, and surely it was his own fatherhood that allowed him to add with a sincerity that could not be denied, "Sons are gifts from God, but daughters are gifts straight from the women we love. Dominic loved nothing in this world so much as you, *madame,* and now the daughter you have given him in death must know from you both her mother's love and her father's."

Still hiccupping from sobs, Minuette worked hard to keep her arms steady as they curved around the baby girl. Her own crying seemed to have stopped the child's, and she studied her mother with wide eyes of the indeterminate bluish-gray of infants. What colour would those eyes settle on? Minuette wondered. Her father's green? Her mother's hazel? Or the bright blue of England's king ...

At that thought, Minuette knew it would never matter. Not to her, certainly, but not to Dominic, either, if he had been here. She'd known him well enough to be sure of that. Her daughter was a Courtenay, born and bred, and Minuette would make sure she knew everything about her father as she grew.

During the long, terrible months of her pregnancy, she had not given thought even once to a name, for that had seemed an act of folly when she'd been certain she would never be allowed to long outlive her child's birth. She let herself ponder this question for a few minutes, drinking in her daughter's face, all round cheeks and faintly indignant expression and pointed chin. She thought of the women she herself had loved and could honor: her mother, Marie; Queen Anne; Elizabeth; Nicole LeClerc; Carrie. But her daughter continued to look at her as though she knew her own name and was just waiting for her mother to recognize it.

The women were cleaning the chamber, tending the fire, moving around the heavily shrouded space like wraiths. "Draw back the curtains," Minuette said to Carrie.

She complied, though only with the long windows farthest from the bed, in order to keep both her and the baby from the drafts of oncoming winter. But it was enough, for the sun had risen and the light that streamed in through the leaded glass brought with it not only the promise of a future, but the certainty of a name.

"Lucette," Minuette said, looking first to her child, who seemed contented, and then to Renaud's rock-solid masculine face. He had the gift of being an island of security wherever he was, very much like Dominic. "Lucette Courtenay, for she is a light in darkness."

Renaud's hand curved gently around Lucette's head and Minuette saw a glint of tears in his eyes. "Well named, *madame*," he whispered. "And welcome to the world, *Mademoiselle* Lucette. Your home is here, for as long as either of you shall desire."

After William's first visit to the dungeons, Dominic had prepared himself to expect anything, from hourly visits to taunt him to more long days and weeks of solitude. It was a combination: over the next two days, William descended to the cell five times in all. He veered between brooding, watchful silence, and long descriptions of Dominic's "execution" and how devastated Minuette had been. At first Dominic closed his ears to all talk of Minuette. He might have urged her to put herself into William's chancy care, but that didn't mean he wanted to hear about it. But it soon became clear, from William's tone if not his words, that things had not gone well between them. There was a mean, selfish part of Dominic that was glad of Minuette's defiance, though he did not want to see her die.

And that was surely what all this was about, wasn't it? To punish him to the very limits of his life by either turning Minuette into William's mistress or by being treated to the specifics of her death and knowing—irrational though it was—that Dominic had failed in his promise to catch her when she jumped out of this world.

After two days came the solitude, with only the silent man to remove his waste bucket and Eleanor to bring him food. She was much worse than William, for she could never stop talking, and Dominic would gladly have choked her to death by the end of a fortnight if he could have reached her. But he remained chained and tried to tune out her light flow of vicious chatter that never told him anything useful.

He forced his mind to work, to scratch out the days as marked by food, to sleep at regular intervals, to wash his face and limbs in the cold water brought every third day, to recite to himself scripture and poetry and mathematics and the history of battlefield tactics. He couldn't decide if it made him saner or crazier to speak aloud, but sometimes he could not bear his own silence any longer and would talk to Minuette. Words of comfort, of encouragement, of safe delivery of the child, of mercy, and of hope.

It was late December, he thought Christmas Day itself by his reckoning, when William appeared once more. The moment he saw William's eyes, Dominic's hope died. It was the face of a man who has been cheated of the one thing he wanted, desperately angry and lost even though he himself has thrown it away.

"She's dead. The execution was ten days ago. I thought you would want to know."

There were a million things Dominic wanted to know, but was not willing to ask. *Did she die well? Was it quick and painless, as I promised her? Was she frightened? Did she cry for me? Where is she buried?*

But only one question mattered enough to ask. "And the child?"

William's eyes shuttered, locking away his own anger. "A son. I've claimed him as mine and given him his own household."

Dominic wanted to shut his eyes and pretend none of this was happening, but he would not weaken before William. Was it better or worse that the child survived? Better, surely, for the child was, after everything, part of Minuette and it was important that her son be safe.

William turned away from the cell and Dominic called after him, "Are you finished with me now?"

Are you going to kill me now? he meant. And surely William understood that, for he paused and threw an almost casual glance over his shoulder. "Not until your hope is gone. I will know when it is."

Only when William said it did Dominic realize he did still have hope. Knowing that Minuette's son (*My son?* his heart whispered) lived gave him a hope of purpose.

"You're a cold-blooded bastard."

William didn't turn back this time. "I know."

CHAPTER TWENTY-FOUR

WHEN WILLIAM LEARNED of Minuette's escape from the Tower, he had grimly begun to compose the lies he would tell Dominic about her. Her husband must not be allowed to know that she had slipped to safety, for then he might be content to die. And Dominic could not be allowed to die as a reward. His death would be agony, not release, breaking him beneath the weight of all his failures.

So when word reached William from his spies in France that Minuette had given birth to a girl, he ignored the fact that it was December and the roads grew progressively worse the farther one traveled north and that he would miss Christmas at court and that Elizabeth was still in the Tower ... He ignored it all and rode to Lakehill House. Where he told Dominic the lies he thought would hurt him the most: that the child was a boy, that the child was in England under the king's name, and that Minuette had been executed as threatened.

William did not find it as satisfying as he'd expected.

After only one night (in which he rebuffed Eleanor's company and slept alone), he rode away without seeing Dominic again. It took him nearly three weeks to make it back to Greenwich, for he grew feverish along the way and spent five days in one of his father's old hunting lodges that had not been regularly lived in since William's coronation. These fits of illness were growing increasingly troublesome, leaving him with only the blurriest of memories. He saw that his men's faces were wary when he emerged from the lodge ready to ride again, and wondered if it was fear for him or fear of him that caused it. Either way was as well—he would never again make the mistake of having friends.

Jane was at Greenwich, having overseen the Christmas festivities in his place, no doubt with punctilious generosity and personal devotion. She was now six months along with child and looked to be carrying well, though she had always been rather pale.

She was also, as she had always been, relentlessly good. Which was a valuable trait in a queen, but one that William found tiresome when pointed at him and his actions.

Of course she did nothing so direct or combative as ask precisely where he had been or why. No doubt she assumed it was a woman. If Jane was jealous, she gave no sign. William could never decide if that was insulting or a relief. She did worry about his health and the strain of traveling poor roads in poorer weather and having only men and local servants to treat him at the outlying lodge, and would he like her to make him a tisane, she had a receipt for one that was most efficacious—

"Jane," William cut her off. "What is it you want to ask me?"

Whenever she had a request to make that she was uncertain about, she would twitter on as though she could slip in something distasteful in a long flow of words and he would be lulled into agreement. He didn't remember her being like that when they were younger; Jane had always been rather direct. Was it possible his own wife was afraid of him?

It would appear not. "I would ask you to release your sister from the Tower," Jane said, meeting his eyes without blinking. She was the only one other than Lord Burghley who had spoken directly to William about Elizabeth since her imprisonment.

"Elizabeth is my family and that is not a matter you need concern yourself with."

"Elizabeth is my family, also. And what good is a queen who cannot move a king to mercy?" Jane observed.

"Elizabeth earned her punishment. I did not choose it for her."

"But to what end? Surely your displeasure has been well noted. And you cannot change the past. No punishment you can devise will bring her back to you, William."

She did not mean Elizabeth. Only Jane would be principled enough to bring up the woman her husband had loved to his face. Or foolish enough.

"Do you think I don't know that?" he lashed back, knowing that she would hear the warning signals in his voice. "Do you think I do not know every single thing that has been taken from me forever? Don't tell me about changing the past. Are you not proof that I am living for the future?"

William curved his hands around her stomach, feeling the movement of his child within. It was the most intimate touch he'd bestowed on Jane since she'd conceived—and even perhaps before, for there had been no grand passion. Only duty performed, on both their parts.

"You carry my future," he said, trying to soften, trying to remove the taint of anger or regret or bitterness that remained in him from his earlier words.

But Jane was shrewder than he'd guessed. Or braver. "You cannot bring Minuette back, but you can have your sister. Consider it, Your Majesty. Please."

He did as she had bid, despite himself. It was true that he didn't know himself what he intended for Elizabeth, other than make damn sure she knew how angry he was. He would not go to see her, for he had no desire to ever set foot in the Tower precincts again. While the deepest weeks of winter froze around him, William pondered an appropriate end to his sister's imprisonment. What punishment fit Elizabeth's crime of stealing away the only woman he had ever loved?

It wasn't until the end of February that the appropriate solution presented itself. It was Lord Burghley who brought him word that Robert Dudley had been seized in Dover where he had attempted to enter the country in disguise.

William actually laughed aloud when he heard it, at the folly of the grand romantic gesture. "Did he intend to slip into the Tower and spirit away my sister?" His own words made him pause and consider.

"Your Majesty?" Lord Burghley prompted after the silence grew awkward.

It was perfect. Elizabeth had ensured William would never again lay eyes on Minuette—he would do the same for the only man his sister had ever come near to loving.

"I think I've had enough of Dudley follies," William said coldly. "Like father, like son . . . well, this is one son who will not live longer to rise against me."

The months Elizabeth spent in the Tower did not pass, as she might have hoped, like a vague, hazy dream. Rather, each hour was etched in lines deep and sharp upon her mind and soul and body. Her physical comfort was assured, for angry as he was, William would not see her anything less than well-clothed and fed—for his own pride, if nothing else. But Elizabeth had to school herself to the indignities of being confined at all.

At least she was allowed books and paper, though she did not bother to write many letters, knowing they would all be censored and just as likely never delivered. She did not write to William at all, but she did write to Jane, who was allowed to maintain a correspondence with her disgraced sister-in-law. Through Jane, Elizabeth knew that William's winter consisted of regular bouts of illness and that the physicians were uncertain of their cause.

Guilty conscience, Elizabeth decided. For William was not a monster, just an angry and lonely man who could find no rest.

Lord Burghley visited her twice in the Tower. Although Walsingham was not allowed to see her, he kept in touch with Burghley, and Elizabeth had the impression of connections being made and reinforced beneath the surface of events, like a web in the center of which sat herself.

She was beginning to grow tired of winters and the inevitable uncertainty of spring and summer with its better weather for military campaigns. How many springs now had dawned with the threat of invasion and civil war? She counted back to William's eighteenth birthday four years ago and his victory in France. When would the cycle of vengeance end?

When Lord Burghley appeared the third time in her cell, it was mid-April 1558 and it was with news that William summoned her from prison to Hampton Court.

"A temporary reprieve?" she asked lightly, though not so lightly as she wished.

"Only the king wholly knows his own mind," Burghley answered gravely, "but I believe he feels you have been amply punished."

Something in his tone warned her and she narrowed her eyes. "What else has William done?" she asked sharply.

Burghley's eyes flicked to the Tower constable who stood near enough to overhear. "The king has commanded silence on this matter. But you should prepare yourself, Your Highness."

The constable's expression gave away nothing except a devout wish to be elsewhere, far out of reach of either Tudors' temper. Elizabeth straightened her shoulders and raised her head, for she would never be caught being afraid for herself. "Then best lead me to the king that I might have my answers."

She took nothing with her, simply walked out of the cell as solitary as she had walked into it, accompanied by men but sufficient within herself for whatever might await. Royalty was not a matter of apparel or jewels—for Elizabeth had dressed for warmth rather than fashion while in prison—but a matter of attitude. Today she wore a kirtle the shade of summer grass and a wool gown in a green so dark it almost looked black, but she carried herself as though she was arrayed for the most solemn of court ceremonies.

During the months of her imprisonment, Elizabeth had felt herself more surely her mother's daughter than she ever had before. For a woman—even a princess—would always be at the mercy of a king, and it took a woman of no small self-possession to maintain her integrity of spirit when faced with a king's anger. Anne Boleyn had never cowered in her life, and Elizabeth would do no less.

Her self-possession frayed as they made their way to Water Gate and she was helped into the chancellor's barge for the river trip to Hampton Court. But it was only when the barge cut across the Thames toward the southern tower of London Bridge that Elizabeth began to suspect the truth. The southern tower of the medieval bridge had been known for one thing since William Wallace in 1305: the spikes upon which the heads of traitors were impaled.

Who was it her brother wanted her to see?

There were several heads atop the spikes, but even from the great distance below on the river, Elizabeth could see that all but one were left over from the rebellion the previous year, the heads ragged and picked at by birds. Only one looked newly dipped in tar, giving the features a gruesome aspect. She was not near enough to distinguish individual features. It was her own imagination that made the leap, knowing her brother as she did.

Burghley confirmed it. "I'm sorry, Your Highness. Robert Dudley did not take your advice to remain in France. He was caught last week in Dover trying to reenter the country in disguise. Your brother ordered a hasty trial and execution at Dover Castle."

Burghley, wisely, did not continue speaking. Elizabeth bit her tongue so hard it bled, but she would not make a sound. She fixed the sight of Robert's head firmly in her mind, refusing to turn away, carrying the image with her all the way to Hampton Court.

That was a mistake, William, she thought coldly. If her brother believed he had cowed her, he was entirely wrong. She could not be cowed. She could only be hardened.

LETTER FROM ELIZABETH TO FRANCIS WALSINGHAM

> 17 April 1558
> Hampton Court Palace
>
> Walsingham,
>
> I am returned to court, though rather less than warmly welcomed. However, my brother has consented to your presence at court as well. I beg you to join me as soon as convenient.
>
> HRH Elizabeth Tudor

William did not summon his sister to his presence until nearly two weeks had passed. He chose to greet her outdoors, in the privy garden that held so many painful memories of Minuette. But he almost welcomed painful memories, if only to feel something—anything at all—in the long march of days that were beginning to wear on his soul. Women brought him little pleasure, and he could not even drink to forgetfulness any longer. Anything beyond a single glass of wine made him ragingly sick, a pounding head vying with a burning stomach, and he would retch for hours until he was bringing nothing up. If he could not drink and he could not whore, all he had left was to rule.

And even that was fraught with obstacles. Lord Burghley continued to speak dispassionately, but his evenness did not conceal an iron purpose that was often opposed to William's. The council was growing restless and impatient and William knew he should bite back hard, but he had not the patience for anything but blunt orders that, as often as not, were delayed until they didn't matter any longer.

The changes in Elizabeth's appearance were slight but unmistakable. A new gravity to her expression, a wariness in the very way she moved, as though suspicion had become a permanent part of her being. And so you should be suspicious, William thought scornfully. That is the life of royalty.

She curtsied so low she was almost kneeling. But her humility had its limits in her very nature, and there was a familiar tartness to her voice when he gestured to her to rise.

"It is good to set eyes on you, brother. I had almost forgotten how handsome you are."

A subtle reproof, or a subtle jab at his scarred cheek? One could never be sure with Elizabeth. "Jane is right glad you have come," he managed. "I hear you've been keeping her company as she prepares for her confinement."

"A pity she has to retire to a closed chamber just as the weather is becoming so lovely."

William waved away the mysterious female etiquette of childbirth. "The spring will be all the more lovely when she emerges with my son."

He almost heard Elizabeth's retort (*What if it's a daughter?*) but she neatly swallowed it. "Do you have any use for me here besides entertaining your queen?"

Not when I've lately impaled your lover's head upon a spike, he thought. But would not say. Not ever. Nor would his sister ever allude to it. She was, above all else, a survivor. Very much like their mother.

But the fact that she would not speak of it meant there would forever remain an unbreachable barrier between them. William felt a fresh wave of desolation at the loss of his single remaining relationship; it was no comfort to know that he had built that barrier himself.

He drew his breath sharply and said, "Try to keep out of trouble, Elizabeth. I should hate to be forced to remove you from court once more."

She swept into another low curtsey, but he could not help seeing disdain in the lines of her body. "Heaven forbid I force the king to anything."

He had to stalk away then or risk losing his temper openly. His head pounded and there was the strange light that preceded a period of pain and weakness and the blurriest of thoughts.

He kept to his own darkened chamber for the next three days and was still gripped with illness when Lord Burghley himself intruded to let him know that Jane had been taken by her childbirth pains a full five weeks before her expected time. William forced himself to dress and leave his bedchamber for his privy chamber, where low-voiced attendants whispered among themselves. William would listen only to Burghley himself as the day passed, fading into a lovely, spring-scented twilight that he thought hazily could only betoken good fortune. Minuette had been born more than a month early, he reminded himself—his first thought of her in months without pain—and she had positively blossomed with health her entire life.

But when Burghley bowed low before him, he read the news on his face instantly. "The child," William said flatly, and it was not a question.

"Your Majesty, I grieve to bring you this news, but—"

"The child is dead. Well, that is a common enough grief in this world. My queen will recover. She will bear me sons and to spare in future." He spoke the right words instinctively, not knowing if he really believed them.

Burghley flinched. "I am sorry, Your Majesty. The queen did not survive the ordeal. Both mother and babe are gone to God."

William had thought he was past feeling pain, but this overturning of all his plans, the efforts he had made to move forward and secure himself a future, pierced what little was left of his heart. Burghley waited, but when William did not speak, he bowed himself away.

"Wait!" William snarled after him.

Burghley halted and everyone in the chamber held still, waiting for the king's rage.

"Was it a boy?" he ground out.

"Yes, Your Majesty."

Elizabeth paced her privy chamber at Hampton Court, watched once again by Walsingham and Dee and Lord Burghley. *Am I really running a shadow council?* she sometimes asked herself. *And if I am, is that all to the bad?* Someone had to think beyond personal sorrows to the welfare of England.

Not that she didn't truly grieve for Jane Grey and the lost prince. She had liked Jane well enough for herself, but what that loss meant to William was the true worry. He had tried to move on, done the rational thing in marrying Jane, and God had laughed in his face. Or at least, she imagined that was how William saw it. Imagination was all she had to go on, since William had left Hampton Court for Richmond the day after Jane's death, where he remained with orders not to be disturbed except on the most urgent business.

Burghley had come to see her at Hampton Court for the day at his own initiative, but Elizabeth would have summoned him if he hadn't. Their minds clicked along well together, and he was the first to comment on Walsingham's report that the French king had allotted the Duke of Norfolk three ships in which to make an exploratory thrust into England.

"Will he come ashore near Framlingham, do you think?" Burghley mused. "It's the Howard stronghold and passions still run deep about Mary's execution."

"It's likely," Elizabeth agreed. "But we cannot overlook less obvious avenues, if only because Norfolk is smart enough to know how we'll think."

"So watches all along the southeast coast and nearer to Scotland as well," Burghley offered. "I'll give the navy orders."

"Has the king shown any interest in this news?"

"No, Your Highness. The king shows interest in nothing. He scarcely eats at all, and if he sleeps, his face does not show it. He will answer a direct question, but only if it is repeated more than once."

Elizabeth rose and the men followed suit, standing while she circled the chamber. "I've been thinking," she said musingly, "of Henry VI. The poor, mad king whose venomous French wife cost him his throne nearly as much as his own madness. But if that Henry had not been so often ill, unable to govern, and if his wife had not been quite so openly ambitious, then there would have been no Edward IV to take his place. And without the Yorkist

Edward and his brother, Richard, to oppose, my grandfather might never have come to the throne that he filled so well."

She stared out the tall, narrow window through which she had once watched carefully for glimpses of Robert in the courtyard below, and said, as though to herself, "Truly, God moves in mysterious ways. It is all men can do to catch a glimpse of His plan, and our own place in it."

It was a delicate matter to read a royal mind, particularly when that mind was none too certain of itself. Elizabeth felt the minds of the three men tracing her careful threads and was not surprised that Walsingham spoke first. "Who could have guessed your father's quest for a son, that took such a crooked path, would end in tears and grief?"

"Your Highness," said Burghley. "The king has made no provisions for a regent since he appointed me that task last year. But you remain his heir, and the privy council supports you in such a role. If the king is too ill to act when Norfolk lands in England, you must be prepared to lead."

"You think the king will not act?" Elizabeth swung restlessly away from the window. "I think battle will be the only thing that can still stir him. If—when—Norfolk lands, I would wager all I own that the king will ride to meet him."

"Is that what you would counsel?"

"I do not counsel the king. But if I were to be asked my opinion, I would urge negotiation. For all his talk, the French king has not actually given Norfolk that much. Three ships, when he might as easily have offered three dozen? And talk of a French marriage has not led anywhere just yet. I think Norfolk is proudly English, and would prefer to return home. Why not make it easy for him? Offer pardon, with suitable monetary punishment upon his estates, and provide him with a Protestant bride. I thought Margaret Clifford might do. She has proved her fertility with her ill-conceived

Dudley son and is near enough to the throne to not be an insult to Norfolk."

"A generous offer," Burghley remarked.

"An entirely hypothetical offer," Elizabeth countered. "But you asked what my counsel would be."

John Dee, who had remained watchfully silent throughout all of this, stirred at last. "It is not your counsel England needs so much as your action. What does your wide view tell you, Your Highness?"

"That the king will ride to battle . . . and that misfortune awaits kings who fight from a position of despair rather than hope." And that you once came near to calling me queen, she thought, and knew from John Dee's expression that he remembered.

The air hung heavy with unspoken possibilities, perhaps even hopes. Who would dare to speak more? It was, not surprisingly, Walsingham. "It is true that despairing men are not as careful of their persons as they might be. A battlefield is a messy place. It would be best to be prepared for all ends."

He would not ask—and if he did, she would not answer. But Elizabeth met Walsingham's gaze and inclined her head the barest inch in acknowledgment, not only of his words, but of his thoughts.

Then she turned away from all of them, and said stiffly, "You are dismissed."

She stood for a long time at the window, long enough that the shadows moved toward night. In those shadows she allowed herself to see William as he had once been: beloved brother, joyous friend, enthusiastic king. And with deliberation, she took every single one of those memories and locked them away into a corner of her heart.

The first intimations of fresh trouble came from the mouth of the Humber River. Three French carracks, along with five hastily converted merchant cogs with single square sails, were sighted by coastal defenses the last week of May. William received the news in silence, knowing that his advisors thought him insensible. He was not insensible—he was just conserving his strength for what mattered. Clearly God did not intend his marriage to matter, so he saved his energy for swift vengeance against Norfolk and the Catholics he was rallying to his cause.

Burghley, faithful Crown servant that he was, continued to update him daily despite William's outward lack of interest. And so William knew that Norfolk's ships had withdrawn, perhaps to make a play for a landing farther south at the Howard family's East Anglia stronghold near Framlingham. "Don't overlook the feint," William told Burghley, and noted the slight hesitation of surprise from the Lord Chancellor that the king was indeed paying attention.

"No, Your Majesty."

And feint it was, for in the end Norfolk managed to land his mercenary troops along the north side of the Humber near Ravenscar. Yorkshire was well chosen, for it had been the site of the Pilgrimage of Grace twenty years ago and the old Catholic ways held strong sway. Norfolk was calculating—but William was more calculating still. And the King of England had God on his side, at least in the matter of religion.

From the depths of his retreat at Richmond, William issued a rapid list of commands. Troops ready to march north and block Norfolk from sweeping to London. Burghley to take charge of the government from Whitehall. And, finally, the figurehead his people needed. "Bring me Elizabeth," he told Lord Burghley, and received a relieved acquiescence. You prefer her to me? he thought cynically. That is only because she is not actually monarch. It is easy to be liked when one does not have to make the hard decisions.

Elizabeth came without demur. William met her in his presence chamber at Richmond, seated on a gilded throne beneath the canopy of estate. He was dressed as though to ride out, but he wore a circlet of gold and rubies and faced Elizabeth as her king and not her brother.

"Your Majesty." Elizabeth curtsied a precisely calculated depth and waited for William to acknowledge her.

"Rise," he said abruptly, and leaned back as Elizabeth stood straight and square, hands folded across her skirt. She had judged her attire as nicely as he had, her gown of black and white suiting her pale skin and bright hair.

She had always been more patient than the rest of them, and that patience had not deserted her in times of crisis. She waited, apparently unruffled, and William felt a twist of old and bitter amusement at the familiarity of their positions.

"I ride out tomorrow to intercept Norfolk and his hired mercenaries," he told her. "Fewer have flocked to him in the North than surely he had hoped. This time I will not leave the field until the Duke of Norfolk is taken or dead. This cannot be allowed to continue."

"I agree," she replied. "England grows weary of strife. The people must have peace."

"Lord Burghley will assume government power in London, but it would please me if you would act as regent from Hatfield as necessary. We have had our troubles, but I do not forget whose daughter you are. The people need to have Henry's children before their eyes."

"I will gladly serve."

His eyes narrowed. He leaned forward, arms resting on his knees. "Can I trust you in this, Elizabeth?"

She did not answer immediately, or indignantly. Rather, she fixed her eyes on his as though seeing deeply into him as she used to do, and he remembered asking her once when she would teach him to read people as she did. *When you learn to control your countenance,* she had answered. He wondered if she found it harder to read him now than she once had.

Elizabeth curtsied once more, answering as she did so. "I can always be trusted to put England's good before my personal interests."

That phrase sat with him uneasily throughout the night. Once, she would have laughed at the notion that he could not trust her, or scoffed at his need for a spoken vow when he should be able to trust her without words . . . But in a world where everything else had tilted and altered, why not his sister?

The march was quick and easy, for the early June weather seemed to smile on military ventures with clear skies and dry roads. William was glad they did not have to stop and stay in any one place for long, for he did not miss the resentful mood along the way. Instead of cheers, his army was met with sullen silence and occasionally a catcall. Elizabeth had been right—his people wearied of the constant conflict. It made William all the more anxious to confront Norfolk and finish the job with the duke's death, for what pleasure was there in ruling a country that was mocking and ungrateful?

And when he had finished with Norfolk, he would ride on to Cumbria. It was time to put an end to Dominic once and for all—perhaps, William thought, his refusal to deal with the past had caused God to destroy his present. When Norfolk was dead, and Dominic as well, then perhaps this burden of listlessness and illness would be taken from him and he could think clearly about the future of England and his own legacy.

The battle was joined at last south of the cathedral city of York. Clearly, Norfolk had not advanced as far as he'd hoped, nor had he gathered many local troops to support the small number of mercenaries. The fighting was sharp and began under clear skies, but within an hour the clouds that had been absent for so long erupted and rain began to pour fast and hard. William was aware of being wet, but fighting allowed him a chance to escape his own head and he refused to be sidetracked or retreat. They were winning the fight, Norfolk would be taken on the field, and William at leisure to return him to the Tower or execute him on the spot. It was the nearest he had been to feeling happy in almost two years.

The blow came at him from behind, catching the side of his helmet hard enough to stun him. The second blow (a mace? a stave?) struck his shoulder and sent him fumbling for his horse's neck. But his horse had been struck as well and went down to its knees, sending William to the ground. He shook his head to clear it, but the ringing in his ears mingled with the sounds of battle as he hefted his sword and swung round to meet his foe.

Two mercenaries on horses had managed to slip through his guards and William braced himself for a brief fight and, at the worst, a briefer surrender. No doubt they saw Norfolk's end as well as he did and wanted to use the king's safety to negotiate their own retreat from the field. William didn't care about the mercenaries— let them return where they'd come from.

He almost didn't even mind, for at least the feeling of anger and disappointment was clean and sharp. After so long of muddled emotions and even more muddled motivations, it was nearly a pleasure to at least know what he was feeling.

But the mercenaries on horseback made no move to take him and suddenly William felt himself seized from behind. Before he could grasp what was happening, there was a sharp, almost liquid pain beneath his arm and then a second, similar, piercing pain beneath his other arm, and the rational part of William's brain supplied the information that a dagger had been carefully thrust between the plates of his armor. The last blow came to his knees, a blunt thrust from the flat of a sword that spun him to the muddy ground, cursing and bleeding and wondering how the hell he could have been so stupid as to imagine Norfolk would fight with honour. Apparently he wasn't the only one who'd intended to leave his enemy for dead today.

DISPATCH FROM WILLIAM CECIL, LORD BURGHLEY,
TO HER ROYAL HIGHNESS, ELIZABETH

Norfolk is defeated and his mercenary army dispersed back to Europe. The duke is being returned to the Tower of London. The king was seriously wounded on the field. He has been taken to Pontefract Castle.

William hated being at Pontefract, but he'd been unconscious when borne from the field and the royal castle was deemed the best refuge. He'd never stayed at Pontefract before, for it was tainted by betrayal and death: the royal guardian had handed it over to the rebels during the Pilgrimage of Grace; Edward II had executed his cousin for treason at Pontefract; and most awfully, Richard II had died in its dungeons, starved to death by Henry of Lancaster.

In the first two days, William had hopes of quickly moving on, for though the wounds pained him greatly they seemed to have missed anything vital. He followed reports of Norfolk's surrender and dispatch to London and agreed with his commanders' decision to let the mercenaries retreat across the sea. A man who is being paid to fight will not return when the paymaster is removed.

But the pain did not ease, despite the ministrations of several physicians. And soon pain became something worse—a poison of infection spreading from the dagger wounds through his whole body, bringing with it weakness and fever. William began to drown in dreams, and whenever he emerged to wakefulness he was seized by an awful fear at the familiarity of his position. It was the smallpox all over again: a lost, dark wandering through the blackness of his own soul.

I'm going to die. He'd had that thought more than once during the smallpox, but Dominic's steady voice had found him in the darkness and brought him back. There was no Dominic to save him now.

Lord Burghley came, and several hours later (or was it days? William had lost time entirely) a dark-haired, dark-eyed man whom he associated with Elizabeth.

From somewhere deep, William dredged up a name. "Walsingham," he croaked, for the fever and pain had stolen his voice along with his strength.

"Yes, Your Majesty." Walsingham waited, as though he expected William to say something else. And William realized there was something he desperately needed to say. Needed the women to know.

"Box," he croaked again, and was able to point so that Walsingham found the plain oak box on the table at the foot of the bed. William had carried that box with him everywhere since burning Wynfield Mote, and his attendants knew to keep it within his reach.

At a nod from William, which sent pain flaring bright and hot through his head, Walsingham opened the box and withdrew the simple linen bag that had been taken off Minuette's maid in the camp outside Wynfield Mote.

Walsingham looked questioningly at William but did not open the bag. William knew he could feel the outline of a diary, the fluid shape of jewels, and he wanted to tell him ... no, not him, it wasn't Walsingham who needed to know ... it was Minuette's, it should return to her ... but she was never coming back. And Dominic ...

As William's exhausted body slipped back into restless sleep,

Dominic's eyes followed him, dark green and hate-filled, watching him from the squalor of the dungeon at Lakehill House.

Dominic knew he was beginning to go slightly mad as the days and weeks and months passed and William did not return to see him. What was the king doing? Leaving him to die of grief and solitude? If that were William's plan, he should never have mentioned that Minuette's son—possibly Dominic's own son—lived. The thought of some part of his wife left behind—and in the king's hands—was just sufficient in the worst hours to keep Dominic moving in both body and mind.

But then there came a stretch of days when absolutely no one came, not even the mute servant who brought his food and emptied his fetid waste bucket. Dominic passed a bad few nights when he thought that William had sent orders to let him starve in the darkness, but before despair could quite sink into his bones, Eleanor appeared.

He had not seen her since William's last visit, for she had apparently lost interest in taunting him at the same time the king had. But she had not changed. Dominic could still see in her the lovely, scheming, utterly amoral young woman she had been when she first appeared at court and in William's bed. Of them all, it seemed Eleanor was the least affected by the years.

For all that, her voice had a new edge to it, like broken glass stroked across his skin. "I've had word. Your fate has been consigned into my hands. Now what," she wondered softly, studying him as she might a dog, "shall I do with you?"

Seriously, Will? Dominic thought. You cannot even finish me off yourself, but must leave me to her?

Her eyes traveled his body, still chained but now wearing the rough homespun brought to him by the mute servant some time ago. His hair was a tangle to his shoulders and crawling with various unsavory life forms, and his beard itched awfully. Most of him itched.

"It would not do for you to meet your fate looking quite so revolting," Eleanor continued. "I shall send a man to clean you. And then ... the ax, I think. Is that not what you have been waiting for all these months? Do you even know how long?"

His voice was rough from disuse, though he'd made himself speak aloud in the emptiness of his cell as often as he could stand. "Just kill me, bitch, and be done with it."

Her eyebrows shot up. "Well, well, well ... who would have guessed the oh-so honourable Dominic Courtenay had it in him to say such things? But then, we all have our darker sides."

She left then, but was as good as her word. The mute servant returned, this time with another man who looked marginally more intelligent if just as uninterested. They stripped Dominic—undoing the wrist chains one at a time—and scrubbed him harshly and methodically and sluiced away more dirt and filth than Dominic cared to think about. His hair they simply cut, ruthlessly cropping it, and though they didn't shave the beard completely they at least made it manageable. Dominic was ashamed to admit what a difference it made, to feel clean.

And then he waited, dressed not in homespun but in soft hose and clean linen that had probably belonged to Giles Howard at some point, and waited for the promised deliverance of the ax.

CHAPTER TWENTY-FIVE

DISPATCH FROM WILLIAM CECIL, LORD BURGHLEY,
TO HER ROYAL HIGHNESS, ELIZABETH

The king's wounds fester and grow foul. His previous bouts of ill health have weakened his constitution. The physicians are uneasy. Perhaps Your Highness should come to Pontefract.

Elizabeth sent Walsingham as her envoy to Pontefract, dispatching him with a curt written message rather than speaking to him. And then she waited.

The previously glorious early summer weather had turned violent on the day of the battle, and Elizabeth felt the heavens mirroring her own internal struggle. She could not stay still, but she would not leave Hatfield. She would not go to Pontefract. She would not go to London. As long as she remained at Hatfield, time seemed suspended and all that had come before and all that might follow after were held in the balance of one man's breath and one sister's choice.

When the weather forced her indoors, Elizabeth paced through the confines of her favorite home and thought back to the deaths of those she'd loved. Her father, always larger than life, who might have been terrifying in his tempers if his affections had not been just as wide and deep; Elizabeth had been thirteen when Henry died, and she well remembered the keen sense of loss that filled the very air of England. Then her mother, four years ago, with whom Elizabeth had sat until her last hour, watching the vibrant Anne fade with every painful breath until her vital spirit slipped free of her injured body.

She thought of Dominic, whom she had perhaps not realized she loved until too late, for he was the very embodiment of self-effacement, and one tended not to notice him until he was gone. The last time she'd seen him had been the day he'd fled court with Minuette, to escape William's reach for a time. But in the end the king had his revenge on the scaffold.

And Robert . . . her last memory of Robert Dudley was three days after Dominic's execution, when she asked him to risk his life for Minuette, to escort her friend from the Tower to safety in France. He had taken Elizabeth's hand in his and kissed it, not as a friend or a would-be lover, but as a subject. And he had said: *I serve at your pleasure, Elizabeth, and I am your man until the last day of my life.*

After two weeks of storms and flooding, the sun made a feeble return, like a new colt trying out its legs. Elizabeth had heard nothing from Burghley for two days when, on June 28, horsemen riding fast approached Hatfield.

Elizabeth met them outside, dressed in a gown that hinted at childhood in pale blue and white, her hair dressed high at the crown and left to hang to her waist. She noted Lord Burghley at once, but it was the nobles of the privy council who took center stage.

Not a duke—for Rochford and Dominic were dead, and Norfolk imprisoned—but the Earls of Pembroke and Oxford stepped forward of the others and were the first to kneel.

"Your Majesty."

She could not have told who spoke those words first, but they were repeated as the remaining men—and her own few ladies—also knelt to offer homage to their new monarch.

My brother is dead, she thought. And John Dee was right. Elizabeth the queen.

She had practiced her response and spoke without faltering. "This is the Lord's doing, and it is marvelous in our eyes."

8 July 1558
Chateau de Blanclair

William is dead.

10 July 1558
Chateau de Blanclair

I did not mean to break off writing so abruptly before, but I found that I could not go on. Not for sorrow's sake, or rage, or relief . . . I think it is more that I do not know how I feel.

The news came through Walsingham's contacts. William had been wounded at the battle outside York and his general state of ill health led to a festering of the wounds and a weakness of spirit that could not be overcome. He died the day before our shared twenty-second birthday.

Now Elizabeth is queen. And yet I find that I remain far more interested in the fact that Lucette has light brown hair that curls slightly against her perfect scalp, that she is wonderfully chubby and good-natured, that she sits up perfectly well unassisted, and that she has cut her first two teeth. What are kingdoms and politics next to that?

27 July 1558
Chateau de Blanclair

Today I received a letter written in Elizabeth's own hand. She begs
me to return to England. "Not to court, unless you wish it," she
writes. "And I cannot imagine that you do. But I have carpenters
hard at work restoring Wynfield Mote, not just the manor house
but the cottages of your people that were burnt. Your home will be
waiting for you, Minuette, whenever you desire to return."

My home. I once thought my only home was Dominic. But
now?

Her letter came with a gift: my old diary, my mother's rosary,
and the sapphire and pearl necklace Dominic gave me so long ago.
I touched the filigree star hanging from the jewels and wondered if
Dominic could see me from Heaven and knew how much my grief
for him is mixed with love for Lucette.

It seems it was not Elizabeth alone who returned them, for she
wrote that in his last days William had given them into
Walsingham's hands, along with a few cryptic words that she
transcribed: "Minuette . . . tell her . . . Dominic. Sorry."

I think Dominic would not grudge me the tears I wept for
William at that.

August in the Loire Valley was a succession of sunny days that
were a continuous astonishment to the English guests. Minuette
took advantage of the weather and spent hours each day in the
gardens with Lucette and Carrie. Harrington had made himself
useful around the estate, and with France at temporary peace with
Spain and refraining from pushing the advantage lost by Norfolk,
Renaud was home much of the time. Minuette watched him with
his sons, old enough now to be taught the beginnings of swordplay,
and remembered Dominic and William testing themselves against

each other all the years of childhood. Nicolas was the image of his father in both face and temperament, and at nine years old was already a serious horseman. Seven-year-old Julien had his mother's happy temperament and a wide streak of mischief that Carrie said knowledgeably was a common trait of second sons.

The boys were too old to be interested in babies, and too young to care about their English guests. But wherever Lucette was, so was Renaud and Nicole's daughter, Charlotte. The girl was three years old and absolutely enchanted with baby Lucie. Charlotte kept up a constant stream of lisping French babble directed Lucette's way and today was no exception. While Minuette dead-headed roses, Charlotte informed Lucette that "next summer, when you are big, we shall go to the river for a picnic."

It was Carrie, who had picked up quite a lot of French this year, who said to Minuette, "Shall we be here next summer?"

She had told Carrie and Harrington of Elizabeth's letter, and then avoided the subject for weeks. But it had to be broached, and sooner rather than later if they meant to sail home before winter.

Minuette continued removing the brown-spotted and faded roses as she considered her answer. Or, more properly, how to phrase the answer.

"I will not go to London," she said finally. "But I should like to go home. Lucette is English, and I want her to know her people. And where better than Wynfield?"

She looked at Carrie's dear, faithful face. "I'll speak to Renaud. Let Harrington know that we will prepare to cross the Channel in September."

And though she meant to avoid political entanglements in future, there was one more favour she would ask the new queen: if possible, to discover where Dominic was buried and to have his body reinterred at the old chapel near Wynfield where they had been married.

The first months of Elizabeth's reign passed swiftly, as she accustomed herself to the trappings of power as well as to the realities. Lord Burghley she named her chancellor, and when Archbishop Cranmer died of causes incident to age in late September, Elizabeth appointed Matthew Parker Archbishop of Canterbury. Parker had been Anne Boleyn's chaplain during the early years of her marriage and it gave Elizabeth pleasure to bestow a favour. Not that she didn't expect him to work hard and at her command. He and Burghley between them were busy planning her coronation. Elizabeth had insisted on consulting John Dee as to the date, and at his advice settled upon January 15. Though it was a long stretch to wait, Elizabeth would be glad to leave 1558 behind and begin her official reign in a new year.

It was mid-October when Walsingham asked for a private audience as soon as convenient. He had been out and about through England, no doubt checking with his spies that all was well and keeping abreast of those who protested her succession either because she was a woman or because she was Protestant or both. She expected him to deliver a report on the state of her kingdom, but he had something more personal to say.

"I was approached in the North by Eleanor Percy, lately sister-in-law to the Duke of Norfolk."

"Don't tell me Eleanor wished to plead for the duke? She has no feeling for the family she was born into, let alone that of her ill-chosen marriage."

"No, Your Majesty. She said that she has endeavored to contact you and has heard nothing in reply."

"If she wants to know what I intend to do about the child of hers that William recognized, she will simply have to wait. Unless she would prefer me to decide immediately that the child will be removed from all contact with her as long as I am paying for her upkeep."

"It is not the child she spoke of." Walsingham sounded unusually diffident. Almost hesitant.

"Whatever is it that you cannot say directly, Walsingham?"

"It seems, if she is to be believed, that the late king visited her in Cumbria several times in the last year of his life."

Elizabeth remembered William's absences in the North and frowned. "So? She is not claiming another child, is she?"

"No. She is not precisely claiming anything—hinting, rather, no doubt hoping to extract various promises from Your Majesty in return for . . ." Walsingham shrugged his shoulders. "Perhaps in return for nothing."

"It is not like you to speak so guardedly."

"With Your Majesty's permission, I would like to travel to her home in Cumbria and examine matters for myself before I speak further."

Elizabeth waved her permission. "Please do. I will speak with you on your return."

In the event, Walsingham did not return. It was Elizabeth who traveled to meet him, despite the fact that it was already November and for no one else would she have set forth on this journey without specific information. But Walsingham had never failed her, and so when he wrote, *You will wish to see this for yourself,* she believed him.

Perhaps the best part of being queen was not having to explain oneself to all and sundry. Elizabeth gave her orders, left Burghley to run things in London, and rode the long way north to Cumbria. She took her time, visiting overnight with several noble families, and arrived at the windswept, desolate, absolutely depressing Lakehill House on a grim November afternoon.

Walsingham met her in the hall. "Mistress Percy has been sent to Kenilworth with the Howard family," he told her. "I thought it best when I discovered the secret she'd been keeping at the king's behest."

"William had her keeping secrets? I would have thought Eleanor incapable of discretion."

"Not where her own interests are concerned. I can show you the cell below where he was kept later, but for now he is in the family wing. He likes open windows and open doors, and I cannot say I blame him."

"Who?"

But Walsingham would not say. Growing impatient, Elizabeth followed him through the hall and up the stairs to a low-roofed corridor off which several doors opened. The one at the far end was not shut. Walsingham rapped lightly on the door frame and then stepped back to allow Elizabeth entry.

A man sat with his back to her, looking out the window onto the bleak landscape beyond. For a moment she thought the man hadn't heard her entrance, but then he turned his head and Elizabeth felt herself spin into dizziness.

Gaunt and shadowed, his black hair cropped ruthlessly short and more heavily bearded than he'd ever been, but unmistakably Dominic Courtenay.

He looked at her without interest, perhaps even without recognition, while Elizabeth's mind put together the pieces of the past shaken loose into a new picture. Robert had attended his execution, but Dominic had been beaten, she remembered. And blindfolded. And his tongue had been cut out so that he—or someone else—might not speak.

William had gone to great lengths to spirit Dominic away privately to a hell of his own imagining.

A harsh voice came from him, hardly recognizable in tone or attitude. "Now will someone tell me what is going on?"

He stood up and faced her, and Elizabeth saw with a jolt to her stomach that his left hand was gone, the arm ending in a neatly bandaged square of cream linen. What had William done?

But before she could speak, Walsingham said behind her, "Your Majesty—"

"Majesty?" Dominic interrupted, and narrowed his eyes. "What does he mean?"

Feeling more vulnerable than she had in many months, Elizabeth met Dominic's emerald-green gaze and said, "The king is dead."

She didn't know what reaction she expected, but it wasn't the bitter laughter that ensued. With a bow that was half mocking, half savage, Dominic said, "Long live the queen."

Dominic was glad enough to leave Lakehill House, though "glad" was a strong word for an emotion that was muffled and distant. It had been hard enough to adjust to being pulled out of his prison cell by Walsingham, told only that Eleanor was gone and he was safe . . . to have Elizabeth appear and discover that she was queen and William was dead was almost more than his mind could take.

Was it comedy, he wondered, or tragedy—that he lived and the king was dead? Dominic didn't know how to feel about any of it . . . except that his hand ached. The left hand. The one the promised ax had struck off rather than his head. Dominic knew enough of events from Walsingham to be certain the taking of his hand had been Eleanor's idea, after William's death.

As he rode south from Cumbria in a closed carriage with Elizabeth, Dominic wondered why Eleanor had not simply killed him. But he knew the answer to that—Eleanor might be vengeful but she was also a survivor. She would not have risked Elizabeth discovering that she had killed a man once held dear by the new Crown. Probably she had tried to blame the loss of Dominic's hand on William as well.

And why not? Dominic thought savagely. William so thoroughly stripped me of everything that mattered—might as well hate him for the loss of my hand as well.

Except, even now, he couldn't quite hate William. Fury, yes. A desire to beat William as thoroughly as the king had battered him. A wish to have William at his feet, begging for mercy . . . even now, Dominic's instinct would be for mercy.

If it were not for Minuette. Her death was the one blow Dominic could never forgive his friend. Surely this was why William had left him alive—to be eaten up by guilt and grief until death would be a sought-after release. *Just like a king. Leaving me to finish his dirty work.*

Three days out of Cumbria, Dominic finally asked, "Where are we going?"

"Where would you like to go?"

To the past . . . "Where is she buried?" he asked abruptly. "At the Tower?"

There was a long, fraught silence. Then Elizabeth said, "No, she is returned to Wynfield Mote."

"Then I will go to Wynfield."

The next day, after more long hours of silence, Elizabeth asked him, "Why do you think Walsingham didn't tell you about William's death when he found you? And didn't tell me that you were alive until I saw with my own eyes?"

Dominic shrugged, uninterested.

"I think maybe he wanted the pleasure of seeing my face when we both learned the truth."

The last day's approach to Wynfield was exquisitely painful, for

Dominic knew every mile of that road. He knew that there were things he needed to ask and to do. Did Minuette's son truly live? Was he in Elizabeth's keeping? But all Dominic could think of was lying down next to his wife's grave and allowing himself to finally rest.

He saw the evidence of building where new cottages had been erected in stone and thatch. The fields had been turned over for winter, ready for new planting next spring. Elizabeth had done her best to restore the damage her brother had wrought here.

And the house itself . . . the walls were the same, a few streaks still showing where smoke had left its mark, but the roof was rebuilt and the moat filled. Dominic closed his eyes and remembered riding in here another November, three years ago today.

Our wedding day, Dominic . . . one body and two souls . . . for to deserve everlasting life, whatsoever that they have done here before.

It had been far easier to return than Minuette had feared. Lucette had adored the crossing of the Channel, wailing when taken below and burbling with delight on deck with the sea and sky surrounding her. Renaud had accompanied them to the French coast, and offered Minuette a final hug and word of advice.

"To live for your daughter is a fine thing. But you are very young as yet, and to live for yourself also would not be a sin."

"And would you live for yourself if Nicole were gone?" she asked.

With that ineffable French shrug, Renaud answered, "Who can say? Farewell, *Madame* Courtenay. May your life be long and happy."

Returning to Wynfield was mostly happy, for Elizabeth had extended herself and the estate cottages were tidy and snug and already half filled. Some of the families burnt out the previous year had gone elsewhere, to family or London, but Minuette discovered that the surrounding community had done much to care for those left behind. Emma Hadley, Alyce de Clare's sister, who had always treated Minuette with mingled envy and dislike, had provided house room and work for a widow and her young children, and Wynfield's steward, Asherton, had remained in the area determined to put things right as soon as he could.

It was almost a relief that the interior of the house was new, for it felt as though it were a place for her and Lucette to move forward rather than looking back. But still Minuette rejected the larger space of her parents' former bedchamber for her own smaller one where she and Dominic had always lain together.

On November 17, Minuette was in her mother's rose garden with Carrie and Lucette. Some of the rosebushes had not survived the heat of the fires, but new roots had been planted alongside a few hardy remnants of the original garden. The two women were entertaining themselves with the child's first faltering attempts to walk. She could stand nearly steady as long as she held onto someone's fingers, but she was so plump that her balance was all wrong every time she took a step. Minuette supposed it wasn't very kind to laugh so joyously whenever Lucette sat sharply down, but her creased frown of indignation was delicious.

She and Carrie were laughing when she heard horses approaching, and a few moments later, Harrington's deep voice called out, "Royal standard."

Crimson and azure, lions and lilies . . . time spun through memories but swiftly righted itself. "Her Majesty," Minuette said. "This is unexpected. Carrie, alert Mistress Holly as gently as possible. I don't want my housekeeper dropping dead of shock."

She scooped Lucette into her arms and waited at the edge of the roses, not inclined to welcome the queen too warmly until she knew what was wanted. She was a little surprised that Elizabeth came in a carriage rather than on horseback, but her friend appeared perfectly upright and healthy when she was handed out of the interior. Elizabeth had always dressed well, but there was something indefinably weightier about her deep-red gown and ivory kirtle that better suited a queen than a mere princess. The intricate coils of her red-gold hair were another symbol of position, as though Elizabeth were using her body itself to proclaim her status.

Elizabeth nodded in greeting but did not move toward her friend, and Minuette was just thinking crossly that really, standing on one's dignity could go too far, when a man stepped out of the carriage behind Elizabeth.

She would have known him in her sleep, or her dreams, from his scent alone, or the quality of his stillness, or the sharp line of his jaw. Only when Lucette let out an aggrieved wail did Minuette realize she was squeezing the breath out of both of them.

"Dominic," she whispered, and in the way he stood, she realized that he was as shocked as she was.

And then they moved, both at once, and Minuette knew that she had finally, absolutely, come home.

17 November 1558
Wynfield Mote

Dominic is sleeping, truly resting for the first time in more than a year. He did not want to close his eyes, for fear I would vanish, but I promised him I would stay awake and watch for both our sakes. He is stretched out in the bed behind me, and so I write this at an awkward angle that I may not lose sight of him.

I did not know until today that joy could be nearly as terrifying as grief. But I survived the grief . . . we shall survive the joy. Dominic was so dazed at first that I had to tell him three times that Lucette was a girl before he quite grasped it. If I'd ever harbored a doubt that Dominic would not be able to love a child of

whose birth he was uncertain, it vanished the moment he took
Lucie in his arms and stared at her as though she were the most
marvelous creation God had ever granted.

And now I understand those broken words of William's that
were passed to me across the sea. "Minuette . . . tell her . . .
Dominic." As he died, William wanted me to know that Dominic
still lived. "Sorry," he said.

I forgive you, Will.

And thank you for my husband.

Elizabeth stayed one night at Wynfield, a matter of hours in
which Minuette despaired of Mistress Holly's nerves. But Elizabeth, like her brother, had a gift with the common people that set
them at ease and made them love her. Perhaps almost worship her.

Minuette rose alone to bid Elizabeth farewell at dawn. Without
Dominic to care for in his uncertain state of health, Elizabeth
would ride rather than take the carriage. Minuette embraced her
in the courtyard. "Thank you," she said with all the fervor of her
grateful soul.

With a gaze that took in the building work around them, Elizabeth asked, "I trust you are content with the work done here?"

"You have been very generous."

"And if I were to ask you for something in return?"

"It would depend on what was asked."

"I could use good men and women at my court."

Minuette was silent as she chose carefully each word of her response. "You will be a wonderful queen, Elizabeth, and I will never
be able to thank you for my own safety and Dominic's return. But
we are finished with royalty and courts."

Her friend smiled ruefully, as though she'd known the answer.
"May I at least crave your presence at the coronation? I do not

think I can take those vows without my dearest friend to anchor me. You are all I have left, Minuette."

Minuette knew she was being manipulated, but all the ties of loyalty and long friendship tugged at her. "I will come to the coronation. On the condition that you promise, afterward, to let us be."

Only then did Elizabeth's eyes—blue like her father's and her brother's—harden. "Your daughter is lovely, Minuette. And her eyes are blue."

That was a mistake, Your Majesty, Minuette thought. I have grown almost as hard as you these last years.

She allowed Elizabeth to see all the implacability and fierceness of her mother-love, and with a chilliness that would have done Anne Boleyn proud, spoke only one word. "Don't."

Elizabeth would not apologize; her nod was as close as she would come. "Goodbye, Minuette."

"Farewell, Your Majesty."

Minuette did not stay to see the queen depart. Her husband and her daughter awaited, and nothing on earth mattered more.

POSTLUDE

SPEECH OF ELIZABETH TUDOR TO THE PEOPLE
OF LONDON, 14 JANUARY 1559

"I thank my Lord Mayor, his brethren, and you all. And whereas your request is that I should continue your good Lady and Queen, be ye ensured that I will be as good unto you as ever queen was unto her people. No will in me can lack, neither, do I trust, shall there lack any power. And persuade yourselves that for the safety and quietness of you all, I will not spare, if need be to spend my blood. God thank you all."

On the morning of 15 January 1559, Elizabeth rode through the streets of London in a litter pulled by two donkeys—one of them led by Robert's older brother, Ambrose Dudley—to the acclamation of her people. She had heard nothing but cheers for the last twenty-four hours. Yesterday she had processed through the city to behold various composed pageants in her honour, and by day's end her conquest of London was complete.

Today, however, was the moment when God would set His seal upon her reign. Elizabeth might be skeptical by temperament, but she could not deny her deep craving for the ritual that would signal to the world that England had a queen regnant and none could oppose her with impunity.

She entered Westminster Abbey to a flood of music and an impression of a great multitude raised to Heaven on the viewing stands built for the occasion. Awaiting her at the altar were Matthew Parker, her new Archbishop of Canterbury, and the chief nobles of her current realm. There was not a duke in sight, for though she intended to pardon Norfolk, he remained for now in the Tower. The only other duke in England was Dominic, to whom Elizabeth had returned his title and estates without his consent. They could fight about what it meant later, but for now he had refused to attend the coronation or even to leave Wynfield. Minuette, though, was here as promised. Not bearing the queen's train, as would have been Elizabeth's wish, but somewhere in the pressing throng.

She remembered every moment of her brother's coronation twelve years ago, and only through force of will was she able to hold back the images that kept threatening to impose themselves on today's investiture. William wasn't the only spectre: Elizabeth fancied she felt both her mother and father hovering near and wondered if Anne's pride outweighed Henry's disappointment.

The ceremony had been meticulously composed down to the very last syllable. Much of it was in Latin, as it had always been, but at several key moments Elizabeth had insisted that English be spoken instead. A symbol that the old world was passing and the new world was upon them. And when it was time for the archbishop to read her the oaths, it was Lord Burghley who handed over the sheet on which they were written. Burghley was no cleric—he was not even noble—and Elizabeth knew the action would displease the more reactionary of her subjects. So be it.

Sitting stiff and straight in St. Edward's throne, draped in the heavy weight of her gold coronation gown and ermine-lined robe, Elizabeth watched Archbishop Parker raise her crown to Heaven.

"I crown thee, Elizabeth, Queen of England, Ireland, and France," Parker intoned, and placed the intricately arched crown set with jewels on her long, loose hair.

I will make you proud, she vowed. And whether it was her mother or her father or her brother—or God—that she promised, not even Elizabeth knew for certain.

ACKNOWLEDGMENTS

How do I begin to say thank you to those who have touched the Boleyn books and my life in equal measure? The task is so daunting I keep putting it off ... but the story I began in 2004 has finally come to an end and so must my reluctance to bid this experience farewell.

Tamar Rydzinski was the first professional to believe in me and in the world of *The Boleyn King*. Thank you to the best of agents and the most patient of guides through the bewildering labyrinth of publishing.

Kate Miciak is a force of nature, and this book in particular bears the marks of her brilliant editing. Thank you for your kindness to me, for loving my world as I do, and for working so hard to bring it to others.

Ballantine/Random House has provided me only the very best of publishing experiences. Lisa Barnes in publicity, Maggie Oberrender in marketing, production editor Shona McCarthy, and a host of others who have touched these books and made them shine from cover art to the very last comma: Sophia Wiedeman, Pamela Alders, Hannah Elnan, Caroline Teagle, Victoria Allen, Robbin Schiff, Susan Corcoran, Priyanka Krishnan, and Julia Maguire.

When I began this story ten years ago, my oldest child was ten and I lived in the mountains of the West. Now my *youngest* child is twelve and I look out my window to the woods of New England. Within these ten years of change, some constants have remained. My friends at the Bluestocking Literary Guild, whom I love fiercely and devotedly. My parents and in-laws, whose constant faith in me almost make me believe I am as good as they think I am. My children, who may be bigger and more expensive in their schooling and entertainment than ten years ago, but who remain the very best creations I will ever be part of. Katie Jeppson, who is my first reader, secret-keeper, shopping and travel partner, and best friend. And my husband, who believed in my dreams when I was eighteen (of course, that dream was to be the first female Chief Justice of the U.S. Supreme Court) and in more than twenty years of marriage has never failed to be proud of me.

And some parts of this life have been wonderfully new since *The Boleyn King* was published last year. And so my final thanks is to you, dearest reader, wherever you may be. I dreamed of you for years and it was the hope of you that got me through the pain of repeated rejections. And you have repaid me in spades. To the reviewers and book bloggers (hooray for you!) who have generously shared my books with your own readers, to the strangers who have gone out of your way on Facebook and Twitter to let me know you care about my fictional world, and to all of you who care passionately about words and stories. You are my people. Thank you for making me one of yours in return.

The Boleyn Reckoning

LAURA ANDERSEN

A Reader's Guide

3 July 1546
Hampton Court Palace

Only when forced to move his uncomfortably corpulent body did King Henry VIII feel the burden of his age and ill-health. In his mind he was still in his prime: rising forty, limber on horseback, three steps ahead of everyone in his court, passionately wed to a queen who might frustrate at times but just as often satisfied his every physical and intellectual desire. These days he moved as little as possible, preferring to make the world come to him in only slightly more literal a manner than during the more than thirty-five years of his reign.

But today he endured the indignities of being helped into the privy gardens of Hampton Court, settling into a wide gilded chair beneath a portable canopy of estate that shielded him from the erratic summer sun, then dismissed the hangers-on in order to ponder the tableau before him.

He fancied for a moment that Cardinal Wolsey, so long dead, looked approvingly over his shoulder at the gardens that had once been the Cardinal's own. How could Wolsey complain of his treatment at the king's hands when at the far end of the gardens stood the living proof that Henry had been right all those years ago? Henry's son, royal and healthy. A dark-haired boy like Anne, but with the king's own sea-blue eyes and an unconscious litheness of body that Henry envied. He shifted restlessly in his seat, the pain of his long-injured leg stabbing a reminder of his own rapid aging. Prince Henry William Tudor (it was the king who had insisted on the second name, harking back to William the Conqueror) had just celebrated his tenth birthday, born forty-five years to the day after King Henry himself.

"Should I summon him?" Anne's seductive voice had not changed in fifteen years. She leaned gracefully over his shoulder and smiled at their son. "I think you're making all the children nervous."

"They'll not be children for long." Henry, like Anne, studied the quartet of youths, who knew perfectly well they were being watched but had been instructed by the royal guards to continue with their own amusements.

William, naturally, was the center of the group, although often as not he was twinned with the Wyatt girl who was of an age with her future king. The child's hair was the color of honey, and Henry thought she would grow into a beautiful woman. Her mother had certainly been, though in the days he'd known her Henry had been obsessed almost wholly with Anne.

The other two in the group had something of the same watchful, wary aspect to them though physically they were nothing alike. Elizabeth was a daughter to be proud of, so very Tudor with her red-gold hair like a banner and her mind as sharp as a blade. She reminded Henry of his youngest sister, Mary, though he hoped his daughter would behave with rather more sense where her personal life was concerned. And then there was the Courtenay boy—though not so much a boy. He was fifteen, a skillful swordsman and an instinctively talented soldier. More importantly, he was naturally self-effacing and loyal, qualities that would stand him in better stead than the ambition and deviousness of too many court members.

"Send William and Courtenay to me," Henry told Anne. "You may take the girls off with you. I wish to speak to the boys alone."

Dominic followed two paces behind William, wondering why he'd been included in what was obviously meant to be a father-son discussion before they parted ways. Tomorrow William would return with his own household to Ashridge while King Henry and the court moved on to Whitehall. Dominic knew the girls were as curious about his inclusion as he was. Elizabeth had turned considering eyes upon him, thoughtful as was her wont, and Minuette had very nearly spoken up in surprise. But, in Queen Anne's presence, she'd managed to turn her surprise into a charming farewell.

The royal privy gardens of Hampton Court were alight with brilliant colours and awash in the heady fragrance of flowers and cut grass. Because of the constant pain in his legs, King Henry was rarely seen standing and today he waited for them in his great carven chair, so heavily gilded it outshone the summer sun.

Dominic made his quiet obeisance expecting to do no more than shadow the young prince as usual. But it appeared the temperamental king had something specific to say to him.

His blue eyes fixed piercingly on Dominic, King Henry announced, "Lord Rochford has recommended that you be knighted at Christmas. What say you to that?"

Caught by surprise, and never easy with words, Dominic fumbled his response. "Lord Rochford is very kind, Your Majesty."

Henry treated that statement with the contempt it deserved. "My brother-in-law has never been kind in his whole life, boy.

If he says you're ready, then you are. But why wait until Christmas? You'll return to court next month, both of you, when the Admiral of France arrives to ratify the peace treaty. We'll conduct the knighting then."

The king turned those intense eyes on his son, who was trying to suppress his delighted grin. "I take it that pleases you, William?"

"Yes, Father. May I knight him?"

The king huffed in disbelief. "You're a child, yet, and no knight yourself. Think you to step into my place so soon?"

For all his youth, William had his mother's shrewdness. "No, Father. But how shall I be prepared to rule if I am never allowed to do anything?"

"Ha!" Henry gave a genuine shout of laughter. "A question I long pondered with my own father. Now there was a man for holding tightfisted to power. And money. And every possible privilege he could grasp. I daresay he thought he'd live forever and he was not overeager to teach me to follow him."

"But you are wiser, Your Majesty." William's submissive tone didn't quite hit the right note, and Dominic winced inwardly. King Henry did not care for clumsy flattery.

With narrowed gaze, the king said, "Don't try to finesse me, boy. Only your mother has ever dared that. No, you may not knight your friend here, but perhaps ... What say you, Courtenay? Is His Highness the Prince of Wales prepared to assume more royal responsibility?"

"I am certain your wisdom will guide you, Your Majesty." And please stop asking me questions, Dominic thought desperately. He was always afraid of putting a foot wrong and losing the capricious king's affection.

But today there was real approval in the king's expression. "A careful man you will make, Courtenay. Mark that trait, William, and value it. When one is king, any friend is to be cherished. But a careful friend all the more so. Charles Brandon was as good a friend as I ever had, but his lack of care led him very near the edge on occasion."

"As when he married my aunt?" William said thoughtlessly.

Under his breath, Dominic muttered, *"William."*

For the length of several seconds, King Henry seemed to gauge how offended to be at his son's impertinence. At last, he said with only slight coolness, "As when he married your aunt *without* my knowledge or permission. I hardly know myself why I forgave them, save I loved them both so well. And what is a man without family or friends? As long as no one forgets there is only one king."

"Well," William said, and this time his tone of teasing was perfectly judged, "I don't think Dominic would run away with Elizabeth without my permission. Dominic never looks twice at any girl."

"There's a world of difference between the ages of ten and fifteen," King Henry said knowingly. Wondering how the hell he kept being dragged into this awkward conversation, Dominic endured the king's look of sly amusement with burning cheeks. "I'll wager he looks twice, and more than looks."

Then that amusement—as though the king knew all about Dominic's awkward encounters last winter with the innkeeper's daughter—was replaced by the unmistakable bite of authority. "But it's true, Courtenay, and I take my son's point: you have not Charles Brandon's recklessness. Nor your uncle of Exeter's. And all the better for you."

Dominic swallowed against the memory of his uncle's treasonous end and his own father's possible entanglement in the affair, and bowed. "Yes, Your Majesty," he said, in fervent agreement.

The king leaned back in his chair, looking all at once tired and heavy with every one of his fifty-five years. "Rochford will make the arrangements for your knighting. And when you return to court, William, you may be my deputy in some of the matters with the Admiral of France."

William bowed solemnly. "Thank you, Your Majesty."

The king dismissed them and Dominic felt air return to his lungs as though he'd been underwater during the entire encounter. As they walked toward the river, he caught the unusually pensive expression on William's young face. "What are you thinking?" he asked.

"That I don't want to get old," William said. "I don't want to be ... I want to be young, Dom, and strong forever."

"Better to grow old than to die young, Will." Surely Dominic's own father would have gladly traded the chance to be old and infirm rather than to die of a brief illness in the Tower before the age of forty.

But the practicality of Dominic's words were lost on the young prince. "I may grow older, but I will not end confined to a litter chair whenever I wish to move."

And then, with a familiar stubborn expression and the lofty tone of one born to rule, William announced, "Just wait, Dom. I will rule myself as well as I rule my kingdom until the very last day of my life."

QUESTIONS AND TOPICS FOR DISCUSSION

1. The Duke of Norfolk declares: "William is his father all over again—what he wants, he gets" (page 257). Do you agree with Lord Norfolk's assessment? Why or why not?

2. Elizabeth tells William that she can always be trusted to put England's good before her own personal interests (page 367). Are her actions in England's best interest? Do you agree with her assessment of her motives, or is she serving her own personal interests? Had William not murdered Robert Dudley and confined Elizabeth to the Tower, do you think she would still consider William's death and her own ascension to be in England's best interest? What are Elizabeth's defining characteristics that make her a more desirable monarch than William?

3. Discuss the theme of loyalty in this book. William and Elizabeth often are faced with choices related to balancing loyalty to their family versus loyalty to their country's interests. Minuette and Dominic are forced to choose between loyalty to each other and their own personal happiness and loyalty to their life-long friends and personal senses of honor and duty. What choices

would you have made in their positions? Which character do you consider to be the most loyal?

4. On page 278, Minuette asks herself: "Am I whore, or am I savior?" What do you think of her bargain with William? Are her actions disloyal to Dominic? What would you have done in her position? Does Minuette's history with William and the fact that her heart, "so long twined with William in friendship, would demand its share of [that] hour" (page 278) color your opinion of her actions? Why do you think Minuette later refuses to make a similar bargain with William in exchange for Dominic's life?

5. After William had all-but announced his engagement to Minuette, was there any reaction he could have had to the news of her secret wedding and miscarriage (short of labeling her a traitor) that would have enabled him to save face at court? How could he have reacted differently without becoming a laughing stock in England and abroad? Considering how much he fought for the right to marry her (with his council and foreign ambassadors pushing for a strategic marriage) was his reaction reasonable in the context of the time? How would you react if similarly betrayed by a close friend?

6. On page 224, Minuette asks herself "At what point could pain have been avoided?" How would you answer this question? Was there a moment at which Minuette could have acted differently in order to spare William's pride and feelings? If so, what should she have done?

7. At one point, the Duke of Norfolk tells Dominic "You were a traitor the moment you took [Minuette] from [William]"

(page 261). Do you agree? Was Dominic a traitor? If so, at what point did his actions become treasonous? If not, what label would you give his choice to deceive the King?

8. What do you make of Minuette's refusal to tell William the last lie that could have granted herself and Dominic safety? Considering they had been lying for a year, why do you think she chose the moment before they were scheduled to flee to come clean?

9. William had to make several difficult decisions regarding the lives of family members, significantly his half-sister Mary and his uncle George Boleyn; how do you think those decisions impacted him? Did they pave the way for his later decisions to convict Dominic and Minuette of treason, and to imprison his sister? What would you do if a family member or close friend posed a serious threat to your position, success, and happiness, personally or professionally? What if the threat were to your country?

10. How have the various relationships between the four central characters evolved over the course of the series? Compare the William in *The Boleyn King* to the one who rides to battle the Duke of Norfolk in *The Boleyn Reckoning*. How has his leadership style changed over the course of his reign? To what do you attribute these changes?

11. Is it possible for royalty to have true friendships, or is William right in thinking otherwise? Is it necessary for those in power to have an attitude toward mistrust? If so, can friendships exist anyway, or is perfect trust required for true friendship?

12. What is your reaction to William's decision to execute Mary Tudor? Was this the right choice for his government? What about for him on a personal level?

13. What impact (if any) did the death of Jane and the loss of his son have on William?

Also by Laura Andersen:

THE BOLEYN KING

Long live Henry IX!

Just seventeen years old, King Henry IX, known as William, is anxious to prove himself. With the French threatening war and the Catholics' rebellion, he trusts only three people: his older sister Elizabeth; his loyal counsellor, Dominic; and Minuette, a young orphan raised as a royal ward by William's mother, Anne Boleyn.

Against a tide of secrets, betrayal, and murder, William finds himself fighting for the very soul of his kingdom – and for his right to marry for love not duty. . .

EBURY
PRESS

Also by Laura Andersen:

THE BOLEYN DECEIT

Torn between his kingdom and the woman he loves. . .

William Tudor, now King Henry IX, sits alone on the throne.
But England must still contend with those who doubt his le-
gitimacy. William is betrothed to a young princess from France,
but still he has eyes only for his childhood friend Minuette, and
court tongues are wagging.

Even more dangerous – if discovered – is that Minuette's
heart and soul belong to Dominic, William's best friend and
trusted advisor. . .

EBURY
PRESS

DELICIOUS!

By Ruth Reichl

Dear Mr Beard,

I sent my Magic Moments off yesterday,
and that made me think of you.

I hope the cookies will remind Father of our life here.
Or maybe I should say what life used to be,
before the war changed everything . . .

Hidden in the library of *Delicious!* magazine young intern Billie discovers the wartime letters of twelve-year-old Lulu Swan, written to distinguished food writer, James Beard. Lulu's can-do spirit in the face of food shortages and other hardships helps Billie come to terms with her own tragic past. Until one day it occurs to her: Lulu may still be alive.

EBURY
PRESS

Also available from Ebury Press:

THE HAREM MIDWIFE

By Roberta Rich

Safiye had more to worry about than simply birthing this child.
Her only son might not live to hear the call for morning prayers.
If there ever was a time when the Empire required a
male heir it was now.

In the opulent royal palace of Murat III, on the shores of Constantinople, midwife Hannah Levi is charged with ensuring the Sultan's harem provides him with a male heir.

If she fails, the entire Ottoman Empire will collapse. But the slave girl who has been stolen away to be the Sultan's latest concubine is not all she seems...

EBURY
PRESS